Born in Aberdeen, Scotland, the daughter of a Polish army officer and a Scottish businesswoman, Jennifer Bacia came to Australia as a child.

After finishing her degree at Queensland University she worked in the fields of education, public relations and corporate management.

She has lived in Rome, London and Los Angeles and has travelled widely in the Far East and former Eastern Bloc countries. She now divides her time between Europe and Australia.

As a successful candidate for the Australian Film Television and Radio School, she is also developing her skills as a screenwriter.

She is the author of the international best seller, *Shadows of Power*.

Also by Jennifer Bacia

SHADOWS OF POWER
WHISPER FROM THE GODS

ANGEL OF HONOUR

JENNIFER BACIA

PAN
AUSTRALIA

First published 1991 by Pan Macmillan Publishers Australia

This edition published 2001 by Hinkler Books Pty. Ltd.
17-23 Redwood Drive, Dingley, Victoria 3172 Australia

National Library of Australia
cataloguing-in-publication data:

Bacia, Jennifer
Angel of honour.

ISBN   1865156310

I. Title.

A823.3

Printed and bound in Australia

For my parents with love and gratitude

With thanks to my first-rate agent, Selwa Anthony; also to Jennifer and Scott Wilson, Donna Garibaldi, Lyn and Phillip Christensen, Pam and Bruce Hudson, and Philippa Power.

PROLOGUE

The killer was in no hurry. He knew his victim's schedule, and the Citroen was parked just minutes away. He had plenty of time.

As he sipped at his espresso, he watched the passers-by on the Rue de Rivoli. It was the end of September and the tourist barbarians were almost gone. Once more the city belonged to the Parisians.

It was surprisingly warm and the man sweated in his English tailored suit. His stylish clothes gave little clue to his nationality: Lanvin shirt, silk tie from de Casi in New York, French calfskin shoes by Lobb's of St James. Long ago the killer had recognised the universal human failing which prejudged a man by his dress. At all levels, officialdom was always more easily deflected by the appearance of distinction and elegance. Neither the firm from which he'd hired the Citroen nor French Customs or police had presented him with any problem.

Not that he'd expected any. The assignment was simple enough, the victim's routine as predictable as the Swiss.

He put down his empty cup and glanced at the gold Rolex on his left wrist. Fifteen minutes after ten. His target would soon be leaving for the offices close to the Musée d'Orsay.

The killer had never set foot in the museum. Art of any kind left him cold. In his opinion, there seemed much better things to spend one's money on than rotting pieces of canvas. His eyes lit up behind the dark glasses. Like the fresh-faced boys of Marrakesh, for example . . .

It was their first serious confrontation.

'But Felix! You don't understand. This is the one personal task I must attend to before I leave France. It will not take me long. All I need is twenty-four hours — I'll be back in Paris before anyone realises I've gone.'

Felix Noverro was over sixty. He didn't like arguments. As he studied the explosive combination of beauty and determination that was Noella de Bartez, it occurred to him that this was the first time she had ever appeared irrational.

His face stern with warning, he confronted her over the small polished table strewn with paper.

'It is you who do not understand, Noella,' he emphasised. 'The mission you are about to undertake carries risks even here in France. For the next nine days until you leave Paris, I want you close by where we can be assured of your safety. I have — '

She interrupted him impatiently. 'Felix, there can be no danger! Balo is thousands of miles away. What harm can he do me here?' Angrily, she pushed back from the table and began to pace restlessly around the tiny apartment.

Felix Noverro sighed in frustration. Noella de Bartez, he decided, had her father's temperament. She had inherited her mother's beauty, but looked more Spanish than English: the thick dark gold hair, the fiery brown eyes and the full, lush figure. Although it had never been his good fortune to meet the late Catherine de Bartez, Felix had been one of her greatest admirers.

Now he did his best to make her younger daughter understand the seriousness of his warning. 'It is not Rodriguez Balo who concerns me, Noella. He is a mere puppet for men whose resources are infinite and for whom Balo's survival is paramount. Their network of evil can easily cross oceans.'

Noella de Bartez spun to face him. 'Felix, I have waited more than a decade for this opportunity. Do you think I would take risks now? Now, when we are so close to success?'

The old man looked at her appraisingly. He had learned to trust his instincts and there was something here he did not quite understand. Something else, he sensed, lay behind this unusual display of temperament.

With no clue to the reason for her vehemence, he could only repeat his warning. 'You must not take the risk of leaving Paris, Noella.'

Noella de Bartez swung away from the old man's penetrating gaze. She was afraid her own dark eyes might betray her. She must be careful. For so long she had kept her secret.

Taking a deep breath, she forced herself to speak calmly. 'It is almost time for my weekly meeting with the director, Felix. I must leave now.'

Felix Noverro nodded his grey head approvingly as he rose slowly to his feet. 'Yes, it is important that your routine is seen to continue as normal these next few days. That way they will be kept off guard as long as possible.'

He walked her to the door and, as they kissed their usual warm goodbye, Felix was reassured. Noella would listen to reason.

But already, as she made her way down the narrow flight of stairs that led to the street, Noella de Bartez was dismissing Felix Noverro's warning.

Felix worried unnecessarily, she thought. Balo or the others would never dare touch her here in France.

As she stepped out into the sunshine, her mouth set in a determined line. Nothing, or no one, was going to stop her doing what she had to do...

From his first floor window, Felix watched with troubled eyes as the tall elegant figure walked away.

Noella frowned. Out of the corner of her eye she could see him. The man on the opposite sidewalk.

He appeared to be matching her pace, watching her closely as he walked. Quickening her stride, Noella glanced sideways again to check if the stranger was still with her.

He was.

In that split second of appraisal she had seen the distinctive dark patch covering his left eye, while some sixth sense told her he was not a native Frenchman.

She forced herself to shrug off the sudden tightness in the pit of her stomach. Listening to Felix had made her imagination work overtime, she chided herself. She had nothing to worry about in France.

Distracted by her thoughts, Noella stepped out onto the Avenue Vantinon with barely a glance at the approaching traffic.

She was halfway across the wide avenue before she saw the danger.

A dark Citroen. Bearing down on her at frightening speed.

For a fraction of a second Noella hesitated, her brain racing as she gauged the distance to safety.

Then she spun around, and was running, back to the sidewalk she had stepped from just seconds before.

But it was too late.

With deliberate precision, the Citroen too altered course, never lessening its speed as it tore relentlessly towards her.

Fear iced Noella's blood. Surely, it wasn't — *No! Dios!* NO!

The impact knocked her sideways, tore the breath from her lungs, as she was hurled against the rough cobblestones. Tumbling over and over in a flurry of limbs it took the hard edge of the gutter to at last bring her to a bone-jarring stop. Paralysed with fear, white with shock, she lay gasping for breath. But she was unharmed.

Carefully untwining his body from hers, her saviour enquired anxiously, 'You are all right?'

His French was heavily accented and as he reached out to help her to her feet, Noella saw for the first time who had saved her.

'You!' The word came in a raw whisper from her dry throat.

Up close, she saw the full horror of his face. Not merely the eye patch, but the flesh puckered and raw, grotesque. Some terrible accident...

Yet undoubtedly, he had saved her life.

'Who — who are you...?' Her voice shook.

As concerned and curious onlookers began to gather round them, the man spoke quietly and urgently. 'Never mind who I am. What they tried just now is the proof you need. You must not underestimate the danger — they are determined to stop you.'

Dazed, Noella tried to speak, but the stranger interrupted her. 'I promise that from this moment on, you will be in my care. I shall always be close by.'

With her hand still gripped in his, Noella shivered as the full force of the stranger's passion flowed through her like a live current.

BOOK ONE

CHAPTER ONE

'Noella! Where in the name of Jesu is the girl?'

Dark eyes glittering under his heavy brows, Victor de Bartez stormed down the cool stone hallway of the *hacienda* and flung open the door to the kitchen.

Ignoring the other staff, he confronted a plump, grey-haired woman dressed in black. 'Nona! Where is Noella? The guests are assembled and still she has not put in an appearance. How dare she disgrace us all on a day such as this?'

The woman quaked in the face of her employer's anger. It was not often the senor lost his temper but when he did, these days, it was mostly thanks to his younger daughter.

'I have been busy here, senor,' she muttered. 'I have not — '

Victor de Bartez cut short her excuses. 'She is in your charge, Nona. Find her at once!'

Turning on his heel, the President of Martiguay strode out of the house and, adjusting his expression, rejoined the elegant, well-dressed guests who were gathered in smiling groups on the well-manicured lawns of the sprawling homestead. The sun shone warmly as uniformed waiters offered refreshments from silver trays; it was perfect weather for the celebration of the engagement of Victor de Bartez's eldest daughter, Gabrielle, to Eugene Ravell.

Inside the house, the nurse muttered angrily as she

hurried from room to room searching in vain for her charge. That vixen! Where in the name of the saints had she got to? Today of all days to go missing — her sister's betrothal party, and the very best families in the country assembled for the celebrations. Nona's lips tightened in fury. Where *was* the disobedient minx?

'Yes... oh *yes*, Paolo. There, touch me there...'

The naked boy looked into that lovely face and felt certain he must be dreaming. Any moment he would wake up and find himself alone. Surely this could not be Noella de Bartez who lay beneath him? Surely the daughter of *el Presidente* would not choose to lie with the boy who tended her father's horses?

Over the four years he had worked at the *hacienda*, Paolo Avende had developed a warm friendship with the younger daughter of Victor de Bartez. With her sister five years older, and her father so often away, it was to Paolo that Noella had so often turned for companionship. She was an expert horsewoman and together they had spent many happy hours roaming the surrounding countryside. But Paolo never allowed himself to forget that the beautiful, fiery-eyed girl was the daughter of *el Presidente*. That was why he felt certain he must be dreaming now...

The fire in Paolo Avènde's body convinced him it was no dream.

Noella de Bartez cupped a hand around one of her full, firm breasts. 'Kiss it, Paolo. Kiss it.'

Even in her excitement she spoke with the assurance of one used to being obeyed, and Paolo did as he was told. Lowering his head, he touched a tentative tongue to those soft pink buds and immediately they became hard and erect.

'You see, Paolo,' she breathed hotly, 'you see how you excite me?'

The boy felt the urgency of his own response as

the girl thrust herself eagerly against him. Already at sixteen, he thought tremulously, she has the body of an angel.

'I want you, Paolo.' Even though the words were whispered there was no denying their force. 'It is you I have chosen to make me a woman. Today . . . Now . . . Before they come looking for me.'

And then, unexpectedly, she broke into a giggle. 'Not that they are likely to search for me here.'

They were in the hayloft of the stables at the rear of the *hacienda* and Noella felt certain that none of her father's elegantly dressed guests were likely to come tripping through the straw and horse shit.

Her words made beads of sweat break out on Paolo Avende's face while his belly clenched in apprehension.

He was eighteen, and had made love dozens of times before, but this was different. Noella de Bartez was not one of the simple village girls he had grown up with; she was special, the daughter of *el Presidente* and a member of one of Martiguay's richest and most illustrious families.

'I want to know what it is like to have a man inside me, Paolo.' Noella murmured the words close to his ear. 'You are the most handsome man I know, more handsome even than Eugene Ravell, whom my sister is to marry.'

Her voice quavered when she spoke the name but the boy didn't seem to notice. Her compliment had flattered him, given him confidence. He would prove to Noella de Bartez that birth meant nothing when a man and woman lay together.

Carefully, tenderly, he eased his aching penis between her silky thighs, expecting resistance, surprised when none came. Then he remembered that Noella de Bartez was an excellent horsewoman. That was how it happened sometimes.

She clung to him eagerly, wrapping her long legs

around him as he began to move slowly back and forth, his organ growing fuller as he felt her wetness. She was ready for him.

Instinctively she caught his rhythm, moving in time with his own motions, her breath quickening against his cheek. For Paolo, time seemed suspended as his whole being flooded with desire. Suddenly he could hold back no longer; his body shuddered violently, went rigid, and with a drawn-out cry, he surrendered to his climax.

Noella watched his face in wonder. The human being was gone and had been replaced by an animal — an animal whose features were contorted in pain, yet who groaned in an agony of pleasure.

A shiver ran through her. She wanted to discover for herself the secret of such exquisite torture.

Twenty minutes later, the sensual skill of Paolo's hands and mouth had reduced her time and time again to that same atavistic animal.

'Noella! Where have you been, you wicked child? Your father has been searching everywhere for you. He demands you join him at once!'

In the massive, oak-beamed foyer of the *hacienda*, Noella kept her eyes on the silver-framed mirror as she smoothed her hair. A half smile played around her lips. She looked no different. No one would be able to tell. A pity perhaps...

With a sigh, she answered the scolding nurse. 'Don't fuss, Nona. I'm here now, aren't I?'

'Why do you always give me trouble, Noella? Why can't you be more like your sister? Why is she the saint and you the devil?'

The girl allowed her smile to widen as she turned and made for the door. 'You know, Nona, I am sure that in some things I am much better than Gabrielle.'

*

Late that evening, long after the guests had gone, Noella padded down the stone passageway to her sister's bedroom.

'Are you awake, Gabrielle? Can I come in?'

'Of course, Noella.' Her sister opened the door. 'I am far too excited to sleep.'

Perching herself on the wide, wooden-framed bed, Noella tucked her long legs under her clinging silk nightdress. Gabrielle, she saw, wore her usual nun-like cotton gown, and Noella wondered if after her marriage her twenty-one-year-old sister would wear something more provocative to bed.

She doubted it. Gabrielle had often made it plain that she considered any sort of self-indulgence a sin. 'Just because we are rich, Noella, there is no need to flaunt our wealth in front of those who have so little. We must be especially careful now that Papa is *el Presidente*. The poor have a heavy enough burden as it is. We must show them that we understand their plight.'

How the poor could possibly be affected by what Gabrielle chose to wear to bed, Noella couldn't imagine.

She studied her sister in the soft light of the bedlamp. 'Are you happy, Gabrielle?' she asked.

The elder girl's face broke into a radiant smile. 'Oh, Noella, you would not believe how much. Eugene is everything I have dreamt of in a husband. Intelligent, kind, good-looking, well-read . . . and with the same concerns for social justice that are so important to me. Not only will we bring happiness to each other, but together we will be able to do so much good for our country.'

Noella sighed inwardly. Gabrielle became so tedious when she talked about such topics. More times than she cared to remember Noella had been forced to sit in bored silence over her evening meal while her father and sister spoke endlessly about their concerns for Martiguay. To Noella, there seemed no logic in their interminable discussions. Surely there would always be poor, as there would always be rich? Nothing, and no one, she felt certain, could change that.

Now, with studied innocence she asked, 'Perhaps you can answer one question for me, Gabrielle.'

'Of course, little sister. What is it you want to know?'

Noella looked away, her arms hugged tightly around her legs. 'Tell me about Eugene... Is — is he good in bed?'

'*Noella!*' Gabrielle looked askance, her face aflame. 'How can you ask such questions? A woman does not learn such things until her marriage bed. What would the good Sisters say to hear you talking like that?' Flustered, Gabrielle quickly changed the subject. The preparations for her marriage, she decided, were a much safer topic.

But Noella wasn't listening. She was thinking about Eugene Ravell. A year ago, when he had first been invited to her father's house, she had fallen instantly in love with the tall, handsome student.

Gabrielle had met Eugene Ravell at Andorro's Central University where both were enrolled in the faculty of Law. The Ravell family was one of the country's oldest and most esteemed, though mismanagement and wasteful heirs had robbed them of most of their fortune.

After that first visit, Eugene came often to the house, captivating Noella with his dark good looks, his easy laughter and charm. But while she flirted shamelessly, Eugene seemed never to notice. He had eyes only for Gabrielle.

Yet surely, thought Noella, it must be obvious that her sister was no match for her own beauty. Gabrielle was pretty enough — her complexion smooth, her dark hair thick and lustrous — but her features were too heavy for real beauty. And what could a man find appealing in that thin, flat-chested body? To look at the two sisters, it was the elder, Gabrielle, who had the body of a child, and young Noella the voluptuous curves of a mature woman.

For months Noella had spun out her dreams about Eugene until the day he had come to the house to ask her father for Gabrielle's hand in marriage. Later that evening, forced to join in a toast to the happy couple, Noella had been sick with despair.

But Victor de Bartez's delight at the match was clearly obvious. 'You are lucky, Gabrielle. You have found both a husband who loves you and one who understands well the problems of our country. He will be of great support in our struggles.'

The three of them had looked so happy; only Noella felt left out and miserable. It was not a new sensation. She had known for a long time how much her father resented her, how he blamed her for ... for what had happened. In the circumstances it was only natural that Gabrielle was his favourite.

She slipped off the bed and kissed her sister on the cheek. 'I am happy for you, Gabrielle.'

As she walked back to her own bedroom, the soreness she felt between her thighs made sincerity easier. Gabrielle might have won Eugene, but Noella had beaten her in becoming a woman.

CHAPTER TWO

From the rear of the air-conditioned limousine, Victor de Bartez looked out at the never-ending rows of dilapidated houses with their cracked, grimy windows, crumbling paint and missing roof tiles. At a roadside water pump a row of women waited patiently to fill their pails, grimy children playing at their feet.

The President of Martiguay gave a heavy sigh. The task in front of him was enormous. Ten years of dictatorship had left his country in ruins. Poverty, hunger, illiteracy — the social and economic problems seemed insurmountable.

Sometimes Victor de Bartez wondered whether, at fifty, he were strong enough for the task. It was a thought he immediately suppressed, chiding himself harshly for his doubts. He was tired, that was all. The first free elections in ten years had offered him a chance to save the country he loved and he would face that challenge with faith and courage.

For a moment he closed his eyes as he leaned back against the cool leather of the early-model Mercedes. If only Catherine were alive — with his wife by his side his courage would never falter. He muttered under his breath, cursing yet again the fates which had so cruelly taken her from him.

Victor de Bartez had met Catherine Campion while completing his Master's degree at Oxford. The daughter of an impoverished English baronet, she was back in England for a short rest from a career that had taken off at breakneck speed.

At twenty-five, Catherine Campion was the darling of Hollywood. Enchanted by her aristocratic background and captivated by her classy good looks — the slim, lithe figure, the pale blonde hair and ice-green eyes — America could not get enough of her. The studios were more than happy to oblige. Less than five years after arriving on the West Coast, Catherine Campion had starred in almost a dozen films and won her first Academy Award.

As her fame grew, so too did a cult following. All over the world, wherever her films were shown, girls modelled themselves on the cool English beauty. They dressed like her, talked like her, and walked like her, feeding greedily on the image presented to them on the screen and in the fan magazines.

One day when the frenzy was at its peak, Catherine woke in the bedroom of the rambling hillside home she leased on Los Angeles' Mulholland Drive and decided she had to get away. The studio ruled her life, told her how to dress, who to see, where to go, almost what to eat and drink. She had lost every vestige of her privacy.

This isn't what I want, she thought, staring into the bathroom mirror at the face which had graced endless magazine covers but which now seemed suddenly gaunt and drawn. Success had been something she'd always dreamed of, but the price was too high. She had become a commodity.

Stopping only to call her startled agent, Catherine had hidden her famous looks under a red wig and old-fashioned dark glasses and caught the first flight back to London. She needed to take a break and think seriously about her future.

She had been at her father's Buckinghamshire home almost a week before the press sniffed her out. But by that time she had already been introduced to Victor de Bartez at a small dinner party at her cousin's home.

For Catherine it was love at first sight. Not only was Victor de Bartez unbelievably handsome: tall, dark and well-built, with strongly chiselled features and a slow, wonderful smile, but he had the added appeal of being the temperamental opposite of every man she had ever met during her five years in Hollywood. She felt herself drawn like a magnet towards this gently spoken man with his air of dignity and quiet self-confidence.

She was delighted when he called the next day to ask if he could see her again. For the next two weeks before she returned to the States, Catherine stretched her ingenuity with a variety of disguises which enabled her to see the tall, handsome foreigner almost daily. When the time came to say goodbye, she did her best to hide her despair when Victor said nothing about the future. Maybe she had misread his interest, she told herself miserably on the flight back to Los Angeles.

But she found it impossible to get Victor out of her mind. When her agent rang, pushing for a commitment to her next project, Catherine was evasive. She didn't want to think about work. All she wanted was to be near Victor de Bartez. With him by her side, she knew that nothing in the world would ever make her afraid again.

She procrastinated, driving her agent crazy, until the day four weeks later when her prayers were answered.

In his elegant formal letter, Victor told her how he felt, how he couldn't forget her, but hardly dared to ask that she change her life for him. If she would just reply, he pleaded, and put an end to his torture of uncertainty, he could try to get on with the rest of his life.

Six weeks later Catherine Campion became Senora de Bartez, matriarch of a vast estate in a country about which she knew next to nothing.

The news sent the world press into a frenzy. How could their favourite princess turn her back on such a phenomenal career? How could she walk away from all the trappings of success and bury herself in some godforsaken Latin country?

Victor recalled the pandemonium of the first few months of his marriage when hundreds of journalists had descended on Martiguay. Finally, in an attempt to appease them, Catherine had agreed to just one press conference, at which she had made her decision clear. Love had made her choice an easy one, she stated calmly. She was walking away from her career without a single regret. All she wanted now was to be left alone to get on with the rest of her life. She loved her husband and she knew she was going to love his beautiful country.

And it was true, Victor thought. Catherine *had* come to love Martiguay as much as he did. He adored her for that. Once or twice a year she would spend a week or two in England, but was always eager to return to the tropical heat, the prolific vegetation, the space and tranquillity of the vast cattle ranch she now called home. She told him it was as though the years in Hollywood had never existed, and he believed her.

The depth of happiness each found in their marriage was made complete when, two years later, their first child was born. A daughter they named Gabrielle.

Even now, Victor felt ashamed when he remembered that initial instant of disappointment when he learned that his first born was not the son he had hoped for. Yet it was a feeling very quickly dispelled by his growing enchantment with his precious child.

Gabrielle delighted him and he spent every free moment in her company. 'She has your temperament, my darling,' he smiled lovingly at his wife. 'Calm and unfussable.'

As Catherine looked at father and daughter together, she knew a happiness she had never believed existed.

Nothing in her amazing career had ever brought her such pleasure.

But in the years that followed, her failure to carry to full term a brother or sister for Gabrielle was a cause for despair. It took five years and three miscarriages until at last, and with great relief and joy, a second daughter was safely delivered.

But where Gabrielle had been endowed with her mother's placid disposition, the new child was restless and demanding from the start. Strong-willed and stubborn, Noella tested her parents in ways her sister never had. On the few occasions when Victor became exasperated with his strong-minded second daughter, it was Catherine who would gently intervene.

'We cannot expect her to be the same as Gabrielle, Victor darling. The child has her own personality and we must be careful not to suppress such vitality and energy. Directed into the proper channels such traits can be Noella's greatest assets.'

In the years since Catherine's admonition, Victor had had plenty of time to question the wisdom of such a restrained approach to his difficult daughter's upbringing. Many times he had thought that if only he had enforced a stronger discipline on his younger child, the tragedy might not have occurred. Maybe then, Catherine would still be by his side, offering the love and support he so badly needed.

The accident had occurred one summer afternoon when Noella was six. The girls had gone with their mother for a picnic by the lake, a half-hour drive from the house. Under Catherine's watchful eye they had been allowed to paddle in the sandy shallows before they ate.

Nearby, a number of small fishing craft belonging to the peasants who worked the estate were drawn up at the water's edge. Forbidden by her mother to play on the weather-beaten boats, Noella had dissolved into sulky tears. She hated being thwarted.

It was from eleven-year-old Gabrielle that Victor later learned how the accident had happened.

'We were by the edge of the trees... and Mama let us play hide and seek,' the child explained fitfully through her sobs. 'First I hid, then Mama, and finally Noella. But we couldn't find her, Papa... though we looked and looked. I could see Mama was beginning to be afraid. She had warned us not to go too deep into the jungle...'

As Gabrielle remembered, it was just a moment later that they heard the screams. Hurriedly retracing their steps to the water's edge, they had been faced with the terrifying sight of Noella adrift in one of the tiny craft far out on the lake.

'She was waving her arms at us, Papa,' sobbed Gabrielle, forced to recall the terrible scene. 'Mama took off her shoes, her face was so white... She told me to wait just exactly where I was and then she went into the water.' The child threw herself into her father's arms. 'You — you know how bad a swimmer she was...'

Victor's grief at Catherine's death had been overwhelming. He had lost the centre of his being and felt as if something inside him had also died. He could barely look at the child who had cost him his beloved wife.

The funeral was the hardest thing Victor had ever had to endure in his life. And even that ordeal he could not face in private. The Cathedral of San Martino in Martiguay's capital, Andorro, was swarming with members of the international media as, stony faced, Victor followed the gold-handled coffin into the church.

None of the hundreds of journalists ever learned the true circumstances of Catherine de Bartez's death. Even Victor wouldn't wish that burden on his child.

Afterwards, he buried himself in the work of managing his vast estate, leaving the girls to the care of their nurses and other staff. But while he had shut out the rebellious six-year-old who had caused his terrible loss, Victor could not turn so easily from his eldest child.

It was his first born who slowly dragged him back to sanity. It was Gabrielle who became the focus of his life, Gabrielle who became for him the son he would now never have.

In time, on the surface at least, Victor resumed what passed for a normal relationship with his younger daughter. But inside, some irrevocable change had occurred.

As Noella became older, as she grew daily more like her mother, Victor was even less able to break down the inner barriers he had raised against her. He did his best to hide his feelings, and felt sure Noella had no inkling of them.

But the girl knew. She sensed it from the start.

Noella never blamed him. She had been responsible for her mother's death. It was only right that she should be punished, only right that her father should withhold his love.

Victor was still thinking of his younger daughter as the Mercedes bumped along the badly-surfaced roads on the city's outskirts.

The girl was becoming too much for Nona to handle, he could see that. At sixteen, Noella had a mind of her own and even the nuns were finding her difficult to control.

He should spend more time with her, he thought guiltily, but that was impossible at the moment. It was only six months since he had assumed the presidency and his schedule was punishing. Ten years of dictatorship had been marked by corruption, graft and mismanagement, and nothing could be changed overnight.

Victor did not underestimate the immensity of his task, one made more difficult — and dangerous — by the existence of forces still loyal to the late Bernardo

Peres. The death of Peres from cancer had led to the first free elections in years but despite his win, Victor knew there were still those who were bitterly opposed to a democratically elected government.

That was why his limousine was accompanied by two armed motorcycle police, the reason that their route to the helipad was always varied and that a twenty-four-hour guard was kept on both the Presidential Palace and the *hacienda*.

Though it was only a two-hour drive to his family home, Victor knew his safety on the open highway could not yet be completely guaranteed. But he had been determined to return to the *hacienda* for the traditional Easter break. He would try to rest, check on the staff, and spend some time with his daughters.

The helicopter's blades were spinning in readiness when the limousine drew up beside it. As his chauffeur opened the door, Victor de Bartez saw that Gabrielle was already awaiting him. During the university term, he had her company at the palace and today she had gone straight from her classes to the helipad.

As he climbed into the cabin beside her, Gabrielle's face lit up with pleasure. Victor kissed his elder daughter warmly, smiling his greeting above the noise of the spinning blades. He was glad that after her marriage Gabrielle would not leave him alone in the palace.

CHAPTER **THREE**

It was almost dusk when Noella rode into the stables, the gelding's hooves clattering on the cobbles. Sweat foamed on the horse's coat and its sides heaved as she jumped nimbly to the ground.

'You have ridden hard, senorita,' said Paolo, as he caught the reins she threw at him. It was the most he could allow himself; the expression in his eyes showed how he felt at the horse's condition.

'I do what I like with my horses, Paolo, as I do with my stablehands.'

The boy blushed to the roots of his hair at the cutting comment. 'Noella, please, I — '

But she brushed past him as though he hadn't spoken.

She hasn't forgiven me, he thought miserably, as he watched her stride towards the house, her back rigid with angry pride.

If only Noella would let him explain, he sighed, as he led the heaving horse into a stall. Then he might be able to make her understand that there was nothing to forgive, that it had all been a silly mistake. Since that first exciting time with Noella, he had never even looked at anyone else.

As she walked away, Noella felt a perverse pleasure at the memory of Paolo's obvious discomfort.

Good. She had meant to hurt him. Just as he had hurt her. How dare he flirt with that bold kitchenmaid when he was sleeping with Noella! Did he think she was going to stand for that?

Paolo needed to be taught a good lesson, she determined. When he had been punished enough, she would take him back.

But as she entered the house, Noella had to admit that by punishing Paolo, she was also punishing herself. How much longer could she bear to do without the passion and excitement she had found in Paolo's arms?

Noella pulled off her riding boots and dusty trousers and ran water into the deep marble bath. She had seen the helicopter at the side of the house. Her father and Gabrielle had returned.

As she lowered herself into the warm water, she felt the usual gnawing teeth of jealousy. It had been her deliberate plan not to be at the house when they arrived. She knew too well how unbearable it would be to see Gabrielle and her father walking arm in arm across the lawn, laughing at some shared joke, oblivious to anyone else.

Hurt tears welled in Noella's dark eyes. Why couldn't he love her as much as he loved Gabrielle? Why did she have to be burdened with the guilt of her mother's death? It was so obvious that Gabrielle was the only one he cared for — Gabrielle who shared his crazy obsession with politics, who really thought they could change things in Martiguay.

I can't wait to get out of here, she thought. She dreamt of living somewhere exciting, where there were nightclubs and parties, where she could dance until dawn with adoring men who would tell her how beautiful she was, who would love her as much as she needed to be loved. She wanted the life her mother had walked away from . . .

Instead, she thought darkly, stepping out of the bath, she was stuck in this living graveyard. Ordered about by sour-faced nuns during the day, and surrounded by peasants and old women the rest of the time.

For a moment Noella stood and stared at herself in the full-length bathroom mirror. She was so like her mother, they said ... The photographs which filled the house clearly showed the resemblance in the slim straight nose, the generous mouth, the dark golden hair. But the stubborn chin and dark flashing eyes were pure de Bartez.

Suddenly Noella giggled. What would Sister Rosa say if she could see her now, staring so blatantly at her nakedness, indulging in the sin of vanity? Not as much, no doubt, as she'd say if she knew about Paolo. Father Camello would surely die of apoplexy if she admitted *that* in Confession!

Her face quickly became sober again at the thought of Sister Rosa, her teacher. She remembered what lay ahead of her this evening. Her father would be presented with her term report. It wouldn't please him, she felt sure. Still, she gave a sigh, if she were lucky he would at least wait until after they had eaten.

Catherine de Bartez had not been long in Martiguay before establishing her reputation as a gracious and imaginative hostess. Her knack of mixing a wide cross section of Martiguayan society — writers, musicians, actors, judges, the more open-minded of the clergy — to ensure lively and stimulating debate, had made invitations to her dinner table a much coveted prize. Since her death, however, only rarely — on occasions such as Gabrielle's engagement — were guests asked to the house.

As he sat at the head of the long refectory table, his daughters on either side of him, Victor de Bartez wished as always that he could turn back time.

He remembered when the same room used to be full of laughter and good conversation, when candelabra cast soft shadows on the stone walls, intensifying the beauty of their female guests.

In those days, there had been hope among the landed gentry, the judiciary, and the educated elite, that Martiguay would at last fulfil its destiny, would finally emerge from the shadows of the past and find a niche in the modern world.

Instead they had been betrayed, forced to watch helplessly as the country was crushed beneath the heel of a cunning and ruthless dictator. At least, thought Victor morosely, Catherine had been spared the knowledge of that. It had been less than a month after her death that Peres had come to power.

As he spooned up his soup, Victor glanced sideways at his younger daughter. Tonight when she had first walked into the room, he had felt the breath catch in his throat. It had been two months since he'd last seen Noella and absence made him more acutely aware of her growing resemblance to her mother. The curve of her cheek, the soft line of her lips . . . Already she looks like a woman, he thought, taking in the fullness of her bosom beneath the wide-collared dress. It would soon be time, he realised, to talk seriously with Noella, about men, life, and the values a woman needed to preserve if she wished to make a good match.

He dabbed the linen napkin to his lips. Why had he never worried so much about Gabrielle at the same age? But Noella was different. He had always known that. Headstrong and impulsive, she would need careful guidance over these next few years. Victor sighed. He hoped the Sisters might have already begun the delicate task of explaining the facts of life to Noella.

Then he frowned as he remembered the report from Mother Louisa which had been waiting for him on his study desk. He had read it before dinner.

'Noella has the potential to do much better than this,' Mother Louisa had written at the end of the row of scandalous marks. 'She is too easily distracted and puts little effort into her work.'

His daughter's shameful results angered Victor. Noella was not stupid, he knew that. As Mother Louisa said, she did not bother to make the effort.

'Papa...' It was Gabrielle who into broke Victor de Bartez's reverie. The maid was waiting to remove his empty plate.

'Oh, oh yes.' Leaning back against the ornately scrolled wooden chair, he smiled at his elder daughter.

Gabrielle was everything he could have hoped for in a daughter. She had never given him a moment's worry or disappointment. And now, her eagerness to follow his own political path added to his joy. The de Bartez name was one to be proud of in this country. They had always been at the forefront of events. Over a century ago, his great-grandfather had arrived from Spain with a modest entourage of servants and military men to establish himself in this far corner of the empire. It was Diego de Bartez who had built this sprawling house, who had become the first mayor of the neighbouring town and established the de Bartez name as a force to be reckoned with.

Service to country was a deeply-rooted tradition among those who carried the name de Bartez. It was the reason that Victor had at first supported Bernardo Peres. He had assumed that Peres' first concern was for Martiguay and had been happy to support his reforms.

But these 'reforms' had soon been revealed for what they really were: attempts to maintain and extend Peres' personal power, to ensure that he and he alone held absolute veto. With military support — and a ruthless secret police — Bernardo Peres had succeeded in his aim. For over ten years he had ruled Martiguay and been answerable to no one.

In the end, only his death — as well as growing

pressure from the United States, whose economic interests in Martiguay were being destroyed by rampant inflation and civil unrest — had forced free elections and brought Victor de Bartez to power.

Politics ran in the de Bartez blood. As a boy, Victor had attended a local military academy, then studied for his Law degree at Andorro's Central University. A post-graduate qualification in International Law from Oxford had followed and on his return to Martiguay he had combined a successful law practice with the management of the estate.

He had quickly become one of the strongest supporters of Bernardo Peres. A gifted orator, Peres had convinced his countrymen that he shared their passionate concern for their country's future.

Disillusion, when it came, hit hard. As the dictator tightened his grip, it was Victor de Bartez who became the natural leader of an illegal opposition, formulating policies, gathering supporters for when the moment for action presented itself.

Peres' sudden death provided that moment. Two months after the dictator's demise, Victor de Bartez was elected President of Martiguay.

Despite the initial American approval given to his Presidency, Victor knew there was unease about his accommodation of some of the more left-wing peasant parties. The sore point had been a focus of discussion on his first visit to Washington not long after his election. But Victor had stood his ground. The peasants were entitled to a voice, he insisted. To Victor, the definition of democracy meant the right of such parties to exist and contest future elections. The American view, it seemed, was not quite so all-embracing.

Suddenly Victor realised that his daughters were talking together while he, as so often happened these days, was lost in thoughts of his work. Silently he chided himself. What was the point in making the effort to return home for the holiday break, if he now ignored his children?

With a smile, he interrupted them. 'Now, Gabrielle, tell me where you have got to with your plans for the wedding — there are only four months to go, after all.'

As Gabrielle began her excited explanation, a shadow crossed Noella's face. She lowered her eyes.

As usual he was only interested in Gabrielle.

'Come in.'

Noella turned the gleaming brass handle and pushed open the heavy door. Dinner was over and she was presenting herself in her father's study as directed.

Victor de Bartez was sitting behind a magnificent mahogany desk. It held no other papers but the small folded card Noella recognised as her school report.

'Sit down here by me, Noella.'

As she crossed the spacious room, Noella tried to judge from her father's tone just how bad her report really was. Hiding her anxiety, she sat down on a velvet-backed chair her mother had brought from England.

For a long moment Victor de Bartez didn't speak as he unfolded the spectacles he used for reading and placed them on his nose. In the silence, Noella's eyes were drawn to the large oil portrait of her mother that hung on the wall facing her father's desk.

She is an icon, was her sudden bitter thought, a saint he still worships. Every time he looks at me, he must remember what he lost. And none of us is ever allowed to forget...

At last Victor de Bartez cleared his throat and tapped the card that lay in front of him. 'This, I am ashamed to see, carries the de Bartez name on it, Noella. The mark after every subject — geography, mathematics, history, religion — would appear to indicate a dunce, a brainless nothing who is capable of little else but writing her name and adding up two simple figures.'

He paused and looked coldly at his daughter. 'Is that all you can lay claim to after almost ten years of first-class schooling, Noella?'

She lowered her eyes; her palms were damp but a sudden irrational surge of pleasure shot through her. *He is looking at me, giving me his full attention...* Hiding her excitement, she answered softly, 'No, Papa.'

'Then why do these marks not reflect your true capabilities? Why do you waste your time and not apply yourself, Noella?' Victor de Bartez's exasperation was obvious. 'Do you have no pride in your name, do you not wish to achieve what Gabrielle has achieved?'

At the mention of her sister, Noella's mouth set in a stubborn line. Why did she always have to be compared to Gabrielle? She was not like her sister ... did not want to be. All she desired was to be loved as Gabrielle was loved. Loved for herself. Forgiven for her sin.

CHAPTER **FOUR**

Noella felt a warm sense of anticipation as the tall metal gates slowly swung open and the car crunched up the short pebbled drive.

As the car drew up at the entrance to the double-storeyed villa framed with blazing bougainvillea, Inez Sarandon emerged from the house, a smile of welcome on her attractive face.

'Noella! How wonderful to see you. And, of course, happy birthday, my dear. I'm so glad I can share it with you.'

As Noella stepped out into the warm sunshine, Inez Sarandon kissed her fondly on both cheeks. Wrapping an arm around the girl's waist, she led her into the house.

'I'm glad too, Inez.' It was so easy, Noella thought, to respond to the older woman's warmth. 'You are very kind to have this little party for me this evening.'

Inez Sarandon laughed as they walked down the cool, tiled hallway. 'The pleasure is mine, my dear. Have you any idea how young it makes me feel to be celebrating a seventeenth birthday once more?' She squeezed Noella's arm, her delight obvious. 'I have put you in your usual room. I'm sure you want to freshen up before the others arrive. Gabrielle and Eugene should be here by six, and your father, hope-fully, not long afterwards.'

★

Noella had been nine years old. Crouched beside Gabrielle, she had peered down curiously through the wooden banisters at the attractive stranger who had arrived at the *hacienda* with their father.

Later, when they had joined the two adults in the sitting room before dinner, her father had seemed strangely nervous as he made the introductions. 'Children, may I introduce Senora Sarandon? She is a ... a good friend of mine.'

Noella stared at the woman who sat smiling at them from the sofa. Her eyes were friendly, her glossy, copper-coloured hair was drawn up in a heavy coil, and the scent of some wonderful perfume filled the room. As she moved to set down her wine glass, the jewels on her fingers and ear lobes flashed in the lamplight.

A nudge from Gabrielle reminded her of her manners. Noella bobbed a curtsy as the nuns had taught her.

'*Buenas noches*, senora,' she said shyly, echoing Gabrielle.

'I am very pleased to meet you both,' Inez Sarandon replied warmly. 'Your father has told me so much about you.'

Later as they sat at dinner, Noella couldn't take her eyes off this mysterious 'friend' of her father. Who was she? Why had her father told Senora Sarandon 'so much' about herself and Gabrielle?

Later, Noella raised these puzzling questions with her sister.

Gabrielle's dark eyes had looked troubled. 'I ... I think Papa needs a ... a friend, Noella. He misses Mama very much.'

Still, Noella didn't really understand.

As the maid left her to unpack in one of the guest bedrooms, Noella reflected on how grateful she was that Inez Sarandon had become part of their lives.

Since her father's election, the relationship had, of necessity, become more discreet, but Inez had made it clear that she was always on call as a friend and confidante.

Gabrielle had long overcome her resentment of the woman she had seen as taking her mother's place. These days she and Inez were very close. On the other hand, Noella had never had any reason to resent the attractive widow. If Inez Sarandon helped fill the void in her father's life then Noella could only be grateful for any respite from her burden of guilt.

She took her time dressing for dinner. With both her father and Eugene in attendance she wanted to look her very best. Not yet permitted to wear make-up, Noella was glad that her lashes were naturally long and thick and her cheeks had a natural blush. As she leaned into the mirror, biting her lips to give them colour, she was pleased to see how much of her bosom was revealed. She had badgered the dressmaker to cut the neckline lower.

'Surely modesty is more dignified, senorita,' the woman had protested mildly. The child was, after all, the daughter of *el Presidente*.

'I am not ashamed of my body,' retorted Noella, and with a shrug the seamstress had complied.

Tonight they will see that I am a woman, Noella thought, her eyes shining brightly. Eugene would desire her, and her father would notice her at last.

Ramon Artemos froze as the girl entered the room.

Dios! A child with the body of an angel! So ripe, so succulent, so young... He felt the bulge start between his legs and shifted uncomfortably in his seat as the girl kissed first her sister and then her brother-in-law to-be.

A moment later Ramon was forced to rise awkwardly to his feet. 'And may I introduce my cousin, Noella, dear? Senor Ramon Artemos.'

'Enchanted, senorita.' Ramon took the soft cool hand in his own and quickly resumed his seat before his lust betrayed him.

'Senor Artemos is staying a few days with me,' explained Inez as the maid offered glasses of champagne. 'My cousin has made quite a name for himself as a movie director in LA; it is not often that he pays us a visit.'

'I hope you forgive me for intruding on your celebrations, senorita.' Ramon Artemos was all smooth charm. 'I have just finished my latest movie and was forced to attend to a little business in my homeland.'

'There is no need to apologise, senor.' Noella studied the stranger with interest. She had had no idea that Inez had a cousin in the movie industry. Ramon Artemos looked older than Inez, in his late forties perhaps, thickening around the middle but handsome in a rugged way with his smooth, tanned skin and greying hair. His clothes, Noella realised, were unmistakably *norteamericano*: loafers, double-breasted navy jacket with gilt buttons, buttoned-down collar on his shirt.

The way he was looking at her told her that Senor Artemos found her attractive. But Noella turned away from his gaze. Old men did not interest her. It was Eugene she wanted to impress.

A frown creased Inez's face as she sipped at her cocktail. It worried her to see how openly Noella flirted with her sister's fiance. Yet Gabrielle, if she noticed — and surely she couldn't fail to — gave no indication of her feelings. Thank God, Inez comforted herself, that Eugene in no way encouraged the girl. The way she was displaying herself in that terrible dress would have tempted a saint. Inez could see that Noella's wardrobe was something they would have to talk about.

Ramon Artemos, too, was not unaffected by Noella's performance. The response in his groin was unmistakable as he watched her posing and posturing, the neck of her dress dipping temptingly as she bent over to pick up her drink, her hand lingering on Eugene's knee as she made her point. He was finding it more and more difficult to concentrate on the conversation.

Dios. She was driving him crazy. And only seventeen years old . . . a gift.

Finally the provocation proved too much for Eugene to ignore. In a low voice he said, 'Noella, a lady has no need to flaunt herself so blatantly. Forgive me for saying this, but you rob yourself of dignity in a dress which is too old for you while your behaviour is that of a precocious child. Men are not attracted by such antics.'

From where she sat, Inez was unable to hear his words but she saw the young girl's face burn with embarrassment. It was easy enough to guess what had transpired. Yet she couldn't blame Eugene . . . or the child who craved so obviously for love and attention. Anxiously, she glanced at the slim gold watch on her wrist. If only Victor would arrive soon.

Beside her, Ramon noticed her action. 'He is late?'

'Yes.' A frown drew Inez's dark brows together. 'There was a meeting, but he promised he would do his best to get away on time.'

Ramon nodded. It was almost fifteen years since he had left Martiguay; he had little interest in the backward peasant country which had been his birthplace. Yet even he had to admit that since Victor de Bartez had come to power, things slowly seemed to be changing.

Ramon Artemos had been in his thirties when he had left Martiguay for the United States. A Golden Globe award for his second film, a soul-searching look at the nature of love between mother and son, had opened a few doors and given him his start. Now, happy to leave the soul-searching to others, he preferred to direct the sort of mass-market entertainment which made him rich enough to support two ex-wives and four children, and powerful enough to bed numerous beautiful young hopefuls.

In an attempt to distract himself from the sight of the seductive child, he lit a cigarillo and began to tell Inez about his forthcoming movie.

But his cousin was barely listening. Inez was thinking of Victor, of the punishing workload he had undertaken, and how she wished she could more openly assist him.

But she had known from the start that Victor would never marry her. With great honesty and as gently as he could, he had made it clear that no one would ever be able to take the place of the wife he had adored.

'I wish it could be otherwise, my dearest Inez, but I cannot help what is in my heart. If you can accept that, then we can find comfort and companionship with each other, be friends and lovers.'

By the time she had been introduced to Victor de Bartez, Inez had been a widow for almost five years. Her late husband had left her a fortune, but she soon discovered that money did not cure loneliness. It had been difficult to accept that Victor would never make her his wife, but now, at forty-two, Inez was pragmatic. As Victor said, there was comfort in each other's company — and she loved his children as if they were her own.

While their relationship was an open secret in their own circle, discretion was still necessary and Inez had come to terms with the fact that she would never stand by Victor's side as the first lady of Martiguay.

Shaking off such thoughts, Inez got to her feet. It was almost eight-thirty. 'I think we should start or the dinner will be spoilt. I am sure Victor will be here any moment.'

As she spoke the unconvincing words, Inez saw the look on Noella's face and pity welled up inside her. Poor child. Not only had she lost a mother but she also had to suffer her father's rejection.

To Inez, the situation was painfully obvious but Victor had always flatly refused to discuss it. 'I love my daughters equally, Inez. Surely you are not suggesting that I bear a grudge against Noella for... for what happened?'

Inez had been unable to answer. For that was exactly how it appeared to her. She loved Victor de Bartez with all her heart; he was a good man, honest, strong, and moral. Yet for all that, he could not — or would not — recognise that by his distance and reserve, he was reinforcing the burden of Noella's guilt. Victor was slowly destroying his younger child...

They were halfway through their first course when Inez was called to the phone. As soon as she came back into the dining room she was aware of Noella's searching eyes on her face.

'I—I'm sorry, Noella dear. That was your father. He's been held up. He won't be able to make it.'

Inez Sarandon's heart went out to the girl as she saw the flash of pain that crossed the beautiful face. She knew what the child was thinking: her birthday was not important enough for her father to attend; he had let her down again.

'He sends his sincerest apologies, my dear, and asked that I pass on his very best wishes. He — he will try to get to the *hacienda* later this month.'

But Noella had already turned back to her meal. 'Of course,' she said flatly, her eyes downcast.

After the meal was over, Inez, in an attempt to jolly the child out of her disappointment, put a stack of dance records on the stereo. 'Come on, everyone, we must work off that fattening birthday cake.'

It was the answer to Ramon Artemos' prayers. He had spent the meal in an agony of sexual frustration seated opposite the seventeen-year-old temptress. Every movement she made — stretching for the salt, bending over her plate — seemed calculated to allow him a tantalising glimpse of the full young breasts beneath the low neckline of the dress. Very young girls had always been one of Ramon Artemos' weaknesses and Noella de Bartez was driving him crazy.

Now, sweating in anticipation, he smiled as he drew her from her seat. 'Come, little birthday girl, we must try to make you happy on this special night.'

Reluctantly, face sulky, Noella got to her feet, allowing the older man to take her in his arms. Over his shoulder she could see Gabrielle and Eugene smiling into each other's eyes as they too moved to the music and suddenly her sulkiness gave way to anger.

How dare Eugene tell her she was not yet a woman! How dare he think she was a child who could not attract a man!

Her face was close to Ramon's, and she could see the glaze in his eyes, feel his hot breath against her cheek. At least he was responding to her as a woman.

Suddenly defiant, she released herself from the older man's hold and began to dance with wild abandon, her every movement calculated to tease and provoke. She would show Eugene how much of a woman she was; she would show him how she could move this boring old film director.

Opposite her, Ramon Artemos felt sick with desire.

CHAPTER FIVE

'A little closer, senora. *Si, si*, that is splendid. And now, a smile...'

While the wedding party posed for the photographer, the guests mingled on the velvet lawns, bathed in brilliant sunshine. Amidst strict security, the wedding ceremony had taken place earlier in the local stone church which five decades ago had been erected with the assistance of the de Bartez fortune.

It was a day of mixed feelings for Victor. As he walked up the aisle with his daughter on his arm he had wished with all his heart that Catherine might have been there to share this moment. Like him, she would have been so proud of their first born.

Less than a month ago, Gabrielle had graduated with first-class honours. Now she would join the Department of Justice within her father's government. Victor was delighted. He was not old-fashioned when it came to opportunities for women. If all went as he hoped and planned, Gabrielle might one day step into his shoes, carry on the work he had begun. Another de Bartez would take her rightful place in Martiguay's history.

Gabrielle had the brains and drive to do so, he was sure of that; and Eugene would be the perfect supportive partner. Victor had come to know the young man well enough to realise that he would be happy to play a complementary role. Like so many others, he knew the value and influence of the de Bartez name.

At last the photographer was satisfied. As Victor was once more engulfed by his guests, he saw Noella out of the corner of his eye. Oblivious of her duties as always, she was hurrying towards the house. He hid his irritation. What was he going to do with her?

Picking up the skirts of her pale pink taffeta dress, Noella moved quickly up the broad wooden staircase to her bedroom. She felt terrible. Her head was pounding and she felt as if she were going to faint. How had she managed to get through the ceremony in the church? How had she found the strength to stand by her sister's side and pretend that nothing was wrong?

In the spacious marble bathroom she wet a towel with cold water and held it against her forehead. It didn't help.

Back in her bedroom she kicked off her high-heeled shoes and lay down on the bed. Closing her eyes, she tried to shut out the nightmare which was threatening to engulf her.

Dios, Dios . . . let it not be true, she prayed, tears gathering in the corners of her eyes. But the horror would not go away.

Tonight she would have to do something. Before it was too late.

Paolo Avende was dreaming. As he lay on his hard narrow mattress in the shed behind the stable block, he smiled in his sleep.

She had seemed like a vision today in her beautiful dress, her golden hair shining in the sunlight. From his hiding place in the bushes at the edge of the lawn he had seen how the elegant, worldly men had followed her with their eyes and had felt a jealousy he had no right to feel. Noella still refused to have anything to do with him; he had forced himself to accept the fact that everything was different between them now.

Yet for Paolo those days and nights of lovemaking would ever remain in his memory. The feel of her skin, the heady scent of her perfume, the way she had whispered her need of him.

'Paolo... Paolo... ' The boy stirred in his sleep. It was as if she were beside him now.

'Paolo! Wake up, Paolo! Please!'

With a start the stableboy opened his eyes. It wasn't a dream! Noella was here, beside him.

'Oh, Paolo, please, you must help me.' In the moonlight he could see the tears coursing down her cheeks. Still dazed with sleep, he stared in confusion at the weeping girl. What could be wrong? What sort of trouble could the daughter of *el Presidente* be in that she needed a stableboy's help?

Through her sobs, Noella told him.

'This way, Noella. Follow me.' Paolo called the instructions over his shoulder. 'Let the mule have his head; he will find the way.'

Behind him, Noella clutched at the coarse grey mane as the animal lurched down the steep track. Every now and then its hooves appeared to slip in the loose shale and her stomach would clutch in fear. But each time the mule found its feet again.

They had left at eight. Now, with the sun growing steadily hotter, she began to wonder if Paolo had lost his way. Surely they must be close to the village now.

As if reading her thoughts, Paolo called back, 'We are almost there, Noella. See, there is the church tower.'

Squinting against the dazzling light, Noella looked in the direction Paolo was pointing. Yes, she could see it now. A tall ochre-coloured structure topped by a simple wooden crucifix. Despite the heat, a shiver ran through her body. She was dreading what was to come. But she had no other choice. There had been no one but Paolo she could turn to.

It had taken him three days to get the information they needed and Noella had felt nothing but relief when he told her of his success. Now, as the path levelled out and they began to pass the outlying houses of the village, she pulled the dark shawl closer around her face. The rough cotton chafed her skin as did the faded dress Paolo had found for her. She worried again about the effectiveness of such a disguise. But surely here, in this mountain village, the peasants would never recognise the younger daughter of *el Presidente*?

As they entered the single main street, a gang of noisy, dirty-faced children chased after them, calling out and laughing at the strangers. Paolo swore at them, tried to shoo them away without success, while dark-clothed women stared with round, curious eyes from doorways and windows.

At last they found the house they were looking for. It stood at the far edge of the village, a typical peasant's dwelling of stone walls, an earthen floor, and a cracked, tiled roof. In the small front yard a few scrawny chickens scratched in the dusty ground, watched over by a panting, almost hairless dog.

Trying to hide his horror from Noella, Paolo helped her from her mount. 'I am sure it will be okay, Noella. The man who told me about her said she is clean and . . . successful.'

Noella nodded, unable to speak. *Madre de Dios*, how could she dare . . . ?

The woman was waiting by the open door. Her eyes were hard and unfriendly and the heavy creases of her face were seamed with dirt. Without returning Paolo's tentative greeting she turned and led the way into the second of the two rooms.

Noella followed, heart thumping in terror as she averted her eyes from the low couch covered by a greying sheet. She couldn't go through with it! Not here. Not like this.

But she knew she had no choice. Paolo had been the only one she could turn to. Not Gabrielle, not Inez . . . and never, never, her father.

The woman grunted something at Paolo and put out a work-roughened hand. From his pocket Paolo withdrew a folded envelope and the woman opened it at once, licking her dusty fingers as she counted the wedge of notes.

Satisfied, she nodded and said in a surly voice, 'It will take about an hour. Go to the house next door. My daughter will give you refreshment.'

Paolo nodded and turned to Noella. He gripped her hand in his and forced a smile. His mouth was suddenly very dry. 'It will be fine,' he whispered. 'Have courage, Noella. I will not be far away.'

With a final glance into those staring, frightened eyes he turned and was gone.

The next two hours were the worst of Paolo's life. To his horror, he was close enough to hear Noella's screams of pain, the harsh voice of the woman ordering her to lie still. And all the while, the woman's daughter, a thickset girl with a dark moustache, went about her usual tasks unperturbed while her children also ignored the piercing screams. Perhaps, thought Paolo, sweat beading his upper lip, they heard them often enough.

The longer he waited, the greater his fears grew. If only there had been another way. If Noella had been an ordinary village girl she could have been spared this ordeal.

When she had broken the news to him that night he had tried in a shy, halting way to make her understand his frustration. 'Forgive my boldness, Noella, when I say that to offer you marriage would be my greatest joy. But I know how impertinent and impossible is that dream.' His eyes were filled with a sad intensity. 'This guilt stains deep into my soul; I only hope that some day in the future I will be able to make it up to you.'

Turning away from his intense gaze, Noella answered dully, 'You have nothing to blame yourself for, Paolo'.

They called him at last. 'Come, she is waiting.' It was the woman herself who came for him.

Noella was sitting on a low wooden stool by the front door, her face dead white.

'Is it all right?'

Noella nodded. 'Yes. Please, let us leave now, Paolo. At once.' Her voice was a raw whisper.

He helped her to her feet and she walked slowly and shakily into the dusty yard.

'Are you sure you can manage with the mule? I —'

'What other way is there, Paolo?' The words came out tightly.

She was right, of course. The mules were the only way. To keep their journey secret they had had no other option.

For Noella, the return trip over the hills seemed a never-ending nightmare. Every lurching movement of the animal intensified her agony. Her insides felt as if they had been scraped raw with blunt razors and again and again she was forced to bite her tongue to stop from screaming out in pain.

Her flesh began to burn in the blistering sun and to her horror she felt flies settle on the rivulets of blood that ran slowly down her legs. Once, twice, she came close to passing out, but Paolo was always there to reach out and steady her, to offer sympathy and comfort as they covered the dusty miles back to the *hacienda*.

Just ten minutes from the house, they stopped at a small shaded spring. While the animals drank in long, dragging gulps, Paolo bathed the dried blood from her legs and wiped clean her face and hands.

'What are you muttering, Paolo?' she asked faintly as she lay back against the coarse grass.

'Nothing, Noella...' How could he tell her he was praying to the Madonna that everything would be all right? When he'd been given the address he'd been seeking, Paolo was sure they were being directed to a helpful midwife whose hygiene and skills would be beyond question. The primitive conditions they'd encountered had filled him with horror.

What if Noella were to die? he wondered fearfully. How could he live knowing it was he who had caused her death? He, who loved her to the depths of his soul? The thought made his insides turn to jelly.

But he hid his fear from Noella. 'Come.' He helped her to her feet. 'We are close now. Back in my room you can change into your proper clothes.'

Grunting in pain, Noella managed to clamber back into the saddle. She had told Nona she was going to spend the day riding over to the far valley. The nurse had protested, of course, but Noella knew she wouldn't be able to stop her. The fact that her misbehaviour would no doubt be reported to her father at some later date was, at that moment, the very least of her worries.

Dressed once more in her own clothes, Noella hesitated for a moment by the door of Paolo's room. She reached for the boy's hand and said softly, 'I thank you with all my heart, Paolo. And please... forgive me for treating you so badly. I feel so ashamed.'

She leaned towards him and kissed him gently on the lips. 'I will always remember how you have helped me.'

Paolo watched as she walked stiffly towards the house, his fingers pressed against the place where her lips had touched his.

Noella managed to hide the truth for almost twenty-four hours.

Evading Nona's watchful eye, she had made her way to her room unobserved that first evening. There, she soaked interminably in the tub, soaping herself again and again as if to wash away not only the grime and dust but all memory of that terrible experience.

Then not long afterwards, the bleeding started again. Frightened, Noella spread clean towels across the bed to protect the sheets. She would rise early the next day and wash them before Nona saw them.

It was only a moment later that the old woman herself bustled into the room.

'So there you are, you wicked child! Wait until I tell your father what tricks you get up to behind his back. Come downstairs this instant. Dinner will be on the table any minute.' Then the nurse's eyes opened wide. '*Dios*! Look at you! See what happens when you spend so many hours in the sun? You are the colour of a chilli pepper.'

It was the excuse Noella needed and she leapt at it. 'Nona... please. I'm sorry, I was wrong to disobey you. This sunburn is so painful. I do not feel like eating anything tonight.'

At once the old woman was full of concern. She had cared for Noella since she was a baby and while the girl might be a handful, Nona's devotion to her was absolute.

Shaking her head and clucking her tongue in dismay, she said, 'Cold cloths will help ease the pain ... I shall fetch them at once.'

By the time she returned, Noella was deep in sleep.

The next day, Noella awoke drenched in sweat after a restless night. Beneath her, the towels were sodden with blood.

Weakly, she got to her feet and staggered with the soiled linen to the bathroom. Somehow she found the strength to rinse away the blood and hang the heavy towels over the tiny wrought iron balcony where, she hoped, no one would see them.

Her reflection in the bathroom mirror shocked her. Her face was grey, her dark eyes sunk deep in their sockets and her hair clung damply to her forehead. She had lost a lot of blood. Today, she told herself, fighting back panic, she would do nothing but rest and perhaps by this evening she would feel better.

Slowly, like an old woman, she washed and dressed, trying to ignore the burning sharpness in her belly. When, at last, she was ready, she picked up a book and made her way down to the garden. If she stayed in bed Nona might send for the doctor and she knew she must avoid that at all costs.

Her sunburnt flesh was still sore and she sat in the shade of a pepper tree, the book open on her lap while her eyes focused unseeingly on the same few lines. It was there that Paolo found her.

'Are you all right, Noella?' He looked anxiously at her glazed eyes, her pale, sweat-beaded face.

She nodded, gritting her teeth as a spasm of pain gripped her. 'Yes, Paolo. I am sure by this evening I will feel much better.'

Unable to linger, Paolo returned reluctantly to his chores. Noella's words did nothing to allay his fears.

For the rest of the day, Noella managed to stay out of Nona's way. But at six o'clock she was forced to present herself at the dinner table. When her father and Gabrielle were away she and Nona always ate together.

The sight of food made Noella feel sick. She pushed it around her plate, trying to make it look as though she had eaten, but Nona was not deceived.

'Where is your appetite, child? Has your stupidity of yesterday lost you that, too?'

Listlessly, Noella shook her head. She felt too weak even to answer.

A frown creased the old woman's broad face and, rising to her feet, she moved to Noella's side.

Her eyes widened in dismay as she placed a hand on the girl's forehead. '*Dios*! Your face is on fire, child! What are you thinking of not to tell me you are ill?'

Pulling out the chair, Nona helped Noella to her feet. 'Come. You must have a cool bath at once while I see that the doctor is called.'

'No!' The word Noella had meant so forcefully came out as barely more than a whisper.

Upstairs, she continued her weak protestations as Nona ran the bath. The old woman ignored her. 'Now undress and immerse yourself in that, child, while I telephone for the doctor. Sunstroke can be dangerous if not properly treated.'

Five minutes later when she came back to the bathroom the old woman's heart seemed to shrink in her chest.

Grey-faced, Noella lay back in the tub with her eyes closed, while around her the water was stained a deep and terrifying red.

CHAPTER SIX

'Are you warm enough, senorita?'

With a start, Noella turned to see the uniformed nurse by her side. She had been alone on the terrace, so deep in thought that she hadn't heard the woman approach.

'*Si*, I am fine, nurse. *Gracias.*'

The mountain air was crisp but the rug over her legs kept Noella warm as she settled back against the lounging chair.

'Please let me know if you need anything, senorita.' The middle-aged woman gave her a solicitous look as she turned away.

None of the staff in the discreet expensive clinic ever called Noella by name. Here, she was not the daughter of *el Presidente* and the emergency operation which had saved her life was never referred to. The hospital records stated only that she was 'resting' — 'recovering her strength' after an unstated illness.

And after three weeks of constant care and rest Noella did feel well again. Well enough to be driven home the next day.

She was afraid of what awaited her on her return. Both Gabrielle and her father had visited during her stay in the clinic; once he had been assured of his daughter's recovery, Victor de Bartez had demanded an answer to the question Noella was dreading.

'Tell me his name, Noella. Who was it who has

robbed you of your innocence?' His face was pale with anger.

'Please, Papa,' Noella answered weakly, 'I — I cannot tell you . . . Do not ask me this question, I beg of you.'

Tight-lipped, Victor nodded. 'Very well, Noella. I will not discuss it now. But when you come home I promise you I will get to the bottom of this outrage.'

Noella looked out across the valley, her face bleak with despair. Where would she get the strength to keep the dreadful truth to herself? How could she resist her father's pressure to name the man who had not only defiled her but almost cost her her life?

The bile rose in her throat as memory of that dreadful night returned . . .

She had no idea how long she had been asleep when she felt someone gently shaking her. The hand pressed to her mouth kept her from calling out.

'Hush, little one. Don't be afraid. It is I, Ramon.' The words were whispered in her ear and she could smell the heavy odour of his aftershave and the faint whiff of the cognac he had drunk after dinner.

Still half-asleep, Noella twisted her head against the pillow. Ramon Artemos? Here in her room? What could he . . . ?

The bed creaked as the director slid his body down next to hers. He threw back the sheets and she heard his deep, shuddering sigh as his free hand began to caress her flesh. 'I knew you would sleep naked, *querida* . . . '

Again Noella tried to squirm free of the suffocating hold, but the stranger's grip was too strong. Then, as he moved his body over her own, she realised with a shock that Ramon Artemos was also naked.

Hardly able to believe what was happening, she felt his fingers move to her breasts, drag painfully at her nipples. A moment later his hands were moving downward, forcing her thighs apart, searching out the core of her.

'Look, *querida*... see how you excite me...' His voice was husky with lust as he pressed his thickness against her bare leg. 'When you danced so provocatively I knew what you were begging for. I knew what you wanted.'

His breath coming in quick harsh gasps, Ramon Artemos could prolong the agony of desire no longer. With one sharp movement he thrust his aching stem inside her and began pumping savagely, grunting with every thrust. It was the feel of young flesh that excited him, the firm roundness, the dewy freshness...

Pinned beneath him, Noella struggled, staring wild-eyed into the darkness. But as her violator's movements grew more frenzied, she was powerless to resist. A few short moments later, she heard his quick intake of breath, his body jackknifed, and hoarsely he moaned his ecstasy.

Alone on the terrace, Noella shivered as the feelings of disgust and revulsion swept through her once again. What Ramon Artemos had done had left her feeling dirty and ashamed, as if she were a *puta*, a prostitute, nothing more than a receptacle for his lust. With Paolo it had never been like that. Together they had been like two healthy young animals, finding mutual pleasure and excitement in exploring the mysteries of their bodies.

Afterwards, Artemos had stood over her as she lay whimpering on the bed. He knew only too well that she dare not say a word about what had occurred.

'I am not the first, am I, little one? There have been others — who knows how many? And little wonder, if you invite them as openly, as brazenly, as you invited me. Your sister, Inez, Eugene, all who saw your performance this evening would be forced to admit that it was you who were the tantaliser, the seductress... first with Eugene, then myself.'

Filled with shame and disgust, Noella could hear

the smile in his voice as he said, 'No, my little temptress, I do not think you will tell anyone of this'.

And Noella knew she never could. Inez's cousin... How could she tell her father that?

Inez would never forgive herself and the relationship between them all might be ruined for ever.

No, she had made up her mind. No matter what her father threatened, nothing would make her reveal the truth.

It was Gabrielle who stood anxiously waiting as the car drew up the next afternoon at the *hacienda*.

She kissed her sister fondly, her manner gentle and sympathetic. 'It is good to have you home, Noella. Come,' she said, as she led the way into the house, 'I have refreshments waiting in the sitting room.'

As the maid poured the coffee, Gabrielle sat silently and Noella began to feel nervous. She had seen little of her sister since her marriage to Eugene. Already, she thought, they had grown even further apart: Gabrielle with her perfect marriage, her first-class degree, her important position in the Department of Justice. She, once more the disappointment, with her poor school results, her disobedience, and now her shameful secret.

After the maid went out and closed the door behind her, Gabrielle put down her coffee cup and turned to her sister.

'It is not my place to harp on this tragedy, Noella. But perhaps you do not realise how very fortunate you are to be alive. Only the speedy action of the surgeons and our most fervent prayers saved your life.' Gabrielle's face creased in a worried frown and she shook her head. 'Why did you not come to me or Inez, Noella? Surely you — ' She stopped abruptly, aware of her own agitation. Gabrielle had been trained as a lawyer; she knew it would not assist the situation in any way to let emotion displace logic.

When Noella didn't answer, Gabrielle went on. 'From my point of view, what's done is done, Noella. But what you must realise is that Papa does not view things this way. You have hurt him very deeply; in his eyes, your reputation is tarnished and your chances of a worthy marriage are seriously compromised. It is only fortunate that the scandal has been contained.'

She leaned forward, her voice urgent. 'Papa is determined to know who was responsible for this, Noella. You must tell him. It is your duty to do so. For Papa, the family honour is at stake. He will see that this person is made to answer for his violation.'

Still Noella sat stubbornly quiet.

With a sinking heart, Gabrielle was forced to reveal the full ramifications of the tragedy. 'Surely, Noella,' she said softly 'you do not want to see go unpunished the man who has almost certainly cost your right to children?'

Victor de Bartez was having trouble concentrating.

The meeting of the Council for the Interior had been in progress for almost three hours and too often Victor had found his attention wandering to the problem of his younger daughter.

She still refused to give him the name of the *bastardo* who had brought about her tragic condition.

It was a situation he had discussed endlessly with Inez. 'The whole thing is intolerable, Inez! The child continues to defy me and I won't stand for it.'

Watching him pace angrily around her sitting room, Inez had tried her best to pacify the situation. 'I know it is difficult for you, Victor, but Noella has learnt a hard lesson, I am sure. If you are still worried about leaving her with Nona, you know that I have offered to have her here with me.'

Victor's scowl did not diminish. Inez's offer was a generous, if not totally practical, one but he had made up his mind how to deal with Noella.

'Marriage, Inez. A suitable marriage, arranged as swiftly as possible, is the only way to handle this wilful child. A husband and a home to keep her busy will see an end to this wildness.'

Yet not babies, not a family, thought Inez worriedly. What Martiguayan man would accept a woman who could not give him that? And the girl was just seventeen. Victor himself still called her a child, yet now considered her ready for marriage.

Gently, she tried to protest. 'But, Victor, she is so young — '

'I have made up my mind, Inez.' His mouth was set in a firm line. 'She has refused to divulge the identity of her lover so now I shall make it my business to arrange a suitable husband.'

As the keeper of the house in the absence of *el Presidente* or his elder daughter, it was Nona to whom the man was brought when he arrived at the *hacienda*.

He was short and wiry, his dark hair oiled straight back from a high forehead, his hands surprisingly neat and well cared for.

The guards who escorted him to the *hacienda* entrance had already informed Nona that the visitor's name was Franco Calaban. A jeweller, he had told them, but beyond that had refused to state his business.

Perplexed by the unexpected intrusion into her unvarying daily routine, Nona led the man into the small parlour at the rear of the kitchen.

As he took the seat indicated, Franco Calaban cleared his throat uneasily. 'The matter is somewhat ... delicate, senora. Perhaps ... ' He glanced at the open door.

Increasingly puzzled, Nona assured their privacy. Seating herself opposite the visitor, she asked him to state his business.

Franco Calaban opened the small leather case he had with him and brought out a black velvet pouch.

Pulling open the drawstring, he produced a narrow gold bracelet. 'Do you recognise this item, senora?'

Nona's small dark eyes opened wide. She certainly did.

That evening Victor de Bartez received a phone call from the *hacienda*.

'What is it, Nona? Is something wrong?' His thoughts flew immediately to Noella.

As he listened to the old woman's excited tones, Victor's expression hardened. 'I will deal with this at once, Nona. Expect me tomorrow evening.'

Again Franco Calaban arrived at the house. This time he was accompanied by his assistant, a heavy, bespectacled man in his thirties. They were shown into the same parlour, where this time Victor de Bartez awaited them.

Nervous in the presence of such esteemed company, Franco Calaban's explanation become long-winded.

'*Momento, momento* —' Irritated, Victor held up a hand. 'Let me understand this clearly. You recognised this bracelet because my wife had once sent it along to you?'

'*Si, Presidente*. That was a long time ago but I never forget any pieces I have worked on. The clasp was broken and — '

Victor cut him off impatiently. 'But it was your assistant who spoke to the boy?'

The man nodded. '*Si, si*. If I had been in the shop that day I would have recognised the bracelet at once. My assistant was not to know.'

The thickset man shook his head, anxious to shrug off any blame.

'When the boy offered the item for sale, my assistant was happy to negotiate a price. It is a very pretty piece, after all.'

Victor looked down at the bracelet that dangled from his fingers. Catherine's. One of his very first gifts to her . . .

'Of course,' the jeweller continued, 'when I saw it, I realised it had been stolen and came at once to do my duty.'

Victor rose to his feet. 'You have my sincere thanks, senor. Now,' he added slowly, 'we must identify the culprit, and ensure he is made to pay for his crime . . .'

CHAPTER SEVEN

Bristling with anger, Victor de Bartez confronted the white-faced boy in the small cobbled yard behind the stables.

'So, I keep a thief under my roof! Give him food to eat, a bed to sleep in, a living wage. Yet still he cannot be trusted!'

Paolo hung his head. The moment he had been called in front of the jeweller's assistant he knew nothing could save him.

Victor de Bartez stopped his angry pacing and faced his employee. 'I want the truth, boy! I want to know how you gained access to my possessions! Who in my household helped in your despicable deed?'

Still Paolo said nothing. For how could he defend himself without revealing the ugly truth? Better that *el Presidente* think him a thief than discover that.

In the face of the boy's silence, Victor's temper grew. 'So, you have forgotten how to use your tongue! Well, maybe the police will help to loosen it for you.'

'Papa! *No!*'

At the sound of his daughter's voice, Victor de Bartez spun round, his face darkening. 'Leave here at once, Noella! This has nothing to do with you!'

Ignoring the unspoken plea in Paolo's eyes, Noella cried, 'But it does, Papa! It does!' Eyes brimming with tears, she faced her father. 'Paolo is no thief, Papa. It was I who gave him the bracelet... He — he got the money for me!'

In that long moment as his eyes swept from his distraught daughter to the terrified boy and back again, Victor de Bartez suddenly understood.

'*Dios*!' The word exploded from his lips. 'The stableboy! He is the one who has taken your innocence! It is he who has dared to lay a hand on my child!'

Victor de Bartez did not hesitate. A powerfully built man, he grabbed at the collar of Paolo's thin cotton shirt and dragged him across the yard. A heavy, plaited horsewhip hung on the stable wall near the spot Victor let Paolo fall.

Eyes widening in horror, Noella saw at once what her father meant to do. 'NO!' She ran towards him and grasped desperately at his arm. 'Papa, no! I beg you ... the fault was all — '

The backhander caught her a stinging glance across the face and she staggered backward, crying out in shock as much as pain.

'Go! Get out of here! I will deal with you later!' roared Victor de Bartez as he snatched the whip from its hook.

The blind fury in her father's face told Noella the impossibility of attempting alone to save Paolo. She turned and ran desperately towards the house as, behind her, the sound of a whip crack filled the air, followed immediately by Paolo's agonising scream.

Nona was serving lunch in the kitchen to Jose Manerro, the head gardener. They were both shaking their heads over the sad business of Paolo Avende. Paolo a thief ... Who would have thought it of the boy? Still, the evidence —

Startled, they both looked up as the kitchen door was flung open.

'Nona! Nona!' Sobbing in terror, Noella grabbed the elderly nurse by the hand. In her distress she failed to notice the tall, well-built man sitting at the far end of the long kitchen table.

'Nona! In the stable yard... Papa — he is killing Paolo! Please!'

The old woman understood at once. 'Jose!' She turned to her fellow employee.

Only then did Noella see the man she recognised as one of her father's labourers. 'Please!' She was close to hysteria. 'Please save him! Save Paolo for me. Hurry!'

Moments later, Jose Manerro arrived panting at the yard to see the boy lying sprawled on the dusty cobbles. Already his shirt was in shreds, the blood flowing freely from the wounds on his back.

'You dare! You dare to touch my daughter!' His face suffused with rage, the President of Martiguay was raising the lash to deliver yet another blow, when suddenly his arm was caught from behind.

'Senor! No! I beg of you!'

Furious, Victor de Bartez spun round to see who had dared to interfere.

'Senor, please! Look, the boy is half-dead. The scandal... it would destroy us all, destroy all you are working so hard for.'

The words seemed to break the short circuit of rage which had held Victor de Bartez in its grip. Slowly he lowered his arm and looked down at the boy at his feet.

Jesu, what was he doing? Martiguay, the future — he had almost thrown it all away.

In a voice drained of all emotion he said, 'Get rid of him. Tomorrow at first light, send him on his way.' Without looking back, he strode towards the house.

Much later that evening, his rage finally under control, Victor de Bartez dropped his bombshell on his daughter.

'This time, Noella, you will do as I say. You have no choice.' In the privacy of his study he regarded his daughter coldly.

The boy had been dealt with — first thing tomorrow he would be gone. Now Victor was determined to settle the problem of Noella, once and for all.

'My position keeps me from home too often to exercise the sort of control and direction you so obviously require, Noella. Therefore I intend to see that a marriage is arranged as swiftly as possible.'

Ignoring his daughter's gasp of shock, Victor de Bartez continued, distaste creasing his patrician features. 'In the circumstances, I am not about to force a stableboy to do his duty by you. That incident must be forgotten at once and the de Bartez name honoured by an eligible worthy suitor. There are at least half a dozen sons of friends who immediately come to mind. Do I make myself abundantly clear?'

'Yes, Papa.'

Noella knew she had no time to lose.

It was after midnight when Noella slipped out of the house and ran quickly and quietly through the moonlit gardens. In the stableblock the horses moved restlessly in their boxes as she hurried past.

She stood outside Paolo's tiny room for a moment, her belly churning with guilt as the soft groans of pain reached her through the stout wooden door.

How could she ever make it up to him? Paolo had suffered like an animal at her father's hands. And he had suffered for a lie . . .

Forcing herself to turn the handle, she pushed open the heavy door.

He lay face down on the narrow mattress and even in the shadowy light of the single lamp, Noella saw enough to make her gasp in horror. From shoulder to buttock the boy's back had been shredded into a bloody, weeping mess.

'Paolo! Oh, *Dios*! What has he done to you?'

Slowly the boy turned his head, confusion then alarm

showing on his tortured face. He tried to speak but no sound came from his parched lips.

'Paolo... Paolo...' Noella fell to her knees by the bed, stroking his burning forehead as she sobbed his name over and over again.

'Noella...' The word when it came was a broken whisper. 'You — you must not be found here. Please, go back at once.'

'No, Paolo!' She brushed away her tears, defiance giving her strength. 'I am coming with you. Nothing could make me stay here after this... I have everything ready. At first light we will leave together.' Her eyes shone with feverish determination. 'It was I who caused your suffering, Paolo, now I will look after you.'

Nothing Paolo said could make her change her mind.

Travelling on foot along dusty tracks, and on hot, crowded ramshackle buses, it took them three days to reach the village.

At night they bedded down on the fringe of the jungle where Noella would fetch water from a nearby stream and gently bathe Paolo's wounds.

'I can't believe it, Paolo. I just can't believe it was my own father who did this to you.' Her voice was choked with tears as she knelt to peel the shirt away from his weeping flesh.

Gritting his teeth against the pain, Paolo tried to comfort her. 'You must not judge your father too harshly, Noella. In his eyes what we did was not only a sin against the Church but also against the rules of our society.'

Kneeling in the dirt, Noella turned to stare into Paolo's dark troubled eyes. Taking his face between her hands she whispered, 'Beautiful Paolo...'

And he was. With his strong handsome features, his soft intelligent eyes, his thick glossy hair. As she gently ran her hands down his muscled arms, across his smooth, broad chest, she heard his intake of breath and remembered how Paolo had taught her what it was to be a woman, taught her how to find pleasure in her body.

Desire suddenly flamed inside her and at that moment Noella wondered why she had ever cast him aside.

Then her arms dropped to her side and she looked away. After what she was about to tell him, Paolo would never want her again.

It was a shock, but somehow Paolo understood.

Stumbling over her tale, Noella hardly dared to look at the boy sitting beside her on the hard earth.

When she was finished, he was quiet for a long moment but then, tenderly, drew her into his arms. 'Noella... my dearest Noella...'

It was Paolo's open-hearted sympathy and understanding, which she felt had been withheld by her own family, that made her bury her face against his chest and sob as if she would never stop.

'Hush, *querida*, there is no need to cry. I do not blame you. It is that *bastardo* I could kill!'

Noella raised her tear-stained face to look into Paolo's angry eyes. 'I — I felt too ashamed to tell you the truth, Paolo... And there was no one else I could turn to for help. How could I say anything to Gabrielle or Inez?'

Ignoring the pain of his wounds, he drew her down to lie beside him; murmuring words of comfort, he stroked her hair until at last he felt her fall asleep in his arms.

For a long time Paolo stared up into the night sky, silently cursing their world which would always keep them apart. How easy it was to love her, he thought. If only they could have been man and wife, he would have accepted the child as his own. Noella would have been spared the suffering she had had to endure.

But, he sighed heavily, he was only dreaming...

He looked down at her peaceful, sleeping face. It was guilt, he knew, which had made her run away with him, but soon she would see for herself that his life could never be hers. Paolo felt gripped by an overwhelming sense of despair. If it were in his power, he thought, he would give her the stars, the moon, the very heavens themselves — instead, he admitted bitterly, he could not even offer her the shelter of a roof over her head.

Then, with the warm steadiness of her breath against his cheek, the sweet scent of her skin and hair in his nostrils, Paolo made his silent fervent vow.

I shall protect her always, he swore. *For as long as I live, no one will ever hurt her again.*

CHAPTER *EIGHT*

'You have slept well, child?'

Hector Avende studied the girl who sat on the wooden bench across from him.

'*Si*, senor. And I have eaten well too.' With a smile, Noella indicated her empty plate. The *pupusas*, the meat-filled *tortilla*, had been wonderful.

Exhausted and hungry, Noella had almost cried in relief when late the previous day they had finally arrived at Paolo's village. All she had wanted was to sleep and eat and even then she wasn't sure in which order.

The women had ushered her into one of their homes where they had bathed her body and blistered feet, then brought her thick tripe stew with hunks of dark bread. Despite her hunger, after only a couple of bites Noella had been unable to keep her eyes open.

During the two nights they'd spent under the stars, she had found it almost impossible to sleep. The ground was cold and unyielding and the mosquitoes and other insects had feasted on her tender flesh.

After that, even the horsehair mattress on the rough wooden bunk had seemed like heaven. Now, after two nights' sleep, she felt a bit more like herself.

The village where Paolo had been brought up comprised about two dozen simple adobe houses built around a dusty market square. The villagers were curious but friendly, although none but Paolo and his grandfather, Hector, had any idea who she was.

Aware now of the old man's scrutiny, Noella asked, 'Is Paolo all right?'

She was embarrassed to ask the question. How could Hector Avende forgive her for what had been done to his grandson?

The old man nodded. His face was a parchment of wrinkles, and his thin grey hair lay ragged on his collarless shirt. But there was dignity too in his aged face, in those keen dark eyes which reminded her so much of Paolo's.

On their journey to the village, Paolo had explained that it was his grandfather who had brought him up after the accident which had killed his parents. His love and respect for the old man had been evident as he spoke.

Hector Avende answered her question in an even tone. 'His wound is painful, but he will recover.'

'I — I'm so sorry for what happened, senor.'

'Paolo gave me only the barest details, senorita. It would seem that in some way he has angered *el Presidente* greatly.'

Flushed with emotion, Noella exclaimed, 'Paolo was innocent of any blame, senor. What my father did was totally unjust! I don't feel I can ever bear to live beneath his roof again.'

From under shaggy white brows the old man regarded her steadily. 'So ... where then *do* you intend to live, senorita?'

Noella frowned. 'I ... perhaps I shall stay here — in Paolo's village.'

Yet even as she spoke the words, Noella wondered how much she really meant them. She had been brought up in comfort — no, luxury. How could she live a life of toil and poverty like the women she saw around her? Even those hardly older than herself already looked tired, defeated by their lives of drudgery and hopelessness. How could *she*, Noella de Bartez, spend her life as they did? She, who longed for parties and pretty clothes, for charming men in expensive cars ...

And then, experience offering the gift of insight, Noella suddenly realised that there were people for whom running water and proper food counted more than the delights and excitements she so craved in life. For the first time she understood that it was for people like these that her father and Gabrielle were working so hard.

Hector Avende seemed to sense her confusion. In his wisdom he had known it would not take long for the girl to recognise that her place was not here with people like themselves. He said as much now. 'You must think carefully, child. Your father will not cease his search for you ... and it will not take him too long to trace you here. Have you thought what that could mean for Paolo? Do you see the danger it would place him in?'

He watched the conflicting emotions on the girl's face. 'And consider, too, how much damage your impulsiveness can do to your father's cause,' he continued. 'In his distraction his enemies may find ways to move against him. For, believe me, child, *el Presidente* has more than his share of enemies. There are many who are opposed to his government, who are loath to see the reforms he wishes to impose ... Do you understand, child, what I am trying to say?'

Eyes lowered, Noella was thinking hard. Grudgingly, she had to admit that what the old man said made sense. Paolo had suffered enough because of her — how could she expose him further?

She had also been frightened by the talk of her father's enemies. Despite the threat implied by the bodyguards and the security that surrounded him, she had not really worried too much about that before.

Only the thought of an arranged marriage gave her cause to hesitate. Still, if she spoke to Inez, asked her to intercede, perhaps her father could be persuaded to change his mind. If she promised to improve...

Slowly Noella lifted her head to stare into Hector Avende's wise, dark eyes. 'What do *you* think I should do, senor?'

After dinner that evening, Noella told Paolo what she had decided as they strolled hand in hand by the fields of cotton that ringed the village.

'I have no option, Paolo. It is the only way, isn't it?' There was appeal in her voice. She wanted Paolo's affirmation of her decision to return.

'Yes, Noella,' he answered softly. 'The only way.'

For a while they strolled in silence, both realising that this would be their last time alone. Paolo felt his heart twist with sadness. Who knew when they would ever see each other again? How he wished things could have been different.

'The villagers have been so kind, Paolo,' Noella broke into his thoughts. 'They have so little but are happy to share it with me.'

'Poverty need not rob a man of goodness, Noella. Yet where people struggle to survive, only hope can keep the bitterness from their hearts. And hope is what your father's government offers.' Paolo swept his arm in a wide arc. 'You see these fields, Noella? Do you know why they are planted with cotton and not with rice or wheat or maize? Because on the world markets it is cotton which fetches the best price for the rich landowners. It is the same with the coffee plantations — the rich own more than eighty per cent of the land and use it to grow richer, to keep their power. Meanwhile the poor must pay inflated prices for basic foods which Martiguay must import. Or, if they have no money, they starve. It is this your father has sworn to change; this is the reason his government must survive.'

Noella listened in silence, surprised at an intensity

she had never before heard in Paolo. Did he really think Martiguay could change? Could even her father's government make things different? Surely there would always be rich and poor?

As if reading her mind, Paolo added softly, 'Things *can* change, Noella. I know they can. Either peacefully, or through more forceful means. And we will all have our part to play.'

He turned to her and grasped her arms. There was a different sort of emotion in his voice as he exclaimed, 'I have things to do, Noella, important things. And you do too. For now we must part, but maybe some day in the future, our paths will cross again. I hope this with all my heart.'

As they stood there in the moonlight, Noella knew that she wanted Paolo then as she had never wanted him before. Heart pounding, she lifted her head and kissed him lingeringly on the lips.

'Paolo... oh, Paolo... ' She breathed the words against his cheek as she kissed him again and again, and then tenderly, gently, led him to the grassy verge beside the path.

Moments later they were naked and Noella was drawing him down on top of her, impatient, yet careful of his still painful wounds. As Paolo's strong brown body covered hers, she welcomed him into her moistness.

'Noella...' It was a long soft whisper of desire and she raised her head to gaze into his face. His beauty enthralled her. She had seen how the young village girls looked at him as he passed by, knew that in a very short time someone amongst them would make Paolo hers...

Tears filled Noella's eyes. She burned with a passion to possess. Maybe never again in her life would anyone love her as much as Paolo...

★

Early the next morning, a battered local taxi took Noella to the nearest town.

In the cobblestone plaza with its trickling fountain, she found a seat in the shade of a dusty frangipani tree and settled down to wait for the central post office to open.

Fear clenched her belly at the thought of what surely awaited her at home. Her father would be furious and probably more determined than ever to see her married as soon as possible.

Inez was her only hope. Only Inez might be able to make her father change his mind.

As the church bells tolled nine, the tall, solid doors of the post office swung open. Noella entered the cool, dimly-lit stone building and found the solitary telephone booth. She fed in the correct number of coins and carefully dialled Inez's number.

The maid answered and, a moment later, she heard Inez's worried voice.

'Noella! Where have you been, child? Are you all right?'

'I — I'm fine, Inez. Please, can you send a car for me? I want to come to you.'

Inez Sarandon heard the tremor in the girl's voice. Poor, poor Noella. 'Oh, my dear... tell me where you are. I will send my car at once.'

'Victor, please... She has asked to come here. Let us respect her wishes... Yes, yes, of course... But let me speak with her first.'

Relieved at finally having her own way, Inez said goodbye and replaced the receiver. It had been her duty to assure Victor that his daughter had not come to any harm — another thing altogether to make him understand that the situation must now be treated with delicacy.

As she waited for Noella to come downstairs, Inez

paced restlessly around the sunny reception room. Her role was difficult. Like most men, Victor did not like to appear weak. His way of dealing with Noella was to treat her like a child who could still be forced to obey orders.

But it was obvious to Inez that the time for that was long past. The girl was strong-willed and rebellious and Victor refused to acknowledge the role he had played in making her that way. What had begun as a desperate bid for attention from a cold and distant parent had now blossomed into a fully fledged challenge to his authority. Noella was hurting, Inez thought, because the wound inside her had never been allowed to heal. What could be more natural than that she should now seek to 'punish' her father for withholding his love from her, for his inability to forgive?

The older woman sighed. How infinitesimal was the difference between love and hate . . .

There was a tap at the door and she turned to see Noella enter the room. Her hair was still damp from her bath and she was wearing a softly patterned robe Inez had given her.

'Come in, my dear. Sit down here with me. Will I ask Juanita to bring us coffee?'

'No, thank you, Inez. I had sandwiches and juice before my bath.'

'You must be feeling better then.'

The girl nodded but Inez saw the wariness in her dark eyes. 'Papa . . . Did you . . . ?'

The older woman nodded. 'Yes. I told him you were here.'

'Is — is he very angry, Inez?'

'No, Noella. If anything I think your father is very upset at what has happened between you. I know he feels very sorry that he lost his temper as he did. You must try to forgive him. His position puts him under immense pressure and in this case he allowed his emotions to overrule his better judgement.'

Noella hid her surprise at Inez's words. Never before had she heard her father criticised. He was the one who was always right, whose infallibility was never in question.

She looked at the older woman with new respect. So often she had wished that her father would marry Inez. Instead of idolising a dead woman, he should have given this warm, loving, sympathetic human being the recognition she deserved. Then Inez could have shared completely in all their lives.

'Inez, what am I to do? I am not yet eighteen. I want to live, to experience life — not be forced into a marriage with someone I do not love. Please, Inez,' the tears shone in Noella's eyes, 'please help me!'

To her relief and surprise, Inez found that Victor de Bartez had already abandoned the idea of an arranged marriage for his rebellious daughter.

Later that same evening he had come to the house and greeted Noella with cordial restraint. If he had not forgiven her, he at least acknowledged that his own actions had been partly to blame for her running away.

'I am ashamed that I lost my temper, Noella. But in my fury that a peasant boy would presume — ' He broke off and waved a hand, dismissing the comment. 'This incident is best forgotten.

Victor de Bartez saw the relief in his daughter's eyes, and the vulnerability in that lovely face suddenly caught him unawares. Oh, *Jesu*, it was as if Catherine —

Fiercely, he pushed away the painful thought. 'Go to bed now, Noella. I have things to talk about with Inez.'

'You look tired, Victor.' Eyes troubled, Inez stroked a hand over her lover's cheek. 'You are working too hard.'

'There is much to do, Inez — and the situation gets more desperate with every passing day.'

Wearily, Victor de Bartez leaned back against the sofa. He was not exaggerating. The Peres years had cost Martiguay greatly. The economic fabric of the country was falling apart. And now, his own peers were organising against him on the question of land reform. If he could not solve the question soon his entire election schedule was in serious jeopardy.

He sighed heavily. How much longer could the people be expected to suffer? How much time would they give him to accomplish his miracles?

Inez broke into his depressing thoughts. 'What conclusion have you reached about Noella, Victor? Are you certain you do not want her to stay here with me?'

'Your offer is very kind, Inez, but no. I have made my decision. Noella's place is in the Presidential Palace with her sister and myself. There, I can ensure she is under much stricter supervision and her studies given top priority. I am determined she will achieve her University entrance. She may not have Gabrielle's brain but Noella is still quite capable of passing this exam.'

At the risk of arousing her lover's disapproval, Inez said softly, 'I think you underestimate Noella, Victor. Perhaps when you can accept her as she is, you will find that she is more than equal to her sister.'

Irritably, Victor pushed himself out of his chair. 'Please, Inez. I am too tired for such cryptic remarks.'

At the front door, his goodnight kiss was subdued. It was always the same, thought Inez, watching the taillights of the limousine disappear into the darkness. The issue of why Noella was as she was could never be confronted.

CHAPTER NINE

'Come, child! Concentrate.'

The priest's thin, bearded face reflected his irritation. He wasn't accustomed to such fractious students. At first he had been honoured by the request to act as private tutor to the daughter of *el Presidente*. Now he was beginning to regret his eager acceptance of the role.

'But Father,' protested Noella, 'I don't see the point. Why is it necessary to memorise the dates of all Napoleon's campaigns? They are there in the history books for everyone to read. I am much more interested to know why the Church supported Bonaparte. Why did they —'

'Enough!' Swallowing back a most unchristian anger, the priest snapped shut his text. 'That will be enough for today. Please read to the end of chapter twelve before next time.' He stood up. 'Good afternoon, senorita. Please be kind enough to give my regards to your father.' With a flick of his dark brown cassock the tutor swept past her.

Left alone in the vast library that served as her classroom, Noella gave a small sigh. Whatever satisfaction she might have derived from disturbing Father Joachim was dissipated by a sense of growing despair.

Living at the palace was almost like being in a prison. Her every waking moment was strictly supervised and when not at her books she was expected to play an active role in the official duties that occupied so much of her father's and Gabrielle's lives.

Noella hated the restrictions and tedium but could see no way of escape. Scowling, she picked up her books and made her way down the maze of corridors to her own bedroom. It was imposing yet uninviting, with its impossibly high and ornate ceilings, its silk damask walls and heavy eighteenth century furniture.

As she closed the door behind her, Noella felt her depression deepen. How she missed the easy comfort of the *hacienda*, missed even Nona's affectionate scolding.

And Paolo . . . Her heart skipped a beat as she remembered the afternoons of passion, the freedom and pleasure of the chase and the capture. She wondered, as always, what Paolo was doing now.

The crimson taffeta dress was spread out in readiness on the bed and the sight of it did nothing to improve Noella's mood. She had almost forgotten about the dinner this evening. Yet another formal event where she would be expected to smile and make small talk with ugly old men, interested in nothing but foreign aid and coffee, agricultural machinery and schools for the peasants.

She kicked the giltwood frame of the door. She would go mad!

Just two weeks later a rare glamorous event interrupted the boredom of Noella's usual routine.

As the limousine carrying her and Gabrielle drove past the waving, eager crowds and into the racetrack enclosure Noella felt her excitement grow.

A group of smiling officials was waiting to welcome them as they alighted at the grandstand; copying her sister, Noella extended a white-gloved hand to each of the welcoming party in turn.

'We are delighted you and your sister could join us today, Senora Ravell.' The chairman of the Caverro Racetrack Committee beamed as he ushered the two women into the official arena. 'It is only a shame that *el Presidente* himself could not be with us for the start of the season.'

'It would have been his great pleasure, Senor Lopez, but you know how things are for him at present.'

The chairman nodded soberly. 'His is a difficult task, I am sure, senora.' Personally, he did not approve of the programs of Victor de Bartez. The poor, as he saw it, did well enough. The newspapers were full of the government's plans to spend millions of *pesos* on public housing, while at the same time they were to disallow tax rebates for racehorse breeders. A scandal! Such a government would not last long in Martiguay.

Gabrielle moved easily among the elegant crowd. Always aware of her position, she was pleasant and friendly to all, but knew that among this outwardly smiling group there were those who were bitterly opposed to the reforms of her father's government. Their enemies were to be found among their own class, among those to whom poverty and inflation, corruption and decay, meant little alongside the compulsion to maintain their own comfortable life styles.

Gabrielle knew only too well that such people had hoped to find in her father another Bernardo Peres, another leader who could be counted on to maintain the status quo. Now, after almost two years of de Bartez government, they had found otherwise . . .

For once Noella was enjoying her role as the daughter of *el Presidente*. Surrounded by the cream of Martiguayan society she felt, for the first time, the sense of power attached to the de Bartez name. How respectfully they addressed her, how important they made her feel! Confident of her beauty, Noella revelled in the attention.

It was towards the end of the afternoon's race program that Gabrielle left her by herself. 'Excuse me one moment, Noella. I must have a word with Senor Barco.'

She indicated a portly, white-haired man whom Noella knew was one of Martiguay's leading judges.

Noella nodded. She hoped Gabrielle would not be too long; the races were beginning to bore her. After all, this was not Longchamp or Ascot or Deauville. Such an afternoon as this could not dispel her dreams of escape.

'Are you not enjoying yourself, senorita?'

Flustered that her mood had been noted, Noella turned to find a well-dressed man standing by her side. He was tall and appeared to be in his late twenties. He had dark curly hair, surprisingly blue eyes, and a wonderful smile.

'Allow me to introduce myself. Daniel Jarro.'

His hand was extended, and as she took it in her own Noella felt an immediate attraction to the stranger's rugged good looks, his air of ease and self-confidence.

'You have lost money, perhaps, senorita?' There was a mischievous gleam in Daniel Jarro's dark blue eyes as he asked the question.

'No, senor. I do not bet.' Noella could have kicked herself for sounding so stilted.

'You are prudent with your money then. As a banker, I am glad to hear that.' Again he flashed that wonderful smile and Noella felt her heart begin to beat faster.

'Oh, of course, I thought the name was familiar. Your father — he is the chairman of the Central Bank.' Noella vaguely recalled a distinguished looking man with greying hair and finely chiselled features. He had visited the palace on a number of occasions.

'The very same, senorita. And as a dutiful son, I have, you see, followed him into this very honourable profession.'

Daniel Jarro was teasing her, Noella knew, but she found herself tongue-tied and felt a warm flush creep over her cheeks. How gauche and immature he must think her.

'I — ' Just as Noella began to speak she felt a touch on her elbow.

'Come, Noella. It is time for us to depart.'

Noella spun round. 'Oh, Gabrielle.' She tried to gather her composure. 'May I introduce — '

Gabrielle interrupted her, nodding coolly at Daniel Jarro. 'Senor Jarro and I have met before, Noella. Do excuse us, senor. Our car is waiting.'

'Of course, senora.' Daniel Jarro gave a little bow. 'I trust you have had an enjoyable afternoon. And perhaps,' he added, his teasing eyes fixed on Noella, 'we shall meet again soon.'

For the next few days Noella thought of little else but Daniel Jarro. Excitement fluttered in her belly when she recalled the touch of his hand, the way his dark blue eyes had looked into hers, that wonderful lazy smile. And where Paolo had had an almost feminine beauty, Daniel Jarro's handsomeness was overlaid by a raw, almost dangerous, sensuality. With a shiver, Noella wondered how much longer she would have to wait until she saw him again.

As casually as she could, she tried to find out more about him from Gabrielle.

'The Jarro family have a long banking tradition, Noella. As you know Fernando Jarro is the chairman of the Central Bank. From what I hear, his son has just recently returned to Martiguay; he has been living in the United States gaining experience in the *norte-americano* banking system.'

'He is very handsome...'

Gabrielle saw the interest in her sister's dark eyes. 'You must let nothing distract you from your studies, Noella.' Her voice held a sharp note of warning. 'Anyway, a man like Daniel Jarro is too old for you; he is sophisticated and worldly. He would not be interested in a schoolgirl.'

But Gabrielle was wrong.

*

Noella had begun to despair of ever seeing Daniel Jarro again when, by wonderful good luck, they ran across each other once more.

On this occasion she was accompanying Eugene and Gabrielle to the opening night of the Martiguayan State Theatre's latest production.

The long monologues and lack of action on the stage bored her to distraction and when at last the curtain closed on the first act, Noella felt nothing but relief.

It was in the crush of formally-dressed patrons in the foyer that she saw the man who had been so much in her thoughts. In the well-cut dinner jacket which emphasised his broad shoulders and tapering waist, Daniel Jarro looked even more handsome than she remembered.

As if suddenly feeling her gaze, Daniel Jarro turned, his eyes immediately finding hers. He smiled, that same slow devastating smile, and Noella felt her pulses race. Then to her delight and terror, he broke away from his friends and forced a way through the crowd to her side.

'Senorita de Bartez! You look wonderful this evening.'

Noella swallowed, praying she would not blush. 'Thank you, senor.' As before, she felt terrifyingly lost for words.

'Are you enjoying the play?'

'It is . . . interesting.'

Daniel Jarro leaned towards her and a shiver ran through her as she smelt the subtle aroma of his freshly-shaven skin, felt his warm breath against her ear. 'Do you think the second act could possibly be as tedious as the first?'

A sudden desire to giggle overtook her. 'Only if the leading actor is not killed off at once.'

And looking deep into each other's eyes, they both began to laugh.

*

Now Noella's daydreams were devoted exclusively to Daniel Jarro. As she sat at her desk, her eyes read the same line of text over and over again, so completely did the charming banker dominate her thoughts.

Why doesn't he call on me? she thought. Is he interested in me as a woman, or merely being polite to the daughter of Victor de Bartez? The answer to her tortured questions came just four days later.

That morning, just as Gabrielle was leaving for her office, she reminded Noella that they would be having official guests to dine with them that evening.

'Only a small affair,' Gabrielle explained, noticing the sulky look that had appeared on her sister's face. Folding her napkin, she stood up from the table. 'Just the Minister for Finance and Fernando Jarro of the Central Bank.'

Gabrielle was almost out of the breakfast room door when she turned and added, almost as an afterthought, 'Oh yes, and Senor Jarro's son will also be present.'

The rest of the day couldn't pass quickly enough for Noella. When she should have been concentrating on composing an essay on the great Spanish writers she was dreaming of the evening to come, and as soon as her lessons were over she flew back to her room to agonise over what to wear for her next meeting with Daniel Jarro.

Determined to look radiant, she spent hours getting ready. Soaking in a bath of perfumed oils, she allowed herself to fantasise about the young banker. He was so handsome, so dynamic and self-assured.

As she lay back in the warm soapy water, Noella's fingers strayed between her legs. Slowly, dreamily, she began to stroke that part which Paolo had taught her about, the part which made her come alive.

Closing her eyes, she imagined that it was Daniel's hands touching her there, those long slender fingers probing and teasing, unfolding her like a flower as his warm moist mouth found her eager nipples. Her breath quickened and a pulse beat rapidly in her throat as her fingers stroked in a steady, constant rhythm. Moments later she was arching out of the water, fighting to stifle a cry as waves of pleasure swept through her.

Even before Daniel Jarro had laid a finger on her he had brought her to orgasm...

Her entrance was perfectly timed.

The others were already seated with their drinks when Noella entered the opulent reception room with its ornate furniture and gilt-framed paintings.

Murmuring a greeting to Eugene and Gabrielle, she smiled as her father introduced her to their three dinner guests.

'... and I think you are already acquainted with Senor Jarro, my dear, but may I introduce his son, Senor Daniel Jarro.'

Noella met Daniel Jarro's bright appreciative eyes. 'Actually, Papa... Senor Jarro and I have met on a previous occasion.'

Victor de Bartez raised a bushy eyebrow but said nothing further and as the men resumed their seats the conversation returned to the matters Noella had always found so boring. But not tonight, she thought, her face aglow. Tonight in Daniel's company nothing could bore her.

At the long mahogany dining table gleaming with crystal and silver, Noella found herself seated diagonally opposite the young banker. On her one side was Eugene, on the other Fernando Jarro. As the dinner progressed, Noella was surprised when the chairman of the Central Bank, who on earlier occasions had barely spoken half a dozen words to her, now seemed happy to engage her in conversation.

'Are you enjoying city life, senorita?'

Ever so slightly, Noella lifted a bare shoulder. 'To tell you the truth, senor, I am kept so busy with my studies I have little opportunity to taste what the capital has to offer.' She slid a sideways glance at her father, hoping he was listening.

'But, my dear,' Fernando Jarro looked at her in mock concern, 'all work and no play is not good for the soul! You must make sure to correct this situation at once.'

Turning, the banker addressed his host. 'Victor, what is this I hear from your beautiful younger daughter? All the time at her books and no relaxation?'

At the head of the table, Victor de Bartez set down his wine glass. 'Noella knows how important it is that she pass her entrance examination, Fernando.'

But the chairman of the Central Bank was not to be deflected. 'That is all very well, Victor, but have you forgotten that youth also requires some distraction to refresh the brain?'

Without waiting for a reply, he turned to his son. 'Daniel, what about the polo next Saturday? You are playing, isn't that so? I am sure Senorita de Bartez would enjoy such an exciting spectacle in the company of other young people.'

As Noella held her breath, Daniel Jarro smiled, flashing perfect white teeth. 'I would be delighted to escort the senorita to such an event, father... or anywhere else it might be her desire to go.'

'There, Victor, you see?' Fernando Jarro rounded on his host. 'You must allow Noella such pleasures. She is too beautiful to hide away.'

'Fernando,' Victor de Bartez countered, a hint of irritation in his voice, 'Noella has made me a promise she will apply herself to nothing but her studies in readiness for this most important examination.'

'But surely, Victor — '

'I think, Fernando, we should drop the subject.'

This time there was no mistaking the finality and firmness of Victor de Bartez's tone.

The evening was ruined for Noella.

Her father had talked about her as if she were a child with no mind of her own, as if she were invisible at the table! What would Daniel Jarro think of her now? Surely he must be laughing at her!

Choking back her anger, Noella spoke in monosyllables for the rest of the meal. Later, when coffee was served in the reception room she murmured an excuse and made her escape through the open french doors onto the terrace.

In the darkness, she felt overcome by the emotions she had kept under control throughout the meal. How dare he! How dare her father treat her like that! Her cheeks flushed with rage and tears of humiliation stung her eyes.

'Noella . . . ?'

Startled, she spun round to see Daniel Jarro standing behind her. So lost had she been in her angry thoughts she hadn't heard him approach.

'You are upset, I think, Noella.' His voice was soft with sympathy.

It was the first time he had ever called her by name and Noella fought to blink away her tears. 'What my father fails to recognise is that I am a woman, senor. Not a child who must sit quietly and do as I am told. I — '

The touch of Daniel Jarro's hands on the naked flesh of her shoulders cut off the rest of her words.

'But you aren't going to do what he says, are you, Noella?' The words were whispered into her hair.

CHAPTER TEN

'Everything is fine, senorita. Your next appointment will be in six months' time.'

'*Gracias*, senor.'

Noella slid out of the lowered dental chair and walked back to the reception area where her driver was waiting. As they left the dentist's expensive suite and emerged into the bright sunshine, Noella's heart quickened. She wondered if he would keep his word.

'Senorita!'

Noella spun in the direction of the voice and her face beamed with pleasure. 'Senor Jarro! *Buenos dias*. How — how are you?'

The driver was waiting patiently by the limousine, unaware that the performance was being played out expressly for him.

'You are in a hurry, senorita? You must rush? It is not possible that we could take a coffee together?'

Even though she had been dreaming of this moment since the night of the dinner party when they had planned it, Noella suddenly felt afraid at the thought of her father's rage. What would be her dreadful punishment if he found out that she had disobeyed him?

But then all the resentments of the last few months boiled up inside her. She was young, alive, beautiful — why, because of her one mistake, should she be forced to live like a nun? If her father found out, well, too bad!

She smiled up into Daniel Jarro's expectant face. 'Coffee would be lovely, Senor Jarro.'

That evening, Noella could barely sleep. In the short time she had spent with Daniel Jarro she knew for sure that she had fallen deeply in love. The young banker was charming, charismatic, sophisticated, and despite her position as the daughter of *el Presidente*, it was difficult for her not to feel like a country bumpkin when he spoke of the elegant social life he had led outside of Martiguay.

It was the sort of life Noella had always dreamed of: a continual round of parties, dinners, first nights at the theatre, invitations to elegant homes and country estates.

While she listened, wide-eyed, Daniel Jarro spoke of his upbringing in England. 'My father is a great admirer of the English and it was his desire that I receive an English rather than an American education. I was thirteen when he sent me away to Winchester.'

He saw the incomprehension in Noella's eyes. 'One of the better public schools, senorita. Yet still,' he laughed, 'imbued with the traditions of poor food and draughty corridors. However, I survived and the time I spent at Oxford more than made up for those early rigours. The education was first class and the friends I made there were people similar to myself who valued tradition and breeding, who clearly saw their duty as the ruling class.'

Noella was fascinated. She could have listened to Daniel all day, but she had told the driver to pick her up in an hour and even now she could see the long dark car emerging from the traffic.

They said their goodbyes as the driver stood anxiously by the open car door. The man was worried that by obeying the senorita he would find himself in trouble with *el Presidente*. But what else could he have done?

When Noella was seated, Daniel leaned in at the open window and smiled. 'It was a fortunate accident to meet with you today, Senorita de Bartez. I have enjoyed our time together immensely. *Adios.*'

And with a wave of his hand he turned and melted into the crowd.

Retribution came swiftly.

The next evening, Noella was summoned to her father's study.

Victor de Bartez wasted no time in coming to the point. 'So, tell me, Noella... why were you so late in returning from the dentist yesterday?'

Noella shifted uneasily in her seat. 'I — I had coffee with a friend, Papa.'

'A friend?' Victor stopped his restless pacing and turned to stare down at his daughter. 'A girl friend, was it, Noella? Someone I know, of course?'

The note of sarcasm in her father's voice told Noella there was no point in trying to lie. Somehow he had found out the truth.

Eyes lowered, she answered quickly, 'No, Papa, not a girl friend.'

'Oh? Then I must assume you were blatant enough to appear in public in the company of a man without the benefit of a chaperone? Well, Noella, do tell me the name of such an assuming gentleman.'

The same resentment she had felt the day before surfaced again in Noella and raising defiant eyes she met her father's angry gaze. 'It was Daniel Jarro, Papa. The son of the chairman of the Central Bank.'

Victor de Bartez's anger bubbled over. 'This despite what I said the other evening! After the incident at the *hacienda* you made a solemn promise that your studies would take priority and now I discover that still you are not to be trusted!' Victor saw the rebellious set to his daughter's mouth. In an ice-cold voice, he warned, 'You are not to see that man again. Daniel Jarro is too worldly a companion for a girl of your age. Now, do I make myself totally clear?'

Gabrielle frowned. 'But Noella, you know Papa's feelings in this matter. After the . . . incident with the stable-boy —'

'Surely I have been punished enough for Paolo!' Noella's face was flushed with anger. She threw her arms up in frustration. 'I feel as if I'm slowly going crazy in this place. How much longer do I have to listen to tedious speeches, smile at ogling strangers, sit at dinner with men thirty years older than myself?'

Noella faced her sister across the broad, old-fashioned desk. They were in Gabrielle's office in the Department of Justice and Gabrielle hoped the walls were thick enough to prevent the curiosity of her staff.

'It's all right for you,' Noella added, her voice high-pitched with agitation. 'You *chose* this sort of life. You *like* it! But can't you see?' she leaned earnestly towards her sister, 'I don't! I never did!'

Gabrielle sat motionless for a moment, her hands locked in front of her. Finally she asked, 'What *do* you want, Noella?'

The answer was unhesitating. 'Freedom.' There was desperation in Noella's eyes. 'Freedom to live my own life without rules and regulations.'

Gabrielle stared at her a long moment then answered quietly. 'As long as you are a de Bartez in Martiguay, Noella, that will never happen.'

Gabrielle's words lay heavy on Noella's mind. She knew her sister was right. The life she dreamed of would never be hers. Not while she lived in Martiguay as the daughter of Victor de Bartez. And the possibility of escape seemed years away.

Unless . . .

CHAPTER ELEVEN

With Gabrielle's words echoing in her mind, Noella set about planning her escape.

Despite her father's threats she was determined to see Daniel Jarro again. She adored him, completely and utterly. He was everything she had ever dreamt of in a man: handsome, intelligent, sophisticated and worldly. Why should she need the fawning attention of others when she could have such a prize? And Daniel had spoken of how much he preferred life in Europe to his native country. Together they could share the life style she had always dreamed of. She would be free at last.

Noella's eyes shone with excitement. How wonderful true love was! She knew she could never have been happy with a man she had not chosen for herself. And Daniel Jarro, she felt sure, would offer her the love she had always longed for.

All she had to do was make him see that in Noella de Bartez he had found the perfect wife.

With the help of a young palace maid, who carried their notes back and forth, Noella and Daniel were able to meet regularly over the next few months.

No one ever suspected the reason for her sudden devotion to the knowledge offered by the Martiguayan State Library. While her driver waited in the foyer of the immense, white-columned building, Noella would disappear among the racks of books, emerging an hour or two later to be driven home.

But the setting was not exactly ideal for young lovers. Noella felt sure that it must be as maddening for Daniel as it was for her to be always fearful of some prim librarian or unsuspecting scholar coming upon them unexpectedly as they stole their kisses among the rows of books.

More than anything, she longed for privacy, a place where they could relax together, where she could hint to Daniel that he had every reason to look forward to their wedding night.

Noella racked her brain for a solution to this most intimate problem.

Less than three weeks later, it was Amelia Havere, an old school friend now settled back in the city, who agreed to help her.

'But only if you tell me who it is, Noella.' Amelia's thin, plain face was bright with curiosity.

Noella's pride was evident in her smile. 'Daniel Jarro.'

Amelia Havere drew a long envious breath. 'Daniel Jarro! *Dios*, but you are lucky, Noella.'

Noella's smile grew wider. 'Daniel will be luckier, Amelia. He will have me as his wife.'

The plan was simple enough.

It was half-term break and Victor de Bartez was happy for Noella to have her friend spend the night at the palace. The next day as Amelia was about to be driven home, Noella asked if she might accompany her. 'May I spend the afternoon with Amelia, then, Papa?'

Victor's mind was on a meeting later that day with his Finance Minister, and absent-mindedly he gave his consent. Noella hid her delight.

It was a twenty-minute drive to the Haveres'

splendid stone villa with its commanding views to the distant ocean. Setting the two girls down at the portico, the chauffeur drove the limousine to the rear of the house to await Noella's return.

'*Buenos dias*, Mama.'

Amelia put her head round the door of the over-decorated sitting room where her mother was playing bridge with her fashionable friends. Lucia Havere barely lifted her eyes from the game.

'Ah, you are home Amelia. And Noella, how nice to see you. Ask Maria to give you some lemonade. And there are fresh *quesadillas* in the kitchen.'

But Noella had no time for the sweet dessert. 'Cover for me, Amelia . . . I shall be back in an hour or so.'

'There is no need to hurry on my mother's behalf, Noella. As I told you, once she is at the bridge table she notices nothing else.' The girl's voice held a hint of bitterness but Noella didn't notice.

'I take the path at the back of the tennis court?'

Amelia nodded. 'Yes. It is well marked, you will not lose your way.'

'I am sure I will find it. *Adios*.'

Amelia Havere watched enviously as her friend ran quickly across the lawn. She imagined what it might feel like to have Daniel Jarro's hands touch her own small breasts, have his tongue push its way between her teeth. She felt a warm tingle start between her legs.

She would make Noella tell her every single detail when she returned . . .

Daniel was waiting, leaning against his dark blue Alfa Romeo, the smoke from his cigarette curling into the still warm air.

'Noella!'

Quickly he stamped the butt into the ground as he saw her emerge from the trees.

She was out of breath from having run all the way.

The popular picnic area of Azores Park merged with the boundary of the Havere estate and, as she had hoped, at midweek the place was deserted.

'Daniel...' And then, unexpectedly, shyness overcame her. This was the first time they had been utterly alone together.

But a moment later, Daniel's strong arms were enfolding her and all her inhibitions disappeared. She felt electrified by his closeness, giddy with anticipation of what was to come.

'So,' he put a hand to her chin and gently tilted her head so she was forced to look into his eyes, 'now we can relax, no?'

He bent and kissed her, his lips sliding over hers, his tongue at first teasing and playful, then probing and masterful. Noella reeled in pleasure, drowned in a wild riot of joy as she buried her hands in his thick glossy hair.

In a daze, she lay back on the dry springy grass, blinking into the strong sunlight as Daniel slowly unbuttoned the front of her dress. Her mind roared out of control as his fingers pushed aside the lacy cup of her bra and gently kneaded the soft fullness of her breasts. She heard his sharp intake of breath as he bent his head to her rock-hard nipples, circling them with his teasing tongue.

Noella felt her flesh catch on fire. She groaned in delight as his hands moved over the soft lines of her waist and hips, as he raised his head to breathe soft feathery kisses at the base of her throat.

In an agony of desire, she clasped him against her, caressing the strong tendons at the back of his neck, aching for the feel of his naked flesh. With trembling fingers she found the buttons of his shirt, began to undo them, but a moment later Daniel's hand gripped her own.

'No.' His voice was flat, oddly remote.

Abruptly he moved away and sat up, staring out at the distant skyline of the capital.

Beside him, Noella lay catching her breath, trying to hide her confusion. What was the matter? What had she done to upset him?

Brushing stray leaves off her dress, she sat up, her stomach churning with fear. Had she been too forward, too bold? All she had wanted was to prove to Daniel that she knew how to satisfy a man, that she would be able to pleasure him as his other lovers must surely have done.

As if reading her thoughts, he turned towards her, a look in his blue eyes she could not easily fathom. Raising a hand in an impatient gesture of dismissal, he said, 'Not here, Noella. Not like this. You are — you are too special for that.'

She began to speak, to protest, but he interrupted.

'No, listen. I think the time has come. To tell your father about us. It is no longer possible for me to hide my feelings.' Daniel Jarro took a deep breath. 'You understand what I am trying to say, Noella?'

His voice is shaking, he is so overcome with emotion, Noella thought joyously, her fears at once forgotten.

'Yes, oh, yes, Daniel.' Never could she have hoped that so soon . . .

But then a shadow passed over her face. Daniel's proposal meant she would now have to confront her father, and be forced to reveal her lies, her deceit, her blatant disregard of his authority. It was the one stumbling block she had always refused to face in weaving her fantasies of the future. In a tremulous voice she revealed her fears.

'Do not be frightened, Noella.' He covered her hand with his and she was surprised at how cool his flesh felt on such a warm day. 'There is no need for unpleasantness. My parents are close friends of your father. I will ask for their help, ask them to pave our way.

With their intercession, your father must surely be convinced that we can find happiness only with each other.'

As she listened to Daniel's reassuring words, Noella hoped with all her heart that he was right.

Somehow Fernando and Julietta Jarro were able to bring about the miracle Noella was praying for.

Although initially furious at his daughter's deceit, in the end Victor de Bartez had bowed to pressure and given his consent to the marriage. 'With one proviso, Noella.' His face was stern.

'Yes, Papa?' Heart singing, Noella felt she would agree to anything if it meant being allowed to marry Daniel.

'First you must pass your exam. Nothing must interfere with that.'

'Of course, Papa.'

Another three months... Noella wondered how she would be able to bear the wait. Still, she thought resignedly, it was a small enough price to pay.

'And I can only hope,' Victor continued coldly, 'that you will obey your husband more readily than you have your father.'

As she turned to go, Noella's face was set with cold determination. The word 'obey' would be obsolete in her marriage, she promised herself. She and Daniel would have an equal relationship.

The engagement was celebrated at the palace with a small dinner party for the two families.

Seated beside Daniel, her hand possessively in his, Noella felt an overwhelming sense of triumph. She had broken the rules, defied her father's authority, and she had won. She had got what she wanted. In just a few weeks' time she would become Senora Daniel Jarro and no one ever again would be able to tell her what to do.

From across the room where he was chatting with her future father-in-law, Noella saw Eugene throw her a glance. No longer could he call her a child, she thought defiantly. Soon she would be a married woman with a husband and a home of her own.

And then, unexpectedly, Noella's thoughts turned fleetingly to Paolo. He would always be dear to her. Paolo had loved her truly, she knew, but he could never fulfil her dreams.

She looked adoringly at her handsome fiance. Only Daniel could do that.

CHAPTER TWELVE

Three months later, to her immense relief, Noella passed the University entrance exam. She had fulfilled her father's condition and was now free to concentrate all her energies on the forthcoming wedding. There seemed a hundred things to see to at once and as she pored over endless lists, she was grateful for Inez's helpful advice.

Noella changed her mind so often over details of menus, flowers, or choice of wines, Inez began to worry that by the day of the wedding the girl would be too exhausted to enjoy it.

'Oh no, Inez!' Noella happily dismissed the older woman's fears. 'I seem to have boundless energy. Really, it is just so wonderful to have so much to look forward to.' The girl's face was bright with excitement. 'And the Bahamas will surely be the most romantic spot on earth for a honeymoon.'

Inez's eyes grew troubled. 'Are you certain you know your fiance well enough, my dear? After all, a few months is — '

'Enough,' finished Noella airily. 'The Jarros are an excellent family. Fernando Jarro has been an intimate of Papa's since they were at college together.'

Yet Inez could not shake off her sense of disquiet. She hated dishonesty . . .

'I — I don't believe it!'

Her face white as paper, Noella trembled as she

listened to the voice at the other end of the telephone. From across the room, Amelia Havere watched her in puzzled concern.

'*Si, si*, Papa ... I will wait until the *policia* arrive.'

Slowly Noella replaced the receiver, her eyes glazed with shock.

'Noella, what's wrong? The *policia*? What has happened?' Amelia looked anxiously into her friend's dazed face.

Noella felt the numbness spread through her veins. She had been spending a couple of days at the Havere home relaxing before attending to the last-minute preparations for her marriage, and had been looking forward to Daniel joining them for dinner that night.

But not now.

'It — it's Gabrielle.'

The escort of four armed policemen arrived a short time afterwards. Bundled hastily into the bullet-proof limousine, Noella was driven at speed back to the palace.

As the car swept through the palace gates, she noticed with a sense of foreboding that the guard had been doubled. Soldiers carrying automatic weapons patrolled the grounds, and the nearby streets had been closed to traffic.

Ignoring the worried officials gathered in the corridors of the executive wing, Noella burst into her father's office.

'Papa! How is she? What — '

Victor de Bartez was on the telephone and he waved her quiet. '*Si ... si ...* ' He nodded repeatedly while Noella paced in an agony of impatience. '*Bueno ... Adios.*'

'Papa! Tell me!' Fearing the worst she stared wild-eyed into her father's grim face as he replaced the receiver.

'Gabrielle, praise the heavens, is unharmed... but a dozen other innocent souls were not so fortunate.' Eyes dark with rage, Victor de Bartez raised a fist above his head and brought it down with violent force against the polished desktop. '*Bastardos*! Murderers!'

After that, the wedding preparations became a nightmare. What better lure for the terrorist sympathisers of Peres than a gathering of the entire Presidential family and their supporters?

Victor was determined that no one must be put at risk. The attempt on his elder daughter's life had shaken him badly. It meant among other things that the terrorists had been well-informed of her movements.

In her role as a member of the Ministry of Justice, Gabrielle had been on one of her regular visits to the far-flung judiciary. Only a lucky delay in leaving her hotel had saved her life. The bomb which claimed twelve innocent lives had detonated just minutes before her arrival at the local government building. Three blocks away in her car, Gabrielle had felt the force of the shock and known at once what had caused it.

Now, heeding the strongly worded advice of his security chiefs, Victor determined that the wedding celebrations must be transferred from the *hacienda* to the Presidential Palace.

'Try not to be disappointed, Noella,' Inez said comfortingly as she watched the dressmaker pin the white draped gown in place. 'The palace chapel is very beautiful and everyone will feel more at ease if they are assured of their safety.'

With an effort, Noella dragged her eyes from her pleasing reflection in the full-length mirror. Already she had put the incident out of her mind. Gabrielle was all right, that was all that concerned her. And it would surely be only a matter of time before the crazy men responsible were rounded up.

She lifted one shoulder in a shrug. 'Perhaps Papa is overreacting, but I am not upset, Inez. To me, the only thing of importance is that by the evening of May 30, I will be Senora Daniel Jarro.'

Inez frowned as the same feeling of unease stirred again. Noella was still so immature.

For Noella, waking up on the morning of her wedding day, there was an air of unreality about the fact that by evening her life would be changed so dramatically. No longer would she be her father's child — but a married woman able to sleep openly with the man she adored, free to live the sort of life she had always longed for.

After a breakfast Noella could barely touch, she greeted Inez, who had arrived to help with the preparations. Elegant in a St Laurent hyacinth-blue suit and matching wide-brimmed hat, the older woman calmly supervised the hairdresser and other attendants as they fluttered around the bride-to-be.

At last, just before midday, Noella was dressed and ready. As they were about to leave for the pink marble chapel in the far wing of the palace, Inez held Victor's second child at arm's length.

'You look like an angel, darling. Absolutely stunning.' Her voice was tight with emotion as she took in the exquisitely designed dress, the white lace mantilla draped over the dark gold hair.

As she smiled at Inez, it occurred for the first time to Noella that in leaving Martiguay she was going to miss this serene, elegant woman who had always been such a true and loyal friend. Had she ever bothered to tell Inez how much her concern and friendship had meant?

'Oh, Inez,' she cried, throwing her arms around the

older woman, 'you have been so good to me. Sometimes only you made me feel I was worth anything. You are so good, so wise, so honest . . .'

So honest.

As they hugged each other close, Inez was glad Noella couldn't see her face.

From the moment she entered the vaulted marble nave of the palace chapel on her father's arm, Noella felt as if she were living a dream. A wonderful, thrilling dream.

The ceremony itself went without a hitch and Noella shivered in delight as Daniel slipped the slim gold band onto her finger. Now this wonderful, handsome man was truly hers.

After the ceremony the newlyweds had one official duty to perform. Victor de Bartez had decided that the whole family should make an appearance on the palace balcony. From early morning a crowd had begun to gather in the hope of catching sight of the young couple, and in the face of the recent tragedy, Victor determined that a response to the people would do much for morale. The security chiefs, at first understandably nervous, had in the end agreed that the risk was small.

From the moment the wedding party stepped out into the sunlight, a roar that never ceased went up from the crowd. Surrounded by her father, her new parents-in-law, Eugene, and Gabrielle, who had been her matron of honour, Noella blushed with delight as she raised a hand to acknowledge the cheering, waving masses.

Why, she thought dazedly, it was almost like being a princess . . . Almost as if they were *her* people.

It was as she was about to re-enter the palace that she saw him. The boy sitting on the horse at the edge of the crowd.

Noella stopped dead in her tracks. Was it really — or were her eyes playing tricks?

Then the boy raised one strong brown arm above his head, waved in a wide salute, and she knew. The magnetism of his presence crossed the distance that divided them.

Paolo! Paolo had travelled all the long distance from his village to see her on her wedding day.

Beside her, Daniel put an impatient hand on her elbow. 'Come, Noella. That is enough.'

Forced to move, she followed her husband to the French doors. Then, about to step inside, she was unable to resist one last look back.

Already the boy on the horse had disappeared.

For the rest of the afternoon Noella was bathed in a warm glow of happiness. The toasts were drunk, the enormous wedding cake was cut, and finally, to the strains of the twelve-piece orchestra, Daniel took her in his arms for the bridal waltz.

She snuggled against him. 'It has been a perfect day, hasn't it, darling?' She felt shy using the endearment. In so many ways she and Daniel were still strangers to each other.

Noella drew back and looked up into her husband's handsome face. Only now did she realise that he had seemed quieter than usual today. Was he worrying about her? Concerned at her disappointment that they were unable to go to the Bahamas? Instead their honeymoon would now be spent on the American east coast at an exclusive resort where their security would be assured.

The attempt on Gabrielle's life had caused the upheaval in their plans. Yet Noella could not have been more delighted. Thanks to her father's fears, she and Daniel were leaving Martiguay at once. For the next three years they would live in London while Daniel gained experience with a major English bank. Out of such an unfortunate incident had come her chance to escape even more quickly than she'd dared to hope.

Now she beamed happily into her husband's face. 'We will be so happy, won't we, Daniel?'

'Yes, Noella.' His voice was oddly flat but Noella was too excited to notice.

She felt electrified by the power of Daniel's rugged masculinity. Tonight, she thought, almost breathless with anticipation, the ache inside her would be finally eased.

Then a shadow passed over her face. The worry which had nagged at the edge of her consciousness during the months of her engagement could no longer be ignored. She and Daniel had never discussed having children. Yet no doubt, like most men, he too hoped one day to become a father.

With an effort of will, Noella thrust away the disturbing thought. Perhaps, just perhaps, she prayed, there might still be a chance.

Fernando Jarro leaned across his wife and addressed his son's new father-in-law.

'Look at them, Victor. Do they not make a handsome pair?' He closed his eye in a wink. 'We must congratulate ourselves, eh?'

Victor looked at the couple on the floor. He'd had his doubts at first. Daniel Jarro was almost ten years older than Noella. And then there had been those rumours about his time in New York... Yet Fernando had assured him that the boy had sown his wild oats.

He smiled, his eyes still on the dance floor. 'Yes, Fernando, we played it exactly right. They were made for each other.'

He didn't see the look that passed between Fernando Jarro and his wife.

Noella was upstairs changing for the flight to New York when there was a tap on the door.

Victor de Bartez entered the room. He smiled as

he watched Inez fuss with the collar of Noella's lace-trimmed suit.

'You will be the envy of those *norteamericano* women, Noella.'

She blushed. A compliment from her father was all too rare.

'Now, Inez,' he said, seeing that the task was almost completed, 'if you would be kind enough to leave us alone for a moment.'

The older woman caught his glance. 'Of course.' She smiled at Noella. 'I will see you downstairs, my dear. The car arrives in ten minutes.'

'She will not be late.'

Victor waited until the door had shut and he was alone with his daughter. Even then he did not speak as he studied the child he was losing. Catherine, he thought, she looks just like Catherine on the day I first met her.

Clearing his throat, he spoke slowly, choosing his words with care. 'Of course it does not make me happy to see you go, Noella. But I am reassured that away from Martiguay you will at least have a safer existence. The thought that either you or Gabrielle might be made to pay for what I am trying to achieve for our country has always been my greatest worry.'

He moved closer and placed his hands on her slim shoulders. 'At last, Noella, I can honestly say that you are a daughter I can be proud of. At first I was angry you had disobeyed me, had betrayed my trust yet again. I thought you too young, too immature to make a careful choice of partner, but you have proved me wrong. I am certain that in Daniel you have chosen well.'

His dark eyes stared intensely into hers. 'What matters now, dearest child, is that you hold on to the happiness you feel this moment. Life can be cruel and unjust and a strong and loving partner is your best comfort during difficult times.'

For a second irritation flared inside Noella. Why did he have to spoil it? Why even at this moment, did her father have to refer, no matter how obliquely, to his own loss?

Victor didn't seem to notice how he'd stung her. 'You are going far away,' he continued, 'but always remember that Martiguay is your home, the country of your birth. Your family, those who care for you, will always be here.'

He hesitated then, looking down into that open beautiful face. In her eyes he saw the naked need, the unspoken plea for forgiveness at last . . .

In his heart Victor yearned to say the words his daughter so wanted to hear. Instead, he kissed her gently on both cheeks and left the room.

CHAPTER *THIRTEEN*

From their suite on the eighteenth floor of the Ritz-Carlton hotel, Noella looked out at the neon skyline of New York.

Los Estados Unidos... Just a few hours on an aeroplane, yet she felt as if she were on another planet.

All around her gleaming towers reached into the velvet night skies while below, silver lines of traffic crisscrossed the endless streets. Her eyes shone with excitement. How wonderful to spend her wedding night in this famous city.

It was after ten but she didn't feel tired. Wrapped in a silken cocoon of euphoria she never wanted the feeling to end. It had been the happiest day of her life.

Only once, at the moment of parting, had a different emotion intruded, an emotion so intense it had caught her unawares.

In the forecourt of the palace where the limousine and police escort had stood in readiness, Noella found it difficult to choke back her tears as she said goodbye to her father, Inez, Eugene and finally, Gabrielle.

Her sister too was overcome with emotion. *'Vaya con Dios*, Noella.' Then, as they clung together on the palace steps, Gabrielle whispered, 'Mama was with us today, I am sure. Just as she was on my wedding day.'

'Noella'...

With a start, she turned from the view. In the

doorway of the spacious, wood-panelled bedroom, Daniel stood naked, his dark hair still damp from his shower.

'Come . . . ' He beckoned her into the softly-lit room and Noella's heart turned over at the perfection of his body, the broad muscular shoulders, the tapered waist, the strong lean legs.

Mouth dry, pulses racing, she followed him to the bed. Slipping the thin silk gown from her shoulders, Daniel drew her down beside him.

Her response was instant and shameless. 'Daniel . . . ' Her arms slid around his neck and she caught her breath at the sensual heat of his naked skin. 'Oh, yes . . . '

She shivered as his body straddled hers and she arched and moulded herself against him, her mouth eager for his. Eyes closed, she moaned his name, lost in a giddy vortex of lust and love, her body trembling in wild anticipation.

What happened next shattered all her eager dreams.

Without preamble, without a moment of tenderness, Daniel Jarro drove himself between her legs, thrusting his rock-hard shaft into her delicate flesh. Wildly, urgently, he took her with a piston-driving strength until at last, body shaking in violent spasms, he gasped out his climax.

Stunned and confused, Noella lay motionless as he rolled away from her to the far side of the bed. For months she had been anticipating this moment, dreaming of the tenderness and passion she would find in her husband's arms. Instead she lay sore and bruised, shocked at Daniel's brutality.

She turned her head on the pillow. Daniel's eyes were closed, his face relaxed, and the steady rhythm of his breathing told her he had already drifted into sleep.

He was tired, she consoled herself. That was all. It had been an exhausting day for them both. Tomorrow, everything would be different.

Reaching out a hand, she switched off the lamp and for a long while lay staring into the darkness.

She hated herself for her thoughts. Hated herself for remembering Paolo's gentleness and passion.

The next morning Daniel was up and dressed by the time Noella awoke from a broken, troubled sleep.

'Don't take too long getting ready. The car is due in less than an hour.' As he looked up from the newspaper, his tone was coolly impersonal. *As if he were talking to a stranger*, Noella thought.

Doing her best to hide her hurt and bewilderment, she stepped under the shower. She had hoped they might linger in bed, have a leisurely breakfast together before taking the car out of New York.

Why is it so different from what I imagined? she asked herself miserably.

'Oh, Daniel . . . It's beautiful.'

Noella had been tentative on the drive from the city but now, as the car rounded the final curve of the long tree-lined drive and the hotel came into sight, she recovered some of her high spirits.

Westland House was a fantasy of ivy-covered stone, leadlight windows, and towering chimneys overlooking Long Island Sound.

Beside her, Daniel Jarro felt the tension in his bowels. He'd been crazy to go through with it. There must have been another way.

But he knew there wasn't.

A softly-spoken manager showed them to their suite. Tall windows gave uninterrupted views of the Sound and bowls of scented flowers filled the elegantly furnished rooms.

' . . . and may I introduce your housekeeper, Mrs Timpson,' a shapely woman in her early thirties, dressed

in traditional black and white, bobbed a curtsy, '...
and your personal butler, Mr Devlin.' The man was
a little younger, blond, broad-shouldered, with a perfect
smile. 'They are at your complete disposal. It is their
pleasant task to see to your every need.'

The manager gave a little bow as he left the room.
'I trust you will enjoy your stay at Westland House.'

The rest of the day passed easily enough. Together
Noella and Daniel explored the grounds: the deep, tiled
pool, the ornamental lakes, the marked area of lawn
where two couples were hitting a ball with what looked
like outsize polo mallets.

'Croquet.' Daniel answered in response to Noella's
puzzled frown. 'A traditional English amusement.'

After a lunch served on their private terrace by the
quietly efficient butler and housekeeper, Daniel suggested a game of tennis. Noella hid her disappointment
as she went to change. It wasn't what she had in mind
for the afternoon...

Then, almost before she quite realised it, the day
was gone and they were preparing for dinner.

'Why don't we join the others this evening? Meet
our fellow guests?' Daniel called his questions through
the half-open bathroom door and didn't see Noella's
frown.

Who cared about the other guests? she thought miserably. Couldn't Daniel see that she wanted him to
herself? She had hoped they could have dinner in their
suite in order to fall more quickly into bed. Noella's
face grew strained. Wasn't that what a honeymoon was
for?

'Of course, *querido*,' she forced a lightness into her
voice. 'If that is what you wish.'

It was almost midnight before they finally retired to
bed. The evening had been pleasant enough but as each
hour passed Noella had grown more impatient.

Now she changed quickly into a lace-edged gown, so sheer that the outline of her body was clearly visible. Tonight, she knew, everything would be all right.

Daniel was waiting, lying naked, his body dark against the crisp linen sheets. As she slipped in beside him, he smiled and stretched out a hand to stroke her neck.

'Beautiful Noella.' His voice was a silky murmur and as he continued to stroke, hand moving lower, Noella felt her heart begin to race. This was the moment she had been waiting for.

He drew her to him, lips nibbling at her ears, her throat, her moist, open mouth. As she shivered in delight, he tossed the gown aside, bending his head to her naked breasts, teasing her nipples into swollen attention.

Just when Noella felt she could bear no more, he moved down the bed and she gasped as his hungry mouth found her pounding bud. A groan of pleasure burst from her lips and her cheeks burned with shameful joy. Never in her wildest imagination had it occurred to her that lovers did such things!

Enclosed in a cocoon of sensual response, she felt herself soaring towards that urgent peak of delight, trembling on the edge of ecstasy when, without warning, Daniel suddenly drew away.

Noella's eyes fluttered open in surprise. Her body hung suspended in a desperate limbo between pain and pleasure, while on the pillow beside her, her husband's handsome face looked calmly into her own.

In a voice thick with unsatisfied desire, she murmured, 'Daniel, please . . . '

'Hush.' He stroked her damp hair.

'Daniel, please, I — '

He interrupted her, a spark of something indefinable in his eyes. 'A woman should never beg, Noella. That is the way of a *puta*, a whore.'

Then, leaning over, he kissed her gently on the lips

and she could taste herself on his mouth. 'Sometimes, *querida*,' he said lightly, 'there is more enjoyment in waiting for life's little pleasures.'

In the days that followed the pattern remained the same. As they sat at breakfast, swam in the pool, chatted before dinner with the other wealthy guests, Daniel was always the loving, considerate husband.

Yet when they went to bed the dreadful torment continued.

Noella's mind spun with a dozen different explanations for the situation that existed between them. As she lay by the pool in her sleek white maillot, watching her handsome husband execute a series of perfect dives, her eyes grew haunted behind her dark glasses.

Was there something wrong with her? Was Daniel comparing her to his other lovers and finding her inadequate? Did her need of him really make her seem like a whore?

Nerves stretched to breaking point, Noella started to imagine the worst. Even the woman who attended them in their suite aroused her suspicions. Wasn't the housekeeper with her good looks and mature sexuality just a little too friendly and attentive? Stomach churning, she determined never to leave Daniel alone in the woman's presence.

On their last night at Westland House, Noella awoke to find the bed empty beside her.

Puzzled, she focused sleepily on the bedside alarm. It was not yet five o'clock.

Where was Daniel?

Throwing back the covers, she slipped on her robe and padded barefoot through the suite. She was alone.

In growing confusion, she returned to the bedroom. Where could Daniel have gone?

Suddenly her stomach tightened and she felt the blood rush from her face. Her suspicions had been right!

Daniel had stolen away to be with someone else, one of those mature, experienced American women who watched him with hungry eyes as he dived and swam. What other explanation could there be for a man to leave the bed of his new bride?

Her mind in a turmoil, Noella didn't hear the door open behind her.

'Noella . . . ?'

She spun around, heart jumping in her chest. 'Daniel! Where have you been?'

He was dressed in slacks and casual pullover, his hair rumpled and cheeks flushed.

For a moment he didn't answer as he took in her wild eyes, heard the shrill edge to her voice. Then, with a soft laugh, he crossed the room and folded her in his arms. '*Querida* . . . what have you been thinking? Can't a man take a walk before the sun comes up without being looked at as if he has committed the most heinous crime?'

Noella looked down at his dark brown loafers, wet with dew, and suddenly felt foolish. 'I — I just thought . . .'

But Daniel was throwing off his clothes, a strange light in his dark eyes. As he pulled her to the bed, Noella's heart soared. She could see the excitement in his face. This time, she knew, everything was going to be as she dreamed.

But once again, her illusions were shattered. As before, he entered her with a savage intensity.

Tears filled her eyes. 'Daniel, please. I can't enjoy it if —'

'*Enjoy?*' It was as if she had uttered an obscenity. His lips curled as he stared at her in cold disdain. 'Only whores enjoy sex.'

Afterwards, they lay apart. As she watched the dawn light begin to soften the room, silent tears rolled down Noella's face.

It would never be like it had been with Paolo. She knew that now.

CHAPTER FOURTEEN

'Darling, no! You're far too greedy. No more...'

With a silvery laugh, Lady Celia Hartlee evaded her lover's eager grasp and slipped off the massive oak bed with its canopy of Irish lace and pale lavender pleating.

'I'm due at Guy's at five,' she explained, wrapping a peignoir of ivory satin around her pale, rounded body. 'Cocktails for some old schoolchum. Since I haven't seen my sweet, disreputable brother in ages, I promised I'd go.'

'You were wonderful, darling,' her lover murmured from the bed. 'Has anyone ever told you you have the most beautiful breasts in England?'

Celia Hartlee laughed. 'Both my husbands — and it didn't stop me leaving either of them.'

As the only daughter of the immensely wealthy Earl of Saxby, whose title dated back to 1698, Celia Hartlee had always had her choice of aristocratic partners. Married at twenty to the second son of a Duke fourteen years her senior, Celia had known even on the honeymoon that the match would not last. How could she bear to spend her life with a man who preferred long telephone conversations with the manager of his racing stables to satisfying his sex-hungry bride?

Her second union also proved less than satisfying in that department. It mattered not a jot to Celia that her charming Irish husband never made a penny from his poems. Of greater concern was the fact that his potency was directly dependent on the flow of words from the gold Cartier pen she had given him. Long barren periods for Oswald Flannery meant the same for his frustrated wife and that marriage too came to a premature end.

The greatest and most surprising lesson Celia learnt from these vexing periods of her life was how many of her friends were also dissatisfied with their husbands' performances. Over long boozy lunches at San Lorenzo or Le Caprice, she listened in delighted horror to the discussions of the shortcomings and failings of the men her friends had married. And when in earthy, explicit language these well-dressed pillars of English woman-hood began to reveal their fantasies, Celia's fair English skin turned a deeper shade of pink. It had never occurred to her that women could be wilder and more imaginative than men.

Nowadays she didn't blush at all.

'Kiss me goodbye then, damn you, and I'll go.' With sulky eyes, her lover looked at her from the bed.

Smiling, Celia moved back to the bed and did as she was asked.

'There ...' she said, stroking back Angelica Beauman's dark, tangled hair and planting a kiss lightly on her forehead. 'Now you really must go, darling.'

Guy Hartlee welcomed his guests with the easy languid manner of a man supremely satisfied with his life.

He had no reason not to be. A titled and wealthy bachelor of thirty, he enjoyed the sort of life style which made him the envy of his peers.

Sports and gambling were his dual obsessions — an expert marksman, he hunted, raced cars and powerboats, and had skied for Britain in two Winter Olympics.

It was the same craving for excitement and challenge which drew him to risk high stakes at the tables at White's and Aspinall's, as well as in Monte Carlo and

Deauville. And whether he won or lost, Guy Hartlee always had fun. He had, after all, always held the opinion that life was nothing more than an amusing game.

Eyes bright with excitement, Noella sipped at her drink and listened to the buzz of conversation around her. English presented her with no problem. Her mother had spoken the language to her and Gabrielle from the time they were babies and Noella spoke it even better than the French she had learnt at school.

Still, she felt a little shy among these older, self-confident foreigners and stayed close to Daniel as he chatted with their host.

Noella had liked Guy Hartlee at first sight. Small and wiry, with a short clipped blond moustache and bright blue eyes, he had flattered her outrageously. She hadn't realised Englishmen could be so charming.

As she watched him laugh with Daniel at some shared joke, it was obvious that the years of school and university had built a durable friendship between them. The thought made Noella aware that for the first time in her life she was without close friends of her own — and the difficulties of her relationship with Daniel only served to underscore her sense of loneliness. Tonight, as always, he was openly loving and attentive, but in bed the torment continued until she had begun to dread his touch.

Breaking off in mid-sentence, Guy Hartlee placed an apologetic hand on Daniel's arm. 'Excuse me a moment, will you, old chap? Celia's just arrived. She said she'd try to make it.'

Curious, Noella turned to watch as their host greeted a smiling, shapely blonde, kissing her on both cheeks.

'Who is this woman, Daniel?'

'Lady Celia Hartlee. She's Guy's sister.' There was something in his tone which made Noella wonder if perhaps he didn't particularly care for the blonde Englishwoman.

Celia Hartlee seemed acquainted with almost everyone in the room and it took a while before Guy was able to make his way back to them, his sister in tow.

Up close, Noella saw she had the same laughing blue eyes as her brother, a slim, arched nose, and the sort of creamy porcelain complexion which made it difficult to judge an Englishwoman's age.

'Celia, you remember Daniel.'

'But of course! How nice to see you again, Daniel. It's been so long ... seven years?' Celia Hartlee's voice was low and throaty and she stressed certain words with an almost theatrical emphasis.

'Close enough, Celia, but you, I can honestly say, look not a day older.' Daniel Jarro delivered the compliment with mechanical politeness.

Wry amusement lit the Englishwoman's blue eyes. 'Men are quite capable of telling the most monstrous lies.'

'And this, Celia darling,' Guy Hartlee placed a friendly hand on Noella's shoulder, 'is Daniel's beautiful new wife, Noella. As you can see, he never told us that Martiguay produced such stunningly attractive females.'

With a slow smile, Lady Celia Hartlee took Noella's hand in her own. 'There are so many things you men keep secret, Guy ...'

Two days later the telephone rang in the smart townhouse Noella and Daniel had leased near Regent's Park. The place was more than they could afford on Daniel's salary but he had insisted on the importance of the right address. Fortunately, Fernando Jarro was happy to indulge his son's expensive tastes.

With Daniel spending long hours at the bank, Noella was left to cope alone with the setting up of the household. Anticipation soon turned to panic as she realised she had next to no idea how to equip or run a house. And she had no one to turn to for help.

Until now.

Picking up the receiver, she recognised the distinctive throaty voice of Celia Hartlee. 'Noella, darling, so glad you're home. Now, I've been thinking how we can solve your problems.'

From that moment, Celia Hartlee became Noella's fairy godmother. She knew exactly where to hire the best staff, buy the choicest meat or finest wines, find the perfect out of season flowers.

And her influence soon extended beyond the domestic front. Dentists, hairdressers, beauticians... Noella was happy to accept all Celia's recommendations. On their regular shopping expeditions to Beauchamp Place, South Molton Street, or the King's Road, she would change into one designer label after another under her new friend's appraising eye. Soon Noella's wardrobe was bulging with outfits by Jasper Conran, Katharine Hamnett, or Christian Lacroix, and it reached the stage where she could barely trust herself to buy a new handbag without Celia Hartlee's expert advice.

Socially too, Celia expanded Noella's horizons with invitations to lunches, gallery openings, or exclusive charity functions where she seemed happy to introduce Noella to her upper-crust friends.

'Just don't mention Martiguay, darling,' Celia smiled disarmingly. 'No one has the faintest where the place is. Better, perhaps, to speak about your mother.' Her smile broadened. 'The English, you see, like to be able to file people into appropriate boxes, and your mother was, after all, the daughter of a baronet. That's the sort of thing we English understand.'

It was hard for Noella to take offence at Celia Hartlee's words. After all, she knew her new friend spoke the truth. Why should any of these sophisticated, self-

satisfied foreigners be interested in a country as poor
and remote as Martiguay? Hadn't she herself found it
easy to forget?

Then, after she had been in London almost eight
months, a letter from Gabrielle made her thoughts turn
to home.

'At first,' her sister wrote, 'I could hardly believe
it. But I am so happy. The baby will be born in August.
Papa is delighted of course — almost as much as Eugene.
Already he is sure it will be a boy!'

Fingers cold and stiff, Noella folded the letter. Again
it was Gabrielle who would fulfil their father's dreams.

As her friendship with Celia Hartlee grew, Noella barely
noticed the twelve-year difference in their ages. Celia
had cured her of her loneliness, helped her feel at home
in this strange new city.

Yet for all the growing closeness between them,
Noella still felt unable to reveal the problem in her
marriage. She longed to confide in the sophisticated
divorcee but one thing held her back.

She was too ashamed of her failure. Somehow, she
knew, she had let Daniel down. The problem, she felt
certain, must lie with her.

And then, in a totally unexpected way, Noella discovered
just how easily that problem might be solved. Again
it was Celia Hartlee who unwittingly pointed her in
the right direction.

They had just returned to Celia's flat in leafy Holland
Park after a morning spent combing the antique houses
in New Bond Street. Noella was delighted with her
purchase. The eighteenth century Venetian tapestry
would look wonderful in her entrance hall and thanks
to Celia's negotiations, she had acquired it at a reasonable
price.

'Make yourself comfortable, darling.' Celia opened

the door to her sunny sitting room. 'I'm just going to kick off these hellish shoes. What will you have to drink? Tea, coffee, something stronger? It's after one, so a real drink wouldn't be totally obscene.'

Noella smiled. 'Just coffee will be fine.'

Left alone, she settled herself in the blue down-filled sofa enjoying the quiet ambience of the room.

What did it feel like to live alone, she wondered? Celia seemed to enjoy it, even after sharing a home with two husbands.

Idly, she picked up a hard-cover book that lay on the table beside her and began to turn the pages. There were glossy photographs . . .

Noella caught her breath. She could hardly believe her eyes. She had never seen photographs like these before . . . Totally naked men in a state of . . . of excitement; young attractive women clad provocatively in garter belts, panties cut high on the thigh, transparent brassieres . . .

'Quite fascinating, don't you think?'

Noella's head shot up. She hadn't heard the older woman re-enter the room. Face aflame she answered, 'I — I'm sorry I didn't mean to — '

Celia's light laugh cut across her words. 'No need to apologise, Noella darling. It's there for all the world to see.'

Celia could barely hide her delight. Her ploy had worked; the girl had done exactly as she'd hoped.

She sat down close beside her on the sofa and, taking the book from Noella's hands, slowly began to turn the pages. 'You see how tempting a woman can make herself? It's the dressing up; I've always believed that a much greater provocation than total nudity. Men love the game, the fantasy — it whets their appetite — and of course all women are born actresses when it comes to keeping their lovers happy.'

Turning to Noella, she arched a perfectly-shaped eyebrow and said with deliberate casualness, 'But I'm sure I don't have to tell you any of this, darling. You must have a wonderful sexual relationship with a man as handsome and virile as Daniel.'

For the next three weeks, Celia Hartlee was out of town and Noella found herself missing the older woman's company. She realised how heavily she had come to rely on Celia's friendship.

She kept remembering, too, the photographs she had seen, and her new friend's comments about the 'games' and 'fantasies' men so enjoyed. Surely, she thought, a woman as sophisticated and worldly as Celia Hartlee would understand a man's needs...

'Darling, I had an absolutely super time. There's just nowhere in the world like Italy. Sun, sun, sun. And the food! I've put on pounds.'

As Celia chattered on, Noella did her best to seem interested. She had hoped Celia's return would lift her mood, but nothing seemed able to shift the black despair which had settled on her. Nothing had gone as she had hoped.

Suddenly breaking off in mid-sentence, Celia shot her a curious glance. 'Darling, you haven't heard a word I've been saying. What's wrong? Is anything the matter?'

Noella shook her head. 'No. No, nothing.'

But her stomach churned as she turned away from Celia's searching blue eyes. How she hated pretending. If only she could talk to Celia about this. But it was too hateful, too shameful, to reveal to anyone else. What had happened she would have to bear alone.

'Well then, enough of my adventures.' Celia got to her feet and held out a hand. 'Come with me. I've got something I want to show you.'

She led the way up the thickly carpeted staircase to her bedroom above. Noella had never seen the room before and found it hard to hide her surprise.

Celia chuckled. 'Do you like it? I wanted a real eighteenth century boudoir.'

The room was a fantasy of feminine indulgence with its huge canopied bed, a sunken onyx bath with burnished gold taps, and a cushioned love seat.

But Celia was leading the way into the spacious dressing room beyond. From one of the floor to ceiling shelves that lined one entire wall, she drew a hot pink carrier bag, initialled in gold.

'For you, darling,' she handed the package to Noella. 'Isabella Lantini is one of Rome's most inspired designers. She knows exactly how to make a woman look like a princess and a whore at the same time. Do open it.'

'Oh, Celia!' Warmed by her friend's generosity, Noella unwrapped the swathe of tissue. With a gasp of delight she drew out a gown of emerald green and held it up against her. 'It's gorgeous. But you really shouldn't —'

Celia Hartlee waved away her protestations. 'I loved it on sight. If I could have wriggled into it myself I would have.' She wrinkled her nose in mock disgust. 'Not made for English hips, I'm afraid. But I knew at once it'd look absolutely divine on you. Hurry up, darling, I'm dying to see it on. Come through when you're ready.'

Celia was sitting on the love seat, legs tucked beneath her, when Noella emerged in the clinging jersey gown. It had taken her a few minutes to cope with the tiny pearl buttons that fastened from navel to throat.

The Englishwoman's blue eyes travelled slowly over the girl. Her voice was husky as she said, 'It's wonderful, darling ... so very, very sexy. Turn around, let me see the back.'

The dress was deceptively chaste. Buttoned high to the neck, it was slashed low and revealing at the back.

Celia nodded, her mouth dry, as she took in the

bare curve of flesh. A bra was impossible, of course. 'Oh yes, darling, it's utterly fabulous.'

In the privacy of the dressing room, Noella struggled to undo the row of tiny buttons. She was suddenly overcome with despair and desperation.

What was the point in wearing a dress like this? Nothing made any difference to Daniel. No matter how sexy or appealing she tried to be, she knew now that wasn't what Daniel wanted. She had tried the game of dressing up, of tantalising, as Celia had suggested, and his response had shocked her.

Her dark eyes haunted, she slipped the dress off her shoulders and was confronted by the evidence of her husband's disgust.

'Noella, can I help —?' Heart thumping, Celia entered the room. This was how she had planned it. The gift, the chance to see the girl naked, maybe to make the first tentative moves...

Startled, Noella tried to cover her nakedness but the Englishwoman's gasp of shock told her she was too late.

Celia Hartlee's eyes were riveted to the girl's full, perfect breasts, to the enormous ugly bruises that spoilt that perfection.

'Oh, God. How in the world — ?'

She saw the tears spring into those dark, frightened eyes.

'Oh, my dear. Please, what happened? Tell me.' A picture of concern, she drew the naked girl into her arms. A jolt of pure pleasure shot through her. God, how much longer would she have to wait?

Only when Noella's sobs had finally subsided did Celia Hartlee speak. Placing her hands on the girl's shoulders, she drew back and looked into that anguished, tear-stained face.

'Darling.' Her voice was soft and gentle. 'I know what you're putting up with. Believe me, I do.'

Seeing the startled disbelief in Noella's eyes, she nodded. 'I had friends who went out with Daniel when he was at Cambridge. I've heard the stories . . . the way he leads a woman on, leaves her aching for fulfilment.' Her fingers trailed a soothing path up and down Noella's bare arm. 'There are men like that, Noella, men who take some sort of perverted pleasure in hurting a woman.' Her fingers moved with deliberate casualness, brushing the ugly mottled blemishes on Noella's breasts. 'I know why Daniel —'

But Noella cut her off. Slipping free of the older woman's grasp, she protested weakly, 'I don't know what you're talking about, Celia. It — it was an accident. I bruised myself when I slipped and fell.' She grasped at the words, almost willing herself to believe they were the truth.

Celia Hartlee gave a sad, sympathetic smile. 'Of course you did, darling. But please,' her direct blue eyes stared into Noella's dark ones, 'just remember one thing. I'm your friend. I'll always be here for you if you need me.'

CHAPTER *FIFTEEN*

'Senor Avery! I am delighted you could join us this evening. How is Paris? As cold as London?'

Lucia Delmonte didn't bother waiting for an answer as she welcomed her guest into the crowded reception room. 'If I could only have the warmth of Martiguay as well as the culture of Europe, I would be in heaven.'

The wife of the Martiguayan Ambassador to England flashed a wide smile at the tall American. The Nordic type had always attracted her, and Richard Avery, with his sea-blue eyes, thick, golden hair and fair skin, came close to her ideal. They had met only twice before but she had been drawn at once by the young American's quiet charm and self-deprecating humour, qualities Lucia Delmonte had always found rather rare in a *norteamericano*.

'Fortunately I was able to accept your kind invitation, senora.' Richard Avery's accent was pure Boston. 'I'm not often in London as you know, but by lucky coincidence I had an engagement this week at the L.S.E.'

At thirty-four, Doctor Richard Avery was already an acknowledged expert on Latin American affairs. A two-year lectureship at the Sorbonne based him in Paris but occasional speaking engagements took him to other European institutions. His recent paper on radical proposals for the retrenchment of Latin American debt to the I.M.F. had raised more than a few eyebrows at the London School of Economics.

Lucia Delmonte laid a conspiratorial hand on the rough tweed sleeve of the young American's jacket. 'I particularly wanted you to meet our President's daughter, senor. She and her husband are our special guests this evening; you will find them interesting company, I hope. You see,' she pointed discreetly with a gleaming red fingernail, 'the young woman in green velvet.'

'I am a great admirer of your father's reform agenda, senora. I saw for myself some of the atrocities which occurred when Peres was in power. In fact, I was later called upon to testify at a US Congressional Caucus on Human Rights.'

Introduced by his hostess, Richard Avery was interested in discussing Martiguayan affairs first-hand with the daughter of Victor de Bartez. 'However,' he went on, 'it seems that the President's greatest obstacle lies in the fact that his proposals may still be undermined from within. Has he evolved a strategy to overcome that?'

The girl beside him raised one slim shoulder in a shrug. 'This is something I have no knowledge of, senor.'

Richard Avery hid his surprise and disappointment. He had followed the crisis in Martiguayan politics closely. It was his considered judgement that de Bartez was the only man capable of providing the leadership and clear-sighted policies likely to lead his country to peace and prosperity. Yet a more intimate insight into the strategies of the de Bartez government would obviously not be forthcoming from the President's younger daughter. To the contrary, Noella Jarro seemed singularly disinterested in the political workings of her country.

Richard tried a different tack. 'It must please you to see the growing opportunities for women now in Martiguay, senora. Your own sister, of course, has played an important role in effecting these changes.' He smiled down at her, noticing for the first time the beauty of those large, liquid brown eyes. 'Do you have any intention of following in her footsteps on your return?'

Noella felt like screaming with boredom. After the initial cocktail party welcoming them to London, she had managed to find excuses for any further invitations from the Martiguayan Ambassador and his wife. But Daniel had insisted that they attend this evening. It was a matter of protocol, he argued. They couldn't continue to ignore their duty.

Now here she was stuck with this dull American who seemed intent on discussing nothing but Martiguay and its politics. Couldn't he see how much it bored her?

She raised an insolent eyebrow. 'My sister and I have very little in common, senor, and I can think of nothing more tedious than "following in her footsteps", as you put it. In fact, if I were to pass any comment at all on my sister's career, it would be merely to say that she should relinquish it at once now she is about to become a mother.' She gave the tall, blond American a tight smile. 'If you will excuse me?'

Pushing past him, she left Richard to look after her in bemused annoyance.

Arrogant and spoilt, he decided, sipping at his glass of non-vintage Krug.

But beautiful, too.

As he moved around the room, Richard Avery was unconscious of the interest he sparked in the eyes of the well-dressed female guests.

He was a man without natural vanity, whose interest in his fellow human beings transcended any self-conscious concern about his own impact on others.

The only son of a former Senator who had made his fortune in aeronautical engineering, Richard had received a first-class education, graduating from Yale as his father and grandfather had done before him.

It was during two summer vacations spent as a member of the Peace Corps that his future career was charted. At various posts in Central and South America, Richard saw at first-hand the poverty and abuses, the corruption and graft, which had left the mass of ordinary people living lives of abject misery.

A postgraduate degree in Latin American politics was the natural extension of his overriding commitment and concern for America's troubled neighbours, while a series of well-argued articles on the self-interested stance of Washington brought him international academic attention. It was at a conference on Latin American trade policies that he had first met the Martiguayan Ambassador to Britain.

Now, as he mingled with his fellow guests, Richard chatted easily in Spanish or French or English. His skill in languages and his familiarity with Europe he owed to his Danish mother. As a child, many of his vacations had been spent with his Danish relatives; although his mother had adapted to life in the States, she had never ceased to miss her own close-knit family.

It had long been her dream, Richard knew, that one day her only son would meet and fall in love with a fellow Dane. Well, he smiled to himself, there had been girls, but never a Dane . . .

At college he had had two lengthy relationships, each of which could have led to marriage. Both times he had sidestepped the issue. Not from any inherent opposition to the idea of marriage, but rather because at that stage of his life he had had an overwhelming desire to explore the world and its options.

And now, he thought, distracted for a moment from his conversation, there was Michelle.

At thirty-nine, Michelle Valdier was almost five years older than himself. The art critic of a prestigious monthly journal, she was elegant in the classic, understated way of so many Frenchwomen.

She was also married.

Richard had met Michelle and Francois Valdier at a soiree at the home of a fellow academic. He had liked the pair at once. They were typical of their class: urbane, cultured, childless, with a spacious apartment in the fashionable narrow streets of the *sixième* and a rambling country house in the smartest part of Provence.

They led busy, often separate lives, as they explained to Richard on the evening they met. 'Francois' company is involved in computer technology. He must travel all over Europe, sometimes even to the Far East,' explained Michelle Valdier in faultless, slightly accented English. She smoothed a slick of short gleaming hair behind a perfectly shaped ear and smiled over her drink. 'The arts and technology... our careers are diametrically opposed, *n'est-ce pas?*'

Richard was surprised — and strangely excited — when two days after that first meeting, Michelle Valdier rang to invite him to lunch. He hadn't asked questions, drawn no preconceived conclusions from the unexpected invitation — merely turned up at the appointed hour at the busy restaurant in Les Halles.

It was as they were finishing their coffee after an excellent three-course meal and stimulating conversation, that he felt the Frenchwoman's cool hand on his thigh.

'I would like to see you again, Richard.' Her intelligent grey-green eyes stared into his. 'Lunch is always a possibility, but I am not always hungry for food...'

The affair was now in its seventh month. Michelle Valdier was an erotic, experienced lover who gave herself with complete abandon in bed. It always intrigued Richard to see how, as she re-donned her clothes, she reverted once more to her cool, slightly aloof, reserve. A woman very different from the one he knew in bed.

No mention was ever made of her husband and, taking his cue, Richard also avoided the subject. But he was uncomfortable on the few occasions that he found himself at some social gathering where Francois and Michelle were present as a couple. The deceit sat uneasily on his shoulders.

When he finally admitted as much to Michelle one afternoon as they lay naked in each other's arms, she threw back her long white neck in a gurgle of merriment.

'Oh, Richard, you are so American, so puritan. Francois is happy I am not lonely when he is away. Marriage is not meant to stifle. Just because I choose to spend my life with a man I hold dear does not mean I must be denied the thrill of intermittent pleasures.' She stroked his tousled blond hair and gave him a lazy smile. 'I will be old soon enough, *cheri*, now for a while I must relish what can still be mine.'

It was a straightforward response and one Richard decided he could live with. After all, he thought, the relationship was self-limiting. He would be returning to the States at the end of his tenure. In the meantime, he would relish his good fortune with the minimum of guilt.

He was enjoying a lively debate with Ambassador Delmonte on the future of Martiguayan trade when the white glare of flashbulbs suddenly brightened the room.

Turning, Richard saw that it was Noella Jarro who was the photographer's target. She seemed more than happy with the attention, smiling as she clung to her husband's arm, enjoying, no doubt, the envy of the other women.

'She is very beautiful, *si*?' The Ambassador spoke the words close to his ear.

Richard nodded politely, hiding his depression at the sudden realisation of how often beauty was unaccompanied by either intellect or knowledge. He had hoped to find more of both in the daughter of a man as brave and charismatic as Victor de Bartez.

*

Across the room, Noella was indeed enjoying the attention.

When at last the photographer was finished, he smiled and proffered a small black and gold card.

'My name is Giles Roget, madame. I am based in Paris, where I also do a great deal of fashion work.' He spoke quickly and quietly, but the husband seemed more interested in finding a waiter to replenish his drink. 'You are the image of your mother, Madame Jarro. If for any reason you ever wish to make the most of that fact, please feel free to contact me.'

With another smile he was gone, leaving Noella to stare after him.

Noella was alone in the house when the doorbell rang.

Fresh from the shower, her hair hanging damply around her shoulders, she pulled on a soft pink robe and debated whether to answer her caller. It was the housekeeper's afternoon off and her young Spanish maid had just stepped out to the local market.

In truth, Noella was glad to have the house to herself. Solitude gave her a respite from the increasing tension of pretence, from the facade she was forced to live behind, particularly in front of the servants. To them, she knew, she was the fortunate and beautiful Senora Jarro, a woman who had everything: money, status, an elegant home, a handsome and loving husband...

Noella activated the intercom. 'Yes? Hello... who is it?'

'Darling, it's me.'

'Celia!' Noella's eyes lit up. It seemed like ages since they'd seen each other and Celia always cheered her up.

The next minute, she was opening the front door to a smiling Celia Hartlee.

'Oh...' The Englishwoman took in Noella's robe and damp hair. 'Am I interrupting? Are you getting ready to go out?'

'Not at all. Come in, Celia. How lovely to see you.' Shutting the door, she led the way into the sunroom with its view of the small, walled garden. 'All the servants are out. Can I get you a drink? Tea? Or perhaps you would prefer gin?' She had learned about English drinking habits. As long as it was after noon, hard liquor was totally acceptable.

'A gin and twist would be lovely, darling. Will you join me?'

Out of politeness, Noella agreed, though wine was more to her taste, and then only as an accompaniment to a meal.

Celia smiled at her as they settled on the pink and green flowered sofa with their drinks. 'Sorry not to call first, Noella, but I was just passing and hoped you wouldn't mind. It seems ages since we saw each other.'

It was. Almost three weeks in fact. Not since the afternoon when Celia had caught sight of the bruising on Noella's breasts. Noella had even begun to fear that perhaps her refusal to confide in Celia had offended the older woman.

But this unexpected visit and the Englishwoman's cheery manner reassured her.

Celia Hartlee was always amusing company and soon had Noella laughing with her bitchy, sarcastic comments on the London social scene.

'It's incestuous, darling... quite, quite incestuous. Nigel Dempster doesn't know the half of it.' She handed her empty glass to Noella. 'Lovely. Shall we have another?'

Noella felt a pleasant buzz in her head from the effects of the gin. Her whole body seemed heavy and relaxed. How wonderful it was to forget her own problems for a while in Celia's company.

'And tell me, my sweet,' Celia Hartlee laid her arm across the back of the sofa and brushed back a lock of hair from Noella's shoulders, 'how are things with Daniel?'

Immediately Noella's tenseness returned. Was Celia's question personal, or a more general enquiry about Daniel's work? She didn't want to risk offending her friend again. Forcing herself to give a little laugh, she said, 'He's fine, Celia. Always working hard, of course.'

'Of course.' The other woman's hand still rested on her shoulder. 'But I wasn't only referring to his work.'

Noella's eyes grew troubled. 'Celia, I don't want — '

Interrupting, the older woman changed the subject 'You're so tense, darling. I can feel it here.' She squeezed Noella's shoulder through the thin gown. 'Why don't you lie down here and let me rub those horrible knots away?' She gave a slow smile. 'Tension is so ageing...'

Almost before she knew it, Noella felt the gown slipped from her shoulders and next moment she was face down on the wide, comfortable sofa with Celia's small, soft hands stroking at her cool flesh.

'Just relax ... Let me help you feel wonderful.' Celia Hartlee's voice was a silken murmur.

The touch of the other woman's hands was infinitely soothing. Noella's breathing slowed; she felt as if her whole body was beginning to melt against the sofa.

'You have beautiful skin, darling.' Celia Hartlee's cheeks had flushed a dull pink as her hands explored the smooth curve of the girl's spine, circled her hips and gently brushed the roundness of her buttocks. 'Doesn't it feel good?' She had to fight to keep the steadiness in her voice.

'Oh, yes... ' Noella breathed the words softly into the cushions. She could feel the tension pouring out of her. If only Daniel would touch her as gently as this.

'Roll over now, my sweet.' Heart racing, breath shallow, Celia Hartlee felt the gorgeous moisture start to bloom between her legs. Oh God, it was going to be so easy after all...

Turning as instructed, Noella felt a sudden sense of shyness, and at once chided herself for her unworldliness. A sophisticated woman like Celia Hartlee wouldn't give a second thought to another woman's nakedness.

'This is where the tension sits.' Leaning over, Celia drew cool, soft fingers down either side of Noella's long, slender neck and felt her shiver.

Her breath ragged, she drew feathery circles across Noella's chest, her fingers moving closer and closer to the pink buds of nipples. God, how she'd dreamed of this moment ...

Then, with one hand, she was fumbling with the buttons of her own blouse, throwing the silky garment aside, and lowering her milky white breasts against the girl's golden flesh; as their bodies met she gasped in pleasure, her senses reeling in erotic delight.

'Celia!' Noella's eyes flew open. Frozen with shock, she stared in disbelief into the older woman's flushed face.

Celia Hartlee's body was crushed against her own, her mouth agape in ecstasy as her trembling fingers found Noella's nipples.

And then shock gave way to a breathless, pulse-pounding anger. 'NO!' With all her strength, Noella forced Celia away and stumbled to her feet.

Eyes wild, she stood over the dishevelled woman. 'I thought you were my friend! I thought you cared about me! And all the time — '

'Darling ... ' Still breathing heavily, Celia Hartlee struggled to sit up. 'I do care about you. I know what Daniel is doing to you. He can never give you satisfaction. You or any other woman. And I know the reason why.'

'What do you *mean*? What do you know about Daniel?' Noella's voice held a shrill edge of hysteria as she held the discarded robe against her nakedness.

All she wanted was to throw this perverted woman out of her home, never see her again — but the desire to know exactly what Celia meant held her back.

Aware of her advantage, Celia Hartlee reached for her blouse and slowly began to dress. She hadn't lost yet... 'Daniel hates women, Noella. It goes back to the time he was a schoolboy here. There was a woman, the wife of one of the masters. She got her kicks from introducing young boys to sex... then taunting them about their inadequacies.'

Celia stared levelly into those dark, wild eyes. 'I know all about it, you see, because Guy was a victim too. Only he didn't fight his homosexuality like Daniel has tried to do. Daniel has never forgiven women; he wants to, but he can never — '

The stinging slap made Celia Hartlee stagger backwards.

'Get out of here!' Face twisted in fury, Noella spat out the words. 'Get out of here at once, you filthy *puta*!'

When she heard the front door slam, Noella leaned against the living room wall. Wrapping her arms around herself, she wept until there were no tears left.

CHAPTER SIXTEEN

The whine of the engines died away and the jet came to a standstill at the side of the one, low-set building which was Martiguay's international terminal.

As she clattered her way down the steep metal steps, Noella screwed up her eyes against the glare of the tropical sun. After almost two years of grey English skies, the steamy Martiguayan heat seemed to burn with a fiercer intensity; she felt the sweat breaking out between her shoulder blades as she stepped onto the baking tarmac.

But the next moment her discomfort was forgotten at the sight of Gabrielle smiling from the back seat of the waiting limousine.

'Noella!' As she slid in next to her, Gabrielle welcomed her sister into her arms. 'Oh, Noella, you look wonderful... I am so glad to have you home again, even for a short time.'

She drew back, smiling happily as the car with its heavily-armed escort sped off the airport apron.

'It is a great shame Daniel could not come with you, but of course we understood when you said how busy he is at work. Is he well? Are you both happy in London? Is it what you expected?'

As she answered her sister's fusillade of questions, Noella forced a gaiety into her voice she did not feel. Already she feared it might have been a mistake to come home. How was she going to keep up a pretence of happiness for almost two weeks?

But she had had to get away, had been desperate to escape the nightmare that surrounded her in London. Here, far away from Daniel, she must decide what to do. When she had informed him that she wanted to see the baby, spend time with her family, he had seemed barely interested.

Noella forced her attention back to her sister. 'But tell me the most important thing, Gabrielle. How is the baby, tiny Roberto? Does he sleep well already? Is he already calling Eugene Papa?'

And to Noella's relief, for the two-hour drive to the *hacienda*, Gabrielle was happy to do most of the talking.

Inez knew there was something wrong. She could see it in the girl's eyes and wondered if it was as obvious to the others.

They were enjoying Sunday lunch under the shady vines in the garden. The entire family. Even Victor had been persuaded to take the Easter break at home in honour of Noella's visit.

'You look exhausted, Papa. Are you still working as hard? Are things going well?' Noella looked at her father with concern.

Victor sighed and ran a hand over his hair. Noella noticed for the first time that grey strands had begun to appear among the black. They had not been there when she had left.

'If anything, things are more difficult, Noella. The poor grow more restless with every passing day and I do not blame them. The pace of reform is slow — I am hampered on every side by those who do not wish to see their power and influence diminished. My greatest fear is that the *campesinos*, those without land, will grow tired of waiting, of hearing empty promises, and one day resort to violence to achieve their aims.'

Nothing had changed and nothing *would* change,

Noella thought to herself, listening now with only half an ear. Her eyes were on the happy, chubby baby being bounced on Eugene's knee and suddenly a terrifying depression settled on her heart. She would never have a child of her own. For the rest of her life it would be only Daniel and herself.

Since that terrible afternoon, she had been haunted by Celia Hartlee's revelations. Could there be truth in what she said? Could that possibly be the reason for Daniel's strange behaviour? She was naive about such things, knew little about men like that...

But Noella was sure of one thing. Daniel didn't hate her. He had married her because he loved her. No one could dispute that. Already in the few days she'd been away, she had made up her mind: when she returned to England she was going to broach the subject of their sex life openly and frankly with her husband. If, indeed, there was a problem because of something that had ` happened in the past, then with love and understanding they would sort it out.

Her gaze swept across the broad acres of the *hacienda*, to the far green jungle, and the distant smudge of the mountains. Already she felt as if she didn't belong here any longer. This had never been the life she wanted — but if she could no longer live with Daniel, Martiguay was surely where she would be forced to return. She *must* make her marriage work. She had married Daniel in the eyes of God and the Church, and there was no going back.

Hair whipping around her face, Noella leaned low over the horse's neck. A cloud of dust rose behind her as she followed the winding road back to the *hacienda*.

Only the approaching dusk had forced her to turn back. She had ridden hard, exhilaration mingling with an almost overwhelming nostalgia for those carefree days when she and Paolo had covered the dusty miles together.

The house came into view and Noella pulled on the reins, gradually bringing the sweat-soaked mare to a trot. Those days, she knew, were gone forever.

Inez found her standing alone at the rear of the stables. It was dusk and mosquitoes swarmed in the heavy air but the girl seemed not to notice.

It was only when the older woman spoke that Noella became aware of her presence.

'You miss your horses, my dear?' Inez slipped an arm around Noella's narrow waist.

'Yes. Yes I do.'

Something in her voice made Inez turn. There were tears glistening in the girl's dark eyes.

'Noella, my dear. What is the matter? Are you unhappy?' Her face was creased with concern. 'Is it anything you want to speak about?'

With a huge effort of will, Noella bit back her tears. 'It's nothing, Inez . . . nothing.' She gave a choking laugh. 'I'm just remembering what mischief I used to get up to here. As poor Nona always said, I was a devil.'

Inez held her close in the darkness. 'Sometimes,' she said quietly, 'that which makes us devils may also transform us into angels.'

It was raining when she emerged from Heathrow. The car she had ordered was waiting and Noella clambered gratefully into the back seat. As they headed through London's dismal outer suburbs in the late afternoon traffic, her mind was on the decision she had made about Daniel. Now that she had been given a hint of where the problem might lie she wanted to tackle it immediately. That was the reason she had caught the earlier flight home. She couldn't wait to see Daniel and tell him that she understood, that together they could work things out.

The house was in darkness when she put her key

in the lock. She had given the servants time off while she was away, and Daniel, of course, would be still at work. She had plenty of time to bathe and change before he arrived home.

Leaving her suitcase in the hall, Noella mounted the thickly carpeted staircase to the main bedroom. She was half a dozen paces from the door when she heard the noise.

Frowning, she stopped in her tracks.

A long drawn out whimper, as if someone was in pain. 'Daniel?'

There was no reply.

Worried, she turned the handle and pushed open the door.

It was a sight she would never forget.

She heard the scream; it took her a second to register that it had come from her own throat. Oh, *Dios, Dios* ...

Guy was the first to speak. With a look of sardonic amusement he slowly rose from the bed. 'Well, darling Noella. If only you had rung ... '

But Noella barely heard him, scarcely noticed his pale, wiry nakedness. It was Daniel who held her horrified gaze, Daniel who stared insolently back at her from the bed.

'What are you doing to me?' Her voice was a thin whisper of disbelief. 'You are my husband. You love me ...'

Daniel's laugh was an open taunt. 'Love you? Oh, my dear Noella. Please, do not flatter yourself. I married you because it was the only way to escape from a rather pressing problem.'

'What do you mean?' Her burning eyes never left his face.

Daniel waved a hand in dismissal as he sat up on the bed.

Guy, now fully dressed, seemed to be enjoying the scene. 'Oh, come now, Daniel. Be a gentleman. A lady, even if she is a wife, is owed an explanation.'

'Tell me!' Trembling, her fists curled into tight balls, Noella approached the bed. 'I said, *tell me*!' she screamed, her precarious self-control gone now, as she pummelled at his naked torso.

His face contorted in anger, Daniel grabbed her wrists, twisting the flesh until she cried out in pain.

'Okay! You want to know? Sure, I'll tell you!' His eyes were narrow slits of hatred. 'It was blackmail. A man in New York. He found out who I was and sent the photographs to my parents. They paid, but forced me to agree to marry.' His mouth twisted in a sneer. 'It was the loss of his own position as much as anything that terrified my father. Marriage, he said, would silence any rumours. And who better to improve *his* status, consolidate *his* position even further, than the daughter of *el Presidente*? When he put the proposition to your father, he couldn't have been more grateful. After all,' he taunted, 'given the circumstances, his sullied daughter wasn't going to be easy to marry off . . .'

'But,' Noella stammered, confusion clouding her face, 'my father tried to stop me from seeing you, he was angry when he found out — '

Again the derisive laugh. 'Oh, yes! He understood you so well, didn't he Noella? He knew you would always want what was forbidden.' Daniel stared at her with scornful eyes. 'They knew, Noella. They all knew — Gabrielle, Eugene, Inez . . . And you reacted just as they had planned.'

Only when dawn was beginning to lighten the sky was she at last able to fall into a short, brittle sleep.

During the long hours of that terrible night Noella was forced to come to terms with the deception that Daniel and her family had perpetrated upon her. Her face burned with humiliation as she thought of the ease with which she had fallen into their trap. As she paced up and down she knew she must plan her next move with equal cunning and wit.

Nothing would make her share a roof with Daniel a moment longer. It had been one thing to want to save a marriage that she had believed was based on love, another to live with a man who had been manipulated into marrying her and who flaunted his perversion. It was then, during those sleepless hours, that she remembered the night Daniel had disappeared on their honeymoon. She had feared another woman, even the sexy housekeeper, but now the image of the attentive blond butler rose to haunt her. Noella felt the bile rise in her throat.

In her rage and shame, her first instinct had been to accuse and decry — but, as she forced herself to analyse the repercussions of such a reaction, she soon realised the drawbacks of that approach. If her father knew she had left Daniel he would insist she return to Martiguay — and she was not prepared to do that. At last, it seemed, she had a chance of the freedom she had always yearned for.

By the time she fell into an exhausted sleep Noella knew exactly what she was going to do.

'We have to talk.' Her suitcases were packed, her ticket bought, and a car was booked for early the next morning.

Panic flared in Daniel's eyes. He was regretting his outburst of the previous evening. The union he had entered for the cover it provided, for the assurance that his father's fortune would one day be his, was, he felt certain, about to be dissolved.

Nothing could have prepared him for Noella's next words.

Fingers laced tensely together, she said coldly, 'As you can see, I am leaving you — going away. That is the only solution to our immediate problem. However, it is in both our interests, I'm sure you'll agree, to cover up the fact that our marriage is over. The last thing you need is for others to be asking inquisitive questions.'

There was a new authority in her voice as she faced the man who had betrayed her. 'I have a plan which involves my living in Paris. However at those times when for business reasons it is necessary that I appear at your side I will do my best to be there. That way you can live as you wish as long as you make no attempt to interfere with me.'

She stared at him impassively. 'Do I make myself clear?'

Daniel's protest was weak as he clutched at the unexpected reprieve. 'They will find out in time.'

'I will deal with that when it happens.' Noella was going to make sure that if her plan worked, no one would be able to tell her what to do when that time came.

CHAPTER SEVENTEEN

Noella took a taxi from Charles de Gaulle to her hotel. She had booked a room at the Meurice, overlooking the chestnut trees and ornamental lakes of the Tuileries.

Money would not be too serious a problem. She had made a withdrawal from the account she kept with Daniel, at the same time arranging for the transfer of her father's generous monthly allowance. If things went as she hoped, she would not need to be dependent on her father's money.

As they sped past the dark, pewter waters of the Seine, Noella suddenly felt marvellous. She was young and free, and in the most beautiful city in the world!

As soon as she was settled in her room, Noella dialled the number on the small black and gold card. She had kept it from that evening all those months ago.

Giles Roget, photographer. The only person she knew in the whole of Paris. But perhaps the most important . . .

Giles Roget dressed for his appointment with care. He was not typical of his profession, preferring tailored suits and handmade shirts to his colleagues' more customary baggy jeans and scruffy T-shirts. For the sake of image, he had always lived beyond his means, ever certain that one day his fortunes would change.

His elegant appearance was the reason he had landed

the assignment that evening at the Martiguayan Embassy; it helped to blend with the crowd.

A small smile played around his lips. Now, thanks to Noella Jarro, such mundane jobs might be a thing of the past.

He was waiting in the lobby when Noella stepped out of the elevator.

'Madame Jarro.' Giles Roget smiled warmly and took her hand in his. He was not a particularly handsome man — average height, with crisp light brown hair, and the faint evidence of teenage acne on his sallow skin — but in the place of good looks he had developed a well-honed charm.

'Monsieur Roget... I am so glad you were free to see me.' She glanced about the lobby. 'Perhaps we can find somewhere to talk privately together?'

For the first time Noella felt nervous. What if Giles Roget's words that night had been idle flattery? Perhaps now she was here, he would be merely amused at her presumption?

She cleared her throat as they settled themselves in a banquette. 'Monsieur, on the evening we made our acquaintance you mentioned to me how... how closely I resembled my mother. How, if I ever wished to... to capitalise on that fact you might be able to be of assistance.'

Giles Roget nodded, hiding his growing excitement.

Encouraged, Noella went on. 'At the time, of course, I dismissed such talk. I was the wife of a respectable' — she almost choked on the word — 'banker with all the duties that role implied. But now... well, my position has changed and what I am really asking is whether you were serious in your comments that evening.'

Giles Roget gave her a dazzling smile. 'Oh, yes, madame. Very, very serious.'

Noella let out a long soft sigh. Thank the saints...

'Then, monsieur, there is just one thing I must insist upon.'

Giles Roget planned his campaign with all the precision of a man eager to redress life's imbalances.

As soon as Noella had settled in an appropriately fashionable apartment, he set about the process of recreating her in her mother's image. The resemblance had been there before — his photographer's eye had seen that — but now it must be emphasised and embellished.

The first step was to lighten Noella's dark gold hair and style it in the simple, swinging bob which had been Catherine Campion's trademark. Her brows were thinned and arched, her make-up subtly changed, her wardrobe transformed to bring to life a woman who had been dead for almost thirty years. But the final test lay in the camera's eye...

Hour after hour, Giles Roget shot dozens of rolls of film in the tiny loft he used as a studio. As he posed Noella again and again, he prayed that his instincts had been right.

The photographs told him at once that his prayers had been answered.

On film, with the cosmetic changes he had wrought, the resemblance between mother and daughter was uncanny. What Giles Roget hadn't expected and what added immeasurably to his excitement was the unexpected shock of seeing how subtly the camera captured the girl's sexual vitality. It was almost as if the lens had brought to life her deepest desires.

At last Giles was ready to force his way into the inner sanctum of Eveline Marteaux.

The editor of French *Vogue* was a short, birdlike

woman with a sleek cap of shiny red hair and large, burgundy-framed reading glasses. She was dressed as usual in unalleviated black — Chanel — and had the sort of bland, creaseless features which could have placed her age anywhere between thirty and fifty.

Arching an arrogant eyebrow, Eveline Marteaux looked coldly at the man sitting opposite her. Unless they were special friends, she rarely dealt directly with photographers. But Giles Roget had been insistent that he must see her.

'Well, monsieur, what is this "exciting proposal"' — she gave the words a sarcastic emphasis — 'you have for me?'

Silently, a smiling Giles Roget pushed a photograph across the gleaming Empire desk.

Eveline Marteaux peered down at it through her outsized glasses and a frown drew her brows together.

'What is the point of this, monsieur?' There was an edge of annoyance to her voice. 'Why should you bring me a photograph of a woman dead almost thirty years? Catherine Campion was certainly a beauty, a legend, but — '

Giles interrupted her. 'Take a close look, a very close look, at that photograph, madame.'

With a gesture of impatience, Eveline Marteaux replaced her burgundy frames. She stared at the glossy print. The movie star was dressed in the cool classical fashion she had made famous at the time: cashmere twin-set, full feminine skirt, low-heeled shoes. It was exactly how Eveline Marteaux herself had dressed as a teenager. She had been fifteen when Catherine Campion was at the height of her fame, and like millions of other young Frenchwomen, she had been obsessed with the beautiful star. Her bedroom wall had been covered with magazine photographs of the legendary blonde. But otherwise she saw no reason to be impressed by this particular —

Her eyes widened slightly and she raised her head to stare angrily at the smiling man opposite. 'Why do you waste my time with your stupid mysteries, monsieur? Am I supposed to be impressed with your trick photography?' Annoyed, she tapped a blood-red fingernail on the print. 'The background here, it is the Pompidou Centre; it was not built at the time Catherine Campion made her tour of Paris.' Eveline Marteaux pushed her chair back from the desk. 'I have no time for such charlatan — '

'Madame,' Giles Roget spoke quickly, urgently, 'the girl you see pictured there is not Catherine Campion. I took that photograph less than three weeks ago.' He held his breath as he saw the tiny frown, the beginnings of interest, flicker in Eveline Marteaux's eyes. 'This girl,' he continued quickly, 'is the double of the movie star, yet look closely and you will see the fire, the raw sensuality compared to the iceberg blonde.' Giles' hushed voice held a note of triumph. 'She is a woman of today with the beauty of a legend, madame... a priceless combination.'

With her eyes riveted on the photograph, Eveline Marteaux felt her pulses race with excitement. The difference was subtle but she now saw exactly what Giles Roget meant. At once a dozen different ideas for exploiting the remarkable resemblance began crowding her mind.

She looked up into the photographer's expectant face. 'What is her name?'

Giles Roget let out a long inward sigh of relief. 'Isabel Trevier,' he replied. 'I am her manager.'

Three months later the Christmas edition of *Vogue* carried an unprecedented ten-page spread of the new model, Isabel Trevier. Eveline Marteaux had launched her find to achieve maximum effect. On one side of each double-page spread there was a still of Catherine Campion taken from one of her movies, on the other, her uncanny look-alike, attired in the best of young French design.

As the editor of *Vogue* had hoped, the legend of the beautiful English actress provoked a curiosity in her readers that made the edition a sell-out.

With the obsession for nostalgia already influencing a wide spectrum of the arts, the time was ripe for Noella's entrance on the scene. Parisian cafe society — writers, artists, film directors and designers — all were enchanted by this living reincarnation of the woman whose beauty and talent had once lit up the screen and made her a household name.

Wherever she went the whispered comments were the same. *'C'est incroyable! Elle resemble exactement Catherine Campion.'*

Over the months as her fame grew, Noella became increasingly busy with assignments for *Vogue* or *Elle* or *Marie Claire*, and it became more and more difficult for her to lead her double life, though she still made her sporadic visits to London, usually when some bank function necessitated her presence at Daniel's side. A turban solved the problem of her lighter hair, and her clothes and make-up again became those of a conservative banker's wife. So far, she had managed to keep her true identity a secret from the French paparazzi just as she had successfully hidden her new career in Paris from her family at home.

She knew she was walking a tightrope, yet when she wrote to Gabrielle or Inez or her father, sending the letters via Daniel in London, she felt not a moment's guilt. After all, hadn't they all collaborated in the monstrous deceit which had been perpetrated against her?

Her work brought her satisfaction and a sense of self-worth she had never experienced before, and she was excited by the strange and interesting people who seemed so eager for her company. Paris, she realised, was a city which embraced the avant garde as completely as it did history and the past. Among her new friends Noella found herself confronted with views and ideas completely different from anything she'd ever been exposed to. It was an exhilarating, at times even frightening, experience.

She remembered one party at the house of a diplomat. The fashionable set had all been there, writers, film directors, radical journalists, and a bevy of young, attractive women, some models like herself. The champagne was flowing freely and the strange sweet scent of some exotic cigarette filled the air. Then at midnight a large coloured balloon was lowered from the ceiling. The host, a suave, grey-haired man in his fifties, had touched the end of his cigar to the thin plastic. The balloon burst, and Noella stared in surprise as a cloud of white powder drifted over the room. The well-dressed crowd went mad. Holding up empty glasses, cupping their hands, they fought to catch the falling mist.

'What is it?' Puzzled, she turned to the young, long-haired man beside her. They had been introduced earlier and she vaguely recalled he was something to do with films.

'Their kiss of life,' he answered cryptically, giving her a long, lazy smile. 'For me, my nose is too dear a friend to wish to partake.'

It took a few more parties before Noella understood what he meant. Even then, she viewed the habit as strange. Life itself was so exciting she could not fathom why people needed the added sensation offered by dangerous or illegal substances.

The only one who tried to place restraints on her new-found freedom was Giles Roget.

'These late nights are not good for you, Noella. Your looks will suffer if you do not get sufficient rest. Things are going well for you now but I have even bigger plans for the future; it is important that you always look your best.'

But Noella took little notice of his gentle scolding. She felt answerable to no one. She was happy to let Giles plot her career and handle the money that seemed to be rolling in. What mattered most to her was the excitement, the fun of living the life she had always dreamed of. For the first time in her life she felt like a truly independent and grown-up woman and no one, not even Giles, was going to tell her what to do.

CHAPTER EIGHTEEN

'We just finish the bottle and then we go, *oui*, Richard?'

Michelle Valdier smiled and reached across the table to pat her lover's hand. 'You are good to indulge me, cheri. I think you do not really enjoy these places, *n'est-ce pas?*'

Richard Avery returned her smile as he poured the last of the Lanson. 'Nightclubs seem depressingly the same wherever they happen to be in the world. Dark, smoky, and full of people trying to look intensely interesting.'

'Like the little party who have just arrived?' Michelle nodded across the dance floor to a group of about a dozen people who were seating themselves at a cluster of tables. One girl stood out from the others: tall, blonde, perfect features — and laughing too loudly, as if she had already had too much to drink.

Richard frowned into the darkness. There was something about her...

Michelle followed the direction of his gaze. 'Our latest star, Isabel Trevier — the model every designer is fighting for.' Her voice took on a sarcastic edge. 'Success seems so easy to come by these days. In this girl's case, one merely has to exploit one's resemblance to a long dead film actress and — *voila!* — one is instantly celebrated and rich as the twin of Catherine Campion.'

Richard didn't reply. His eyes were still fixed on the girl. Catherine Campion. Wasn't that...?

Hiding her irritation, Michelle put a hand on her lover's thigh. 'Tell me, *cheri*, did you see the outrageous way Claude was flirting with me this evening? He has never hidden his desire to have an affair, despite the fact that Yvette clings to him like an oyster.'

Michelle Valdier thought it prudent to remind Richard that while she might not have the youth of Isabel Trevier, there were plenty besides himself who were attracted to her.

Richard knew what was expected of him. Bringing his attention back to the woman beside him, he kissed her soft, cool cheek. 'I am so lucky, then, that you chose me, aren't I, darling?'

Seeing the gleam of relief and satisfaction in Michelle's eyes, he wondered as always that such an attractive woman could still need so much assurance.

Richard wasn't the only one staring at the tall, blonde model whose face was now so familiar to the fashion-conscious of Europe. The eyes of most of the other nightclub patrons were also drawn to the girl they knew as Isabel Trevier — though as much for her behaviour as for her beauty and celebrity. Loud and obviously drunk, the girl was insisting on still more champagne. Moments later it arrived and at once she sent it back, complaining of the vintage in a shrill, slurred voice.

As he finished his drink, Richard found his eyes drawn again and again to the tall, blonde model. When the music restarted, he noticed that she was the first to get to her feet and find her way to the tiny dance floor. There, she moved her body in the clinging white dress in a way, it seemed to Richard, that would have tempted the Pope.

Michelle Valdier raised a cynical eyebrow. 'She risks her reputation with this one,' she nodded at the girl's dancing partner, a thin, fashionably-dressed man whose fair hair was drawn back into a short ponytail. 'He is

Jacques Coubert, a writer who already has his name in police files for cocaine possession. His friends are usually the sons of wealthy families, boys with the money to afford the drugs Coubert can provide.'

Richard took in the group of stylish young men seated at the table with their attractive escorts. Michelle, he knew, could always be relied upon to have all the gossip on the arts world.

He turned as she pushed back her chair. 'I will go to the powder room and then we can leave, Richard.' Her voice had a chilly edge and he knew she was annoyed at the interest he was showing in the young model.

'I'll ask for the bill, darling.' He gave her a distracted smile as she moved away.

And then it happened, and Richard realised the astonishing truth.

Isabel Trevier was dancing wildly, close to his table, when one of her long, slim arms caught the tray of a passing waiter. The loaded silver platter went flying, bottles and glasses hit the floor, and a spray of deep red burgundy splattered like blood over the model's tight, white dress.

The spontaneous oath, delivered in Spanish, made Richard catch his breath.

As the girl hurried for the powder room, he was on his feet, pushing through the tables after her.

'Senora Jarro!' He caught up with her in the small private space next to the telephone booth.

It was the final proof he needed. She spun around at once and he saw first shock, then recognition on her made-up face.

'Senora... do you remember me? Richard Avery. We met at the London Embassy. We spoke — '

'My name is Isabel Trevier,' she interrupted icily, the slurring less pronounced.

But Richard knew he was not mistaken. 'Senora,

what is this masquerade? Where is your husband? What — '

'I repeat, monsieur, my name is Isabel Trevier. Now if you will excuse — '

She turned away, but Richard caught her shoulder.

'Listen to me.' He spoke now in rapid Spanish. 'I don't know what game you're playing, but when this gets out, it will do serious damage to your father. Do you know how precarious his position is? If the opposition press were to discover that his daughter is hanging out in Paris with drug addicts and the obscenely rich, can you imagine how they would use that ammunition against him?'

Noella gave him a long, cold look. 'Mind your own business,' she snapped in Spanish, before turning on her heel and disappearing into the powder room.

Noella quickly recovered from the shock of bumping into Richard Avery. She felt sure her secret was still safe. If nothing else, the American's paranoia about her father's position would ensure that.

She refused to believe her new career and life style could possibly have political implications for her father's Presidency. She was an adult now, independent — what she chose to do with her life had nothing to do with her family or anyone else. At least, that's what she kept telling herself . . .

'*Si . . . Si*, Mama . . . No, I am sorry, you cannot speak to Noella just now.' Daniel Jarro drummed his fingers nervously on the desk as he spoke into the receiver. 'She is not here. She has gone out to . . . a movie. Yes, yes of course . . . She will be as delighted as I am at the news . . . *Adios*, Mama.'

Cursing softly to himself, Daniel hung up. It had been weeks since he had seen Noella. Now he must speak to her at once.

Over the next twenty-four hours he repeatedly dialled the number she had given him. There was never any reply. In the end, Daniel discovered from the operator that the number had been changed.

That left only the office of Giles Roget.

'I must get in touch at once with ... with Isabel Trevier,' Daniel demanded of the girl who answered the phone. 'It is a matter of urgency.'

'Mademoiselle Trevier has given strict instructions that her number be given to no one.' With a bang, the officious-sounding secretary put the receiver down in his ear.

In the end, Daniel booked a flight to Paris. Time was running out.

It was Noella's landlady who told him where she had gone. With a twinkle in her dark eyes, the elderly woman looked the handsome young man up and down and approved of what she saw. Who was she to stand in the way of young love?

'Ah, monsieur, mademoiselle looked a picture when she left. If my ailing memory serves me right, even Catherine Campion herself was not so beautiful.' She gave Daniel a devilish grin. 'You better hurry, monsieur, before some other fortunate gentleman enchants her.'

She told Daniel where he could find his true love.

A warm, sunny day made the open-air restaurant in the Bois de Boulogne the perfect location for the launch of Yves St Laurent's latest perfume.

Waiters in snow-white, ankle-length aprons circled through the fashionable crowd, offering crystal flutes of champagne and platters of tempting hors d'oeuvres while in the background a twelve-piece orchestra played classical selections.

Noella was enjoying herself immensely. Dressed in a soft knit dress in hot pink, her hair tucked under a wide-brimmed matching hat, she could feel the admiring eyes upon her as she was greeted by one after another of her new friends. In just a few short months, she thought happily, she had met so many wonderful people. They fluttered around her like butterflies, made her feel like a princess with their flattery and compliments, offered her the sort of love and friendship she felt had always been denied her till now. Eyes bright with champagne, Noella stifled a sigh of pure happiness.

'Mademoiselle Trevier ... *excusez-moi*.'

Noella turned to see one of the broad-shouldered security officers at her elbow.

'*Oui?*'

'I am sorry to disturb you, mademoiselle, but there is a gentleman at the entrance. He says he knows you, must speak to you urgently.'

Noella frowned. 'A gentleman? Looking for me? What is his name?'

'He would give his first name only, mademoiselle. Daniel.'

Madame Nina Repois had barely taken her eyes off the girl since she'd arrived. The resemblance was uncanny. She had seen all of Catherine Campion's films and this girl was her double.

Yet Nina Repois was intrigued by Isabel Trevier for more than the obvious reason. Her first husband, Luis Sarandon, had been a Martiguayan and for the first three years of their marriage they had lived in his country. Nina had been fortunate enough to meet Catherine Campion on a number of official occasions and had been enchanted by the young actress's beauty and breeding, as well as her obvious devotion to her husband and his country.

Now, as she saw the young model hurry in her direction, Nina Repois wondered if Catherine Campion's daughters were aware of this girl who was trading on her uncanny resemblance to their dead mother. Surely the younger girl, Noella, now living in London, must have seen the fuss in the press?

Nina had kept in touch over the years with the woman who had married her first husband's cousin. Though younger than herself, Inez had become a good friend and the relationship had been maintained through regular correspondence and Inez's occasional visits to France.

Even when she married again — although her second husband too had now passed away — Nina Repois had not lost her interest in Martiguay. She had been delighted when Victor de Bartez had come to power, though saddened by the fact that he seemed unwilling to legitimise his union with her old friend. Inez had never said as much openly, but Nina could read between the lines. It was a great pity, she thought. Inez would have made a dedicated and honourable first lady.

Madame Repois looked over her shoulder to where the girl stood to one side of the entrance talking animatedly with a man who was obviously not an invited guest. As she stared at the young couple, Nina Repois' brows drew together in a frown. There was something familiar about the man's face.

Curious, she moved closer to the line of shrubs which formed a natural boundary to the restaurant. The security personnel were kept busy with the line of arriving guests and the young couple had removed themselves a few paces from the entrance.

As she heard the first angry whispers in a language she understood, Nina Repois realised why the young man's face was familiar. She had seen it in the photographs Inez had sent her of the wedding of Victor de Bartez's younger daughter.

'It is *imperative* you return.' Daniel was speaking in rapid Spanish, his anger obvious. He was humiliated that these ill-mannered security buffoons had made him stand outside like a nobody.

'My parents are arriving at the beginning of next week. It seems my father has an urgent meeting to attend in London — and they are "so looking forward" to seeing us.' Daniel gave sarcastic emphasis to the words.

'You shouldn't have come here! What if someone should ask me who you are?' Nervousness made Noella edgy. Up till now, her plan had worked wonderfully. She didn't want Daniel's unexpected appearance to spoil things.

'Listen, Noella, what else could I do? I couldn't reach you at the number you gave me, and whatever bitch I spoke to at Giles Roget's office refused point-blank to give out your new one. The matter is urgent. If you want this charade to continue then you must come back at once.'

Noella frowned. Her schedule was tight. Giles would be furious if she disappeared now.

But she knew she had no choice.

She looked at the man who already felt like a stranger. 'How long are they staying?'

'Just three days.'

'I will be there.' Somehow she would manage it.

On the other side of the shrubbery, Nina Repois dabbed a lace-trimmed handkerchief to her upper lip.

Madre de Dios! It was unbelievable!

CHAPTER NINETEEN

'They are both well and happy then, Julietta?'

Inez had made a point of talking to Julietta Jarro during the interval. She was not enjoying the concert; she lacked the concentration needed to appreciate the music. Normally she could lose herself so easily in Mozart. But not this evening. Not after what she had just discovered.

Julietta Jarro drew the mink stole more closely around her bare décolletage — she liked to imagine she bore more than a passing resemblance to a younger Gina Lollobrigida. 'Like cooing doves, Inez. Daniel is very happy with his work and Noella seems to have had no trouble settling into London. The house is close to the park and really quite charming.'

If none too clean, she thought, smiling a goodbye to Inez in answer to the bell summoning the audience back to their seats. The dust on the picture frames, the flowers left to stand just one or two days past their best — Noella, she was afraid to say, still had something to learn about keeping staff up to scratch.

Still, Julietta Jarro had no real complaints. What mattered above all was that the marriage seemed to be working; that the problem with Daniel had been satisfactorily dealt with and her own position left unassailed.

She gave a little shudder as, with a rustle of silk, she settled back into her seat. How unbearable, if due to a scandal with Daniel, Fernando had been forced to step down.

Julietta waved in a manner that would have done justice to royalty to a woman she recognised four rows away. Her position as wife of the chairman of the Martiguayan Central Bank brought her immense satisfaction.

Inez applauded mechanically as the conductor appeared on stage. Her brief exchange with Julietta Jarro had done nothing to answer the questions that were buzzing around in her head. The Jarros had returned from London just two days ago, and it would seem that as far as they were concerned, nothing was amiss. Daniel and Noella were a happily married young couple leading the life expected of them.

If Julietta was right, worried Inez, what did her old friend Nina Repois mean by her letter? It had arrived that morning and Inez found its assertions almost impossible to believe.

Noella . . . living in Paris? Making a career for herself as a model? Using an alias? The whole thing was crazy, preposterous. But Nina Repois had insisted it was true . . . and sent the photographs to prove it. As she looked at the glossy pages cut from a variety of fashion magazines, Inez felt a cold shiver run down her spine. It was as if Victor's dead wife was staring out at her.

But how could Noella possibly . . . ? She wrote regularly to them all and the letters were always postmarked London. There were phone calls too; not often, but every couple of months or so. Inez's eyes grew troubled. Of course, it was always Noella who placed the calls to them. The antiquated Martiguayan telephone system was notoriously unpredictable.

Less than twenty-four hours later, she had made up her mind. There was only one way to get to the bottom of all this. She would go to Paris herself. Victor need know nothing; he had enough problems to see to at home. During these difficult times she had been loath to leave his side to make her usual visit to Europe. But now she had no choice.

Nina Repois was waiting with a chauffeur-driven car when Inez arrived at Charles de Gaulle. She greeted her old friend warmly, then they headed at once for the Hotel Charles V. It was where Nina always stayed when she came to Paris. She had left the city eight years before. 'The pollution,' she complained to Inez in a letter, 'is unbearable. That, and the traffic, the noise, the streets full of badly-dressed tourists, have made up my mind for me. I cannot bear it a moment longer.'

Now Nina lived in a bright airy apartment on the Côte d'Azur. She filled her days playing bridge and backgammon with other wealthy widows and taking her two bad-tempered chihuahuas for long, bracing walks.

'You saw the photographs I sent, Inez?' Nina was glad her friend had seen fit to act so promptly.

'I saw them, but even then I could hardly believe . . . The hair is lighter, the style — '

'Easily changed, Inez.' Nina Repois spoke earnestly. 'I am certain it was the daughter. The language they spoke, the husband whose face I recognised. What is going on, I asked myself? That is when I wrote to you. And now I hear rumours that a leading cosmetic house is about to put her under contract, and a range of swimwear bearing her name is about to be launched with the girl herself appearing in the advertisements!' Nina Repois raised a scandalised eyebrow. 'I ask you, Inez, where is the dignity? Does the child not know what harm she can do her father's cause? And even more astonishing, why does the husband allow it?'

Inez stared blankly at the flat fields on either side of the speeding lanes of traffic. 'I don't know, Nina.'

But it wasn't completely the truth.

*

The moment she opened the door, Noella knew her secret was out.

'Inez!' Stunned, she stepped back from the doorway. 'How — how did you find me?'

Inez followed her into the sitting room. 'I finally made your manager's very rude assistant understand that I was not going to go away until she gave me the information I wanted.'

Not waiting to be asked, she took a seat and came straight to the point. 'Now, my dear, tell me what is going on.'

Noella stared back defensively. 'It's all right. Daniel knows. He has no objections.'

'But that doesn't explain why you are doing this.'

'Because it's fun, Inez! Because at last I am free of all the rules, the restrictions, and responsibilities.'

'But you're a married woman now, Noella. Marriage carries its own responsibilities.'

'Oh, please!' Noella gave a harsh, humourless laugh. 'Surely you are not so bold as to talk about my marriage, Inez? Tell me,' she leaned forward, her dark eyes glittering with hurt and anger, 'did it amuse you all to see how easily I fell into your trap? Did you not all sigh with relief when I insisted I had found the man I was going to marry and that no one was going to stop me?'

'Darling, I — ' Inez's face was clouded with misery. She had always dreaded it might come to this. How could she explain that it had been done for Noella's own good?

'None of you will know what you have done to me.' The bitterness in Noella's voice shocked Inez.

'But darling, you did love Daniel! You — '

'I loved a man who played his part as well as all the rest of you,' Noella retorted fiercely.

'What do you mean?' Inez was genuinely puzzled.

'I mean I am never going back to him. My

"marriage" is over. Here in Paris, I have a wonderful job and kind and trustworthy friends; never in my life have I been happier.'

'Darling Noella... ' Inez shook her head, concern lining her face. 'The sort of life you are leading does not bring genuine friendship. Perhaps at the moment everything might look fine but you must not count on such fleeting acquaintances. It is your family who really matters, who will always care for you. But you have a responsibility to them too. You will not be able to keep your identity a secret much longer; can you imagine what it might do to your father's cause once the press find out how his daughter — '

'I don't care, Inez.' Noella spoke with a cold finality. 'I simply don't care. Martiguay, its crazy politics, the never-ending problems and crises... none of that is my concern. Now, at last, I am going to please myself.'

When Inez, defeated, finally stood up to leave, Noella asked, 'Are you going to tell him?'

Inez shook her head dully. 'No. I love him too much to add to his worries.'

Noella looked down into the street from behind the blue silk drapes and watched Inez walk away. Her eyes shone with tears. How close she had come to telling the truth about Daniel. But she loved Inez, would always love her. How could she burden her with that guilt?

Giles Roget looked up and smiled at the man who was going to make him rich.

For the chairman of a cosmetics empire, he mused, Philippe Montserrat was one of the most unattractive men he had ever seen — tall, almost cadaver thin, with bulging eyes the colour of wet stones and plump, protuberant lips that reminded Giles of overstuffed pink cushions.

Surrounded by a phalanx of dark-suited lawyers, Philippe Montserrat sat motionless waiting for Giles to finish working his way through the eight closely-typed pages.

Giles hid silent laughter as he pretended to study the convoluted clauses. He knew he wasn't going to sign this mountain of paper.

'Messieurs.' He coughed delicately, evening the pages as he placed them on the desk in front of him. He had been looking forward to this moment. It was what he had planned from the first. Only the timing had to be right.

It was right now.

'Messieurs,' he repeated, smiling directly into the reptilian eyes of Philippe Montserrat, 'how much more would this contract be worth if, instead of Isabel Trevier, you were to have the services of Catherine Campion's own daughter?'

'But Noella! Listen to me. Please, I — '

'No, Giles! You listen to me!' She swung round on him, her face flushed with anger. 'That was the only condition I made — that no one should know my real identity! I insisted on that point alone and you *promised* me you would do as I wished. And now,' with one hand she swept the pile of newspapers and magazines onto the office floor, 'every paper is screaming the name de Bartez!'

'It would only have been a matter of time — ' Giles began weakly.

'But you had to help things along, didn't you, Giles? Why? So the contract with Montserrat would make us a fortune?' She stood in front of him, her chest heaving as she spat out the words. 'Well, I told you at the beginning, the money wasn't important to me.'

Cold anger overtook him. 'Unfortunately, Noella, there are others of us who do not have quite the same cavalier attitude to earning a living as yourself. Do you think I knocked myself out selling you to the people who counted in this city just so I could earn enough to buy a retirement cottage in the country? Money is what most of us are in this business for, cherie; we're not all like you who think it's enough to have a bunch of nouveau riche hangers-on telling us how beautiful and successful and clever we are!'

She stared at him for a long moment. 'We're finished, Giles.'

Without another word Noella swept out of the office.

The intrigue surrounding the true identity of the model who had taken France by storm was increased by Noella's resolute refusal to make any comment to the press.

The revelation merely served to heighten her notoriety and raise her asking price, causing the more cynical to suggest that perhaps the whole affair had been carefully orchestrated with those goals in mind. Indeed, the deluge of startlingly lucrative offers that followed the announcement meant that now, more than ever, Noella required the services of Giles Roget. He had tried a dozen times to talk to her but her anger at his betrayal had not abated. She refused utterly to work with someone she could not trust.

'That's great . . . Beautiful! . . . Okay, got it, sweetheart, you can relax.'

Noella dropped her pose and moved out of the hot glare of the studio lights. She felt exhausted. The shoot had taken hours and now she had to change and rush to a meeting with the chairman of one of France's leading perfume houses.

Noella wished she felt more alert. The company's proposal to develop a new perfume for her exclusive promotion was an exciting one but she was not looking forward to handling the intricacies of the negotiations. Still, she thought, gritting her teeth as she dressed, somehow she would manage.

'You free for a drink this evening?'

On her way out of the studio, Noella turned in surprise at the photographer's invitation. Jeff Matlin was an American, a freelancer she had worked with just once before. Compared to the French photographers, she found him easy-going and undemanding.

She looked at him now in his casual checked shirt and faded Levis. There was an expression of friendly expectation on his attractive face. Suddenly the idea of spending a few hours with someone who was nothing to do with business seemed immensely appealing.

'Not this evening, I am sorry, Jeff.' She saw his disappointment. 'But tomorrow, yes... I would love to.'

She was rewarded by a white, even grin of perfect American teeth.

Noella found it relaxing to be in Jeff Matlin's company. He was funny, witty, and never wanted to talk about work, or the fact that she happened to be the daughter of a screen legend and the President of Martiguay.

'Hey, babe, that's your business,' Jeff had said that first evening. 'I just want to have fun with a pretty lady.'

He had taken her to an unfashionable, out-of-the-way restaurant free from the prying eyes of the press, and Noella was surprised to find herself enjoying the anonymity. She had discovered that there was a strain involved in being on continual public display.

Then one evening, two weeks later, after a late supper, she accepted Jeff Matlin's invitation to return to his small apartment on the Left Bank.

'I want you to see it's not only beautiful women I've had in front of my lenses, babe. Some of the shots

I took in Africa — the sunsets, the wildlife gathered at the waterholes — are out of this world.'

He settled her on the rather shabby rattan sofa and pointed to a pile of albums lying on a nearby table. 'Take a look through those while I make us coffee.'

He was right, thought Noella, slowly turning the pages, the photographs were stunning. She wondered how he could stand the confines of fashion shoots after the grandeur of nature.

She said as much when he returned with their drinks.

'Hey,' the sandy-haired American said lazily, lifting one shoulder in a shrug, 'it pays the bills.'

'More coffee?' Jeff Matlin raised the pot in anticipation and was gratified when the girl nodded.

'*Merci*, just one more. Otherwise I will not sleep.'

The American hid a smile. *Oh, you'll sleep, babe. You'll sleep.*

He had used just the right amount, and the coffee had been strong enough to mask the taste.

Moving closer on the sofa, he trailed his fingers down the girl's throat to the tiny pearl buttons at the start of her cleavage. One by one he began to undo them to reveal the lacy bra beneath. She shuddered as his hands touched bare flesh but made no protest as he removed the flimsy garment.

The trousers came next, slipping easily over her cool, smooth thighs. Jeff Matlin felt a stirring in his groin at the sight of her nakedness — but tonight at least, that wasn't what he had in mind.

He put his arm around her and helped her to her unsteady feet. 'Come on, babe, let's have some fun now, eh?'

She leaned heavily against him as they made their

way down the narrow hallway and into the small second bedroom.

The handsome, naked boy on the bed grinned under the harsh glare of arc lights. 'About time, pal, it's beginning to feel like a weenie roast in here.'

As he adjusted the focus and pressed the shutter to finish the last of the film, Jeff Matlin could barely contain his glee. This little lot was going to make his name and fortune.

'Okay, honey,' he grinned down at the daughter of the President of Martiguay who lay supine in the boy's arms, 'why don't we put you back in your clothes and get you home?'

Staring back at him from heavy-lidded, bloodshot eyes, Noella merely giggled.

CHAPTER TWENTY

Avery... Richard Avery. He was her only hope. Some-how the American's name had come to her mind as the only one who might be able to save her...

In an agony of frustration, head thumping mercilessly, Noella waited for the operator to connect her. Thank God she had remembered where he worked.

At last she was put through to the correct department.

'Monsieur Richard Avery, *s'il vous plait*.'

'*Moment*, madame.'

There was a click, a moment's silence, and then finally, she heard the calm, self-assured American voice.

'Senor Avery! It is Noella de Bartez.' Panic made her breathless and automatically she fell into Spanish. 'Please, senor... I must see you. As soon as possible. It is a matter of great urgency!'

If he was surprised, Richard Avery didn't show it. Without asking questions he took down her address and promised to be there within the hour.

Her appearance shocked him. In place of the glamour and nightclub chic he saw a wild-eyed girl with dishevelled hair, wearing a cotton blouse and crumpled trousers.

Richard frowned as he followed her into the sitting room. What could have happened to reduce Noella de Bartez to such a state?

Slowly, haltingly, she began. 'You were the only one I could think of, senor, the only one who might know what to do. I — I am so frightened — and ashamed.' She twisted a handkerchief in trembling fingers, unable to look at him directly.

'Tell me what it is, senora. Start at the beginning and I will do my best to help you.'

Noella told him.

'... and it wasn't until I woke up here this morning, still dressed in last night's clothes, that I began to realise that something — something terrible had happened. Everything is so vague ... even now, my head is still beating like a drum ... But I tell you, senor,' she stressed, raising her pleading, tearful eyes to meet Richard's, 'there was something in the coffee he gave me, I swear. Never, never, would I have agreed to let him do such things with me.' She bowed her head again and sobbed. 'Please, senor, you are American. You must have friends, perhaps in the Embassy. Please, somehow help me get those ugly photographs back. Otherwise ... otherwise they will surely destroy both my father and myself.'

God ... Richard Avery would have had to have a heart of stone not to be moved by the pitiful figure across from him. She was just a kid, after all. Spoilt and shallow, sure, but that didn't mean some ruthless sonofabitch could be allowed to get away with such a low trick.

And there was also what it could do to Victor de Bartez — both as a father and politician. She was using her family name, after all.

He stood up, the beginnings of a plan already forming in his mind. 'I can only say I'll do my best to get you out of this, senora. But there's no time to lose.'

★

'Matlin? ... Jeff Matlin? Yeah, sure Rick, I can look into that for ya. How soon d'ya need it?' It was the only question Johnny Cohen asked.

Richard told him.

'I'll get back to you a.s.a.p.'

Johnny Cohen was as good as his word. Within the hour a call came through to Richard from the Embassy where his friend was in charge of personnel. The two men knew each other from the days when Richard's father had been a Senator.

'Got somethin' for ya, Rick. Security picked it up straight away. The guy's got a record. Interfering with a minor; happened when he was twenty-two. I checked with the frogs — of course he never mentioned it when he applied for his *carte de sejour*.'

Richard cringed at Cohen's French pronunciation.

'That the sort of thing you were after, Rick?'

'Spot on, Johnny. Thanks a million.'

'Any time, buddy.'

After that it was easy. Confronted with evidence of a criminal charge, one that would have meant the immediate withdrawal of his visa, plus the end of his employment as a photographer of young, naive women, Jeff Matlin saw the virtue in handing over the negatives of the photos he had taken just twenty-four hours before.

Richard personally delivered the sealed envelope to Noella.

She blushed as she took the package from his hands. 'I cannot thank you enough, senor. You have done me a great service. Especially after ... after I was so rude to you on an earlier occasion.'

Earlier 'occasions', Richard corrected silently.

Aloud, he said, 'I am only glad I was able to help, senora. This time you were lucky but you must keep in mind that now your real identity is known you will be easy prey for the unscrupulous.' He studied her as he stood up to leave. 'How has your father reacted to the press having discovered the truth?'

Noella forced herself to speak calmly. 'Such news does not travel fast to a place like Martiguay, senor. As yet, he does not know.'

Yet for all her bravado she knew that it was just a matter of time before the showdown with her father.

'How dare she! How dare that crazy, senseless child do this to me?'

Inez sat white-lipped as Victor threw the magazine against the wall. She had been dreading this moment, but was amazed that it had been so long in arriving. In the end, it had taken a phone call from a leading French magazine to the Palace press secretary to uncover the secret she had kept hidden since her visit to Paris.

Victor rounded on her. 'You knew! You must have known, Inez! You saw her. Why did you not tell me — or try to stop her?'

Inez forced herself to respond evenly to his anger. 'Noella is a married woman now, Victor. If her husband does not interfere with what she chooses to do then I don't feel it is our place to do so. After all,' she shot her lover a cool look, 'we can't always force those close to us to behave exactly as we would wish, can we, Victor?'

She turned and left him standing alone in the room, trying to fathom exactly what she meant.

The phone call woke Noella just after midnight.

Groping for the receiver, she struggled to sit up.

'Allo?'

'Noella! Are you awake enough to take note of what I am saying?'

The sound of her father's voice made her instantly alert.

'Papa! What — '

'No, Noella, I will do the talking and you will listen — very, very carefully. There must be an end to this craziness at once. Do you hear what I say? At once! I don't care what your husband allows or doesn't allow, I am insisting you return to London immediately. I demand it! Do you hear?'

Noella's grip tightened around the receiver and her tone was openly defiant. 'I hear exactly what you are saying, Papa and I am telling you now that I will never do as you ask. I am no longer a child. No longer can you "demand" that I play the roles you so generously choose for me!'

At the other end of the line, Victor de Bartez sounded close to losing control. 'A married woman does not live apart from her husband, nor does she appear half-naked in photographs for voyeurs to drool over. I will not have such a scandal! Do you have any idea — '

'Don't talk to me about scandal, Papa!' Noella was shaking, her voice shrill with fury. 'Believe me, it is I who can tell *you* all about scandal — the scandal of forcing a marriage between a normal young woman and a perverted, unnatural man!'

At the other end of the line, Victor de Bartez felt as if his heart had stopped in his chest. All he could hear were his daughter's wild, abandoned sobs. At last he rasped, 'What do you mean, child? Tell me . . . What do you mean?'

'I mean, Papa, that you trapped me into marriage with a depraved man who is sickened by the touch of female flesh, who appeases his lust in the arms of his own sex.' She gave a deep, shuddering sob. 'That is what you have done to me! That is what you would have me go back to!'

For a long time after the line went dead, Victor de Bartez stood motionless, his hand still clutched tightly around the receiver.

Dios. What had he done? *What had he done?*

He finally replaced the receiver, ending the high-pitched burr of the disconnected line. Seconds later, as his brain once more began to function, he snatched up the instrument and with trembling fingers began to dial Inez's number.

'I must go to her at once. I must beg her forgiveness... for everything.' Repeating the words almost like a mantra, Victor de Bartez clicked shut his attache case.

'Oh, Victor... ' Inez's heart went out to him. She too had been shocked by the news, but its effect on Victor had shocked her equally. Never had she seen him so disoriented, so completely inconsolable.

'Darling... ' Her concern obvious, Inez put a hand on his arm. 'Do you want me to go with you?'

'No, Inez. This is something I must do alone. I can only hope that if I go to her at once, she will forgive me my blindness and selfishness. Business, politics... nothing is more important to me now than that.'

But Inez had another reason for anxiety. 'I understand your impatience, Victor, but surely in these dangerous times you should take an escort? The route to the airport is — '

'No.' He cut her short. 'More than anything I want to keep this journey private. If all goes as I plan, I shall be back within twenty-four hours. That way no questions will be asked.'

By the side entrance to the palace, a worried-looking Gabrielle was waiting behind the wheel of a small unmarked sedan. In the rear seat, Roberto, now a sturdy toddler, gurgled happily to himself.

With one foot in the car, Victor kissed Inez distractedly on both cheeks. '*Adios, querida.* Give the excuses I have told you and I will be back soon.' For a moment his dark, tortured eyes held her own. 'So often I have not been there when my daughter needed me. This time I will not let her down.'

And then he was gone.

Gabrielle was a good driver and they made their way quickly through the dark, quiet streets of the capital towards the airport where the Presidential jet and crew were standing by.

Staring into the darkness, Victor talked quietly, distractedly, almost as if he were alone. 'I can only blame myself. For the sake of the family name and honour, I have betrayed my child. All that mattered was making sure Noella caused no more trouble.'

He turned to look at the profile of his elder daughter and his voice broke as he continued. 'I betrayed her in so many ways, Gabrielle. I blamed a six-year-old child, an innocent child, for the tragic accident that caused her mother's death. I let that come between us in so many ways... I see that now. Oh, my daughter, I have been a fool, such a fool, but at least now it is not too late to take Noella in my arms and tell her how much — '

The bullet ripped through the muscles in Victor de Bartez's neck and choked off the rest of the words. He turned wide horrified eyes just in time to see the grey sticky mass of Gabrielle's brains spatter the windscreen.

The car bounced, flew high in the air and the final sound Victor de Bartez heard in this world was the scream of terror from his mortally wounded grandchild.

BOOK TWO

CHAPTER TWENTY-ONE

At his desk in the far corner of the long living room, Richard Avery read over the typewritten pages spread out before him.

Commissioned by *Le Figaro* to write an article commemorating the first anniversary of the death of Victor de Bartez, Richard had done more than merely pay homage to a man whose ideals and philosophies he had so respected. His main aim had been to draw attention to the true facts surrounding the assassination of Victor de Bartez, and to the role played in his death by the right-wing military government of General Rodriguez Balo.

It had taken Richard many months to separate truth from fiction, to make contact with those willing, under pain of death, to reveal what they knew.

At the time, the assassination of the President of Martiguay, and his elder daughter and grandchild, had been laid squarely at the feet of an extreme left-wing guerilla group dissatisfied with de Bartez's slow progress towards social reform. It had been that spurious fact alone which had provided the excuse for a lightning takeover of the government by a military junta headed by General Rodriguez Balo.

Richard glanced at the clippings of yellowing newsprint that lay on his desk. Most journalists at the time of the assassination, unable to access internal information, had done little to discredit Balo's line of a 'Communist plot'.

The truth had taken time to uncover. And it was that truth on which Richard had based his article.

He sighed as he slipped the pages into a large manila envelope. It rankled that his own country had seen fit to support the new right-wing leaders of Martiguay. There had been too many in the State Department, Richard knew, who had been wary of the effect of de Bartez's radical reform programs on American interests. To them, an unelected military government protective of the status quo was infinitely preferable to a government bent on improving the lot of the exploited and oppressed.

Richard stood up and slipped on his jacket. He would take the article to the newspaper's offices himself.

As he stepped out into the pale autumn sunshine, Richard wondered, not for the first time, what had become of the surviving daughter of Victor de Bartez.

It was as if she had vanished into thin air.

The priest opened the door of the sacristy and saw the girl sitting in her usual place in the last row of the pews.

He found her there two or three times a week, and always late in the afternoon when the church was normally deserted. Once, at the start, he had asked if there was anything troubling her and if she would care to talk, but she had shaken her head. No, she replied, she just wanted to sit.

Cassock trailing behind him, the priest padded down the long, stone-flagged aisle. He murmured a greeting as he passed the solitary figure. The girl lifted her head to give a soft reply and the reverend father wondered momentarily why these modern young women wished so much to look like boys. The short, messy hair, the jeans and shirt, the lack of lipstick or powder... all calculated, it seemed, to erase the distinction between the genders.

Still, such devotion was good to see, he thought approvingly, pulling a small rusty key out of one deep pocket to open and check the poor box. His nose wrinkled in disgust at the offering. A few lousy francs — how was he supposed to do anything for the *clochards* with such a pittance?

The church of St. Therese d'Avignon was in one of the poorer arrondissements of Paris but as Noella walked the two blocks back to her small apartment she barely noticed her surroundings.

In the ten months she had lived there she had grown used to the area: the open doorways of dusty cafes where swarthy men sat smoking over cups of strong black coffee, the *boucherie* whose front window featured its usual curtain of raw pink rabbits, the shoe repair shop with its pleasing smell of new leather, the Arab greengrocer where she bought her fruit and vegetables...

Turning in at a narrow archway, she passed through a tiny, sunless courtyard where small children squealed at play, and pushed open the wooden door beyond.

'*Bonjour*, Mademoiselle Sylvie!' Noella's landlady flashed her gold teeth in a cheerful welcome.

Nothing ever seemed to upset Madame Mellion. She was always happy as she greeted the half-dozen tenants who shared her house. Whatever time Noella went in or out, Cecile Mellion was always at her post with her crinkled grey hair, her shapeless figure hidden under an equally shapeless cardigan, and her feet encased in a pair of men's felt slippers.

'*Bonjour*, madame.' With a smile that didn't reach her eyes, Noella returned her landlady's greeting as she entered the tiny steel cage of a lift. The best thing about Madame Mellion was that for all her friendliness she did not enquire into her lodger's affairs. To her, 'Sylvie Leplaix' was just another hard-up student.

*

Noella opened the door to a room that was small, but clean and adequate. Tossing her denim jacket on the neatly-made bed, she turned on the single gas ring and reheated what was left of her breakfast coffee. She ate most of her meals in cheap student cafes, where she filled her empty hours listening attentively to the talk around her.

How different she found those young, intense students from the people she had once called friends. It hadn't taken long for her to learn the cruel truth of Inez's words. The friendships she had once thought so sure and strong had dissolved with the headlines of her family tragedy.

Suddenly, everything connected with the name de Bartez became anathema. Contracts Noella had been about to sign were torn up, assignments and bookings arranged for months ahead were abruptly cancelled. Almost overnight, her life changed irrevocably. From sought-after, highly-paid celebrity, she had become a symbol of death and violence and ruin.

An early-morning telephone call had first alerted her to the tragedy. After the trauma of the previous evening's long-distance conversation with her father, Noella had found sleep almost impossible. Rising early, she had been about to run a bath when she was disturbed by the ringing phone.

With a frown she picked up the receiver, wondering who might be calling her at such an early hour.

It was the Martiguayan Ambassador to London.

'Senora, forgive me for disturbing you at this hour of the morning... Your number was given to me by your husband.'

The complete unexpectedness of the call and the man's agitated tone, told Noella at once that something was terribly wrong.

'Senora, it is my very tragic duty to inform you

that your . . . your father, your sister and . . . your nephew were murdered a few hours ago in circumstances that are not yet clear. They were on their way to the airport . . . Your father, it seems, had private business to attend to in Europe.'

Noella's heart seemed to shrink into her chest. She heard the words as if they were coming from the far end of a long, dark tunnel. Then she felt the room begin to sway.

The days that followed were a blur of pain and utter disbelief.

Daniel came to Paris and brought her back to London, where she was confronted by a barrage of noisy, jostling reporters and whirring television cameras. Her own high profile made the tragedy which had just taken place the sort of sensational story newspaper editors dreamed of.

Somehow she managed to get through the memorial service held in London a month later in the presence of members of the Royal family and other distinguished mourners.

Face blank, hair draped in a fine black mantilla, Noella stood by Daniel's side, reacting like an automaton to the sympathies of those around her. Her mind seemed frozen as she tried to grasp the enormity of her loss. Somehow, being so far away, and having been denied the formality of a traditional funeral service, she found it almost impossible to believe that she would never see her father or Gabrielle again, never see little Roberto grow into a man . . .

There had been no question of her returning to Martiguay. The military were in complete control. They had sacked the de Bartez government, placed de Bartez's key supporters under house arrest, and ruthlessly hunted down leaders of the left-wing opposition groups they blamed for the murders.

Censorship of the press made the situation difficult to assess but there seemed little doubt that the country Victor de Bartez had been trying so desperately to reform and set on the road to prosperity was once again under the yoke of a harsh right-wing dictatorship.

Not that any of that mattered to Noella. She spent her days in a state of shock, still unable to believe that cold-blooded murder had robbed her of those she most loved in the world.

Even Daniel's angry railing at the fact that the new leaders had frozen all funds to Martiguayans abroad, which meant he would be forced to move out of a house he could now no longer afford, didn't penetrate the cocoon of dazed silence she had woven around herself.

It took Inez's letter, smuggled out of Martiguay three months after the assassination, to shake Noella out of her shell-shocked state.

With glazed, empty eyes she read the neat, looped writing.

... is essential you know the truth, Noella. The army lies to the people, blames the left-wing rebels for the atrocity that took your father, Gabrielle, and poor, innocent Roberto. But the people are not fools; they knew how hard their President was working to end the primitive despotism of the land barons whose only aim is to control the labour market and keep the people slaves.

Noella, the people loved your father. In the days following his death there were mass rallies and rolling strikes all over the country. Ordinary Martiguayans never accepted the official line. They know that the murderers of their President are the same evildoers who are now imprisoning students and union activists, outspoken priests and teachers.

Oh, Noella, I pray this letter reaches you. Not only so you can know the truth of your father's death but so you can find comfort too in knowing that it was you who were in his thoughts and heart at the moment he left this world.

The truth about your marriage devastated him. It was as if a veil had been lifted from his eyes; his only thought then was to go to you at once, take you in his arms and beg your forgiveness. All that mattered was to make right the wrong that had existed too long between you.

I will never forget his last words to me, Noella. They were spoken, I know, from the bottom of his heart. 'So often,' he said, 'my daughter needed me and I was never there. This time, I will not let her down.'

Through a blur of tears Noella read Inez's final sentence:

Remember those words, my dearest Noella, and keep them in your heart forever. Then your father will always be by your side.

CHAPTER TWENTY-TWO

It was the day Noella had been dreading. The first anniversary of the deaths of her father, Gabrielle, and little Roberto.

The weather, grey and bleak, matched her mood as she walked along the pathway by the Seine, hands thrust deep into the pockets of her overcoat.

A year ... Noella found it hard to believe. How was she going to get through this same day for all the years to come for the rest of her life? How was she ever going to find any peace from the anger and despair, the overwhelming sense of regret and hopelessness?

Three days ago there had been a letter from Inez — a letter full of gentleness and reasoned argument, urging her not to succumb to despair.

We have lost those dear to us, my darling, but we cannot help them, or ourselves, by also losing our hope and faith in the world where we must still live on. One day, I truly believe, the work your father began will come to fruition and Martiguayans will achieve the freedom and dignity they deserve.

Noella knew the words were meant to bring her comfort but nothing could ease the bitterness in her heart. How could Inez allow herself to dream so foolishly? Martiguay would never change. Her father, her sister, and her sister's innocent child had given their lives for a worthless ideal. Inez herself wrote of being under constant military surveillance while Eugene, it was rumoured, was imprisoned somewhere north of the capital. Everything and everyone with a link to the de Bartez government was viewed as a threat.

Overcome with misery, Noella stopped by a narrow stone jetty and leaned against the cold metal railing. How easy it would be, she thought, staring down into the thick grey waters of the river... how easy just to let herself fall, let her wet, heavy clothes drag her down... down...

'Hey! Mademoiselle! You got a franc so an old man can buy himself a cup of hot coffee?'

Noella spun around. The tramp was right behind her, grizzled hand outstretched, the wrinkles in his grimy unshaven face etched deeper by his grin.

Noella nodded, feeling for some change in the bottom of her overcoat pocket. Money mattered as little to her as it had ever done. Her father's assets had been frozen and she was living on the little she had saved as a model plus what she managed to earn working three mornings a week in a bookshop off the Avenue Castillion. It was enough to eat, to pay her room — what more did she need?

The answer came into her head as she handed the *clochard* some change.

Something to live for.

A few minutes later, Noella sought refuge from the cold in a small cafe. At midmorning it was empty of other customers and she treated herself to a seat at a table, ordering coffee and a sandwich. She had eaten nothing since the previous evening.

While she waited to be served, she scanned a customer copy of that morning's *Le Figaro*.

When the waiter brought her order, he had to speak twice to draw her attention from the open newspaper. When finally she looked up, he saw the tears wet on her cheeks and wondered what the girl had read to so upset her.

*

She rang him from the call box at the rear of the cafe. The footnote to the article made it clear he was still in Paris. 'Dr Richard Avery, lecturer in residence at the Department of International Affairs at the Sorbonne, is an expert on Latin American affairs.'

To her acute disappointment Noella was told that Dr Avery was taking a class. She said she would call back.

Filling in time, she walked the streets and avenues of the city, completely preoccupied by Richard Avery's article. Not only had he written of her father with respect and admiration, but for the first time Noella had seen in print what Inez had told her in that first smuggled letter. Richard Avery had written the truth about those who had murdered her family . . .

He would never have recognised her.

As Noella took a seat in the corner of his living room, Richard hid his surprise at the changes in her appearance. She was thinner, her long, swinging hair was cut practically short, and the glamorous clothes had been replaced by a pair of Levis and bulky pullover. He studied her face as he handed her a glass of wine. It was devoid of make-up, but if anything, he decided, it merely emphasised her natural beauty: the large dark eyes; the glowing, translucent skin; the perfect bone structure.

Yet he would never have picked her as the girl whose face had stared out from a dozen different magazine covers.

He knew what that day's date must mean to her and seeing the fragility in those dark eyes, he said gently, 'I wondered what happened to you, Noella'.

'So . . . so much has happened to me, Richard —' And with a heartbroken sob, she succumbed at last to the overwhelming grief and pain.

*

'Your father sealed his own fate when he took the dangerous step of seeking to overthrow those who had controlled the country for almost three hundred years.'

The tears had brought an oddly calming sense of release and now Noella sat listening without interrupting as Richard spoke.

'Victor de Bartez was seen as a traitor to his own class... and I have it from impeccable sources that he was killed on the explicit orders of Rodriguez Balo himself. The blame, as you know, has always been laid at the feet of a radical left-wing opposition. But in the aftermath of the murders, that contrived Communist threat has become a reality and its emergence has not only given the Balo government greater reason to assert its authority but also handed it the legitimacy of US support.'

Richard's mouth set in a cynical line. 'The Communist bogey has always had the unfortunate result of making Washington the bedmate of the strangest partners.'

He looked at Noella as she sat, pale and silent. 'Your father was a popular and charismatic leader, Noella. He was the greatest chance your country had ever had to throw off the shackles of privilege and poverty. The rich support Balo because he has assured them he will never take their lands — but the die is cast. The people are prepared to fight for liberty. What your father tried to achieve through peaceful means will now be gained through bloodshed.'

She spoke then, quietly and earnestly. 'Tell me, Richard. Tell me exactly what my father was trying to do.'

He saw the burning interest in her eyes and took her at her word.

Later, as she rose to leave, Noella said softly, 'Compared to the things which drove my father and Gabrielle, I feel I have led a completely pointless existence. Clothes, nightclubs, fun and excitement... those were the things that mattered to me. And now I see the falseness of it all. I came back to Paris because I thought that here I would find the comfort and support I so desperately needed. But,' her eyes hardened and she gave a humourless laugh, 'my "friends" had no wish to be confronted with the ugly realities of existence.'

At the front door she held out her hand, thanked Richard for his time and hospitality and added, 'Until now, I have never understood the nightmare of a life without purpose.'

Richard took the thin, cool hand in his own. His intelligent blue eyes stared into hers. 'There is no need for it to be so, Noella. There is much you can do — for Martiguay and your father's cause.'

He saw the puzzled query in her face.

'Yes, Noella. As one who bears the name de Bartez you can still, even now, play an important role in returning your country's honour.'

He told her what he meant and watched her eyes open wide in amazement.

'Oh, no, Richard! No... that is not possible!'

For almost ten days, Richard Avery's words reverberated in her mind. How could he possibly think — ? She wasn't Gabrielle, she didn't have her sister's application and cool analytical brain. She couldn't possibly undertake what he had suggested.

Richard found it difficult to concentrate on his work. Noella had left no address, no number at which he could reach her. He wondered if, indeed, he had judged her correctly. Would she take up the challenge he had thrown at her? Was she truly her father's daughter?

And deep inside him, almost unacknowledged, was the growing realisation that, apart from everything else, he wanted desperately to see her again.

CHAPTER TWENTY-THREE

The girl carried the tin plate of stew to the figure who sat alone in the shadows at the edge of the jungle.

Around the campfire in the clearing they had hacked out of the tangle of trees, the others ate together, laughing and joking as they passed around the skin of red wine. As usual, however, the one they called El Chacal did not join in their merriment.

'*Comandante . . .?*' The girl called softly into the darkness but the man had heard her and was already on his feet.

He took the plate from her hands. '*Gracias*, senorita — it smells good — a man fights best on a full belly. You are to be admired for daring to join us and help the cause.'

The girl felt her cheeks redden at his words. 'To avenge the murder of our President and his family, and to rid our country of Rodriguez Balo, we must all do what we can, *comandante*. There has been too much bloodshed.'

The man they called El Chacal made no reply. As he resumed his seat and took the first mouthful of his meal, the moon emerged from behind a cloud, illuminating the pitiful horror of his face.

Suppressing a shudder, the girl turned away. A bomb, she had been told — the same bomb which had killed his pregnant wife and four-year-old son — part of the military's campaign of terror against those who dared to oppose them.

El Chacal had not waited long to seek his revenge. Three days later, according to local legend, he had walked alone into the local garrison and fired until sixteen uniformed men lay dead.

Overnight, the price on his head had quadrupled. But for almost eighteen months he had evaded capture, staying one step ahead of the authorities to organise the fight that one day would mean liberty for all their people.

Her chores over, the girl made her way to her tent at the edge of the camp. As she pulled the rough blanket around her, her thoughts were still on the man who sat silent and alone.

El Chacal exuded a magnetism, an air of confidence and ruthless authority that, despite the nightmare of his face, made her unable to ignore his powerful masculine presence.

When at last she fell asleep, the girl's dreams were filled with lust and shame.

Noella packed away her notes and joined the stream of students filing out of the lecture room. Her classes were over for the day but with exams just two weeks away she hurried down the crowded corridors towards the central library.

As she pushed through the revolving glass doors she wondered again at the pleasure she now found in study. Never had she felt like this at school in Martiguay. Then, books and learning had been a tedious chore, her final examination an irritating hurdle to be cleared to win her father's approval for her marriage.

But for the twelve months in which she had been a student at the *Institut des Sciences Politiques* she had revelled in the acquisition of knowledge, in the debates and discussions which opened her mind to a completely different world.

At first she had been taken aback by Richard's bold suggestion. 'Educate yourself in the political process, Noella. Arm yourself with knowledge. That way you can put your case more strongly for Martiguay's future... For you are still a de Bartez and when you choose to speak, people will listen.'

Initially, she remembered, as she found herself an empty desk, she had been tortured by self-doubt. It had been only Richard's encouragement and faith which had kept her going, given her the will to succeed.

Whenever she had needed help in clarifying or analysing the torrent of new concepts and ideologies her classes had exposed her to, Richard had always been there, quietly offering the benefit of his knowledge and advice.

'Question everything, Noella,' he stressed. 'Just because a philosophy or a social system exists does not necessarily mean it works or is the best. Ask yourself how a satisfactory balance may be achieved between society's needs and the needs of the individual.'

Richard stimulated and challenged her. He gave her the confidence to engage in heated debate with her lecturers and fellow students, to express succinctly and clearly her developing political vision.

Now the skills that she had learned would be put to formal test in the forthcoming examination.

Noella opened her books and prepared to take notes. Somehow it mattered more than she would admit that she make Richard proud of her.

The news went round the campus like wildfire. Examination results had been posted!

Joining the crush of students around the department notice board, Noella stood on tiptoe, desperately scanning the long list of names to see whether she had passed or failed. She prayed her name would be there.

The results were listed in order of merit. Trying

to stay calm, she began to read from the bottom of the page. As her eyes moved slowly upwards over the column of type, her belly tightened in panic. The name Sylvie Leplaix did not appear anywhere.

White-faced, Noella turned away, pushing blindly through the mob around her. She had failed. The future Richard had drawn so optimistically for her was over before it had begun. Tears stung her eyes. How foolish she had been to take this step, to believe that one day she could somehow make her mark. And now to face Richard...

'Hey, Sylvie! Congratulations! Now I know why we never saw you out of the library.'

Noella spun around to stare into the grinning, freckled face of a girl she knew from one of her tutorials. Yvette Debray belonged to a student theatre group and cut a lot of classes; she was always asking to borrow Noella's notes.

'What do you mean?'

The girl's grin grew wider. 'Even if I'd worked as hard as you did I'd never have made it into the top ten.'

The top ten... Noella's heart began to race as she pushed her way forward for another look at the results. She hadn't dreamed of looking look for her name so high up on the list.

But there it was.

Fifth from the top.

She could hear Richard's delight on the other end of the phone. 'I knew you could do it, Noella. Now you have proved it to yourself. I am so proud of you.'

When she replied, her voice was low and husky with emotion. 'My father would have been proud too, wouldn't he, Richard?'

'Yes, Noella,' he answered gently. 'Very, very proud.'

*

The restaurant was small and intimate, the food and service excellent. It had been a fitting place for a celebratory dinner.

Now, as the waiter poured their coffee, Richard fell silent. He wished he didn't have to tell her tonight. But he had no choice. It was something they had never before discussed.

He studied her across the small table. The low, soft light gave an added glow to her beauty. She had let her hair grow longer again and tonight, for the first time in months, he noticed, she was wearing light make-up and a softly feminine dress in pale lavender.

Richard's eyes grew troubled. Over the last twelve months he had come to know Noella well. The time they had spent together had brought him immense satisfaction. She had a quick intellect and he had enjoyed watching her gain the confidence inspired by knowledge.

But hard as he tried to ignore it, he'd been forced to admit that, for him at least, there was more to their meetings than that. More and more frequently he found himself thinking of her when they were apart, counting the days until the telephone rang and it was Noella asking if she could possibly come round ... possibly impose again ... there was just a point she would like to discuss. It was always difficult to keep the eagerness out of his voice as he assured her she was always welcome.

But Michelle had sensed a difference. She was, after all, a Frenchwoman — with all the intuition that implied.

'Who is it, *cheri*? Tell me, so I do not make a fool of myself.'

They had just finished making love, and her question caught him completely unawares. He was glad of the darkness to hide his discomfort.

'No one, Michelle. There is no one else, I promise you.'

But he hated himself for the words that came so uncomfortably close to a lie. For the whole time he had held his lover in his arms, buried his face against her hair, he had imagined it was Noella whose naked body was wrapped around his.

As he watched Noella put sugar in her coffee, Richard said, as casually as possible, 'Well, I'm glad I'll be leaving Paris on such a high note, Noella. I feel sure you'll have no difficulty coping with the next two years of your course.'

'Leaving ... ?' She stopped stirring and frowned up at him. 'What do you mean, Richard?'

'My tenure at the Sorbonne is up. I leave for home in less than three weeks.'

For a moment he saw something happen behind those dark liquid eyes.

'Oh, Richard ... I never dreamt it would be so soon. I'm — I'm going to miss you.'

It was then he knew how much he loved her.

After Richard left, Paris seemed a much lonelier city to Noella. She realised just how heavily she had come to depend on Richard's company, on his advice and wisdom; how much she missed his quiet good humour and easy-going nature.

Never once during the time they had grown to be friends had she given thought to the fact that one day he would leave to go back to the States. In just a few short months, Richard Avery had come to occupy a unique place in her life. He was older than her by more than ten years, yet for the first time Noella felt she had met a man who treated her as an equal.

They kept in touch by letter but she missed Richard as her friend, her mentor ... and she couldn't help remembering how sometimes, when they had sat close together, she had found herself dreaming, wondering what it would be like to hold him ...

But she was still the wife of Daniel Jarro, no matter

how corrupt and ugly their marriage. Nothing would ever make her return to him, but the question of divorce left her frightened. She had been married in the Church, taken her vows in the sight of God and that had left her in the limbo in which she now existed.

But still her wild fantasies about Richard refused to be suppressed.

With the beginning of the new term, Noella threw herself back into her studies. She had no interest in socialising with other students, in going to soirees or parties or dances. Her only diversion became a growing interest in the student newspaper.

She began to contribute regular articles that were unambiguous attacks on Martiguay's military government. Thanks to her continuing clandestine communication with Inez, she had access to information seldom revealed by the government-controlled media. It was from one of Inez's letters that Noella learned for the first time about a new and insidious menace to her country.

Ever aware of the need for financial support to maintain its authority, the military government of Rodriguez Balo had been quick to offer sanctuary to a unique group of Martiguayan 'businessmen'. It was the spectacular increase in the demand for cocaine, particularly in the United States, which had allowed this small but powerful cartel to establish itself so firmly with the military.

Inez wrote of the terrifying changes being wrought by this deadly new alliance:

Now those who have held power for centuries see that power base being eroded, Noella. Finally they can see how they have been duped, where they have made their mistake. For it is not the elite which the army now has to appease, but those who reap billion-dollar profits through the sale of the white death.

Balo allows them to go about their business unhindered in return for the financial support he needs to stay in power.

Noella, my dear, there are few outside who realise it yet but it is this trade more than anything else that will change things irrevocably for our country.

Inez's words stayed alive in Noella's mind during the long months ahead, spurring her on as she sat at her books.

The one thing that mattered now was to achieve her goal, to complete her degree. Only then, she knew, would she feel she had the credibility to make her voice heard.

On the rare occasions that she faltered, exhausted by the difficulties of studying and earning a living, she gained strength by reminding herself that her success would mean that the deaths of those she loved had not been in vain.

A short time later, to her pride and delight, Noella was offered the position of co-editor of the student newspaper. She accepted without hesitation.

The experience she gained proved invaluable. Working on the paper forced her to focus on a diverse range of topics: human rights, apartheid, nuclear disarmament, the growing wave of drug abuse ... It was an exhilarating opportunity to crystallise her views on important and fundamental issues and Noella grasped it with both hands.

Sometimes, when a deadline kept her at her desk late into the night, it would occur to Noella to wonder at how far she had come, how much she was capable of. She regretted only that it had taken such a tragedy to reveal her true potential.

CHAPTER TWENTY-FOUR

It was the happiest day of her life, made happier by the fact that Richard was there to share it.

'You couldn't keep me away, Noella!' His pride had been obvious at the other end of the line when she'd rung with the news. 'I wouldn't miss it for anything.'

The sound of his voice had made her heart turn over.

And he'd been as good as his word. At the graduation ceremony in the *Institut's* assembly hall, he had sat four rows from the front, smiling proudly as she'd been called up to receive her diploma.

Noella accepted the scroll from the *Directeur* with tears in her eyes. If only, she thought, her family could have been here to share this precious moment.

But you know, Papa, don't you? You are watching me now... The words were spoken silently from the depths of her heart.

Afterwards, they celebrated with dinner at Le Globe d'Or.

As he touched his glass of champagne to hers, Richard knew that the two years away from Noella had done nothing to diminish his feelings for her. She was as he remembered, but now maturity and confidence had added their appeal.

God, how he wished...

Her hand reached across the table, rested gently on

his own. 'Thank you, dearest Richard,' she said softly. 'Not only for being here with me now, but for making it all possible.'

Her touch electrified him and his longing became a physical ache. As he gazed into those dark, blazing eyes, caught the scent of her perfume, he felt his senses spinning out of control. *I'm a fool*, he thought. *A crazy fool. She's not interested in me like that*.

Later, as Richard walked her back to her apartment, Noella described the moment of confusion when she had revealed her true identity to administration officials at the *Institut des Sciences Politiques*.

'I wanted to ensure my diploma was issued in my own name, in the name of de Bartez. Of course, they were surprised, but they understood. Anyway,' her voice took on a firmer ring, 'the time for secrecy, for anonymity, is over. Now I am ready to call attention to my father's cause.'

'You are going to remain in Paris?' Only a foolish hope made Richard ask a question to which he already knew the answer.

'Yes. I have found a position with the International Institute for the Release of Political Detainees. My work will have a direct bearing on what I am trying to achieve in Martiguay.'

He heard the fervour, the determination, in her voice and felt compelled to give a gentle warning. 'Do not expect miracles, Noella. The government of Rodriguez Balo is firmly entrenched, thanks in no small part, I am ashamed to say, to the support of the United States. As long as those opposing the junta are uniformly branded Communist, Washington will do its best to keep Balo in power regardless of the abuses of his regime.'

But Noella would not allow her hopes to be dampened. Her voice was low and intense. 'That is why,

Richard, it will be my life's task to make the world see the truth.'

It was late but she asked him in for a nightcap. Noella knew it was only prolonging the torture but she couldn't bear to end the evening. In the restaurant she had hardly noticed what she'd had to eat and drink as her mind spun fantasies of Richard — of how it would feel to have his mouth on hers, to have his hard, lean body covering her own...

Now, as she looked up into those clear blue eyes, it took all her self-control to keep her voice even. 'It has been such a pleasant evening, Richard, and who knows when we will see each other again.'

Richard felt his heart slam against his ribs. Had he imagined it, or was there something more behind those simple words? His fingers were not quite steady as he accepted the small glass of brandy.

She smiled as she sat beside him on the sofa. 'Not cognac, I'm afraid, but you forgive me, yes?'

Her closeness made his head spin. 'I would forgive you anything, Noella.'

Instantly, she caught the nuance in his tone, turned to see the message that his eyes could not hide.

And moments later their lips met in a breathless eager hunger that thrilled them both.

Emotions suppressed for so long erupted with volcanic force as they tore off their clothes and clung to each other.

'I didn't dare believe... I didn't dare.' Richard panted out the words between wild, demanding kisses, his hands eagerly exploring the soft, naked curves of her body.

'I've wanted you so long. Oh so very long, my darling.' Noella's voice was a sob of joy and relief. To know that his need and desire had been every bit as intense as her own...

And then she was welcoming him into her body, yielding to the force of his maleness, moulding her burning flesh against his. At that moment, as ecstasy exploded in her veins, Noella knew she had found the man she would love all her life.

Thankful that he had planned his business affairs around a further ten days in Paris, Richard spent every spare moment in Noella's company. He felt as if reality had been suspended, as if, having dreamt for so long, nothing happening now could be real.

Every morning when he woke with the woman he loved beside him, his joy was such that it felt as though he'd been only half alive until the moment he'd taken Noella in his arms.

The same joy caught Noella in its explosive force. Lying in Richard's embrace, trembling in the ecstasy of sexual fulfilment, she discovered once more the passion she had known with Paolo, the passion she had despaired of ever feeling again.

And with senses so acutely heightened, she understood for the first time that only the presence of love brought such exquisite and total fulfilment. What she had felt for Paolo had been real, as real as the feelings she now had for Richard. But where Paolo had known only a capricious, shallow child, Richard knew the woman she had become — and Noella understood that his love embraced both her body and her mind. For the first time in her life she felt herself worthy of another's love. It was a heady, poignant feeling.

During those ten wonderful days, she tried not to think of the ever-present hurdle of Daniel and her marriage. For the moment what she had was enough. But she vowed that nothing, not even love, must distract her from her task.

★

Less than twenty-four hours after she had said a wrenching goodbye to the man she loved, the French press finally discovered what had happened to Noella de Bartez.

Noella was prepared. She had known it wouldn't take long before someone on the college staff leaked the news of her identity to the media.

Bombarded by the press, hounded for interviews, Noella vowed that this time the publicity she generated would be used for a much more worthy purpose.

CHAPTER TWENTY-FIVE

'You are happy in this work then, Noella?'

In the quiet elegance of the Hotel Charles V, Nina Repois asked the question of the woman she had invited to tea. Never once did she make a visit to the capital without meeting with the daughter of the late Victor de Bartez.

She watched as Noella placed the delicate china cup on its saucer. It was almost seven years since that afternoon in the Bois de Boulogne when Nina Repois had first realised the truth about the model who called herself Isabel Trevier.

Then she had seen a carefree, flirtatious girl, wearing the latest couturier fashion, a small fortune in jewellery and obviously revelling in the attention of the paparazzi. In stark contrast, the serious young woman who sat opposite her now was dressed in a sensible off-the-rack suit, her only adornments a plain leather-banded watch and a slim gold ring set with a small single ruby. Nina Repois didn't know whether to applaud or regret the changes.

Noella sighed as she answered her friend's question. 'My work affords me both immense satisfaction and utter frustration, Nina. While the release of political detainees is our main goal — and we have had our rare successes — the regimes that perpetrate these atrocities and injustices continue to hold power. It is my difficult task to keep the facts before a press who seem always too eager for new stories, new sensations, to sell their newspapers.'

A worried frown drew Nina Repois' perfectly arched brows together. 'You must not exhaust yourself too much, *cherie*. Why don't you come and spend a few days with me again? The weather is wonderful in the Midi this time of year.'

Noella smiled gratefully. 'You are very kind, Nina. And I appreciate your invitation. But at the moment it is impossible for me to get away. Next weekend I am to address a rally at Chantilly. The nuclear disarmament lobby knows that if I am scheduled to appear they stand a much better chance of attracting press coverage.'

Nina Repois hid her disappointment. She led a comfortable but boring existence. It would have been a treat to have the girl's company for a few days. Noella had visited two or three times before and they had enjoyed each other's company. Nina had been glad to see the girl relax; she knew how much Noella was driven by her work, in particular by her continuing campaign against the military government in Martiguay... But to be too earnest, too serious, was not good for one's health.

A lover, of course, was what she needed, the older woman mused as she raised a bejewelled finger for the bill. Noella had never mentioned a man, and Nina did not feel she could raise the subject — there was something in the younger woman's demeanour that did not invite such intimate questions.

As she signed for their tea, Nina asked, 'You are, of course, still in touch with dear Inez?'

Noella nodded. 'The official mail is open to inspection at any time so it is not easy to write openly, but we manage through more devious means.'

'Please give her all my love when next you make contact, *cherie*.'

Nina Repois took Noella's arm as they left the dining room. 'Poor Inez, how dreadful it must be for her to have to live daily with seeing the ruin of everything your father worked for. And now the country must face the added threat from these drug criminals Balo shields ... How totally heartbreaking it must be — for her and for all Martiguayans.'

Noella's eyes grew stony as they walked through the hotel foyer. 'The rebels continue in their resistance, Nina. They lack arms and organisation but they do not give up — despite the killers Balo sets on their trail. That is why it is my duty to do all I can to publicise their cause.'

As they kissed each other fondly on both cheeks, Nina clasped Noella's hand tightly. 'I can only admire your dedication and zeal, my dear Noella. One day, I am sure, Martiguayans will be happy to welcome you home.'

The man stood watching from the edge of the crowd as the young woman spoke volubly into the microphone, first in French, then in Spanish.

A month ago he had heard her at Chantilly when she had addressed herself to the topic of nuclear politics; her charisma and command had been unmistakable.

Today, if anything, she was even more electric. But of course, he thought, the subject was closer to home.

With the visit to Paris of the US Secretary of State, a protest rally against America's support for the Balo regime in Martiguay had been organised outside the US Embassy. It was only natural that one of the principal speakers would be the daughter of the late President.

The man saw for himself the effect of her fiery words on the assembled crowd; heard the roars of approval as Noella de Bartez condemned the 'blind self-interest' of Washington.

What struck him in particular was the size of the

turn-out. Despite the fact that Paris was well known as a refuge for dissidents and exiles, for the way its citizens rallied to any number of causes, he was still surprised to see how completely the small circle of expatriate Martiguayans had been swamped by local supporters. Students, teachers, union officials, artists and writers — a wide cross section of Parisian society — had joined in the denunciation of US policy in Martiguay.

The man was convinced that Noella de Bartez was the driving factor.

Turning, he walked past the line of watching gendarmes to the corner of the avenue. His face was expressionless as he slid into the battered Peugeot that immediately drew up beside him.

The months passed quickly for Noella. She lived for her work and the only break in the driving tempo of her life came when Richard visited Paris.

The moment she saw him, fell into his loving arms, she felt her tensions melt away. He recharged her, instilled her with a new energy, so that when she was left alone again she felt able to resume her heavy workload.

They exchanged long letters and whenever she had made some impact in the press, she sent Richard the clippings, 'I know you are interested...'

He was. More than she could know. An idea had been forming in his mind for some time. It depended on so many uncertain factors but he had convinced himself it was no longer a fantasy.

One of those uncertain factors had become a distinct possibility by the time Richard made his next visit to Paris.

He broached the subject with Noella over dinner on the night he arrived.

'Senator Larry Kirk is emerging as the frontrunner

in the next Presidential elections, Noella — and he has indicated he's ready to make changes in Latin American policy. Kirk is the best chance Martiguay has of getting rid of Balo. The drug problem is just one of the reasons Larry Kirk and his supporters want to see the military kicked out in Martiguay, but it's an area that has enormous appeal to the electorate. The people want a President who'll take a hard line with the drug bosses.'

Later that evening, relaxed and sated after a passionate reunion, they lay in each other's arms and continued to discuss the possibilities inherent in Larry Kirk's victory at the polls. One hurdle in particular worried Noella.

'Kirk might appear prepared to discard the policies of the present administration, Richard. But no American President will work with an opposition led by the rebels. That is the stumbling block.'

'I've met Larry Kirk, Noella.' Richard stroked her arm as she lay against his chest. 'He's a man who's learnt to jump over stumbling blocks.'

The four men met in an apartment in one of the soulless concrete towers that had grown like mushrooms beyond the Périphérique, the ring road that circled the capital.

The respect with which they treated the older, grey-haired man made it clear he was the leader.

It was he who spoke now. '*Alors*, Leon, tell us what you have discovered that is so important.'

The man he addressed was small, with a dark, lined face and sharp eyes. He broke the news in his usual terse style. 'There is a man, a lover. A *gringo*.'

There was a muffled oath from one of the others.

None of them had expected that.

CHAPTER *TWENTY-SIX*

The meeting took place in one of the situation rooms in the West Wing of the White House.

Larry Kirk, the newly inaugurated President, sat at the head of the long conference table flanked by his secretary of state, his national security advisor, the director of the CIA and two other aides.

Already, after only four months in the White House, President Kirk projected the aura of power and assurance that surrounds a natural leader. At fifty-two, he was tall and well-built with a full head of sandy hair and the ruddy, weather-beaten face of a yachtsman. It was a sport he still enjoyed — but he knew he would have little time for such pursuits over the next four years. Larry Kirk had a lot he wanted to achieve.

He smiled at the man who sat across from him. 'Rick, welcome aboard. You've met everyone, haven't you?'

Richard nodded but made no reply. Seconded to the State Department immediately after the inauguration, he had already learnt enough about Larry Kirk to know that small talk irritated the new President — he liked to cut through the preamble to the business at hand.

Now Richard waited expectantly for the President to continue.

Kirk's intense blue eyes travelled slowly over the faces of those present. 'As everyone in this room knows, one of my immediate priorities is the reformulation of policy on Latin America. And top of the agenda is Martiguay. That sonofabitch Balo has made a laughing stock of the US for too damn long. He happily accepts millions of dollars in aid yet the country is an economic shambles; and at the same time the drug cartels are allowed a virtual free hand in running their criminal activities as long as they underpin Balo's regime.'

The President's face grew grim. 'It seems to me the time is ripe for helping General Rodriguez Balo say good night.'

He nodded at the dark-haired bear of a man across the table. 'I'll let you fill in the rest, Ben.'

Ben Christensen, the director of the CIA, cleared his throat and addressed the meeting without interruption for the next fifteen minutes. He spoke with the giveaway vowels of a native Texan.

The current situation in Martiguay, he reported, was at flash point; inflation was running at almost 400 per cent; unemployment had trebled; and there were shortages of even the most basic commodities. On top of this came reports of increasingly brutal crackdowns by Balo's troops on those brave enough to speak out against the regime.

'Despite this witch-hunt by the military there have been persistent strikes and street demonstrations in the cities, while the rebels have intensified their guerilla activity in the country.' Ben Christensen's eyes blazed under thick, unruly brows. 'Balo's worried and he's got every damn right to be.'

Stabbing a finger in the air to emphasise his words, President Kirk resumed control of the discussion. 'What Balo must be made to see is that he has no option but to agree to democratic elections. And an immediate trade embargo is one vital way we can force his hand.'

The President noticed the change of expression on some of the faces in front of him. 'Sure it'll mean howls from certain sections of the business community, but it's the most convincing way we have of showing Balo that this administration means business; that he has no choice but to agree to go to the polls.'

Clark Reiner, the national security adviser, asked the question that was bothering him. 'But Mr President, who is there to stand against Balo? We can't be seen to support a guerilla-led opposition ... and there is no other legitimate contender.'

The President allowed himself a small, self-satisfied smile. 'That's where you're wrong, Clark. There is someone.' He looked across the table. 'Tell them, Richard.'

As the others filed out with their copies of the dossier on Noella de Bartez, Larry Kirk motioned Richard to stay behind.

The President stood by the tall windows, his back to the weak winter sunshine. 'Ben knew what we were considering, of course, but to the others it came as a shock.'

From where he still sat at the polished conference table, Richard asked, 'Do you think you'll get consensus?'

Larry Kirk clasped his hands behind him and turned to look out at the snow-covered grounds of the White House. 'The dossier you compiled is very convincing, Richard. As you say, the name de Bartez commands immediate respect, and the woman appears to have the same leadership qualities as her father, to be driven by the same democratic ideals. As well, she is a proven orator and seems to have a very clear grasp of what is happening in the country ... And then, of course, there is no one else ... '

'Noella de Bartez is the only one capable of uniting the opposition, Mr President, I know that.' Richard spoke with utter conviction. He'd had long discussions with Ben Christensen, knew that the CIA had already sounded out the various opposition cells. Even the small group of expatriate Martiguayan activists who had seen Noella in action in Paris.

The President turned and fixed Richard with his keen blue eyes. He said slowly, deliberately, 'Then you must know too that if she says yes, you'll have to give her up... Martiguayans would never accept either a divorced woman as leader, or one married to a *gringo*... especially with anti-American feeling running so high.'

So they had known. For the CIA such a discovery would have been easy...

In a voice he prayed would remain steady, Richard answered, 'Yes. I've known that from the moment it became obvious there was no one else.'

Richard asked only one concession. That he be allowed to put the proposal to Noella himself... and at a time of his own choosing.

He wanted to relish those last bittersweet moments in his lover's company before confronting her with the knowledge that would change everything between them forever.

Noella was surprised and delighted by Richard's suggestion that they spend a few days together on the Italian lakes.

'Is the President not keeping you busy enough, *querido*?' she joked as she took his long distance call. She had been overcome with joy and pride when she'd heard about Richard's secondment to the State Department soon after Larry Kirk's inauguration as President. It had been concrete proof to Noella that the new administration really did mean to change things in Latin America.

Now she rearranged her own schedule and looked forward to the rare pleasure of spending an uninterrupted few days in the company of the man she had grown to love so deeply.

The distance between them and the infrequency of their meetings could not diminish the intensity of their passion for each other and their commitment to a common cause. To Noella, Richard was her inspiration and fulfilment, her friend, her mentor, her lover . . .

Yet always the unresolved question of her marriage shadowed their relationship, lent it an edge of tension and poignancy. Noella never allowed herself to wonder where it would all lead. That was a decision best left to fate.

It was the perfect time of year to spend in northern Italy. The weather was warm and the skies were a dazzling blue. As the steamer chugged past the ancient villages and towns that edged the lake, the snow-capped alps of Switzerland were visible in the distance.

Richard had booked a room in the Grand Hotel at Bellagio. It was an idyllic setting and afforded a breathtaking view over the water and the neighbouring hills. Every morning they awoke in each other's arms, enjoyed a breakfast of strong coffee and crisp warm rolls on their small private terrace, before exploring the surrounding countryside until lunchtime. Then, after plates of steaming pasta and a bottle of local wine in a vine-covered *ristorante*, they would return to the hotel to spend the rest of the afternoon in bed.

Richard had always been a passionate and exciting lover, but now as his hands and lips explored her bare flesh, as his body became one with her own, there seemed to Noella a heightened intensity to his lovemaking. She felt electrified by his passion, intoxicated by his uninhibited need as he buried his face in her hair and moaned out his love again and again.

And forgetting everything else, she surrendered herself to the dark, thundering waves of ecstasy that clouded her brain and brought her to the edge of exquisite madness.

Afterwards, when they lay satisfied and exhausted in a tangle of creased damp sheets, Richard continued to hold her close, as if, it suddenly occurred to Noella, he couldn't bear to release her, as if he feared she were suddenly going to disappear from his life...

'I love you, my darling. I love you so much...' He breathed the words against her hair as he stroked her cheek.

Smiling in contentment, Noella fell asleep. She had found at last the love she had always dreamed of...

'Richard, what is it? There's something on your mind, *querido*. I know there is.'

Noella watched her lover as he stood by the open French doors and gazed over the darkening lake. They were about to spend their last evening in Italy before leaving for Paris the next morning.

Their lovemaking that afternoon had been wonderful, a harmony of body and soul that for Noella had seemed to surpass even the best of their previous times together. But her mellowness, her feelings of peace and contentment, were disturbed by the tension she now sensed in Richard.

For the last hour and a half he had barely spoken as, face withdrawn, he had restlessly paced the room.

'Darling...' She stood up from the dressing table and crossed the room. 'Tell me. What is troubling you?'

He turned then to face her, the expression in his eyes impossible to fathom. 'You're right, Noella. There is something on my mind.' He forced his voice to remain normal. 'But I've deliberately waited till now to bring it up.'

Noella frowned but said nothing as she waited for him to continue. What could be troubling Richard so much? Had something happened with his work, something that might stop them seeing each other?

'Noella, President Kirk has asked me to set up a top secret meeting with you in Washington as soon as possible. He has a proposition to put to you.'

He told her what that proposition was.

It was a long time before Noella found the words to speak.

After that, it was only natural that for the rest of the evening they would discuss the implications of Larry Kirk's proposal. Yet there was one area that they deliberately avoided. Both knew exactly what it would mean to their relationship if Noella agreed to the proposition put by the President of the United States.

Much later, as they lay together in the darkness, it was Noella who finally voiced what weighed so heavily on their minds.

Cradled against Richard's chest, her fingers tracing gentle patterns on his bare skin, she whispered, 'If I decide to go ahead with what Washington proposes, *querido*, it will be the most important decision of my life. In so many ways my life will change dramatically, I know, but I must be prepared for that.' A hot ache grew in her throat and she struggled for control. 'But until I make up my mind, we must live each day as happily as we have the past. Until I decide if I am the right one to take up my father's cause, we must share each precious moment as if nothing will ever change. Do you understand, *querido*, what I am trying to say?'

Richard was grateful for the darkness as he buried his damp face against the softness of her hair.

Noella was met at Washington airport by Richard and two unsmiling White House aides. Bypassing Customs, they slid into a waiting limousine and were driven to a nondescript apartment complex three blocks from the White House.

'This is a government "safe house",' one of the burly aides explained as they crowded into the elevator. 'There'll be no publicity, and we can assure ourselves of your safety at all times.'

The words, spoken so casually, suddenly brought home to Noella just how quickly things were happening in her life. What was being proposed would make her a danger to a regime that had already killed thousands. Her life would undoubtedly be at risk.

A shiver ran through her. Would she too become a martyr, like her father and sister before her?

Beside her, Richard sensed her reaction. It was only natural, he told himself, squeezing her cold hand in his behind the broad backs of the two officials. But already he had begun to doubt his own role in bringing things to this pass. Jesus, if anything should happen to her ... how would he be able to live with himself?

'We will leave you now, senora.' The aides had shown her into the small, blandly decorated apartment, and were ready to go.

The man with the hard, dark eyes and glossy moustache added, 'The President hopes you will be free to dine with him this evening. The confidential nature of your mission dictates that the meal must, of course, be informal.'

'I should be happy to accept the President's kind invitation.'

The man nodded. He had expected nothing less. 'A car will come for you at seven sharp.'

A short time later, Richard also left her to rest.

'It's just gone two, darling. If you're hungry all you have to do is pick up the telephone and ask for what you want. The kitchen staff are on duty twenty-four hours a day.'

They kissed at the apartment door.

'I can hardly believe this is happening, Richard. None of it seems quite real.'

He gave her a slow smile, masking his inner torment. 'Wait till this evening before you say that, Noella.'

Richard was right.

From the moment the limousine passed through the security checks and entered the White House grounds, Noella had to keep telling herself she wasn't dreaming.

Ushered into a side entrance and then down a wide corridor to a small, formal reception room, she was greeted moments later by President Larry Kirk.

Tall and commanding, the President was accompanied by his top aides, men who until then had been merely names Noella had read in newspaper reports.

Exuding a sincerity and charm that immediately put Noella at her ease, Larry Kirk apologised for his wife's absence. 'She's spending a few days with her sister in Chicago.' He smiled as the butler served their drinks. 'I'm afraid Helen hasn't quite had time to get used to the goldfish bowl effect of living in the public eye.'

The talk over dinner was inconsequential but Noella was well aware that she was being closely studied by these powerful men. They owed her no allegiance — she was useful to them only if she could be seen to further their own national interests. She had no illusions about that.

Larry Kirk did not keep her late.

'I'm sure you'd like an early night, Senora de Bartez.' It was the form of address that had been used by all those present. Like Noella, they knew it was the name de Bartez that would galvanise and unite Martiguayans. 'Tomorrow we will talk of more important matters. I have called a meeting for ten; I hope that suits.'

Noella took his extended hand. 'I look forward to that time, Mr President.'

*

Richard was present at the next morning's meeting along with half a dozen of the President's most senior advisers. As Noella entered the room and took her place at the large round table, he gave her a discreet, supportive smile.

How beautiful she looks, he thought, admiring the simple cream coloured suit, the row of pearls, the glossy curve of her hair. Only then did it occur to him to wonder whether such beauty might not work against her with this powerful male coterie. But surely, Richard surmised, the world has moved past that . . .

Yet if there were any present who might have been prejudiced by her looks, they were soon made to realise that Noella de Bartez's beauty was no impediment to her grasp of the issues at hand.

The discussion ranged widely over the current situation in Martiguay, the power of the drug cartels, and an assessment of the vulnerability of Rodriguez Balo's position.

'The rebels must be brought into line under a credible opposition leader,' Ben Christensen emphasised. 'A leader who is prepared to take the difficult steps of stabilising government by establishing democratic principles, instituting real economic reforms, and stamping down on the drug cartels with the full weight of a purged judicial system. Because at present, the drug barons are undermining the banks, the police and the judiciary — judges are afraid to sentence even those few who are charged.'

President Kirk further clarified the situation. 'The problems for Martiguay are enormous on all fronts but the US is prepared to reinstate aid and investment to fully back up a new government provided we are positive the criteria for reform are being met.'

Clark Reiner, national security adviser, gave Noella a cool appraising look. 'The rebels, some with strong leftist leanings, have strengthened their position, senora ... Tell me, if you adopted our proposal, and if you were elected leader, what steps would you take to ensure the processes of democracy were carried out?'

Noella didn't hesitate. 'The people are crying out against injustices, Mr Reiner. My first move would be to convince Martiguayans that under a de Bartez government there would be real changes, the changes they have been waiting for for centuries.' Her dark eyes scanned the silent, appraising men. 'To begin with I would have the plantations remeasured; that will prove that much of the land the rich claim to own is not legally theirs.'

Richard saw the expressions change on the faces around him and had to stop himself from applauding. No one had expected that! But it was a point Noella had made often to him.

From that moment, Noella held the complete attention of six of the world's most powerful men as she outlined the rest of her plan to rescue her country. Crop diversification into food production; the formation of peasants' banks; economic incentives of grants of land plus 'starter kits' of tools, seeds and fertilisers; cuts in spending; free market policies; a complete overhaul of the judicial and police systems ... The list went on, until Noella saw that her listeners were finally convinced.

Richard saw it too. He tried to be happy for her sake and for what it could mean to the future of the country she loved, but a sense of desolation and despair overwhelmed him.

He had lost her, as he'd known he would.

Two days later, as Noella was boarding her return flight to Paris, Ben Christensen was discussing his impressions of the meeting with one of his senior staff.

'The situation with the husband come up?'

Christensen shook his head. 'It never seemed to occur to her.'

His colleague gave him a long steady look. 'It won't be a problem, will it?'

'You know it won't,' his boss answered flatly.

CHAPTER *TWENTY-SEVEN*

On the long journey back to Paris, Noella's mind was focused on nothing but the decision that now faced her.

'We do not expect an answer right away, senora,' the President had stressed at their parting. 'The proposal carries difficulties and the threat of great personal danger — I am sure you understand that. You are faced with a very difficult choice.'

Noella learnt the truth of those words over the next forty-eight hours as she struggled with the most momentous decision of her life.

More than anything, it was her love for Richard that gave her cause to hesitate.

Yet she knew, as she had always known, that she would never be able to forgive herself if she passed up the chance being offered to her — the chance to give some meaning to the otherwise pointless deaths of those she had loved; the chance to seek salvation for her suffering countrymen.

But to do that meant the sacrifice of everything she had found with Richard . . .

Although she had moved from the area a long time ago, Noella found her steps returning to the cold stone arches of the church of Saint Therese d'Avignon.

She knelt and fixed her troubled dark eyes on the enormous silver crucifix suspended over the altar.

Silently she begged for guidance. 'Lord, help me . . .

give me the strength I need for this task, the courage to sacrifice what I love most in this world.'

Four days after her return, Noella rang the telephone number given to her by Ben Christensen.

In Washington, the CIA director had handed her a sheet of unheaded paper with a name and number written on it. 'When you have made your decision, call this person. Felix Noverro is completely trustworthy, an expatriate Martiguayan who is utterly committed to the overthrow of Balo.'

The phone was answered after just two rings.

'*Oui?*' The voice was terse, cautious.

She spoke in Spanish. 'I am Noella de Bartez... I wish to speak with Senor Felix Noverro.'

The tone changed instantly as Felix Noverro greeted the woman who, he hoped and prayed, would be the saving angel of his country...

Noella was introduced to the others in Felix Noverro's small apartment close to the Madeleine. It was a happy occasion — the expatriate Martiguayans were obviously delighted with her decision.

Felix Noverro, a greying, elegant man of quiet dignity, paid her the greatest compliment. 'We have observed you over many months now, senora. You have the de Bartez gifts of leadership and oratory, the ability to unite the country against the dictator, Balo. You are your father's daughter.'

Noella swallowed back her emotion at the words. *Her father's daughter* ...

Then the six men were on their feet, standing almost shoulder to shoulder in the tiny living room while Felix Noverro proposed the toast. 'To Senora de Bartez, the future, and democracy.'

Noella saw the fervour on the faces around her as her countrymen raised their glasses, and elation flooded through her. These men were patriots — they believed in her, had faith in the name de Bartez. She must not let them down.

The bombshell came just as she was about to leave.

It was Felix Noverro who dropped it. Casually, innocently . . .

'Of course, senora, you realise it will be necessary to reunite with your husband.'

Noella froze. When she regained her voice, she answered, 'My marriage is over, senor. It was over long ago. There is no hope of reconciliation.'

The rest of the room had gone silent.

Felix Noverro tried to explain. 'But a single woman —'

Noella cut across him, her tone emphatic. 'I can do this without a man, senor. Believe in me.'

The discomfort of the elderly Martiguayan was obvious. 'I do not think you understand, senora. Martiguayans are staunch Catholics — they will never accept as leader a woman who is estranged from her husband.'

They discussed it long after she had gone.

'She must be made to see sense!' Xavier Illandro could barely control his anger. 'It is impossible for her to stand as a candidate if she is seen to have rejected her marriage.'

Felix frowned. At one time they had worried about the *norteamericano* — for never could they have contemplated a divorcee remarried to a *gringo* — but their contacts in Washington had reassured them that was no longer a threat.

The others were staring at him, waiting for him to come up with a solution.

Felix pursed his lips. 'She will not be convinced by us,' he said slowly. 'The pressure must come from those she loves and respects.'

*

'You understand, senora, what I am trying to say? That is the only weakness. She *must* reunite with her husband — even if it is only for the sake of appearances.'

Inez turned away from the window. The garden was overgrown; the gardener had left a long time ago to join one of the guerilla units outside the capital.

'Yes ... yes, of course,' she replied. These people obviously did not realise the sacrifice involved; could Noella do as they asked even for 'the sake of appearances'?

Inez looked at the hard-eyed man who sat on the edge of the sofa, hat in hand. He was a patriot, in touch with those abroad who had found new reason for hope. In another de Bartez...

It was more than Inez would have ever dared to dream. But now, she realised, it made so much sense. If only Noella could be persuaded...

'I can only do my best, senor,' she answered quietly.

In the end it was from Inez that Noella once more drew strength. She read the letter again and again and acknowledged what she had known all along.

She had no choice. Her personal feelings were of no importance in the face of her duty to her country.

But before she told Felix Noverro of her capitulation, she placed a call to Richard. She struggled to keep her emotions under control.

'I know there is no other way, *querido*,' her voice shook and her knuckles were white around the receiver. 'None of them, of course, know the truth about Daniel. They do not realise what they are asking me to do. But I — I cannot let my own selfish concerns jeopardise my country's chance for freedom.'

A sob caught in her throat and the next moment her fragile control was broken. 'Oh, my darling, oh, Richard, how can I bear it? Not only to lose you, but to return to the sham of a dead and ugly marriage...'

Across the miles, Richard listened to her heartbreaking sobs and saw nothing but darkness in the cold lonely years of his future.

Felix Noverro was sensitive enough to hide his pleasure and relief at Noella's decision.

'I have considered the matter seriously, senor, and realise that of course you are right. I must do everything I can to ensure I am accepted as a credible contender.'

A frown drew her brows together. 'But, tell me, have you thought that my husband might refuse to play his role?'

Felix Noverro gave her a measured look. 'Your husband, senora, is from a wealthy family. He is used to the privileges money brings and does not enjoy being denied the free flow of capital under the present regime. I am quite certain Senor Jarro will understand at once the advantages his cooperation will bring.'

Of course, thought Noella, he is right.

As soon as he was alone, Felix Noverro placed an urgent call to the Martiguayan Ambassador in London.

Quickly and succinctly, the expatriate leader explained what was required.

'*Si*,' the Ambassador nodded into the phone. 'I will arrange an appointment at once. And senor... have no worries. I know Jarro, I am in no doubt he will see sense.'

Daniel couldn't hide his surprise, his astonishment even, at the proposition put to him. Noella...? Noella entrusted with this vital role? He had read about her activities, of course, and knew of her continuing campaign against the Balo regime, but had never dreamt...

The Ambassador brought him back to the point. 'You would be willing then, senor, to re-establish your marriage to this end?'

Daniel's mouth curved in a slow, cynical smile. 'I can do my duty as well as the next man, senor.'

As soon as the news reached him, Felix Noverro reported to his CIA contact. They met in the usual busy cafe three blocks away from Felix's apartment.

'All is well, senor,' the Martiguayan beamed. 'Senora de Bartez will reunite with her husband. He will be no problem.'

The old man didn't notice the change of expression in his contact's eyes.

CHAPTER *TWENTY-EIGHT*

Daniel informed them he would need a month to give notice at the bank, wind up his affairs and relocate to Paris.

'There is no need for undue haste, senor.' Felix Noverro was sitting in Daniel's London flat. As soon as the banker had indicated his agreement to a reconciliation, it was Felix who had made contact. 'For now we must wait in readiness until Washington does all it can to force Balo's hand. But as soon as an election is called,' Felix snapped his fingers, 'then we move at once.'

Daniel listened with a growing sense of anticipation. How difficult and humiliating he had found it without the family money he was so used to. He would do everything he could to change *that* situation.

He drew back deeply on his cigarette, his eyes bright with wry amusement at the thought of seeing Noella in her new role. How she must have changed ... and how she would despise being forced into playing out this farce.

Felix Noverro felt bone weary as he made his way back to Paris. He was no longer a young man and the journey to London had exhausted him. But he could not stop now, not when his goal was so close to being achieved.

For it was Felix Noverro's long-held dream to see his country rise above the ruin and decay forced upon it by its ruthless exploiters.

During the reign of the dictator Peres, Felix had been the editor of an important provincial Martiguayan newspaper. His relentless and vehement attacks on the government had soon brought him to the attention of the authorities. Felix had escaped Martiguay just a few short hours before the *policia* arrived at his office with a warrant for his arrest on the charge of sedition.

He had found refuge in Paris and, in time, married a Frenchwoman. When Victor de Bartez had come to power, Felix was ecstatic. But his plans to return to Martiguay had been disrupted by his wife's unexpected and serious illness. Still, he had managed to interview the new President for the journal on international affairs to which he was a regular contributor. Impressed by the de Bartez government's plans for reform, Felix had been torn between loyalty to his wife and a burning desire to return to his homeland. And then the ex-patriate's vision of the future was abruptly shattered. Victor de Bartez was assassinated.

Lately, however, he had begun to dream again ...

'The estrangement must be explained to the press in a way that will work to enhance your future image.'

As Noella listened silently, Felix explained what he had in mind.

'It is important to emphasise that your husband was always waiting for you to come to terms with your immense loss; that he realised you needed time alone to ponder the tragedy — and to seek solace and new optimism for the future. We will state that he had made it clear he was always there if you needed him.'

Felix walked back to his apartment lost in his thoughts. Noella had agreed to all he proposed but he had seen the blankness in her face, the flicker of something indefinable in her eyes ... He wondered again what had really gone wrong in the marriage.

He chided himself as he turned into the tiny cobbled lane that led to his home. It was none of his business. What mattered was that the problem had been solved satisfactorily.

It was only a two-day business trip to London but Richard couldn't bear to be so close and not to see her. He knew that the husband had not yet arrived in Paris.

His meetings over, he made a wild dash to Heathrow and found a seat on one of the last evening flights.

As he took a taxi in from de Gaulle, Richard knew he was only drawing out the torture by seeing her one more time. But how could he pass up this last chance to hold her in his arms?

She didn't know he would be in London. He hadn't been sure if he could get away and hadn't wanted to disappoint her. As the cab turned into Avenue Colonel Bonnet, he prayed she would be at home.

Noella opened the door, wondering who could possibly be calling so late.

There was no need for words. With a sob of joy she fell into his arms.

They made love with all the sweetness and desperation of knowing it would be for the very last time. For hours they gave each other pleasure, over and over again, until the sky turned pink with dawn. Neither felt like sleeping as they embraced amid the tangle of bedclothes.

'These last moments are too precious to waste with sleep,' she whispered against his cheek. 'They must live in my memory for the rest of my life.'

Richard felt as if his heart would burst with love and anguish. His hands moved feverishly over her body and seconds later he was ready to enter her again.

'Take me, *querido*,' Noella arched her back and

opened herself to his desire. 'Lock me into your body and your heart one final time.'

Their orgasms were simultaneous, shattering like an explosion of stars while the tears slid down their cheeks.

Less than forty-eight hours later Noella was reunited with the man she despised.

Felix Noverro met Daniel at the airport and dropped him at Noella's apartment. The elderly man made a speedy withdrawal, leaving the couple alone for the first time in many years.

As she showed him into the sitting room, Noella noted the changes that time had wrought in the man to whom she was still legally bound. Lines of grey threaded his jet black hair; fine lines creased his forehead and traced a path from his nose to the edges of his mouth — but Daniel Jarro was still a handsome man. Still able, no doubt, thought Noella, to attract those who could satisfy his desires. She did her best to suppress a shudder.

When at last they were seated with their drinks, she made her position coldly clear. 'I am sure this is as distasteful for you as it is for me. However you are aware of the position: my acceptance as a viable opposition leader requires that my marriage appear intact.' She saw the bold amusement on Daniel's face as he sipped his drink and her eyes hardened. 'You, of course, have your own reasons for agreeing to the arrangement, and I am sure it is mutually understood that whatever facade we present publicly will have no implications for our private lives.'

Daniel gave her a cold-eyed smile. 'Why the pussy-footing around, my dear Noella? Why not come straight out with it? What you are trying to say is that I am not to expect a restoration of my conjugal rights, yes?'

The insolence in his voice made Noella's eyes blaze. 'You impress me with your perspicacity, Daniel.'

He matched her mockery with his own. 'I shall be the perfect consort, *querida*.'

Just two days later, Noella made her first public appearance with Daniel at the launch of the latest novel by one of France's premier authors. While the paparazzi might have become bored with her political proselytising, her appearance at the side of her estranged husband drew them like bees to honey.

As the flashbulbs popped, the same question was thrown incessantly at Noella. 'You have reconciled with your husband, madame? You are together again?'

Somehow she managed to keep the smile on her face even at that obscene moment when one of the more insolent photographers had asked, 'So maybe, monsieur, there are now even plans for a family?'

Turning to give her a tender look, Daniel had folded her hand in his. 'All things are possible when one has found love again,' he replied softly.

Noella saw the hidden laughter in his eyes and swallowed back her repulsion. How long, she wondered, would she be forced to endure this abhorrent charade?

They left half an hour before midnight. In the taxi they sat without speaking, keeping the maximum distance between them on the rear seat. Yet despite that, the smell of alcohol reached Noella's nostrils. Daniel had drunk heavily and she had watched nervously as his condition deteriorated throughout the evening — the glazed eyes, the too-loud laughter and the slurred words.

It hadn't been easy to persuade him to leave.

'Why, *querida*?' He gave her a lopsided smile. 'I am enjoying myself. After all, it is not every night I get to escort a celebrity.'

He mocked her, drawing out the final word, while he reached defiantly for a fresh drink from the tray of a passing waiter.

In the end she had managed to get him away.

The success of their charade made it inevitable that Daniel would have to move into her apartment.

Now, with the front door closed behind them, she went to push past him and climb the short flight of stairs that led to her own bedroom.

Without warning, Daniel suddenly barred her way, his hands grasping her shoulders. 'Let us talk a while, Noella.' His face was close to hers, and the stink of liquor disgusted her.

She tried to twist away but his grip was too strong.

'Let me be... I told you never to touch me.' Her voice was icy but controlled.

'But, *querida*, it is not often a woman excites me... and maturity has certainly added to your appeal.' He was grinning at her, forcing her backwards.

'I said no! *Leave me*!'

Eyes bright with lust, Daniel threw her down across the sofa, at the same time ripping off her thin silk blouse.

'But you need me, Noella, no?' His breath was heavy, as he pinned her down with a knee and one hand, unzipping his trousers swiftly with the other. 'Without me, even you cannot get what you want...'

She swore furiously in Spanish, kicked and twisted wildly against his hold, but to no avail. If anything, her struggles seemed to heighten his excitement as he lowered his body over hers.

Her head was hanging backwards over the edge of the sofa, and she screamed as he tore off her panties and drove himself inside her.

'You see, *querida*,' he breathed hotly against her neck, as he pumped his organ against her painful dryness. 'You see how much I enjoy fucking a powerful woman, a celebrity...?'

By then, she was choking on her own sobs.

★

He awoke with a start.

His eyes blinked against the light then widened in terror.

'Listen to me . . . and listen well.' Noella's voice was as cold and steady as the blade of the knife she held at his throat. 'Lay a finger on me once more and I will make sure no man ever looks at your face again.'

The fire in her eyes told him without a doubt she meant what she said.

CHAPTER TWENTY-NINE

After that evening, Noella made sure she spent as little time as possible alone in the apartment with Daniel.

That was easy enough to arrange, given her strenuous schedule which, apart from her normal employment, now included regular evening meetings with Felix and the others. Together they tackled the difficult task of framing a reform program that would go some of the way to meeting the diverse demands of the various opposition groups. Noella knew that her name and background would give her a head start, but success could only be guaranteed by a program with wide-ranging appeal.

There were moments when, weary after hours of heated discussion, she found herself overcome with doubts.

We're counting on so much that is still unsure, she told herself: on the fact that Balo will be forced to call an election some time soon; on the fact that our campaign will appeal to an eclectic opposition and rally our disenchanted countrymen...

When occasionally she would admit these doubts to Felix, he was always reassuring.

'We must trust the Americans where Balo is concerned, Noella. When the time is judged right, there are ways and means of ensuring the dictator has no option but to call a general election. As for the opposition, yes, they are a motley collection ranging from the right to the extreme left, and certainly to some you are only grudgingly accepted as a candidate. But no one will stand in your way. Yours is the best known name in Martiguay, written already into our country's history, and given greater reverence by the martyrdom of your father and sister.' The old man patted her arm comfortingly. 'Have faith, Noella. We have come so far, and soon, very soon, will come the time to act.'

Daniel smiled happily to himself as the limousine Charles Aveline had sent for him purred past the expensive residences of St Cloud.

He was looking forward to the evening ahead. It made a change from drinking in some over-priced bar or sitting alone in the apartment. The role of the dutiful husband had very quickly started to bore him.

By good fortune, Charles Aveline had come to his rescue.

Daniel had met the wealthy businessman when he'd had dealings with the bank in England. Charles Aveline was in his sixties, grey-haired, charming, debonair and at the time had seemed pleased with the way Daniel had handled a rather pressing business matter.

When they had bumped into each other a few days before in the foyer of the Paris bank where he was now employed, Daniel was surprised that the elegant Parisian remembered him.

'*Mais, naturellement*, Monsieur Jarro,' Charles Aveline's blue eyes gleamed as he extended his hand. 'There are men who always make a certain impact.'

Was he imagining it, Daniel wondered, or did Charles Aveline's hand linger just a fraction too long in his own?

The wealthy businessman seemed in no hurry and Daniel was forced to make small talk until, a few moments later, as if he had suddenly made up his mind, Charles Aveline interrupted, 'With your wife so busy it must be tedious for you to spend so much time alone, monsieur. If you are free next Saturday evening, I am giving a small private party at my home at St Cloud. I would be delighted if you could join us.' His eyes held Daniel's. 'My parties are always . . . interesting.'

Daniel knew then he had read the signals correctly. He felt a pulse begin to beat in his temple. Smiling warmly, he replied, 'I would be delighted, monsieur.'

The car was slowing. It turned between imposing gateposts and came to a halt at the brightly lit portico of an eighteenth century villa.

A footman greeted him in the foyer and he was escorted up a wide circular staircase to a salon on the first floor. For a moment, as the door closed behind him, Daniel stood motionless, taking in the scene that confronted him.

In the elegant, wood-panelled room with its gold leaf cornices and extravagant chandeliers, groups of dinner-suited men and glamorous women were being served champagne by a dozen or so stunningly handsome youths. The shock lay in the fact that the latter wore only leather jockstraps and, as they moved around the room, the guests they waited on showed no inhibitions in stroking their naked buttocks or the organs highlighted by the tight-fitting sheaths.

Daniel felt the instant response in his groin.

'Monsieur Jarro! I *knew* you would come.' Charles Aveline was by his side, as elegant as ever, exuding the bonhomie of a well-mannered host. Before Daniel could find the words to reply, the older man leaned forward and kissed him on the cheek. 'Now you must relax and enjoy yourself, cheri. Come, I will introduce you to some enchanting company.'

The hand he folded around Daniel's felt as cold and dry as a lizard.

*

What really surprised Daniel, given the presence of such beautiful young men, was that it was a woman who excited him the most.

Rachelle had caught his eye almost at once. It was her presence and authority as much as her beauty that made his heart beat faster. She was tall, statuesque, with a high, full bosom and generous hips. A real woman.

In her tight-fitting, strapless gown Rachelle Clairveau projected all the glamour and aura of an old-fashioned movie queen; she was exquisitely made up, eyes darkly lined, full lips gleaming crimson, her dark brown hair swept up in an extravagant coiffure.

As he stood close beside her, Daniel felt overcome by the same feelings he had had the night he had been driven to take Noella by force... Again, it was the combination of an almost masculine power and self confidence with undeniable femininity, that so strangely excited him.

Sipping at her drink, Rachelle teased him with her mocking barbs, insulting his profession, his accent, his Latino good looks. Her voice was low and husky.

'Oh, that dashing profile, cheri.' She pursed her lips coquettishly and ran a gloved hand boldly over his cheek. 'Let me think... Yes! Errol Flynn! When I look at you that is who immediately springs to mind.'

She leaned close and Daniel felt giddy with the scent of her perfume as she whispered hotly in his ear, 'Tell me, *cheri*, do you have his endurance? Can you service a woman all night long, as he could?'

It was a challenge Daniel Jarro could not resist.

The first room they entered was already occupied and with a laughing apology, Rachelle retreated, closing the door.

Hand in hand, they hurried up the broad staircase to the floor above. The next room they tried was empty and Rachelle turned the key in the lock behind them.

'No interruptions,' she whispered as she pulled off Daniel's jacket, began to unbutton his shirt.

He was trembling with anticipation, his breathing rapid as she threw aside his clothes.

When he stood naked, Rachelle held out her arms.

'Undress me.' It was an order, delivered in that low powerful voice.

Pulses beating, Daniel drew off the long gloves. Then reaching behind her, he fumbled for the zip fastener on the gown. Slowly, he rolled the dress down to her waist and caught his breath. Her breasts were impossibly large, pale, heavy melons tipped with dark pointed nipples. The response in his shaft was instant.

Blood roaring in his veins, he reached out to knead the ivory softness between his fingers. But Rachelle gripped his wrist with surprising strength.

'I must be completely nude.' She gave him a long seductive look. 'Then, *cheri*, we can do whatever you want . . .'

In an agony of tormented desire, Daniel forced the dress downwards. The tightness made it difficult. But there was another reason too . . .

Beneath the gown, Rachelle Clairveau was naked and Daniel saw at once why he'd had difficulty peeling the dress down over her hips.

The penis was hard and erect, enormous.

A sob of ecstasy escaped Daniel Jarro's lips. Rachelle Clairveau was his fantasy come true . . .

After that first evening, Rachelle Clairveau became Daniel's obsession.

Every moment possible he spent in her company. They met regularly at her apartment and once, when Noella was away on business, even managed a weekend at Rachelle's small stone cottage in the hills near Berthillion.

Daniel couldn't get enough of the man-woman who held his mind and body in a perpetual trap of excitement and lust. His only dread was that she would tire of him and deprive him of the most stimulating and fulfilling sexual experience of his existence.

Daniel never wanted their affair to end.

'Jesus H. Christ!'

Ben Christensen banged his clenched fist heavily against the polished oregon of his desk top. 'It's even worse than we imagined! Faggots were bad enough but a goddamn closet queen!'

'Transvestite,' corrected the man sitting across from him. Jack Tailor had just flown in from Paris. It had been his job to keep watch on Daniel Jarro, to find out if the next step would be necessary.

'Transvestite, queen, faggot — who gives a running fuck!' exploded the director of the CIA. 'If the press smells this it'll be all over. The plan will be worthless. De Bartez will be out before she even has a chance.' He glowered at Tailor, his face still flushed with rage. 'Nothing must be allowed to jeopardise this operation.'

Jack Tailor gave him a level look. 'Then we have no choice.'

'I never thought we had,' Ben Christensen answered tartly.

Two hours out of Paris, Daniel turned off the autoroute onto the winding mountain road that led to Rachelle's cottage. He could hardly believe his luck at being able to manage another overnight rendezvous so soon. The moment Noella had informed him she had to spend the weekend in Lyon, he couldn't wait for her to leave the apartment so he could place a call to his lover.

'Yes, *cherie*, a whole weekend. Please, please, tell me you are free.' A film of sweat had broken out on Daniel's upper lip. God, if this time was anything like the last, he would die in Rachelle Clairveau's bed.

His lover's memory seemed every bit as clear as his

own. She was ecstatic, she assured him. 'But do not trouble yourself to drive across town on Friday evening to pick me up, *cheri*. The traffic is far too horrendous. Go to the cottage direct on Friday — I will take the train to Berthillion station and you can meet me there on Saturday morning, yes?'

That way, thought Rachelle happily, she could still keep her Friday evening rendezvous with the good-looking tennis player she had met last weekend.

As he replayed the conversation picked up by the tap he'd placed on Noella's line, Jack Tailor knew he had to work quickly.

Daniel drove quickly, swerving the rented Alfa around the hairpin bends. At that time of the evening there was little traffic on the narrow, twisting road and the approaching headlights would alert him to any oncoming vehicles.

He was humming softly to himself, anticipating the pleasures of the next two days, as he changed into lower gear for another roller-coaster descent. Lost in lustful thought, it took him a moment to notice that the Alfa had failed to respond.

Daniel frowned. Instead of slowing, the car was gathering momentum down the steep gradient. The gears had not engaged.

Cursing the inadequacies of rented automobiles, he applied his foot to the brake.

The blood drained from his face. Again and again he pumped the pedal. Nothing!

The road was flattening out, curving into the next tight corner, but there was nothing he could do.

His scream was lost in the sound of tearing metal as the Alfa crashed through the guardrail and hurtled into the darkness of the valley below.

CHAPTER THIRTY

As soon as the arrangements were made to fly Daniel's body back to Martiguay and his shocked parents, Noella had left at once for the Cote d'Azur.

It was the relentless harassment from the press that had finally convinced her to accept Nina Repois' kind offer.

The attention which had been focused on her in the two weeks since Daniel's accident was almost too much to bear.

Especially when she had to assume the demeanour of a woman enduring a tragic loss...

Now, as the afternoon drew to a close, she sat alone on the elderly widow's tiled patio. The Mediterranean and some of the most expensive real estate in Europe stretched before her, but Noella's thoughts were far away.

Fate, or a loving God perhaps, had relieved her of an intolerable burden. An accident on a treacherous mountain road had freed her of the man she despised. And yet, as Felix had pragmatically reassured her, her political aspirations would not suffer from Daniel's demise. There was, after all, a dignity and respectability in widowhood that was denied the estranged wife.

Shaking off her cynicism, Noella pushed herself out of the comfortable wicker chair. Perhaps she should take a stroll. Her clothes felt uncomfortably tight. Nina's chef was feeding her too well.

For a moment she stood at the edge of the patio

and looked over the panorama spread before her. Such wealth and complacency, she thought reprovingly. Such insularity and self-interest.

The feeling of nausea came from nowhere. Her hands clutched tightly at the cold metal railing and she felt the sweat break out on her face. Vertigo, she decided, swallowing hard. From standing so foolishly close to the edge.

Turning, she pushed through the drapes into the living room, breathing deeply as she sought to calm the giddiness.

'Noella! Are you all right, my dear?' Nina Repois had come back into the room, her two chihuahuas bobbing around her feet.

Noella nodded, a hand clutched to her belly. The nausea was worse, making it impossible to speak.

'My dear! Quickly, come and lie down, let me get you a drink of water.' Face creased with concern, Nina helped her to the sofa. 'Oh, you poor creature, you aren't well. It's the stress of these last few weeks, it has all taken such a toll.'

But iced water and the cool towel Nina held against her head did little to help the nausea pass.

'I'm going to fetch a doctor.' Nina Repois rose determinedly to her feet.

'Nina...' Reaching out, Noella grasped the older woman's hand. She forced out the words from between pale lips. 'We — we must be careful. I think... I think something has happened to me that I never dreamed possible.'

Claude Pridoux, a small neat man with a greying goatee, was not only Nina Repois' physician but also a close friend. He could be counted on to be discreet.

He looked down at Noella as he closed his medical bag. He had read about this woman. It was difficult to know how she would feel about the news.

'I would say four months, madame. For greater accuracy you would need tests, of course, and I suggest you see your own physician when you return to Paris. In the meantime, rest and a good diet is all that is required.'

'But Noella! *Quel horreur*! That monster attacked you — assaulted you?' Nina Repois looked wide-eyed at her friend.

Noella was sitting up, her queasiness settled by the cup of herbal tea Nina had prepared for her.

'I tried to put it out of my mind, forget it had ever happened. But it never occurred to me this might be the result.' Noella looked at Nina in bewilderment. She was still trying to come to terms with what Claude Pridoux had confirmed. 'You see, I — I was told long ago that the odds were against my ever bearing a child. So I never questioned my missed periods. They were never really regular, and I assumed the stress of these last few months, Daniel's assault...' Her voice trailed off.

Nina Repois drew a deep breath. Her question couldn't be avoided. 'What are you going to do now then, *cherie*? Have you considered how this might affect your plans? We are dealing with men here, Noella. If it's known you are pregnant the offer of candidature might well be withdrawn. A widow is one thing; a pregnant widow quite another.'

Despair clouded Noella's face. 'You are right, Nina, I know. But what choice do I have? How can I destroy what is surely my only chance to bear a child of my own, no matter what the circumstances of its conception?'

But Nina Repois was more than a match for the crisis that had come upon her so suddenly. 'Noella,' she said urgently, placing a hand on the girl's arm, 'listen to me. If you sincerely wish to have this child, everything can still happen as you plan. All we must do is ensure your pregnancy remains a secret.'

She saw Noella's eyes widen and nodded her head encouragingly. 'Yes, *cherie*, it is possible. You are slim, you can dress to camouflage your condition. And then, in the last two months, you will say you need a rest after the difficulties of the year and come here to stay with me. When I explain the circumstances, Claude Pridoux will deliver the child, I am sure. He is a loyal and trustworthy friend.'

She patted Noella's hand, willing her to accept the ease of the solution. 'The baby is due at Christmas; people will be busy with their own plans. There will be no awkward questions.'

Noella stared at the older woman. Hope was beginning to catch fire inside her. It could work. If she was careful. If the elections being forced on Balo did not occur within the next few months.

It was a risk she had to take.

With a sob of happiness, she threw her arms around her friend. 'Oh Nina, how lucky I am to have you in my life. I'm sure you're right. As long as I can get through these next few months without anyone suspecting, my position will be unchallenged.' Her voice was bright with relief. 'And afterwards, when the baby is born, it won't matter. I will be free to do whatever is required of me.'

Nina held the girl close. She was sure the plan would work.

But the strain of keeping up her usual pace took its toll on Noella. Most evenings, she fell exhausted into bed, asleep almost before her head touched the pillow.

Her regular meetings with Felix and his group continued as before. Hours of fiery discussion had led to the development of overall guidelines for reform, with the economy and social services receiving top priority.

'The US embargo is having the desired effect,' Felix reported to Noella and the serious-faced men who filled his tiny living room. 'The government is beginning to panic. But the tightrope we walk is that the domestic economy will be decimated before Balo is forced to the polls. If that is allowed to happen it will take us decades to recover.'

'Why do the *norteamericanos* not move now?' demanded a small, surly-eyed man. 'We know only too well how an "incident" can be manufactured so that Balo will be pushed to the edge.'

'*Paciencia*, Leon, *paciencia*.' Felix tried to soothe his impetuous colleague. 'We must allow the Kirk administration to handle things their way.'

The small man's mouth twisted in contempt. 'Bah! The gringos always put their own interests first. I say we should take action ourselves — act at once. El Chacal is the one we should turn to. He would know —'

'El Chacal?' Noella looked questioningly at Felix. 'Who is El Chacal? What can he do for the cause?'

'El Chacal is the name given to one of the most daring of the rebel leaders,' Felix explained. 'He is aligned with no political group. His base of support is the ordinary people, those who have lost relatives to Balo's death squads, who have lost their land to the growing needs of the drug barons. He leads a tightly organised band of men and women who regularly engage in terrorist activity against army and government personnel.'

'But who is he?' Noella repeated.

Felix shrugged. 'His real identity is concealed. All that is known is that he lost both his child and pregnant wife in a military action against those who dared to oppose the regime. Since then he has exacted a terrible retribution on Balo's troops. From what I am told, he is one of the most wanted men in Martiguay. The target the army most wants to capture.'

'And I say, El Chacal should be our spearhead in

Martiguay.' The outspoken man waved his hand in the air. 'An all-out terrorist action, supported by the various opposition groups would do more than anything else to make the *bastardos* at the top shit-scared. Then they would very soon agree to a general election.'

'I think, Leon,' Felix gave his agitated colleague a warning look, 'we should talk about more practical matters.'

Noella buttoned the front of her loose-fitting dress.

'Well, doctor?'

Claude Pridoux gave her his usual thin smile as he drew off his surgical gloves. 'Everything is progressing well, madame. The baby is developing as expected.'

Noella was always reassured after her check-ups with Nina's friend and physician. Understanding the need for discretion, Claude Pridoux had agreed to make regular visits to Paris to monitor Noella's pregnancy. On every occasion everything had been completely normal. Noella was especially glad of that verdict today.

'So I shall be able to make the journey to Washington without worry, monsieur?'

Claude Pridoux pursed his lips. 'You have less than ten weeks to go, madame, but . . . if you are careful not to exhaust yourself I see no reason for concern.'

The summons to another meeting in Washington had come just five days earlier and for the first time Noella had felt the beginning of panic.

Surely this did not mean that the plan was about to become operational? A cold knot formed in her belly. Not now, she prayed. Oh, please, God, not now. Not when the child was so close . . .

Noella made the long journey in a state of nervous tension, fearful of what she would learn.

She stayed in another impersonal suite in the same block of apartments, this time on a different floor.

Although she'd been half hoping it might be Richard

who would meet her again at the airport, Noella was relieved rather than disappointed by the two broad-shouldered men who greeted her instead.

What she had had with Richard was over, she told herself. They had made their decision and to meet again would be unbearable for them both.

Noella was ready and waiting when the limousine arrived to take her once more to the White House. Dressing carefully in a softly-fitting dress and long-line jacket, she had nervously checked and rechecked her appearance in the full-length mirror, assuring herself that no one could possibly guess.

This time the meeting was presided over by Ben Christensen, who apologised for Larry Kirk's absence.

'The President is in Japan at present, senora, but he wanted us to meet so we could exchange up-to-date information on the Martiguayan situation.' He handed her a bound report. 'Now, according to our operatives in the field...'

Noella gave no outward sign of her relief. So no major move was imminent. If her luck continued to hold, she would get away with it.

Later, as she was being led back down the broad hallway to her waiting limousine, the aide accompanying her slipped an envelope into her hands.

'Dr Avery asked me to see you got this, senora.' The man's voice was as expressionless as his face. He made it clear he had no curiosity about his task.

'Thank you.' Noella struggled to match his neutral tone but her heart was thundering in her chest.

She opened the note in the privacy of her apartment and read the words of love: '... I shall be out of Washington when you arrive. No doubt that's all for the best, though, God knows, it can't change a thing about the way I feel. It doesn't get any easier, Noella my love.

You are constantly in my thoughts. I shall miss you until my dying day.'

She folded the single sheet of notepaper and sobbed aloud.

With just eight weeks left till her baby's expected arrival, Noella laid the groundwork for her disappearance.

She had no trouble absenting herself from her regular employment. Her commitment to her work had always been total, involving her in long out-of-hours activities. No one begrudged her a protracted vacation — especially after the events of the previous few months.

The *Directeur* had been effusive in his sympathy and understanding. 'You have had a very difficult year personally, senora. Such stress can be extremely debilitating. You must feel free to take all the time you wish to recuperate.'

Felix, too, accepted her explanation without question and with equal sympathy. 'Yes, take the rest you deserve, Noella. You will feel refreshed and strengthened for what lies ahead. The time for action cannot be far away.'

It was with a sense of overwhelming relief that she at last took the train south to await the moment when her child would be born.

To ensure their privacy, Nina had taken a villa in the hills behind the coast. But despite the beauty of her surroundings, the tension of keeping her secret for so long at first made it difficult for Noella to relax.

Then, at the end of the first week, a new mood enveloped her. As she sat out of doors, with the sunshine on her face, enjoying the scent of lavender, basil and thyme that grew in profusion in the villa's garden, she felt imbued with a sense of serenity and peace. She read, chatted with Nina, or merely sat and thought. Those days of waiting were ones of utter contentment.

*

The first movements came late one evening. Noella was prepared, but a little surprised. Claude Pridoux had advised her that first babies were usually late. But not this one, it seemed.

Nina sent at once for her friend and the physician arrived a short time afterwards accompanied by a midwife.

The eccentric rich, insistent on a home birth, Claude Pridoux had offered in explanation to the nurse. The plump, red-haired woman was too engrossed with her preparations to be curious.

Wrapped in an elegant peignoir, her hair pinned up for the night, Nina stood by Noella's bedside during the long hours of the labour.

'*Bon, cherie . . . oui . . .* push a little harder now . . . just a little harder.' Dabbing a lavender-scented towel to Noella's damp forehead, the older woman whispered encouragement as the doctor and midwife monitored the baby's progress.

Claude Pridoux had begun to worry that perhaps a Caesarean might be called for when just ten minutes later, the slippery, wriggling infant made its entry into the world.

'*Un fils!* A son! You have a healthy son, madame!' The midwife cried out in pleasure as she quickly wiped the whimpering child and wrapping it in soft muslin, placed it in its mother's arms.

Tears of joy sprang into Noella's eyes as she held her new-born baby close against her nakedness. Euphoria and wonder filled her heart. Her son. Her child.

Turning her head on the sweat-stained pillow, Noella raised her eyes to Nina's. Nina was staring at the baby, incredulous. Noella smiled. She would explain later. When they were alone.

Explain how she had come to give birth to a child with bright blue eyes and soft golden hair . . .

CHAPTER THIRTY-ONE

Lieutenant Alfonse Marchez held his rifle loosely across his knee as the jeep bounced over the narrow jungle track. His was the lead vehicle; a second jeep followed, and two others brought up the rear behind the three canvas-covered trucks whose cargo the soldiers had been sent to protect.

Marchez squinted against the smoke curling from the cigarette that dangled from his lips and surveyed the thick undergrowth around him. He was alert but not unduly anxious. This job was easy compared to some of the things he'd been ordered to do back in the capital.

He took extra comfort from the knowledge that El Chacal had never been known to penetrate this far south. In the last few months the most wanted man in Martiguay had launched a ruthless campaign against the industry whose output did so much to keep the government of Rodriguez Balo in office.

In a series of well-planned, lightning manoeuvres, El Chacal and his supporters had struck ruthlessly at the convoys taking the white powder to the coast for export. As a result, dozens of army personnel had been killed, and their dangerous cargoes destroyed.

Suppressing a shudder, Alfonse Marchez tossed away his butt. *Gracias a Dios* El Chacal was hundreds of kilometres away.

The first shot caught the lieutenant in the upper chest.

Instinctively he threw himself sideways into the under-growth at the side of the track as a deafening volley of shots exploded around him.

Terrified, in agony, the young soldier flattened himself against the leafy dampness as, seconds later, a massive blast threw the heavily-laden trucks high into the air.

Alfonse Marchez was vaguely aware of the weak return of fire from his own men before he lost consciousness.

The men emerged cautiously from the surrounding jungle. There was a strong stench of burning rubber and oil, and a soft mist of cordite hung over the scene of the massacre.

They watched as their leader pulled aside the torn canvas cover of one of the overturned trucks, ignoring the bleeding corpse that hung headfirst out of the driver's window.

'You see?' El Chacal kicked angrily at the plastic-wrapped packets of cocaine. 'You see how they defile Martiguay and its people with their trade? Every month they grow more powerful, filling Balo's pockets and needing him less and less . . .' Contemptuously, the man with the disfigured face spun on his heel. 'Destroy it!' he ordered curtly.

As he strode away he heard the groan. It came from the undergrowth to his left. He gestured to one of his men, and together they pushed through the bushes to find the source of the noise.

'A *soldado*. He is still alive,' the rebel announced.

Impassively, El Chacal looked down at the young man whose torn and bloodied uniform still carried the stripes of lieutenant.

Stark terror showed in Alfonse Marchez's eyes as El Chacal calmly levelled his revolver and fired.

*

Three hours later the dozen footsore men regrouped at their base camp in a remote mountainous area to the north. As they squatted on the stony ground their fatigue was offset by the euphoria of a mission successfully accomplished.

Gradually, over the preceding few weeks, the optimism of the rebel cell had been growing stronger. Their information told them that the situation in Martiguay was changing at last. The US economic sanctions had had their effect: inflation had doubled to a record high, and now the slump in world coffee prices had brought the Martiguayan economy to the edge.

The Balo government was in a panic, divided, chaotic — it was only a matter of time before Balo bowed to the international pressure to hold a free election. His record on human rights abuse and his close links with the powerful drug barons meant he had little hope of surviving a democratically conducted poll.

The man they called El Chacal was pondering these points as he ate his simple meal of rice and beans. It was an open secret who would stand against Balo. After months of rumours it had been confirmed that the daughter of the assassinated President Victor de Bartez was the agreed opposition candidate.

What worried El Chacal most was that by now Balo too must have heard the rumours, must know that despite his certain attempts to manipulate the polls, he would stand little chance against a candidate bearing the name de Bartez.

El Chacal was certain that the life of Noella de Bartez was in mortal danger.

Noella glanced surreptitiously at her watch. The meeting had run well over time and she was aching to get away. Time was so precious these days.

Finally, to her relief, the *Directeur* wound up his

report on the fate of the Chilean detainee whose case they had agreed to take on.

While the other committee members stretched and slowly pushed back their seats, Noella was already snapping closed her briefcase, saying her speedy farewells...

'Please excuse me, everyone,' she smiled distractedly at her colleagues. 'I have another appointment this evening...'

Fifteen minutes later, having opted for the Metro rather than a taxi in the face of the usual Friday evening traffic snarl, she let herself into the apartment. It had two bedrooms, was close to the Bois, and had replaced the Hotel Charles V for Nina's regular trips to the capital.

'She's here! You see, I told you, Mama is here.'

Nina greeted Noella with a smile, as she bounced the child gently in her arms, murmuring soothingly to him as his mother tossed aside her briefcase and threw off her coat.

And then, her face aglow with joy and relief, Noella reached out for her baby son. 'Oh, my darling. My sweetest Alessandro. How I have longed for this moment...'

He came easily to her, his face wreathed in smiles, his blue eyes bright with pleasure and recognition. He had the unmistakable colouring of his Danish ancestry...

Holding her four month old son close, Noella rubbed her cheek against the soft golden fuzz on his head, gave him feathery kisses wherever she saw bare flesh.

'You have not forgotten me yet then, little Sandro? You still are happy to see your Mama?'

When at last she had assuaged some of her longing, she raised her head, her mouth curved with tenderness. 'He looks so well, Nina. So healthy and happy.'

Nina looked fondly at mother and child. 'He is eating like a baby rhinoceros, Noella. In the last two weeks alone he has put on almost a kilo.'

Noella gave her friend a long grateful look. 'You

have been wonderful, Nina. I miss him dreadfully but I know that with you he is well looked after.'

The older woman's eyes grew gentle as she said softly, 'He has brought me a joy I never expected at this time of my life, Noella. Little Sandro has made up for the children I could never have.'

Everything had worked as they'd planned. For the first three weeks after the birth, Noella had stayed with her baby, attempting to come to terms with the shock of his obvious paternity.

When she had first held her newborn son in her arms she had seemed almost delirious with joy, proclaiming laughingly to Nina, 'Do you know, they say when a woman loves a man enough, the child always looks like the father!'

But her euphoria was short-lived. With a sickening jolt Noella suddenly realised what Nina had seen from the start . . .

'I never dreamed it could be Richard's child, Nina!' Noella was swept with relief at finally being able to tell her friend about the man she loved.

'Never in my wildest fantasies did the thought occur to me. When I realised I was pregnant, it was only the memory of that terrible night with Daniel that stayed in the forefront of my mind . . . And now,' she laughed bitterly, 'the indisputable fact that Alessandro is obviously not my husband's child means he must be hidden away, kept a secret so I can carry out the role my country demands of me.'

Her dark, tragic eyes brimmed with tears and suddenly she was sobbing against Nina's breast. 'I'll never be able to call him my son. It's too high a price, Nina . . . Too high a price!'

★

But somehow Noella had once more found the strength and faith she needed to face the future. For the present, her anguish at being separated from the son she adored, her fear of not knowing how long she must continue to conceal his existence, were submerged in the vision she had carried in her heart for so long. To avenge the murders of her family, to seek freedom and honour for her countrymen — that was her mission.

Afterwards, she thought, her eyes blank with unhappiness, she would think about the problem of Alessandro...

For the benefit of her friends and neighbours, Nina had kept the story simple.

Such 'tragic circumstances', she explained, seeming so utterly bereft that none of the elegant, well-mannered widows felt any inclination to press the matter. Her godchild... three days from giving birth... a terrible automobile accident which had killed the poor husband outright and taken the mother's life a mere four hours after the child was safely delivered. A tragedy beyond all bearing, Nina had declared... and with no one else to help, it had been only fitting that she step in and do her duty. After all, she was fit and in excellent health; why should she not think to raise the child?

Anyway, she shrugged, wouldn't it give her something better to do than walking her spoilt dogs and playing endless games of cards...?

The weekend, as always, passed too quickly for Noella. Simple pleasures that most mothers took so much for granted were, for her, moments of intense happiness.

Hair tucked under a scarf, eyes shaded by dark glasses, she pushed Sandro's pram slowly along the shaded paths of the Bois. She and Nina indulged in the sort of chatter common to doting mothers, aunts, and grandmothers. 'He is so beautiful'... 'Look at the intelligence in those eyes' ... 'I'm certain the little *mignon* knows exactly every word we're saying' ... For Noella it was a complete escape from the increasingly pressing matters that were shaping her future.

On the Sunday afternoon, as she watched Nina's car disappear into the traffic for the long journey home, her sense of emptiness and loss was overwhelming.

As she turned away, her lips moved in a silent prayer. *'Dios, make it all worth it. Please, please, make it worth this terrible pain.'*

The telephone was ringing as she let herself into her own apartment.

'Senora de Bartez?'

The call was from Washington. 'One moment please, senora.' An official-sounding male voice. 'I have Mr Christensen on the line.'

The telephone emphasised the CIA director's Texan accent. 'Senora! ... I have been trying to get you all weekend.'

'I —'

But Noella was spared her explanation.

'There's great news. On Friday evening, Balo finally made it official. Martiguayans will go to the polls in free elections.'

Noella felt her heart begin to race. 'When?'

'Six weeks from yesterday.'

CHAPTER THIRTY-TWO

The meeting took place in the ruins of an old windmill. The surrounding countryside was bare and flat, minimising the risk of an ambush.

The *gringo* was accompanied by one of the very few men El Chacal trusted implicitly. It was the only reason he had agreed to the meeting.

Jose Tristano held out his hand to the rebel leader. He was a bear of a man with a head of thick grey hair and a nose that dominated his craggy features. The local schoolteacher, he was also the organiser of a strong resistance cell, and underneath his coarse shirt his back and chest still bore the scars of torture by Balo's terror squads. Only by finally convincing the soldiers that he was a simple country bumpkin who knew nothing had he managed to escape death.

Now he introduced El Chacal to the sharp-eyed, athletic-looking *norteamericano* by his side. 'Steve Burgess, *comandante*. He speaks Spanish, of course.'

The American did his best to hide his reaction as he took in the shattered face. My God. He'd been warned, of course, but nothing could have prepared him for the reality. And the bomb had taken out his wife and kid too... No wonder the poor bastard was fearless in his opposition to Balo. Burgess took the extended hand in his own. El Chacal was just the man they were looking for...

While the young armed guards kept watch, the

American outlined his mission, explained why the CIA had sought out El Chacal.

'I am sure you understand that the US can't be seen to be supporting or aiding Senora de Bartez in any way. It'd give Balo the perfect excuse to say we were trying to rig the elections. But our sources tell us that he's well aware she's his most serious rival — and he'll do everything possible to keep her from returning to Martiguay. If she tries to re-enter the country legally he can find loopholes — accuse her, for instance, of being affiliated with subversive overseas groups. The only option is to arrange for her to re-enter Martiguay secretly and conduct a lightning campaign around the country, keeping one step ahead of government troops.'

Burgess looked at the man who was squatting in the dirt beside him. 'I am sure, *comandante*, you understand what I am leading up to. Balo wouldn't dare to try anything in Paris, but here, in Martiguay, the senora will require a protector, someone to ensure she is not endangered by Balo's terror squads; someone who will help her move quickly and secretly from town to town, and keep her safe until polling day.' The American sat back on his heels. 'We acknowledge, of course, your non-political stand, *comandante*, but hope you will undertake this mission for all Martiguayans.'

For a long moment, El Chacal was silent. Then, at last, he spoke. 'I will be honoured to help, senor. But one condition must apply.'

He told the surprised American what it was.

The telex from Steve Burgess was waiting on Richard's desk when he arrived at his office the following morning.

As he read it, Richard felt relief spread through his body. El Chacal had agreed. Noella now had at least a fighting chance.

The daring and ruthless raids against Balo's troops by the rebel leader and his men had been well documented for Washington and the idea had been developing in Richard's mind for a while. Who else would know the country so intimately? Who else could give Noella such vital and effective protection? The CIA, no matter how capable, would be no match for the jungle-trained locals.

Luckily, President Kirk had agreed. 'I see what you're getting at, Richard.' He pressed his palms together and held his fingers against his lips. 'This rebel leader, you think, could provide the means of smuggling de Bartez into Martiguay and then conjointly with the CIA offer her the protection she will certainly need.'

Larry Kirk turned to Ben Christensen. 'Sounds okay to me, Ben. Can you see any problems?'

'Not from where I'm sittin'.'

In the end, Noella had to leave her office early. Telephone calls from the press were driving her crazy. The news that General Rodriguez Balo was being forced to call Martiguay's first free elections in more than a decade had made the headlines, and journalists everywhere wanted the reaction of the politically astute daughter of the last democratically elected President. The gossip press, too, were eager to pick up the story. For them, the glamorous daughter of Catherine Campion and Victor de Bartez had never lost her appeal.

When she stepped out on the street, Noella got further reminders of the overwhelming interest she held for the media.

'Madame! *S'il vous plait.*'

'Noella! Your comments please!'

'Senora de Bartez, what are the chances Martiguay will have a democratic government in less than six weeks?'

Microphones were pushed in her face, flashbulbs popped, and television cameramen followed her as she tried to force her way through the milling mob.

'Madame, are the rumours true that you are a possible candidate in the forthcoming elections?' A tall, hard-eyed reporter asked the question.

Noella was not caught off guard. She had been warned that the press might start to sniff out the story.

A taxi was pulling up to allow its passenger to disembark.

'No comment,' she replied tersely as she jumped into the cab and slammed the door behind her.

It was important they keep Balo on knife-edge as long as possible.

Back in the relative sanctuary of her apartment, Noella placed a call to Nina.

The older woman knew that events were now moving quickly. 'But you must see Sandro before you leave, Noella.' Her voice was sharp with concern. 'Shall I bring him to Paris again this weekend?'

'Nina, it is impossible. The press have me under almost constant scrutiny.' Noella felt drained, torn by conflicting emotions. 'I have just ten days to finalise things here before I must leave for Martiguay. But somehow, whatever happens, I will find a way to see you both one more time. Believe me.'

Ten days.

That was all they could give her, Felix had explained at the emergency meeting after Balo's official announcement of the polling date. At the same meeting, Noella had been introduced to Jack Tailor, another of Ben Christensen's men, who had told her of the audacious plan to smuggle her into Martiguay.

'The rebel leader has agreed to work with us in assuring your protection as you move around the country, senora. Already the campaign brochures and pamphlets are rolling off the opposition printing presses and once any of those fall into government hands, Balo will know with certainty what he is up against.' Jack Tailor could hardly hide his sense of satisfaction at the ease and speed with which the operation was being put into force.

Noella's excitement mixed with apprehension as she listened to the plans that were being made for her future. A future that did not — could not — include her child.

And then the event occurred which might have taken her from Sandro for ever . . .

BOOK **THREE**

CHAPTER **THIRTY-THREE**

'I — I don't understand...'

With one hand on her elbow, the man with the disfigured face was moving her swiftly through the curious onlookers.

'Do you mean it wasn't an accident? That they were trying to...' Her voice trailed off. She didn't want to believe how close she had come to death. Felix had been right...

'Senora, you allow that we speak Spanish?' The crowd was beginning to disperse and he stopped beside her on the sidewalk.

Noella nodded, beginning to regather her composure.

Suddenly she swung round at the sound of her name. It was Felix, ashen-faced, hurrying towards her.

'Noella!' He was out of breath. 'I was watching... I saw what happened. You —' He broke off, noticing for the first time the man with the eye patch who stood protectively beside her.

His flinch at the disfigurement was barely noticeable before Felix Noverro's mouth widened into a smile of relief. 'So, senor, already you have saved us from disaster.'

Noella stared from one to the other of the men. Her bewilderment was obvious.

Felix was delighted to explain. 'Noella, this is the man who will see you safely ensconced in the Presidential Palace. We know him only as El Chacal.'

*

Jack Tailor's face was thunderous. He had rushed to Felix's apartment as soon as he'd been told the news.

'*Goddamn it!*' He slammed his fist into the open palm of his other hand. 'It was always a possibility, but we never thought they'd try it here! I mean, they don't even know for certain yet that you *are* their opposition.'

'The rumours have been circulating for weeks in Martiguay, senor. Men like Carlos Olivero do not take chances.' El Chacal spoke quietly but his eyes reflected his disapproval.

From the moment he had agreed to safeguard the opposition candidate, he had insisted that his protection must begin from the moment Rodriguez Balo called the election. The *gringos* had been sceptical but now, El Chacal thought, his caution had surely been vindicated.

Tailor stared sourly at the rebel leader. He didn't like making mistakes. And underestimating the tentacles of Martiguay's most powerful drug baron, Carlos Olivero, had certainly been a mistake. But, he thought irritably, he didn't need to be reminded of it by this hick dude, no matter how subtly.

Noting the American's annoyance, Felix said soothingly, 'All has ended safely for the moment. But this incident must surely bring home to all of us the ruthlessness of our opponents.'

He turned to where Noella sat listening, her hands cupped around a small glass of brandy. 'You see now, Noella, that my fears were not without basis. Will you swear that from now on you will go nowhere without protection?'

For a moment she didn't answer. Slowly she looked from one to another of the three men. Her eyes came to rest on the man who had saved her life and for a moment Noella felt the mesmerising effect of that single glittering eye.

She nodded her head. 'Yes, Felix, I promise.'

But regardless of the risk, she told herself, nothing was going to stop her saying farewell to her son.

During the next few frantic days, Noella did her best to avoid the press as she finalised her affairs in Paris. Her departure from the Institute for the Release of Political Detainees was low-key. There was an unspoken agreement amongst her colleagues that the resignation of their most high-profile employee would be kept secret from the media as long as possible. While Noella had never once hinted at her plans for the future, it was obvious to those who now wished her well that the rumours which had been circulating for the past weeks must be true.

'Our prayers will be with you, Noella.' The *Directeur's* sincerity was obvious. 'We hope with all our hearts that you are given the chance you deserve to play your part in your country's history.'

And when she walked out of the building for the last time, there, waiting for her as always, was the man who had sworn to protect her.

In just a few days, Noella had come not only to accept El Chacal's presence, but to appreciate the force of his personality. There was a magnetism and cool self-confidence about the rebel leader that allowed one almost to forget the shattered nightmare of his face. As she listened to his views on the current situation in Martiguay, Noella found herself increasingly drawn to trusting his judgement and clear-sighted perceptions. She knew that he would be a first-rate ally in her campaign to topple Balo — for El Chacal was a man who understood the hearts and minds of the people.

But... would he understand what she had to ask of him now?

His face betrayed no emotion as she explained her

request as they made their way back to her apartment. 'This is the one final thing I must do before I leave, senor. They are... very good friends, people who have shown me great kindness during my years in France.' She could feel his scrutiny as he walked beside her and a faint flush came to her cheeks. 'Felix Noverro is fearful for my safety — which is only to be expected — but with you by my side I know I will have nothing to worry about. Please,' she tried to keep the desperate need from her voice, 'please say you will do this for me.'

El Chacal saw the colour in her cheeks. His instincts told him at once that she was lying. But why? 'You are perfectly certain these people you wish to see can be trusted, senora?'

Noella nodded, keeping her eyes on the avenue in front of her. 'Yes, senor, perfectly certain.'

The next moment she did her best to hide her relief, as El Chacal agreed to her request.

For added safety they drove instead of taking the train. As they sped along the autoroute south, Noella at the wheel, there was little conversation between them. Noella was relieved. Her emotions were at fever pitch as she fought to brace herself for the dreadful moment to come. Beside her, the Martiguayan seemed equally lost in thought.

At last they arrived at the tall, wrought-iron gates that led into the villa grounds. As she switched off the engine, Noella took a deep breath. This was the only dangerous moment...

She turned to the man beside her. 'Senor, I must ask that you wait for me here. I wish to say goodbye to my friends in private.' She saw his sudden frown and hurried on. 'I promise you I will come to no harm inside these gates. Give me one hour, that is all I ask. Just one hour.'

He seemed to hesitate but then to Noella's

overwhelming relief, El Chacal nodded. '*Bueno*, senora. Just one hour.'

Nina was waiting in the garden at the rear of the house. Try as she might, she couldn't keep the shakiness from her voice as she greeted Noella.

'*Cherie* . . . at last. I was so afraid.'

Noella hugged her close. 'I told you I would make it, Nina.'

And then her darling Sandro was in her arms, heavy now at over six months, his golden curls shining in the sunshine, and a smile of delight creasing his chubby face.

Swallowing hard, Noella held him tightly against her breast. *Dios . . . Dios . . .*

'Come, *cherie*,' Nina put a gentle hand on her shoulder. 'Have some coffee with me; I have a fresh pot ready.'

Noella nodded, not daring to speak as she placed her baby son on the rug by her feet. They had an hour. She could not waste it with useless tears.

'When do you leave?' Nina asked as she handed a fine porcelain cup to her friend.

'In two days' time. We fly first to Florida and then a small reconnaissance plane will take us to a covert airstrip just north of the Martiguayan border. When it is dark we will make our way through the patrols.'

Nina paled. 'It is the only way?'

'The only way,' Noella repeated. 'But I am in safe hands, Nina, I assure you.' Without mentioning the attempt on her life, she explained about El Chacal. 'He is a patriot, Nina. His men will be my escorts as I speak to the people. You must not worry too much.'

It was hot in the sunshine and El Chacal was restless as he leaned against the car. But it was a restlessness caused by more than the heat.

He had vowed to protect her, ensure her safety. Now he had let her out of his sight.

Despite her assurances, how could he be sure there was no danger behind these gates? The net of Carlos Olivero was spread wide. Even the gringos had to see that now.

With a sudden resolution, El Chacal decided he could not merely stand and wait. He had to see for himself that she was all right.

'Oh, Nina, how am I going to bear it?' Noella whispered, as she buried her face against her son's sweet-smelling hair. Her heart was breaking as the time came to say her final goodbye. She had thought that leaving Richard was the hardest thing she had ever had to do — but this was harder still.

'You — you will do it because you must, Noella. Because of the suffering and the evil that have poisoned your father's dreams.' The older woman's voice broke with emotion. 'And you must believe that one day the time will surely come when your son can openly be part of your life.'

Lifting her head, Noella struggled for control. 'You are right, Nina. If I achieve my goal then I must find a way to have my son accepted by my side. But,' her voice wavered as tears rolled down her cheeks, 'if — if anything happens to me I know that he will have you, that you will love him as if he were your own.'

But he will never know his mother . . .

The thought cut into her brain as she held her son's warm sturdy body against her own for what might be the last time.

From where he stood, hidden by the bushes at the garden's edge, El Chacal felt the breath freeze in his throat.

A child. There was a child.

A son no one ever dreamed existed.

And even a man with only one eye could see that it carried not a drop of Daniel Jarro's blood . . .

CHAPTER **THIRTY-FOUR**

After so long she had almost forgotten the intensity of the tropical heat. As the aeroplane door was slid back, it invaded the tiny cabin, catching in her nostrils, wrapping itself around her like a thick, stifling blanket.

Hands reached out to help and next moment Noella was standing on the rough bitumen of the hidden airstrip. In the faint light of a crescent moon she could see the encroaching jungle just metres away.

'*Buenos noches*, senora. You okay?' The American accent was unmistakable but the darkness permitted only a vague impression of the speaker. Tall, broad-shouldered, light-coloured hair.

'*Si*.'

El Chacal had dropped down beside her, and as the second American slammed the aircraft door, Noella felt overwhelmed by a sense of unreality. Who would have dreamed that this was how she would return to Martiguay . . . that so much would have changed in the years since she'd left?

'Quickly!' One of the men put a hand on her elbow and hurried her to the edge of the trees, while on the runway the engines of the craft that had brought them from Florida burst once more into life.

The two Americans took them the short distance to the Martiguayan border.

While they waited with Noella in the blackness of

the trees, El Chacal moved cautiously forward. Cupping a hand to his mouth, he gave the prearranged signal. Seconds later the sound was repeated from somewhere on his right and he hurried back to the others.

'All is well. My men are waiting.'

The taller American nodded into the darkness. 'Good.' He turned to Noella. 'We can go no further, senora, but you are in safe hands. Good luck and *vaya con Dios*.'

Her mission had begun.

There were six in the advance party who had come to meet them. Young, lean, hard-faced men who carried their weapons in readiness, alert for any sound that might mean a border patrol.

They moved rapidly through the dense undergrowth, and dressed in shirt, pants, and heavy boots, Noella was soon sweating freely. Insects tormented her bare flesh, branches whipped her face, and her muscles were aching with the unaccustomed exertion.

When, after an hour, they stopped for a short rest, El Chacal put an anxious hand on her arm. 'You are able to keep up this pace, senora?'

Breathing heavily, Noella nodded her head. She knew that the first stage of their plan meant regrouping with El Chacal's supporters in an area not far from where she would meet with the major opposition figures. It was essential they reached there before daybreak.

'Yes,' she managed, feeling the sticky dampness of the shirt against her back, the beginning of a blister on her heel, despite the thick socks. She forced a smile. 'I am fine.'

They were less than an hour from their destination when suddenly the advance scout heard the noise.

He froze, and behind him the others followed suit.

Noella's heart hammered in her chest as the signal was given to drop to the ground.

At once El Chacal was by her side, pulling her backwards beneath a canopy of leaves.

His mouth was close to her ear. 'It is sure to be a patrol. Balo's men. They know the resistance groups move by night and are always on the look-out.'

Pressed against the hard, damp ground Noella held her breath as the sound of movement grew closer. *Dios*, she prayed, keep us safe . . . do not let them find us.

Footsteps. A muttered oath. A stifled cough. The soldiers passed so close that a whiff of pungent cigarette smoke reached Noella's nostrils.

Beside her, she could feel the warmth of El Chacal's body and suddenly realised how dependent she had become on this man for the success of her mission. His knowledge and cunning were her only defence against the forces that threatened her.

And then the sounds were receding as the soldiers moved past their hiding place. Relief poured back into her body and Noella began to breathe again.

El Chacal helped her to her feet. 'God is on our side once more, senora.' She saw the quick flash of his teeth before he turned and once more set a rapid pace through the jungle.

The rest of El Chacal's men — about a dozen in all — were waiting at the camp they had set up in the rocky foothills. To Noella's relief she was allowed some rest before meeting with the opposition leaders who were being brought there. She felt utterly exhausted after the non-stop, four-hour march to the rebels' base and as soon as she lay down on the narrow bunk in the rough lean-to that had been prepared for her, she fell into a deep sleep.

It was El Chacal himself who woke her, shaking her gently until she opened her eyes. Blinking against the sunlight, still not fully awake, Noella felt a moment's wild panic. Where...? Who...?

Then she recognised that shattered face and reality returned.

'There is warm water here to bathe with, senora.' El Chacal spoke softly, indicating the basin he had brought. 'When you are ready, the others are waiting to meet you.'

As he rose to his feet and left her to wash, Noella wondered at how so ruthless a man could also be so gentle.

There were seven of them. Seven Martiguayans, all of whom had relinquished their hope of leadership to a woman who bore the name de Bartez.

As they talked, Noella studied each face in turn, searching for signs of resentment or dislike. If they were there, she thought, they were well hidden. Differences had been put aside in this all-out, last-ditch attempt to end the dictatorship of Rodriguez Balo.

As she listened, Noella realised how thoroughly the ground had been prepared for her return. Washington had worked hard behind the scenes — compromises on the agenda for reform had been reached amongst the various groups, and the machinery was in place for her campaign to begin at once.

But she was left in no doubt of what she was up against.

'Balo is determined to retain power — but he is just a figurehead.' The speaker was Arno Mazar, a tall, slightly-built man who had been a mayor of one of the northern provinces during Noella's father's Presidency.

'The source of real control,' Mazar continued, 'lies with the drug cartels — and in particular with Carlos Olivero. At his fortress in the south, protected by his own private army, he carries out his evil trade with complete immunity. Balo is his puppet and the elections will change nothing if Olivero has his way. The so-called "opposition" candidates have all been hand-picked by Balo himself. He intends to use these "democratically conducted" elections merely to establish a legitimate base to his power.'

'But the people are not fools,' another of the group cut in. 'They know what the government is trying to do. Yet even the presence of UN observers can do nothing to alter this subversion. That is why it is vital to present Martiguayans with a legitimate choice, an opposition leader they can be assured has no links to the regime or the drug cartels who support it.' The man gave Noella a piercing look. 'No one would doubt the integrity of a candidate who carried the name de Bartez.'

Humbled by such obvious respect, Noella at the same time felt proud at the reverence shown to her family name. It merely served to emphasise the enormous responsibility that now rested on her.

The one task left to accomplish was to decide on a name for the opposition coalition. A vote was taken and Noella given veto. The choice was unanimous. Noella would head the National Salvation Front.

When the meeting finally broke up, each of the seven men shook Noella's hand and wished her luck. Arno Mazar, the former mayor, was the last to say goodbye.

'You have just under four weeks to reach the people, senora — and your task is made harder by the law which forbids the gathering of more than five citizens in any one place.' He squeezed her hand. 'We pray that with El Chacal's help, you will be able to stay out of reach of Balo's forces until it is too late. Our country's future depends on it.'

'And our children's future,' answered Noella softly.

The news spread like wildfire around the large provincial township.

From shops and factories, schools and warehouses,

offices and homes, people came in curious anticipatory droves.

'Noella de Bartez!'

'Speaking at twelve noon at Lazon Park!'

'Standing as an opposition candidate!'

On the raised platform, under a grimy square of tarpaulin which offered sketchy shade, Noella addressed the crowd. Her voice was distorted by the old-fashioned p.a. system, but the message she conveyed was unmistakable.

'My fellow Martiguayans . . . the time has come to win back our country! To dispose of the corrupt and unjust, the murderers and thieves who have robbed us of our freedom and opportunities, and taken the lives of those we loved.'

Oblivious to the sweat beading her face, Noella looked out at the gathering crowd, saw the stunned looks and the growing excitement.

'Now is the time for Martiguay to rise from the ashes of the past! As the leader of the National Salvation Front, the only true opposition to the forces of the dictator Balo, let me outline the plan that will feed our poor, educate our children, save our sick and despairing, bring justice to our oppressed . . .'

And under the blazing heat of the noonday sun, while her supporters moved among the crowd distributing the pamphlets outlining her platform, Noella de Bartez spoke with a passion that electrified her listeners, that kept them motionless and silent until her final sentence.

'So, my fellow Martiguayans, do not be afraid for the future. Have faith. Believe with all your hearts that this time our country will find its way out of the wilderness of the past . . . That the success and prosperity, the peace and equality all Martiguayans dream of will no longer be denied them!'

The reaction was tumultuous. After years of fear

and suppression, Martiguayans had at last found reason to hope. The crowd surged around the stage, chanting Noella's name over and over again, cheering and clapping as the symbol of their hope tried to make her exit.

'*De Bartez . . . de Bartez . . . de Bartez . . .*!' The chant filled the air as an exhilarated Noella finally reached the dusty car that awaited her.

'Quickly!' El Chacal slammed the door behind them. Half a dozen of his men, weapons at the ready, were in the accompanying escort vehicles. 'We have had word that the soldiers are already on their way.'

With a wild blaring of the horn, the driver forced the car through the ecstatic crowd, heading for the road that led out of town.

Over the ensuing days, Noella addressed her countrymen in a multitude of towns and villages. The reaction was always the same. Joy, hope, excitement. In the National Salvation Front and its charismatic leader the people saw that they had a real choice at last. The sham election that Balo and his evil supporters had felt sure would entrench their power was now threatened with an unequivocal challenge.

By the end of that first week, government troops were out in force with orders to arrest Noella de Bartez on sight. The charges: illegal entry and subversion.

But always, thanks to the cunning and expert tactics of El Chacal and his men, Noella managed to avoid detection. Her seemingly random schedule of appearances meant the soldiers never knew where she would appear next.

It was a punishing program and at night, in the safe houses of supporters, Noella fell into exhausted sleep.

It was at such a house, a few days later, that she had a happy surprise.

'You are about to be reunited with an old friend,

senora.' El Chacal broke the news only moments before they arrived at the solitary stone villa. 'She has been a brave supporter of the opposition forces for a long time; in fact the local underground printing presses are set up in the basement of this house.'

Noella had little time to wonder about the identity of her host — for as the car pulled up at the entrance to the rambling shabby building, she saw who was waiting for her.

'Inez! Oh, Inez!'

Flinging open the car door, Noella bounded up the steps and the next moment the two women were in each other's arms, laughing and crying at once, kissing and hugging, each starting to speak and interrupting the other.

'Oh, Inez! I am so glad to see you!' Noella smiled through her tears. 'I couldn't write to let you know. It was too dangerous. If the letter had gone astray...' She looked at the woman who had been so like a mother to her. The years, the tragedies, had taken their toll. Inez was frighteningly thin, her dark eyes appearing over-large in her pale, pinched face. Once always so elegant, her looks no longer seemed a priority. Gray peppered her flame-coloured hair, and the plain cotton shift hung loosely on her narrow frame.

Swallowing her own emotion, Inez Sarandon nodded as she gripped the girl's hands between her own. 'I know, my dear. I know it was impossible for you to write. But you see, I knew what was being planned. I knew you were about to fulfil your destiny.' Her eyes brimmed with tears and her voice broke. 'He would have been so proud, Noella. So desperately, wonderfully proud.'

Later, when the house was silent, with the guards posted in the grounds and the others gone to bed, the two women sat in the sparsely furnished parlour and Inez spoke of the terrible night which had changed all their lives.

'Oh, Noella, it was such a tragedy. For both of us. I tried to convince Victor to take an escort that night but all he wanted to do was reach you as quickly as possible. He was so repentant, my dear, so ashamed that he had connived in arranging the marriage. He blamed himself and suddenly seemed to realise how, subconsciously, he had punished you over the years — punished an innocent child for his loss. All he wanted was to hear you say that you forgave him . . . Oh, Noella,' she looked up and even in the dim light the pain was obvious in her eyes, 'we have both lost so much.'

'Yes we have, Inez.' Noella nodded gravely. 'No one can deny that. But the time for despair is over. What I am about to achieve will mean that the lives of Gabrielle and Roberto and my father were not lived in vain.'

The older woman stared at her, heard the conviction and strength in her voice. The reality of how much Noella had changed was brought home to her then. All trace of the insecure child was gone and in her place was a woman of supreme confidence and ability. A woman who believed in herself and all she stood for.

The next morning they left just before dawn. As she gulped down the cup of strong black coffee Inez had prepared, Noella had time to ask about the fate of her brother-in-law.

Inez's face grew troubled. 'Eugene is a broken man, Noella. He never really recovered from the death of Gabrielle and his son. For a short time he was imprisoned, but they soon saw there was nothing to fear from a man in his condition. From what I hear he needs drugs to sleep, to wake, to eat . . . And his job was gone too, of course. How could he work with the corrupt judiciary with which Balo surrounded himself? Since I left town and moved out here, I have seen little of him. I hear he is doing some private tutoring of pupils in his apartment but his heavy drinking may soon end even that.'

The assassins' bullets have changed all our lives, thought Noella, as she gently kissed Inez goodbye.

'When next we are together, Inez, it shall be in the Presidential Palace.'

Inez looked up into that confident, beautiful face. 'I pray that will be so, Noella. But do not underestimate the ruthlessness of our enemies.'

As they drove away from the house, the pewter sky was tinted with the pink of dawn. Noella sat silently in the back seat, El Chacal beside her.

Later, she thought.

Later, I will tell Inez about the miracle of Sandro . . .

CHAPTER **THIRTY-FIVE**

General Rodriguez Balo could smell his own sweat as his official car was halted once again. Being summonsed to this meeting with Carlos Olivero was bad enough; now, he was forced to suffer not only the indignity of leaving his personal bodyguards at the entrance to the drug baron's compound but also the humiliation of constant security checks.

His lips tightened under the pencil-thin moustache. Couldn't the *bastardos* see who he was? Didn't they recognise his face? His official photograph was pasted all over Martiguay.

Rodriguez Balo's odour problem worsened as the cold-eyed guard peered wordlessly into the car, the barrel of his automatic weapon only inches away from the Martiguayan leader's right testicle.

Satisfied at last, the armed man gave a grunt and waved them on their way.

With a muttered oath, the general sank back into his seat. Taking out a handkerchief, he unbuttoned the middle two buttons of his uniform jacket and, trying to avoid scrutiny in the rear vision mirror, surreptitiously wiped his armpits. Despite their close liaison this was his first visit to Olivero's home; he didn't want to arrive stinking like a pig.

The two further security checks as they continued along the sealed road did nothing to improve Rodriguez Balo's nerves or temper. But then suddenly, there in front of them, was the house.

Fortress might have been a more apt description, the general thought, as he took in the central tower, look-out post, and the windowless stone walls. To the right he could see Olivero's private landing strip: a helicopter stood in readiness on the tarmac while the open hangar doors revealed two private jets.

Tall, metal gates led into a vast, tiled courtyard where fountains splashed in the sunlight. As his car came to a halt, General Rodriguez Balo arranged his features into a bland smile of greeting.

He needn't have bothered. Olivero was not there to meet him. Instead, a swarthy-faced manservant as uncommunicative as the rest of the drug baron's employees showed him into the house, down a maze of corridors, past an art collection whose worth Rodriguez Balo could only gasp at, and into an antique-filled room of massive proportions. The floor to ceiling windows looked out over an artificial lake extravagantly scattered with flamingoes.

But Balo was in no mood to appreciate the view. He was dreading this meeting with Olivero, dreading having to report that his men had failed. Despite all their efforts, Noella de Bartez was still at large, free to roam the countryside and cause untold damage to his government's well-laid plans for re-election.

Pacing restlessly, the general waited for the man whose patronage had supported him so effectively for so long. He couldn't say when exactly the balance of their relationship had tilted — he wasn't quite sure. All he knew was that now it was Carlos Olivero who called every tune while he, Rodriguez Balo, had become a mere puppet. Yet it was a situation he could endure if it meant keeping the title and privileges of *el Presidente*. That was why the problem of Noella de Bartez had. to be dealt with urgently.

He heard the heavy footsteps seconds before the door was pushed open and Carlos Olivero entered the room.

The leader of Martiguay's drug cartel was a big, fit-looking man in his fifties with close-cropped grey hair and glittering dark eyes. He had a chest like a bull and his legs, clad in tight riding breeches, were as thick as tree trunks.

He didn't waste his breath on greetings. 'So, tell me the news. You have captured the bitch?'

Balo swallowed nervously as the manservant who had followed Olivero into the room, poured his employer a drink and presented it to him on a silver salver. Balo looked longingly at the glass of straight whisky; a similar offer might have helped give him courage.

'Well?' Olivero gulped down the drink and frowned at Balo's silence.

'I — we... no, senor. With El Chacal's aid she is proving most elusive.'

Carlos Olivero thumped the empty glass down on the table next to him, his face thunderous. 'Do you mean to tell me your jackasses are running all over the countryside and can't track down a woman and a gang of ill-equipped peasants?'

Rodriguez Balo thought it expedient to refrain from mentioning that for months El Chacal had eluded Olivero's men too.

Instead he offered, 'Senor, the polling date is more than three weeks away. There is still time —'

The drug baron swore venomously, his face darkening with rage. 'Are you really so stupid? Do you think after all the publicity she has generated we can just ambush her in broad daylight? In front of her supporters? In front of those *bastardos* from the UN? She has made too much noise now. If there was obvious violence how do you think that would make us look?'

He strode across the room and held a thick index finger just centimetres from Rodriguez Balo's sleek, dark moustache. 'Now, listen to me. Again I will do your thinking for you. It is too late for arrest, public capture.

Instead, de Bartez must be made to disappear. There will be no charges, no fuss, but she must be kept captive until the election is safely over. It will seem then as if she has bowed out, abandoned her plans.'

'But... there will be questions, senor,' Rodriguez Balo ventured.

With an angry gesture of dismissal Carlos Olivero turned away. 'Questions are the least of our worries! The official response will merely suggest that the reason de Bartez came to Martiguay was to draw attention to herself, to make a name for herself for her own purposes. For...' he thought rapidly, 'for the political kudos she is pursuing in the States.'

'But she must still be captured —'

Carlos Olivero swung round and gave his uniformed lackey a withering look. '*Imbecil*! You have overlooked the easiest way of all. And maybe now we will catch both birds...'

Eugene was beginning to get restless. It was almost midday, that terrible hour when the blackness and pain would descend once more unless he took the steps to prevent them.

But the stranger who had joined him on the park bench was still talking and, edgy as he was, Eugene couldn't help listening.

'What a sense of pride you must feel, senor, to have such a one as a sister-in-law. She promises much for Martiguay, just as her father did before her. It is a wonder you do not wish to join her campaign, offer her your support.' The bespectacled man in the yellowing panama hat smiled benignly at Eugene. 'But perhaps you have had enough of politics?'

Eugene pushed himself to his feet. The giddiness was getting worse. 'All Martiguayans have had enough of politics, senor. But you are right, I am proud to be related to one who bears the name de Bartez. I have enjoyed our conversation but now, if you will excuse me . . . '

Back in the tiny two-roomed apartment, Eugene's hands shook as he prepared the white powder. He twisted and tied the tourniquet above his elbow, filled the syringe . . . and within moments was immersed in the release that only the drug could provide.

With a deep sigh of contentment, Eugene released the leather thong and lay back against the narrow divan. This was his only relief, the only way he could manage to function. In the months of anguish and torment following the murder of his wife and child, he had wanted nothing more than to die as well.

Unable to eat or sleep or work, he had felt himself driven to the brink of madness. Even his arrest and imprisonment by the new regime had barely distracted him from his emotional turmoil. But it had been in prison that he had had his first taste of the cocaine which had become his only means of blanking out the horror of his loss.

When they had released him a few weeks afterwards his first panicky thought was how to maintain his supply of the drug. To his relief, he soon discovered that availability posed little problem in Martiguay. The white powder had become his lifeline, his means of coping with the tragedy that had destroyed everything he held dear.

Afterwards, the effects already beginning to wear off and the pain gnawing at him again, Eugene propped himself up on the divan. With bloodshot eyes, he took in the squalor that surrounded him: the tiny kitchen littered with caked saucepans and piles of unwashed plates, the grimy sheets and dirty laundry, the remains of a meal he had prepared almost two days ago decaying on the one wooden table.

Tears of self-pity filled his eyes. He had lost everything that mattered. His family, his home, his career . . . and now, he saw with shameful clarity, his pride and dignity. The tears spilled down his unshaven cheeks. What did he have to live for?

It was then, in the blackness of his despair, that the stranger's words came back to him: ' . . . join your sister-in-law's campaign, offer your support . . . '

And at that moment, with the torment once again beginning to devour his brain, Eugene understood where his only hope of salvation lay.

Her heart beating rapidly, Inez pulled on her robe and hurried down the uncarpeted stairs. Who could be knocking at such an early hour if not the police or Balo's security patrols? She prayed that the door which led to the basement and the printing press had been camouflaged with proper care.

She had not expected another visit by the soldiers so soon. On the earlier occasion they had arrived at the house just hours after Noella and the others had left. Inez had managed to convince them she had seen no one. But why, she wondered fearfully, had they now returned?

'Who — who is it?' she called through the heavy wooden door.

'Inez! It is I, Eugene.'

'Eugene!' Inez quickly drew back the thick bolts, relief flooding through her.

'Eugene, what are you doing here? And at this hour? I never expected —'

'Inez . . . listen to me.' He gripped her arms and she saw a light in his face that hadn't been there for years. 'You must tell me where I can find Noella. I must go to her. I must do everything I can to help. Do you understand?'

★

In the end, Inez responded to his pleadings as a gesture of compassion.

'This is my chance to get my life back together again, Inez.' Eugene spoke quickly, eagerly, his excitement obvious. 'If I can be of some use to Noella, I will have found a purpose in existence once more, a reason to keep going. Don't you see?'

She had hesitated at first. Nothing must be allowed to jeopardise these next few vital weeks. Did Eugene have the stamina, she wondered, to undertake such an arduous and dangerous task?

His argument, finally, had been persuasive and undeniable. Inez made up her mind. Surely Noella would see the benefits to both of them in accepting Eugene on her team.

It was arranged easily enough. Less than two hours later, Eugene was being driven to the safe house a hundred kilometres to the south where Noella and her supporters were scheduled to spend the night. No one, it seemed, could raise any real objection to the appearance of their leader's brother-in-law on the campaign trail.

It was close to sunset when the car twisted its way up the rocky hillside to the run-down villa nestled in a grove of dusty trees. As they came to a halt, Eugene began to experience his first misgivings about the venture he had undertaken so impetuously. Confined for so many hours in the car, deprived so abruptly of the drug on which he had become so dependent, the physical effects of his rashness were beginning to make themselves felt.

Offered refreshment, Eugene had to fight to control the trembling in his hands as he accepted the glass of bitter ale. Pale and clammy, he felt as if his heart were about to burst from his chest, while a red-hot vice seemed to have tightened around his head.

For the first time he began to wonder if there was enough left of the man he had been to carry him through.

'Perfect.'

The lieutenant handed the binoculars to his subordinate. 'Take a look.'

Inching closer to the edge of the sharp outcrop of rock, the sergeant focused the glasses on the scene below. He studied the house, and the long twisting road that led up to it. Turning back to the officer beside him, he showed his long yellow teeth in a grin of triumph. 'We have them.'

'But we must move quickly,' the lieutenant replied.

Crawling back to where the rest of the troop were waiting, he was already thinking of the honours he would receive not only for removing the threat of Noella de Bartez, but also for capturing Martiguay's most wanted *bandido*.

They had no inkling of what was to come.

For Noella it had been another exhausting but gratifying day. She had shaken dozens of hands, accepted bouquet after bouquet, talked until her voice was hoarse.

But she knew it was all going to be worth it. Every day, with every crowd she addressed, she could feel the momentum gathering pace. She had seen the dawning hope on the faces in the crowds, the gradual belief that there was at last a genuine alternative to Balo and his corrupt stooges. Everywhere she went, the reception she received was tumultuous.

Now she sat silently, wearily rubbing a hand over one eye. She had undertaken a punishing schedule and the furious pace was taking its toll.

Today, for the first time, she had felt herself distracted from her task. The town in which she had spoken that morning was not far from Paolo's village. It was from there she had telephoned Inez after she had run away with Paolo. And the memories it evoked in her had been strange, unsettling. As she addressed the feverish crowd, Noella had found herself searching for Paolo's beautiful face, expecting at any moment to see him raise his hand in greeting as he had done the day of her wedding. Try as she would to push the memories away, they kept returning.

Just like the ache in her heart.

The soldiers were in place and waiting when the lead car strained up the steep, rutted mountain road.

The instant its headlights had disappeared around the next bend the uniformed men burst through the bushes and rolled the heavy log across the narrow track.

Just seconds later, the vehicle carrying their quarry came to an abrupt halt. The driver had seen the obstacle just in time.

El Chacal's response was immediate. 'Turn off the headlights! Sound the horn!' He roared out the order as he drew the pistol from his belt.

But it was too late.

The rear doors were already being wrenched open.

Noella was dragged from the car. She screamed, kicking out wildly at her attackers, while beside her in the darkness she heard El Chacal's furious struggle and his breathless urgent command. 'Run, Noella! Run!'

She fought with a wild, desperate fury but within seconds was easily overpowered. Her head jerked backwards as a foul-smelling gag was forced into her mouth and her hands, yanked violently behind her back, were bound with a rough rope.

Everything else happened in a mind-numbing instant. She felt herself being lifted, then bounced jarringly against her captor as he crashed his way through the stinging undergrowth. From somewhere to her right came the sound of an engine roaring into life and next moment the breath was knocked from her lungs as she was flung against a rough surface.

Tears of bitter rage ran down Noella's face. Her struggle was over almost before it had begun.

El Chacal fought like a man possessed. Outnumbered three to one, his ruthless, pounding fists brought screams of pain from his assailants as bones cracked sickeningly beneath his merciless onslaught.

Self-loathing gave the rebel leader his ferocious strength. He had vowed to protect her, to keep her from harm, and now . . . He would never forgive himself. Cold fury burnt in his heart. He would kill them all.

There was a warning shout.

Seconds later the headlights of the returning vehicle lit up the bloody scene.

As El Chacal's supporters leapt from the car, the attackers were already disappearing into the blackness of the jungle.

They had their main quarry, after all.

CHAPTER *THIRTY-SIX*

The news spread like wildfire. The official press saw to that.

Martiguayans were stunned. Noella de Bartez had gone. Left as suddenly as she had arrived. Yet the reasons given by the newspaper editors did not ring entirely true. The articles insisted it had merely been a ruse. De Bartez had sought to cash in on her family name; had been using the situation in Martiguay to draw attention to herself for her own ends. What those ends might be were only vaguely hinted at. A preamble to launching a career in the States? Even a suggestion that Noella de Bartez was hoping to bring herself to the attention of American film studios, that she wished to emulate her mother's career.

While the rumours grew more preposterous by the day, one certainty remained — the campaign of Noella de Bartez had come to an abrupt end.

While she did her best to comfort Eugene, Inez also blamed herself. For it was obvious how Noella had been tracked down. Inez knew that by agreeing to allow Eugene to join the campaign, she herself had been responsible for delivering Noella to her enemies.

Guilt and dread consumed her. What would they do to *this* de Bartez?

*

The meeting of Martiguay's five most powerful and dangerous men took place in the windowless room built into the foundations of Carlos Olivero's fortress.

In the last ten years this cartel of drug producers had extended their power to undermine the entire fabric of the Martiguayan socio-legal system. Thanks to the effective corruption and intimidation of judges, lawyers, policemen, and government officials, their operations had continued without check; and their empires had grown and flourished.

Certainly one drum-beating woman was not going to be allowed to disturb the status quo.

The five men were in no doubt that Noella de Bartez had the backing of the Americans. Since his election, Larry Kirk had made no secret of the fact that he was prepared to tackle the drug question as a matter of urgency. Now, any hope he might have had of using Noella de Bartez to this end had been effectively dashed.

'The problem with de Bartez has been handled then?' Alfredo Lopez, grossly overweight, sweating despite the air conditioning, put the question to his host.

Carlos Olivero allowed himself a small smile. 'A simple affair once that buffoon Balo was pointed in the right direction.'

Alfredo Lopez's lips parted, revealing a row of gold teeth. 'Kirk will be kicking a few arses.' He wiped a crumpled handkerchief over his damp face and added, 'She will be dealt with after the election?'

Carlos Olivero's eyes glinted with pleasure. 'In the usual way. No one will ever find the body.'

A livid Larry Kirk called an emergency meeting as soon as he was told the news.

'Goddamn it, Ben, they've near as anything tied our hands behind our backs! What the hell's happening down there?'

Ben Christensen did his best to placate the President, but like everyone else around the table, he knew that unless Noella de Bartez was located and rescued quickly, the whole mission was doomed to failure. The problem was, he thought darkly, in the eyes of ordinary Martiguayans the *gringos* were almost as much the enemy as Balo himself. After the role they had played for years in propping up the regime, their presence and interference was deeply resented. It had made working with the locals a difficult task.

Richard was also at the meeting. He sat, white-faced, as the situation was analysed by the men around the table.

'They wouldn't dare kill her,' he heard himself say. 'They wouldn't risk it. I'm sure they only intend to keep her out of the way until the election is over.'

He wondered if he believed what he was saying or if he was just trying to convince himself.

Five days later, when there was still no news, Richard made an appointment to meet with an ex-CIA operative in a downtown bar. If there was to be no official action then he was determined to take matters into his own hands.

It was an appointment Richard didn't have to keep.

Ben Christensen called him ten minutes before he left his office. 'They've located Noella. They're going in to get her.'

For five terrifying days he had endured the nightmare of not knowing where she was being held. When at last word came through, El Chacal felt as if the blood had once more begun to flow in his veins. If it cost him his life, he vowed, he would set her free.

The cell was stiflingly hot and stank of urine and human excrement. Grime streaked the walls and the single naked bulb was draped with cobwebs. There was no window and the only furniture was a narrow bunk made of two rough wooden planks covered by a thin straw-filled mattress.

Never in her life had Noella experienced anything so primitive and filthy.

She shuddered as an enormous black cockroach scuttled across the floor close to her feet. And when at last exhaustion drove her to stretch herself on the bunk, it was only minutes before her legs and arms erupted in red itchy welts from the lice-infested mattress.

That first night was an endless waking nightmare but worse was to come.

Early the next morning a sharp-featured man entered the cell. In one hand he carried a portion of rice in a battered aluminium container, in the other, a pair of heavy, rusty handcuffs.

He looked at her coldly. 'Turn around. You must put these on at once.'

Noella's contemptuous laugh resounded off the dank cement walls. 'I am not an animal to be trussed up! Get out of here!'

The blow almost knocked her to her knees. As she staggered, the guard grabbed the collar of her shirt and pulled her towards him so that her face was only inches away from his own. Still reeling from the force of the blow, Noella saw the sadistic pleasure in his eyes as he gave her a hard push and knocked her head back against the filthy wall.

'You are no one here, remember that! A nothing, a nobody!' He spat out the words as he wrenched her hands behind her back and snapped on the square brass handcuffs.

Noella gasped as they bit into her flesh. 'They're — they're too tight.'

Now it was the guard's turn to laugh. 'Perhaps you

wish to take your complaint to General Balo? Shall I bring you a pencil and paper?'

He slammed the door behind him and was gone.

Only the gnawing hunger pains in her belly tempted her to try eating a little of the grey, dry rice. She was reminded of the words she had thrown at the guard, for now, indeed, she was forced to eat like an animal — to push the dish to the side of the bunk where he had left it, to lower her head so she could eat from the bowl like a dog.

But every time she bent to take a mouthful of rice, the sharp edge of the handcuffs sawed at her wrists. After just half a dozen attempts it became impossible for her to continue. Tears of pain and frustration filled her eyes as she deliberately knocked the half-empty bowl to the floor. Then, holding her arms at an angle to minimise as much as possible the burning pain in her wrists, Noella lay awkwardly on the filthy bunk. For the first time she began to fear what they would do to her.

By the fourth day the pain in her hands was almost unbearable. The handcuffs seemed to get tighter and tighter and, to her horror, Noella felt something wet and sticky run down between her fingers. Twisting around, she saw the blood and pus where her hands had rested on the stiff straw mattress. It was then she realised there was a chance she might lose her hands.

She felt as if she were going slowly mad in the windowless cell. Brought to the prison in darkness, she had been only vaguely aware of her surroundings. Since then she realised that she was not in a major holding jail, but in one of the local county blocks built to accommodate no more than twenty or so prisoners.

From the sounds she could hear through the barred

door onto the passageway Noella also became aware that she was being held apart from the other inmates. Footsteps and other noises always disappeared in the opposite direction from her own cell.

By now, too, she was weak and faint from lack of food. It was easier, she had found, to do without than make any movement that might add to the torture of her infected flesh.

Her only solace came each morning just after dawn, when she could hear the sound of Mass being celebrated at the far end of the passageway.

As she listened to the faint intonation of the priest's voice, her dry lips moved soundlessly, echoing his prayers. Her strength was failing fast. Only God, she thought, could save her now.

'What is it? What have you got to wail about?'

Through the red haze in front of her eyes, Noella recognised the guard who had first snapped the cuffs onto her wrists.

'Please . . . ' Her voice was a raw whisper. 'Please, I beg you.' She stared wild-eyed at him from where she was slumped on the bunk. 'Have mercy. Take them off before my hands are useless.'

He spat on the floor at her feet before turning away and slamming the door.

The priest moved slowly from cell to cell removing a Host from the chalice and offering it through the bars to the repentant sinner.

He had reached the end of the row and was about to cross to the opposite side of the building when a surly guard barred his way.

'But there is another prisoner here, I think.'

'NO!' The man fingered his weapon menacingly. 'No one is to have access to these cells.'

The priest stared at him a moment with a calm,

expressionless face then, with an almost imperceptible bow of his head, he turned away.

'Father Iola has forgotten the crucifix!' The slightly cross-eyed guard pointed to the heavy metal cross which still hung on the wall.

'So?' His companion gave a shrug of indifference. 'He'll be back again tomorrow.'

CHAPTER *THIRTY-SEVEN*

Pacing slowly around the narrow perimeter of the jail, the young sergeant yawned and waved a hand around his ears to drive away an irritating mosquito.

As he stared out at the blackness of the surrounding jungle, he heard an owl hoot, and another reply. He grumbled to himself yet again at the waste of another night out of his Marita's bed.

At sixteen, Marita, plump, sweet and willing, was his dream come true. A shudder ran through him as his memory conjured up those soft wondrous breasts, those smooth spreading thighs.

Half a second later, the young soldier was blown to kingdom come.

The acrid smell of explosive and the dust of shattered concrete hung heavily on the warm night air as El Chacal and his men charged through the gaping hole in the prison wall.

Inside, all was chaos. Men screamed in the darkness, guards indistinguishable from prisoners, as they sought to push their way free from broken mounds of concrete.

The destruction was confined to the one end of the jail. The section where the crucifix had been so innocuously left . . .

At the entrance to Noella's cell, the dazed guard was easily dispatched and a moment later El Chacal was turning the key in the cell door.

'Quickly, senora!'

There was no response and for one terrible second the rebel leader wondered if their information had been wrong. But the priest had been adamant that she was being held in that part of the prison, away from the others.

He swept his torch around the stifling cell and at almost the same moment that he saw her, he heard the muffled groan.

Dios... He felt the fever in her body as he swept her into his arms. A torrent of curses burst from his lips. What had they done to her?

As he clambered back the way he had come, El Chacal called to his men. 'I have her! Make your escape!'

In minutes they had melted back into the jungle.

For days after the raid that had precipitated Noella's release the countryside was teeming with soldiers, and El Chacal and his men were forced to move deeper and deeper into the safety of the jungle.

The most pressing task was to free Noella of the torturous cuffs.

Pale with fury, El Chacal realised the extent of her wounds for the first time.

Encrusted with blood and pus, Noella's hands were swollen to twice their size and the infection which had already set in was responsible for her delirium.

After the manacles were finally sawn off, the rebel leader moved Noella to the lean-to that had been erected under the trees. His greatest fear was that already it might be too late to save her hands.

He never left her side. Would let no one tend her but himself. By day, he was there to mop her burning brow, to coax a little water between her cracked lips, to bathe and bandage her tortured flesh. At night, he sat unsleeping at her side, haunted by her feverish moans as violent shivers racked her weakened frame.

*

It was three days before the fever broke.

At last Noella was able to sit up and eat.

'A little, senora... just have a little. It will do you good,' El Chacal coaxed gently.

Light-headed and exhausted, Noella managed to swallow a few mouthfuls of the warm gruel. With red, sunken eyes she stared silently at the man who held the battered spoon to her lips. He could kill in cold blood, yet had a gentleness and kindness that moved her beyond words.

'My hands,' she ventured, staring in horror at the thick wad of bandages around her wrists. 'Will — will they be all right?'

He nodded and saw relief transform her face. 'There will be pain for a while yet, but your hands are saved.'

That night Noella lay looking up at the starry skies, savouring the fragrant smoke of the dying fire and thanking God for her rescue. El Chacal had saved her; had given her back to Sandro and to the cause she had lived for for so long.

The next day she felt her strength returning. When El Chacal brought her the evening meal she asked how much time they had till polling day.

'Ten days, senora.'

She had guessed it wouldn't be long. 'Then I must waste no more time. It is essential I resume my campaign at once.'

He watched her as she finished her food and put the bowl aside. 'It is what we have all prayed for, senora. Even at this very moment, the true story of your capture and imprisonment is being revealed both to the people of Martiguay and the international press. General Balo's plan has backfired on all fronts; not only will he be forced to face the questions and scrutiny of foreign journalists, but until the polling booths close your exposure to the eyes of the world press will mean your safety is well assured.'

For a while longer they discussed details of the resumption of the campaign then El Chacal rose to go.

'*Buenas noches*, senora. I will leave you now to get a good night's sleep.'

'Senor...' She was staring up at him in the moonlight. 'Do not leave me alone tonight.'

He stood frozen to the spot, not daring to let himself believe what he had heard.

Her bandaged hand slipped tentatively into his own. 'Stay with me, please.'

Her touch sent a jolt through his body and the plea in her voice was unmistakable. Stunned and confused, he looked down into that beautiful, vulnerable face.

Her lips trembled as she said, 'I want you. I need the arms of a man around me... I need to convince myself that I am alive in every way.'

'Senora...' He crouched beside her and his voice was thick and unsteady. 'Senora, I think I understand what you are feeling but... look at me. You — you who are so beautiful... You cannot wish to have this face lying beside your own.'

Her eyes filled with tears. 'When I am with you,' she whispered, drawing a finger gently over the ugly puckered flesh of his cheek, 'I do not see your face. I see only your kindness and patience, your courage and goodness. I see those qualities which mean real beauty.'

Then her lips were on his and suddenly his body was electrified with desire; a desire that had never diminished, that had always been there to haunt him. Now he had no choice. There could be no holding back.

Heart thundering in his chest, he stretched out beside her and took her in his arms. His lips crushed down on hers and he felt as if he were dreaming — the way he used to feel all those years ago...

It suddenly seemed as if he had fallen down a long black tunnel that spiralled backwards in time.

Her lips still tasted the same, her breasts had the same smooth perfection, her legs opened with the same abandonment and pleasure as they had then.

For Noella, realisation dawned as a crescendo, slowly but inexorably gathering pace.

Memory stirred at the feel and movement of his body, at the way his hands caressed her hips, her breasts, at the taste and ardour of his mouth.

Her response was pure and explosive, her body consumed by desire. And then, at the very moment of ecstasy the shock of truth froze her brain.

'Paolo! Oh, *Dios*! ... Paolo!' She gasped out his name again and again, her body still shuddering against his. '*Dios, Dios* ...'

And he answered her then, voice broken and raw, the terrible face buried against her hair. 'You knew, you knew ... After so many years.'

'Paolo.' She clung to him, tears running down her face as shock and pleasure dizzied her senses. And for one fleeting moment she was that sixteen year old child again, happy and secure in her first love's arms, with the future bright and untarnished before her ...

They talked for a long time. Taking turns to tell of the years in between, the tragedies that had brought them to this unique moment in time.

Noella's eyes filled with tears as Paolo spoke of the loss of his child and pregnant wife.

'The bomb went off just metres from my home. Afterwards there was not enough left of either of them to fill the coffins ...'

For a moment he was silent and Noella's heart ached as she gripped his hand.

'My son was just four years old.' Paolo made no attempt to conceal his bitterness. 'An innocent child robbed of life by men for whom power was the only goal. The day it happened I swore I would never give up until Martiguay was rid of the dictator Balo, or I died in the fight for freedom.'

She kissed him then, gently on the cheek. 'And now it is a fight we will undertake together, Paolo.'

'Oh, Noella...' He was drawing her close to him once more, responding to the sympathy and the bond which time had not eroded. Nothing would make him admit that much as he had loved his wife, no one had been able to take Noella's place, that he had never been able to forget the girl for whom his passion still burned with white hot fire.

Beside him, Noella could feel his arousal, his desire to love her again — but cold reality had returned and with it confusion and despair.

'Paolo.' Her eyes were dark with pain as she drew away from his embrace. 'You — you will always be special to me ... but nothing can be the same as it was long ago. You see, there is someone —'

He put a finger to her lips and managed to keep his voice steady. 'There is no need for explanation, Noella. I know there is another man. He must look so much like the child you were brave enough to leave behind.'

He saw her eyes fly open, heard her sudden intake of breath. 'Yes, I saw you that day, Noella. I was afraid for your safety and...' He let the excuse die on his lips. Swallowing, he went on. 'You know best what is in your heart, Noella. I have no desire to question that. But long ago I vowed to do all I could to protect you. All I ask is that I be allowed to fulfil that promise.'

His lips were cold as ice as he kissed her gently on the forehead and slipped away into the darkness.

CHAPTER **THIRTY-EIGHT**

The reappearance of Noella de Bartez on the campaign trail, the story of her imprisonment and torture, made sensational headlines in the international press. Now that her mission had been made public, a flood of foreign journalists invaded Martiguay, drawn like hungry locusts to a story that proved irresistible in its combination of glamour and honour, intrigue and danger.

Caught in the crossfire of questions from an uncensored press, General Rodriguez Balo failed to convince.

'I knew nothing of this so-called "plot" to remove Noella de Bartez from the election campaign.' He gritted his teeth and spread his thin lips in something approximating a smile. 'I am delighted to have such a worthwhile and honourable rival for the office of President. Though perhaps,' he shrugged suggestively, 'Martiguayans are not yet ready to accept a woman as leader of their country.'

But Rodriguez Balo was wrong. On the eve of the polling date, the whole country seemed galvanised into action. In remote jungle villages, in hillside hamlets and sprawling coastal towns, the people poured forth to join the queues which had already begun to form at the polling stations.

Under the watchful eyes of the UN observers, it seemed as though all Martiguayans wanted to register

304 • ANGEL OF HONOUR

their vote at the first democratically conducted elections in more than a decade.

Surrounded by her aides and supporters, Noella spent the day visiting as many polling centres as possible. Whenever she arrived at a venue, she was greeted with joyous acclaim, bombarded with good wishes and spontaneous applause.

'It is as if you are already their leader,' Felix whispered in her ear as a path was cleared for them through the crowds. Any tiredness he might have felt after the long flight from Paris had disappeared in the excitement of the moment. Nothing could have kept him from Noella's side on this historic day.

Towards evening, they gathered together in the apartment of a supporter to await the first figures from the outlying towns and villages. Tense but controlled, Noella chatted with the men who now smelt victory. She willed herself to be patient. While the figures from outside the major cities would give some indication of their chances, it would take at least forty-eight hours to be sure of the trend.

Just after eleven they received the first reports. It was Felix who was handed the phone.

'Si... Si...' He nodded his head vigorously.

All eyes were on him as he replaced the receiver and turned into the expectant silence.

Relishing the moment, Felix passed on the news, his face aglow. 'A landslide in the provinces! *Eighty-seven per cent of the vote!*'

Amidst the cheers and pandemonium, he drew Noella into his embrace, as they both wept with relief and happiness.

Further results came in every hour — and the trend continued throughout the country. The National Salvation Front was devastating government candidates everywhere. By eight o'clock the next morning, there was no doubt that Noella de Bartez would be the new democratically elected President of Martiguay.

Inez was there ... Eugene ... Paolo. All those who loved and supported her had somehow managed to squeeze into the tiny apartment while in the street below, hundreds more had arrived to share in the jubilation.

'De Bartez! ... de Bartez! ... de Bartez! ...' It was the same joyous chant she had encountered all over the country.

'Oh, my dear, I am so very, very happy, so very, very proud.' Eyes bright with tears, Inez put her hands on either side of Noella's face and kissed her. 'Heaven is looking down on us today, Noella. The past and all its tragedies can be laid to rest in this moment of glory.'

Assured of the result and too impatient to wait for an official endorsement, the international press were clamouring for a statement from the new President-elect.

After a couple of hours of snatched sleep, Noella agreed to hold a press conference in the foyer of the State Theatre.

Dressed in a beige silk suit, looking elegant and relaxed, she entered the baroque interior of the theatre to face a wall of television cameras, a barrage of flashbulbs, and spontaneous cheering and applause. The press were captivated by the victorious return to Martiguay of the daughter of the late President de Bartez and Catherine Campion. Her landslide victory would make sensational copy.

As she stepped up to the bank of microphones, a hush fell over those who crowded the enormous vaulted hall. For a moment, Noella too was silent, her gaze moving slowly over the expectant faces. When at last she spoke, her message was clear and direct.

'Ladies and gentlemen, this is a joyous day for all Martiguayans. As you know, the National Salvation

Front has completely routed the forces of destruction and oppression which have reigned for too long in Martiguay. My essential task now is to restore to my countrymen what citizens of civilised countries everywhere assume as their right — liberty, equality, justice, dignity and peace. That, ladies and gentlemen, is the message I want you to carry to the world.'

Finally allowing herself a smile of triumph, Noella raised her fingers in the symbol of victory, posed a moment longer for the cameras, and was gone.

For the next fourteen days until her official inauguration Noella stayed with Inez, who had moved back to her villa in the capital.

While the older woman set about re-establishing her household, Noella held meeting after meeting with the men who would comprise her ministry. And while the myriad of fine details were being thrashed out, always there in the background to lend support and encouragement, was Paolo. No one questioned his presence. The vital role played by the rebel leader in the opposition's ascension to power was gratefully acknowledged.

That, however, didn't prevent the amazed reaction when Noella dropped her bombshell.

It was inevitable that the name of Carlos Olivero would arise in discussions on national security. All agreed that the problem of the drug cartels must be confronted without delay. Most pressingly, essential US aid was dependent on the new government's tough and immediate stance against the drug lords.

Arno Mazar, the former mayor who had served under Victor de Bartez, had already accepted the position of Minister for the Interior with the responsibility for narcotics control. Now, Noella put the rest of her proposition for defeating the drug cartel to the men who would form her government.

'Senores, in this most serious matter of narcotics

control I wish to appoint an outsider to the ministry. Through his intimate knowledge of the men and practices involved, he brings an experience that can only aid us in our goal to rid Martiguay of this evil trade.'

The men gathered around the table in Inez's spacious formal dining room looked expectantly at the woman who had led them to victory.

Noella turned and indicated Paolo, who sat at the far end of the room listening closely to the proceedings. 'It is Paolo Avende I wish to nominate to head a task force which will make an immediate assault on the corrupt empire of Carlos Olivero and his accomplices. Senor Avende is a true patriot and from this moment on he will assume the rank of major in the Martiguayan Armed Forces.'

As frantic and demanding as the fortnight prior to the inauguration was proving to be, Noella was determined to find a moment to make a personal pilgrimage — to do something she had been longing to do ever since she had once again set foot on Martiguayan soil.

The intensity in her eyes when she informed Paolo where she wanted to go told him she could not be dissuaded. He understood her need, yet felt compelled to prepare her for what she would behold.

'I must warn you, Noella. After the assassinations Balo's men saw fit to —'

'No.' She interrupted him tersely. 'Let me see for myself.'

As they neared the *hacienda* Noella fell silent and Paolo knew she was steeling herself to confront the past and all its ghosts.

Keeping his men at a discreet distance, he watched in sympathy as she walked slowly up the cracked stone steps to where the heavy oak door hung half off its hinges. Every line of her body told him of her pain and desolation as she entered the dilapidated house.

*

The soldiers had torn apart the once elegant homestead. Whole rooms had been stripped; cobwebs draped the broken chandeliers and not one window had been left intact. Through the damaged roof the elements had taken their toll.

As Noella moved through the rubble of her childhood home, vivid images of the past rose up to haunt her. A faded space on the wall reminded her of the ornate silver-framed mirror where, on the day of Gabrielle's wedding, she had studied her reflection in triumph after losing her virginity to Paolo. In the shattered remains of the kitchen she recalled the meals shared with Nona, the old woman's good-natured grumbles as she did her best to deal with a troubled, recalcitrant child. And as she slowly mounted the damaged staircase to the bedrooms above, her memory was flooded by the image of two little girls whispering excitedly as they crouched to peek through the balustrade at the beautiful woman their father had brought to dinner.

Her footsteps echoing on the naked floorboards, Noella made her way from room to room, feeling a sense of loss that was beyond tears.

And then there was just one place left. The room she had deliberately avoided till last.

The door creaked as she pushed it open and she stood stock still in the doorway of her father's study. It was the portrait of her mother to which her eyes were drawn first — the canvas slashed, the tatters hanging from the heavy frame. Stomach churning, she looked at the charred remains in the centre of the room. It took her a second to realise it was all that was left of her father's cherished mahogany desk. The violation was complete.

And it was there, in that room, with its overwhelming sense of the presence of both her parents, of futures lost, and lives broken, that Noella's fragile control finally snapped.

Falling to her knees amidst the ruins, she covered her face with her hands, sobs tearing at the core of her.

'Papa, oh Papa, we were denied our time of peace and healing, but I know you're with me now. I can feel your strength — yours, and Mama's, and Gabrielle's... I know with you all by my side I will be able to bear this heavy burden.'

Paolo watched anxiously as she finally emerged from the house.

The signs of tears were still visible on her face, but at the same time he saw too the light in her eyes, the proud dignity of her bearing. He knew then that Noella's lonely pilgrimage to the past had merely intensified her strength and courage.

At that moment, he loved her more than ever before in his life.

Feverish excitement gripped the country on the day of the inauguration of the new de Bartez government. Rodriguez Balo had quit the Presidential Palace and rumour had it that he had already left the country. He had no wish, it seemed, to humiliate himself by being present at the official transfer of power.

That morning, as Inez fussed over her preparations for the ceremony, Noella was reminded of another occasion.

'Do you recall, Inez, the last time you helped me like this? Then, it was my wedding day.'

The older woman nodded as she picked an imaginary thread from Noella's sleeve. 'Only today,' she said softly, 'you make your vows to your country, instead of a man.' Her eyes caught Noella's in the full-length mirror. 'But you must still make room for a man in your life, Noella. That is something every woman needs.'

Turning to face her, Noella caught Inez's hands in her own. Somehow, in the rush and fervour of the days leading up to the inauguration there had been barely a moment for them to be alone together. There hadn't been time to tell Inez. Noella had promised herself that as soon as the day of inauguration with its duties and ceremonies was over, she would sit down with Inez and reveal the secret that sustained her.

But now, the opportunity had presented itself.

'Inez, I *have* a man in my life. I love him dearly.'

And as the older woman listened in stunned wonder, Noella told her about the miracle that had occurred.

The people stood ten deep along the route that led to the palace. As Noella's cavalcade made its way down the broad avenues of the capital, the cheers of the excited, ecstatic crowds met her at every turn.

In the main square in the forecourt of the palace thousands more awaited her arrival. It seemed that the whole country had flocked to the capital to share in this historic moment.

Dressed simply and elegantly in a white linen suit, with plain gold rings in her ears, Noella emerged onto the balcony to a deafening roar from the seething masses before her. Eyes shining, intoxicated by the adrenalin of the moment, she raised an arm to acknowledge the people who had voted so overwhelmingly for the party she represented.

At last, as the official swearing-in ceremony began, a solemn hush descended on the crowd.

Surrounded by her ministers, Noella faced the recently-appointed Chief Justice and repeated the words of office. Her voice rang out confidently through the bank of loudspeakers as she swore to carry out her duties, 'fearless in the sight of God, for the greater good of Martiguay and all Martiguayans'.

It was a moment Noella could never have imagined in her wildest dreams when she had stood on the same balcony for her father's inauguration and later on her wedding day. But such poignant thoughts were, she knew, best contemplated in private, when the emotions they inspired could be freely indulged ...

Her head was high, her eyes shone with pride, as the presidential sash was slipped over her golden hair.

'Madam President,' the Chief Justice intoned, then kissed her on both cheeks.

A thunderous roar went up from the watching crowd, who could contain themselves no longer. Flowers, streamers, hats were tossed into the warm air, and Noella's name was chanted again and again. Aglow with happiness, Noella turned to face the crowd. With the blue, white, and yellow of the Martiguayan flag fluttering behind her, she spread her arms wide in acknowledgement of her tumultuous reception.

These were the people she loved. She would do everything to keep their faith.

CHAPTER *THIRTY-NINE*

The yacht was the largest of the flotilla of luxury vessels that appeared every summer in the harbour of St Tropez.

It was past midnight and the two men were alone on deck, the smoke from their cigars lingering in the sultry air.

'So, Carlos, you assure me there will be no problem with supplies?'

The speaker was a short, thickset man whose bulk did not completely obliterate his still handsome features. His name was Luciano Passini; for twelve dangerous years he had clung to his title of Godfather of the Sicilian Mafia.

Tossing the butt into the dark waters of the harbour, Carlos Olivero said calmly, 'Why do you talk of problems, Luciano? Why should there be problems?'

'I am thinking of this bitch who is playing President. She is making a lot of noise.'

'That is exactly what it is, Luciano — noise.' Olivero grinned into the darkness. 'But perhaps the tongue that makes such a clamour should be silenced permanently.'

Noella had been in office just four short months but already it seemed as if she had known no other way of life. Her days consisted of endless committees and meetings in which one after another hard-headed decision had to be made. But slowly, steadily, the program of reform was under way.

Acting on two of her most important campaign promises, Noella had already signed legislation to facilitate the redistribution of land and establish peasants' banks. With low-interest loans available to them, the peasants would be freed of their dependence on the rich landowners and be able to grow sustenance crops for sale to the free market. After more than a decade of despotic rule, the people could at last allow themselves to believe that change — real change — was possible.

The other major priority for the government was the problem of the drug trade. The US had made it clear that only when Congress was assured of the de Bartez government's willingness to take immediate and effective action against the cocaine barons would they agree to extending the aid package so badly needed by Martiguay.

Working closely with Paolo Avende, Arno Mazar, the Minister for the Interior, wasted no time in overhauling the judicial system, restructuring the police force, and investigating the lawyers, judges, and police chiefs suspected of protecting the drug cartels.

Whenever a clear-cut case for prosecution became evident, the modus operandi of the task force was to offer immunity in return for information. It was an approach that was beginning to reap rewards — a fifty-kilo haul of cocaine, awaiting shipment from Martiguay's main coastal port, had already been confiscated from its hiding place.

Carlos Olivero called an emergency meeting of the cartel. In the security of their leader's compound, five hard-eyed, deadly men decided on their own plan of attack.

'I am sure we can beat them, Eugene. This recent success proves it can be done!'

In her excitement, Noella let her food grow cold as she faced her brother-in-law across the table in the private dining room.

As soon as she was installed in the palace, Noella had extended an invitation to Eugene to take up residence with her.

'You are all the family I have left, Eugene. It would give me great comfort to have your company. Please say you will join me.'

She had picked her words carefully. From Inez, she knew of Eugene's circumstances, of his deterioration since the murder of his wife and child. Her invitation was prompted as much by a desire to help him, as a need for company. She had been glad when Eugene had accepted; it made it easier then to persuade him to use his talents within the legislature.

'We need people with your experience, Eugene. There is much we have to act on without delay.'

Grateful as he was for the opportunities offered him, Eugene was torn by doubts. In the initial euphoria of victory, he had found the strength to control the addiction that held him in its vice. But as the stresses and responsibilities of his new job took their toll, his resistance grew weaker with every day that passed.

And his craving became stronger.

With a muttered response to his sister-in-law's excitement, Eugene excused himself from the table. 'There is some work I must see to, Noella.'

She watched him go, a frown drawing her brows together. Poor Eugene. There was still a terrible fragility about him. She must do all she could to help him.

The bombs detonated around the capital in a synchronised onslaught of terror: in the homes of three government ministers; in the office building of a judge suspected of informing; in the central railway station to ensure the general public were made brutally aware that they too would have to pay for the crackdown by the de Bartez government.

One minister was slightly wounded, the judge had escaped unscathed but an office worker had lost both legs and a dozen innocent people had been killed.

Immediately increasing security for all her ministers, Noella called an emergency meeting. She faced her shaken cabinet determined to formulate an effective response to the outrage.

But while the discussion ranged heatedly over a number of options, no final decision was reached. Exhausted and drained, Noella finally brought the meeting to a close.

After the others had left, she and Paolo continued to discuss the pressing problem.

'This is a declaration of open warfare, Noella!' Paolo punched his fist into his open palm as he paced restlessly round the conference room. 'And the battlefield is expanding. Now that the cartel is finding it more difficult to use our own ports for shipment, they are beginning to re-route their product across the border to gain access to our neighbours' ports. So the violence and corruption spreads like a deadly plague . . .'

As she listened to Paolo's words a spark suddenly ignited in Noella's brain. *Dios*, if it could only work . . .

'Paolo, listen! I have an idea.'

He heard the new energy in her voice, saw the excitement that had replaced the despair in her face. And as she outlined what was in her mind, Paolo caught that same excitement.

The press were clamouring for government reaction to the bloody onslaught by the drug cartel. As Minister for the Interior, it was Arno Mazar who made it unambiguously clear that the government was at that very moment working out the details of a plan which would see the most daring and innovative step yet taken in the war against those who, as he put it, 'murder our youth, corrupt our citizens and damage our reputation abroad'.

Noella worked her team hard over the ensuing days. She wanted every detail of her proposal in order before her first official visit to Washington in three weeks' time. This, more than anything, would prove to the US Congress the extent of her government's commitment to their goal of smashing the drug cartels.

On the morning that the presidential jet lifted into the skies for the four-hour flight to Washington, no one among the handful of aides accompanying the President would have guessed at the other purpose to her journey.

Noella rested her head against the seatcover adorned with the presidential emblem, barely able to conceal her happy anticipation.

Nina had responded with enthusiasm to the plan, as Noella had been sure she would.

'I think it's a splendid idea, *cherie*,' she had immediately written in reply. 'After all, it is many months now since you last saw Sandro, and children change so quickly in these early years. Leave the arrangements to me. I will see to everything. When all is organised I shall let you know.

'I am so happy, my dear, that soon we will all be together again.'

And now, thought Noella, as the jet broke through the clouds, there were indisputable and pressing reasons for Richard to be told of the existence of his son.

CHAPTER FORTY

The State Dinner at the White House was a glittering affair.

As Larry Kirk escorted his guest of honour to her seat at the head table, he could almost feel the heated response from every red-blooded male in the room.

Dressed in a white, off-the-shoulder, beaded gown Noella de Bartez projected a beauty and radiance that was dazzling; she made every other woman in the room appear dowdy. The senora, Larry Kirk decided drily, wasn't going to win too many female fans here this evening.

Chatting easily to Noella as the first course was set before them, the President wondered yet again at the hint his official guest had given about 'the important initiative' she would reveal at tomorrow's meeting. He felt certain that it would be associated with her need to ensure US aid.

Meanwhile he steadfastly kept his eyes away from the President of Martiguay's tempting décolletage. Helen, he had no doubt, would be watching him like a hawk.

Noella only picked at her food. She had seen him the moment she entered the room. Seated four tables away. Richard had given her a smile, a nod of recognition — and Noella had felt the instant hammering of her heart against her ribs. To be so close to the man she loved... to know that nothing could remove

318 ANGEL OF HONOUR

the chasm that divided them. Time had not diminished the pain.

The men gathered in the West Wing of the White House gave Noella de Bartez their unwavering attention. They listened in complete silence as, lucidly and precisely, she outlined her plan for a concerted attack on the drug traffickers in Latin America.

'... and this is more than a mere proposal. Already I have written undertakings from more than half a dozen countries in the region that they will join, and strongly back, such a union. The violence and corruption associated with the production of narcotics are problems shared by us all, and the idea of forming a union of nations, of pooling resources and information to defeat the drug cartels, will strengthen immensely our chances of success.

'As well,' Noella continued, 'we will attack the problem at grass-roots level — offer the peasants inducements to demonstrate that they can receive even greater financial return from legal crops.'

Larry Kirk listened to her passionate words with mounting keenness. It could work. Such a tack had not been tried before. If a crackdown by all the producing countries was actively imposed it would *have* to have an impact, a serious impact. It might even come close to dealing a fatal blow to an industry that, until now, had faced no such concentrated attack.

When Noella came to the end of her proposal, the President was unstinting in his praise. 'You and your government are to be commended in every way for such a far-sighted proposal, Madam President. I am sure everyone in this room will agree that a union of the Latin American states will provide a most effective means of combating the drug cartels. Of course, we would envisage that the United States would also have an important role to play.'

As he threw the proposal open to general discussion, Larry Kirk had only one regret — that he hadn't come up with the idea himself.

Still, there were ways of presenting things to the press... And then, Larry Kirk decided, he would milk the political potential of President de Bartez's proposal for all it was worth.

Noella knew it was inevitable that Richard would be at that meeting. She had been counting on it.

When at last they broke for lunch, she was relieved when he approached her offering his personal congratulations. 'It's a first-rate proposal, Madam President.' He addressed her formally, as the others were still clustered around them in the conference room. 'There will be potential to do real damage to the drug trade.'

He had tried so hard for normality, but barely recognised his own voice; the lump in his throat made it almost impossible to get the words out.

'Richard...' Noella lowered her voice and spoke in rapid Spanish. 'I must speak to you. Will you come and see me at my hotel? Tonight? Please.'

Caught completely unawares, Richard could only stand and stare as she was engulfed by officials and ushered from the room.

When Noella had announced her wish to take a short break after the heavy schedule of her meetings in Washington, it drew no untoward comment from any of her ministers or advisers.

As soon as Nina had confirmed the arrangements, Noella had broached the subject casually with Felix Noverro.

'I have an old friend in the States, Felix. She has a vacation home outside of Washington — in Chesapeake Bay — and I would like to spend a day or two catching up with her at the completion of my official business.'

'But Noella, of course!' Felix was quick to assure her. After all, she had been working without a break for months. In just a short time so much of the machinery for reform had been already set in place. No one could begrudge the President a well-deserved break.

But he did have one reservation. 'There is the question of security, Noella. We must —'

She waved his worries away. 'I am sure we can trust the Americans to see to that, Felix.'

The Marriott hotel, luxurious and ultra-modern, was on Pennsylvania Avenue just minutes from the White House.

In the entrance foyer, Richard showed his security pass and was escorted by a friendly plain-clothes officer to the private floor where Noella and her entourage were located.

His feet sank into the carpet as he was shown into the spacious living room of the suite. He had barely taken in the beautiful flower arrangements, the modern tapestry and paintings adorning the walls, when Noella entered the room.

He turned and drank in the sight of her.

'Richard . . . ' She suddenly lost her voice as she looked at the man she loved. His hair was as thick and blond as ever; the blue eyes were creased more deeply at the corners but still as bright and intense as she remembered. She knew she was looking at the man her son would become.

'Noella. How are you? You're looking well.' Richard could hardly believe his own triteness, but it was the only way he could maintain some semblance of control. 'But is there anything wrong? This morning you sounded upset --'

'Yes, Richard.' She forced herself to move away from him, did not dare to touch him. Formality was her only refuge. 'Please — sit down, and I will explain.'

He joined her on the long plush sofa, his senses spinning at her closeness, the scent of her perfume, her hair. God, how had he ever had the strength to walk away?

Noella took a deep breath and spoke, not looking at him.

'Richard, there is something I must tell you. You are fully aware of how dangerous the situation has become in Martiguay. The intimidatory attacks by the drug cartels are now a regular occurrence. Everyone is at risk — ordinary people, my cabinet and ministers, and of course, myself...'

His eyes were fixed on her face — he was aware now of the strain around her mouth, the troubled shadows under her eyes. He nodded but said nothing, and she went on.

'Richard, what I am trying to say is that something could happen to me at any time. And that's why... that's why I have asked you here tonight.'

She turned, met his steady blue gaze, and told him about his son.

Built on the water's edge, the house was hidden at the end of a long narrow driveway. The first snows had fallen the day before, peppering the branches of the firs and leaving a soft slush underfoot.

For Noella, the reunion with her son had been bittersweet. Now almost eighteen months old, Sandro had cried and clung to Nina as Noella had tried to take him into her arms.

He has forgotten me, she thought, heart squeezing in anguish. *It's been too long and he has forgotten me...*

But over the next twenty-four hours, as she fed and bathed him, played with him and held him close, Sandro gradually became hers again.

She looked down at him now as he lay sleeping in his crib and her eyes softened with love. Little does he know, she thought, that in just an hour from now, he will be seeing his father for the first time . . .

Tiptoeing out of the room, she joined Nina in the glass-roofed conservatory with its breathtaking views across the bay. The older woman was sitting on a chesterfield by the open fire and she looked up from her tapestry as Noella sat down beside her.

'He went to sleep all right?' she asked with a smile.

'Like a lamb.'

Nina gave a satisfied nod. 'He will be fresh then for when his father arrives.' She was looking forward to her first meeting with Sandro's father. Already, through his beautiful son, through Noella's obvious love for him, she felt she knew Richard Avery.

Noella picked up a magazine but couldn't concentrate on the glossy pages. She was counting the minutes until Richard arrived; she couldn't wait to be close to him again, to show him the son that only a miracle had produced.

That night in the Marriott when she had first told him of Sandro's existence, Richard's face had mirrored his reaction. Shock, incredulity, and then, as her words finally sank in, unrestrained joy.

'A son . . . ' His blue eyes were alight with wonder as he repeated the words. 'A son!'

Suddenly, all the self-imposed barriers that had stood between them were swept away and they were clinging to each other: heart beating against heart; lips burning with a savage hunger; bodies aflame with desire.

A desire neither of them could resist.

A shiver ran through Noella at the memory of that evening. Moments later she heard the sound of a car making its way up the drive.

'He's here,' she announced to Nina, nervously rising to her feet.

*

'Richard.'

Without a word, he opened his arms and enclosed her in his embrace. There in the open doorway, heedless of the cold, they kissed, long and passionately.

When at last they drew apart, Noella led him by the hand through the hallway into the conservatory.

'Nina, may I introduce Richard Avery? Richard, this is Madame Repois. As you are aware, she is a very dear friend.'

'*Enchanté*, madame.' Richard took the hand of the older woman. She was trim and elegant and unmistakably French. 'Even before I know you I feel I owe you a debt of thanks for all you have done to help.'

Nina Repois looked into those steadfast blue eyes, saw the character and strength in Richard Avery's face and knew why Noella had found him so hard to forget.

'I shall prepare coffee, *oui*?' Returning his smile, she discreetly left the room.

Noella threw Richard's overcoat across the nearest chair and once more caught hold of his hand. 'I know you are longing to see him. Come, Richard.'

At the end of the hallway Noella opened a door into a cheerful, wood-panelled bedroom.

'He has just woken up,' she whispered, bending over the crib and gathering the sleep-flushed baby into her arms.

The child blinked, rubbed a clenched fist into one eye, then gave his mother a sleepy smile. Suddenly noticing the stranger, he tilted his head backwards for a closer look.

Richard was frozen to the spot.

His son. His and Noella's child . . .

The soft golden hair and inquiring blue eyes . . .

Then, with a muffled cry, he was accepting the baby from Noella's arms, cradling him as tears of joy filled his eyes. 'Oh, God, Noella, I can hardly believe it. I can hardly believe it . . .'

Stunned, joyous, he dragged his gaze away from their child to look at Noella. He saw her tears and then she too was in his embrace, the three of them enclosed in a warm circle of joy and love.

They clung to each other, laughing and crying, for a long time.

Richard could hardly bear to let his son be put to bed for the night. As Noella looked on in delight, he had played endlessly with Sandro, enchanted with this bright happy child who bore so strongly the features of his Nordic ancestors.

Later, they ate the wonderful meal Nina had cooked, then sat chatting around the dying fire. Not long afterwards the older woman kissed Noella on the cheek and said good night to them both. She had taken the room next to Sandro's, leaving Noella the privacy of the other wing of the spacious house.

'Shall we call it a night too, darling?' Richard stroked her hair.

Noella felt her pulses catch fire as she nodded and rose to her feet.

In the shadows cast by the single silk-shaded lamp, Noella undressed and joined her lover on the bed. At once they moved together in a shockwave of delight, mouth to mouth, flesh to flesh, the blood roaring in their veins.

'Oh, my darling,' Richard breathed the words hotly against her cheek. 'I want you so much.' His heart was bursting with love, his body trembling against hers.

'Richard.' She gasped out his name as their bodies moved in savage harmony, as they drowned in a sea of passion. *Dios*, oh *Dios* . . . She loved him so. Her heart and soul were being torn apart.

★

For a long time afterwards, she lay exhausted in his arms, filled with an amazing sense of peace and completeness. If only, she thought, it could last like this for ever. If only they didn't have to be apart.

'Darling, are you awake?'

She nodded, murmured happily against his chest.

'I have something to tell you.'

With a frown, Noella slowly raised her head to stare into his face. His eyes were soft in the lamplight.

'Tell me . . . ?'

'It's good news. As you know, Larry Kirk is upgrading our Embassy in Martiguay. As well as increasing Drug Enforcement Agency personnel, he wants me, as the State Department representative, to spend some time briefing our staff there. I should be in Martiguay for about ten days.'

'Richard!' Her eyes shone with delight. 'Oh, Richard, that is wonderful! Absolutely wonderful! When? When will you be there?'

He enjoyed her reaction to his surprise. 'In about two or three months. And after that we'll find some way to see each other regularly, darling. If we're careful, if we're discreet, I'm sure it can be managed. And with Sandro —'

She interrupted him then at mention of their son. 'I was going to tell you before you left. Nina has offered to return to Martiguay to live; no one should have any reason to doubt her story that Sandro is her godchild's son. That way I will be able to visit him regularly, until . . . until something more permanent can be worked out.'

Richard's eyes brimmed with happiness and hope. 'You see, my darling, if we're patient, maybe all our dreams can come true.'

Those two days spent with her son and lover were the happiest in Noella's life. Achingly aware of how little time they had together, she treasured each moment of simple joy.

All too soon it was time to say goodbye.

Fighting for control, Richard kissed his laughing, blond son, who was held firmly in Nina's arms. There would be other times, he consoled himself. There had to be.

Then, turning to Noella, he crushed her against him. 'Until next time, my darling.'

One last, long, aching kiss and he was gone.

On the morning of her departure from Washington, Noella appeared with President Larry Kirk at a major press conference to announce the formation of the Americas Union to crush the power of the drug lords.

Addressing the crowded room, Noella ensured her message was clearly understood.

'All seaports and airports out of the region will be closely monitored. There will be total co-operation between the US Drug Enforcement Agency and the police and intelligence forces of all member countries in the search and arrest of the traffickers and the destruction of their processing laboratories.' She paused and her dark, intense gaze swept steadily around the room. 'As well, we intend initiating retaliatory action in the form of extradition to American courts of those responsible for this horrific trade, thus ensuring they will be dealt with without those administering justice fearing reprisal.'

The assembled journalists took in the tall, beautiful woman in the pale blue wool suit, heard the firmly stated goals for which there were no precedents, and could hardly wait to file their copy.

Standing beside Noella, Larry Kirk did not miss the reaction of the press. He had been determined to gain the maximum political exposure for his administration from the announcement of this far-reaching initiative. The presence of Noella de Bartez had made sure of that.

FORTY-ONE

'Noella, he is beautiful! I am absolutely captivated!' Bouncing Sandro on her knee, Inez was as enchanted as always by his fair Nordic looks and sunny nature.

The three women were sitting in the dappled shade of the lawn, the remains of a light lunch on the wrought-iron table beside them. The house Nina had acquired was set in a large walled garden, a mere twenty-minute drive from the palace. She had been in Martiguay almost a month now, and was delighted to renew her long-standing friendship with Inez, to be back in the country which had afforded her so many happy memories and where now, so many exciting developments were taking place.

As Noella watched the two older women fussing over her son, she thought how much she cherished their warm and supportive friendship. And the fact that Sandro was now close by, that she could see him as often as possible, brought her a sense of peace and contentment that had long been lacking in her life. He was the perfect antidote, she thought, to the stresses she faced daily. On every front her ambitious reform program was addressing the problems left by more than a decade of despotic rule — and the forthcoming summit of the Americas Union would attack the greatest problem of all.

As if reading her thoughts, Inez asked, 'You are thinking of the meeting, Noella?'

Noella nodded. 'Yes. The delegates arrive at the end of the week. It is imperative we reach agreement and adopt a united stance as soon as possible against this evil which faces us all.'

'You have certainly attracted the attention of the international press, *cherie*.' Nina picked up the most recent publication of *Time* magazine which lay beside her on the table. Noella's photograph was on the cover; her government's initiative against the drug cartels was the main feature article of that week's edition.

Then Nina's brows creased in a frown. 'These men know what they are up against now, *cherie*. You must not underestimate the danger to yourself. They will stop at nothing to achieve their own ends.'

'I have always been aware of the risks, Nina.' Noella's voice was serious. 'I take every precaution — but I will not be intimidated. That is the reason Olivero and the others have escaped justice for so long — they induce fear in all who oppose them. Well, this time it is not going to work. This time we will take them on and we will win.'

The note of unshakeable conviction rang out clearly in Noella's voice but, as Nina looked at Inez over the child's fair head, she saw her own fear reflected in Inez's troubled eyes.

It was in the car as they drove away from Nina's that Noella raised an issue with Inez that had been troubling her since her return from Washington.

'... I was hoping to ask your advice, Inez, about a small problem.' She spoke softly, even though the bullet-proof glass panel between themselves and the driver ensured her words were not overheard. 'It's about Eugene. There's something wrong, I'm sure of it. At first he had so much enthusiasm for his work, seemed so glad to be doing something purposeful again. And it was so pleasant for me to have his company at the palace.

'But now,' she shook her head, frowning, 'in the short time I've been away, I see changes in him. He seems to have lost all interest and has fallen behind in what he has to do. Then, when we are alone together, he is vague and offhand, barely offers a word in conversation. Sometimes it seems as if he's miles away in a world of his own.' She turned to the older woman. 'I'm worried about him, Inez. What else can I do to help him?'

As Noella had been talking, Inez had grown increasingly concerned. She realised that her hopes for Eugene's recovery had been born of a reluctance to face the truth about him. Despite Noella's return and the promise it offered of a fresh beginning, of a chance to bury the past, Eugene, it seemed, had been unable to throw off his personal devils. For that reason he now represented a real danger to Noella — a danger to her credibility and standing.

The older woman knew it was time to reveal what she had so long suspected.

Noella listened, disbelieving.

'Drugs? You think Eugene is a cocaine addict?' Her voice held a note of sheer incredulity.

'I have suspected it for a long while, Noella. After the deaths of Gabrielle and Roberto, it was alcohol that provided Eugene's shield from reality; when that was not enough he turned next to the legal crutches of sedatives and sleeping pills. Now, his physical deterioration and the other signs you have seen make me certain it is cocaine which has him in its grasp. Apart from what it means for poor Eugene, I am sure you can appreciate the dangers it represents to yourself and your campaign. To have your own brother-in-law an addict, living under the palace roof...'

Inez trailed off. The conclusions were obvious. The scandal that would ensue from public knowledge of

Eugene's condition could hold serious implications for Noella's lofty cause.

Noella still found it difficult to accept what Inez was telling her. 'First I must make sure that what you suspect is indeed true, Inez,' she answered quietly.

Noella wasted no time. That evening when Eugene did not appear at dinner — an increasingly common occurrence — she decided to seek him out.

'Eugene?' She knocked on the tall double doors that led into her brother-in-law's private quarters. 'May I come in?'

She had never intruded on him before but if Eugene was surprised he did not show it. In fact, he gave very little reaction at all. His eyes were dull and his voice expressionless as he led the way into the sitting room and asked if she would like a drink.

Noella declined, and from her seat opposite took in her brother-in-law's appearance. For almost the first time she realised how much weight he had lost, saw the gauntness and strain in his pale face. Yet still she found it impossible to ask directly the question that was uppermost in her mind.

'Eugene, you look terrible. Tell me, what is wrong? What can I do to help?'

He turned away from her penetrating gaze and shrugged his shoulders. 'Nothing is wrong, Noella. I am all right.'

She tried again. 'Eugene, what if I call a doctor? I am sure —'

'*No!*' He swung around to face her, and for the first time showed some emotion. 'I do not need a doctor. I — I admit there were difficulties in the past. The deaths, the shock... And certainly, as you have noted, there are still moments when I must fight hard against depression.' He managed to inject his voice with strength and conviction. 'But I assure you, Noella, I have overcome the past. I have conquered the demons that lay within me.'

Noella heard the earnestness in his tone and felt herself reassured. Whatever Inez had suspected, Eugene was once more in control.

She stood up, walked over to him, and kissed him gently on the cheek. 'We both have, Eugene,' she said softly, 'and together we will give each other the strength to go on.'

The door of the jet was swung open and the American delegation to the inaugural meeting of the Americas Union descended the metal stairway onto the tarmac.

Representing Noella, a smiling Arno Mazar, with key members of his staff, was there to greet them. Hands were shaken, platitudes exchanged and then, to the relief of all concerned, air-conditioned limousines provided an escape from the blazing heat.

Arno Mazar felt pleased with himself as he sat chatting in Spanish to the senior US official. The Americans were the last to arrive. Tomorrow the historic meeting would take place which would set in motion the most concerted action ever taken to smash the power of the drug lords. As the Minister for the Interior saw it, the salvation of his country was at hand.

Noella presided over the official welcoming cocktail party, radiant in a slim, black, high-necked gown, her hair drawn upwards into a golden coil.

By her side, resplendent, if vaguely uncomfortable, in the blue and white dress uniform of a major in the Martiguayan army, Paolo could only admire her performance.

She is the consummate politician, he thought, noting how easily she moved around the reception room, chatting with each of the two dozen delegates. She was the only woman in the room and for all her beauty and charm, it was her dignity and strength of purpose that left their mark on those with whom she spoke. Paolo saw it happening before his eyes.

On occasions such as these, watching her in her official role, it was hard to believe that once he had held her in his arms, that they had shared the ecstasy of abandoned passion.

And now the child was here. The child of the man she loved.

Paolo knew he would protect the boy as fiercely as he protected his mother.

At the very moment that the delegates were dipping their spoons into the *gazpacho*, Carlos Olivero was holding a last-minute meeting with those who did his bidding.

Outraged at the audacity of the de Bartez government's initiative and its strong US support, Olivero was forced to acknowledge that for the first time the cartels were facing a very real threat to their operation.

Now the time had come to hit back. With force.

He gave one last order to his ruthless killers. 'Call me as soon as the deed is completed.'

With an early start planned for the opening meeting the following morning, the dinner ended before eleven o'clock. Under heavy security the delegates were escorted back to their hotels.

Arno Mazar was the last to leave, kissing Noella on both cheeks, full of excited anticipation for the outcome of the three-day summit. 'It is the beginning of the end for them, I am certain, senora. Now at last Martiguay will be able to raise her head again with the rest of the world.'

Noella shared his mood. 'We have a long way to go, Arno, but I am sure you are right. Now they will see we mean business.'

*

At dawn, two blocks away from the Presidential Palace, Silvestro Cortinez was at his usual job, pushing his broad broom along the littered streets.

Pigs, he muttered grumpily under his breath, human beings were such pigs. Why should it be his lot to have to clean up their shit?

A few minutes later he saw the lumpy hessian sack and his swearing grew louder. Now how was he going to shift that from the side of the road? At sixty-two years of age, and bent like a bow with arthritis, how in the name of Jesu could he be expected to get rid of such garbage?

Moving closer, he kicked out at the damp sack, venting his wrath against those who had seen fit to dump it along his route.

Suddenly the elderly street sweeper stood stock still. A foul stench assaulted his nostrils. It was an odour Silvestro Cortinez had smelt before. Eyes wide, face paling, he backed away; then he turned and stumbled as quickly as possible towards the nearest police station.

It was Paolo who brought her the news. Just as Noella was about to leave her apartment for the conference room.

She saw his face and before he could utter a word she knew something dreadful had happened. Another bomb.

But it was worse than that.

Fifteen minutes later, her shock still obvious, Noella was forced to report the horrifying news to the assembled delegates.

Carlos Olivero had left them in no doubt about his power and ruthlessness.

The sack, dumped so audaciously close to the palace gate, contained the raw, bloody body of Arno Mazar.

He had been skinned as cleanly as a rabbit.

*

The summit continued as planned but the mood was sombre and security tightened even further.

The people of Martiguay were outraged by the murder, and Noella appeared on the national television network to make an official address to her people.

'We will not let this tragedy frighten us or sway us from our purpose.' Her dark eyes looked unwaveringly into the camera, her voice was steady and controlled. 'The callous murder of Arno Mazar must only give us a greater strength of will to achieve our goal. The murders, the violence, the corruption of our institutions, and the damage to our country's reputation abroad must be halted once and for all. The drug cartels have openly declared war and we will fight them with every means at hand. The promotion of Major Paolo Avende to head a comprehensive, military-led assault on the ringleaders and their private armies is our direct response to the murder of Arno Mazar. Our enemies will see that this time there is no escape.'

Paolo...

This latest tragedy brought home to Noella just how much she had come to depend on her friend and protector. When he had broken the news to her of Arno Mazar's murder, it was from Paolo that she had drawn her strength. The shock had been devastating but the touch of his hand and the comfort of his presence renewed her, gave her the courage to face whatever lay ahead. The bond of their shared childhood had been enriched and strengthened by the present dangers they faced in fighting for the country they loved. With Paolo by her side, Noella knew she would never feel alone.

The summit ended without further incident. Strategies were discussed, decisions ratified, and Noella was assured by her neighbours of their total commitment and support in the dangerous battle ahead.

But success brought none of the triumph she had anticipated. Instead, she felt drained and utterly exhausted. Arno Mazar, she reflected bitterly, should have been alive to share this first moment of victory.

CHAPTER FORTY-TWO

'How do you see the situation developing, then?' Richard frowned as he asked the question.

Jake Lennox, the stocky, balding chief of the Drug Enforcement Agency, tapped a stubby index finger on the file that lay before him on his desk.

'You've read the latest report, Richard. I don't think the cartels anticipated just how quickly the Martiguayan initiative would take effect. But in less than three months the supply routes have been severely restricted, dozens of processing labs have been located and destroyed, and the courts are at last being forced to press for convictions. It's a unified crackdown by all signatories to the Americas Union, and Olivero and the others are cornered animals — they're lashing out with all they've got.'

Richard's frown deepened as he listened to Jake Lennox. It was clear that the incredible successes of this first concerted effort against the drug rings had brought vicious retaliation in its wake. Terrorist attacks were escalating and hundreds of innocent people had been slaughtered in almost daily acts of indiscriminate violence as the cartels fought to regain their superiority in the trade they had controlled for so long.

'Of course,' Jake Lennox continued, 'things really hotted up after the capture of Olivero's nephew. That was a real coup for the local boys. Two of the cartel's chief honchos picked up in a daytime raid without a shot fired.' He gave a derisory snort. 'Wish we could have claimed a little glory for ourselves but unfortunately we had nothing to do with it. It was local intelligence who pulled that one off.'

Richard knew he meant Major Paolo Avende, the man Noella had appointed to lead the campaign to destroy the drug trade. Her faith in his abilities now seemed well placed.

But from his reading of the D.E.A. report, Richard knew that the arrest of Jose Condorro, Olivero's nephew and one of the cartel ringleaders, had brought the situation in Martiguay to flashpoint. It was clear that until Carlos Olivero himself was captured, no one, least of all the woman he loved, could be considered safe from danger.

The briefing over, he stood up to go.

'You're leaving tomorrow then?' Jake Lennox walked him to the door.

Richard nodded. 'First thing in the morning.'

The D.E.A. chief patted his shoulder. 'Take care.'

He meant it.

The smile threatened to split Eugene's face.

He was suffused with joy, contentment, peace . . .

Impossibly, his grin grew wider as the euphoria slid through his veins, making his skin flush, his pulse race, his legs feel as if they were filled with cotton wool.

Then a second later, as the rush hit his brain, he moaned in wild ecstasy. The pain and nightmare were gone, replaced by dizzying pleasure and delight.

'It is wonderful, yes? You are happy now? Very, very happy.'

The voice murmured close to his ear and through glazed, half-closed eyes, Eugene saw the face hovering above his. He blinked. Slowly. Once, twice, three times, trying to focus on the features. But definition was impossible.

A giggle escaped his slack lips. Who cared? What did it matter as long as they gave him what he had tried so long and hard to avoid.

The man stared down at the comatose figure on the narrow bed.

'Maintain the same level of dosage for at least another three days.' His voice was cold, emotionless. 'Later, when he is screaming for it, he will do anything we ask.'

With a grunt of acquiescence his companion followed him out of the room, locking the door behind them.

Richard found it difficult to concentrate on the niceties of diplomatic small talk as he sat in the rear of the limousine beside the senior minister who had been sent to greet him. Instead, as he looked out at the lush countryside, at the clusters of rustic stone houses and simple peasant churches, his thoughts were on the heritage that would pass to his son. A heritage in which the name de Bartez stood for leadership and courage in Martiguayan history, in which de Bartez blood had been spilt violently on Martiguayan soil.

As the car entered the outskirts of the capital he prayed that there would be no more martyrs.

He called her on her private line the moment he was alone.

'Richard! How wonderful to know you are here at last!'

The sound of her voice made his heart turn over. 'I can't wait to see you, darling. Is — is there any way we can be together?'

She knew what he meant and her voice was heavy with regret. 'I would do anything to have it so, *querido*, but security at the palace makes it impossible. For the moment we will have to be patient until I see what might be arranged.'

And with that he had to be satisfied.

*

They were reunited that same evening at an informal dinner at the palace. Also present were the US Ambassador, the local head of the D.E.A., two senior ministers from Noella's cabinet, and Major Paolo Avende.

As he picked at the food placed in front of him, Richard could only marvel at the woman who presided over the all-male gathering with such grace and presence. It was almost impossible to equate this Noella with the spoilt and shallow girl he had first met in London.

The discussion ranged over a variety of topics including the invitation for Noella to address the next sitting of Congress.

Richard was aware of Larry Kirk's offer. It was part of the President's plan to coax Congress to loosen its purse strings and provide an even more generous package of aid to the fledgling democracy. Larry Kirk felt that a personal appeal by the dynamic President of Martiguay herself, in which she listed her government's spectacular and wide-ranging initiatives, would convince Congress of its duty.

As Noella accepted the congratulations of those around the table, the US Ambassador asked, 'So when do you leave for Washington, senora?'

Noella smiled. 'At the end of this week. Dr Avery does not know it yet, I think, but I am to accompany him back to the United States.'

Startled, Richard looked up from his plate just in time to catch her quick mischievous glance. He hadn't expected that!

From his place at the far end of the table, Paolo did not miss the look that passed between Noella and Richard.

He had known the moment he set eyes on Richard Avery that he was the man Noella loved. The blond hair, the blue eyes... Paolo knew without a doubt that this was the father of her child.

He had relied too long on his instincts to be mistaken. They had been careful, but Paolo had caught the quick glances, the shining eyes, sensed the heightened tension as they conversed across the table.

Behind blank eyes he hid his own despair.

Noella was halfway through her meal when it occurred to her that seated at the same table were the only two men she'd ever loved.

From under lowered lashes, she looked from one to the other — Richard so fair, Paolo so dark — and reflected how each had played his part in making her what she had become.

It was as if an invisible thread bonded her to these two very different men, and at that moment, in a sudden overflow of emotion, Noella realised that in some strange way she loved them both.

Again, it was a grim-faced Paolo who broke the terrible news to Noella the next morning. She had been about to leave her apartment for her first appointment of the day.

'*Dios*,' she breathed, the blood draining from her face.

Five minutes later she had called her cabinet together in an emergency meeting.

'Noella!'

He had telephoned the palace the moment he had heard. Only now, with the cabinet meeting over, had he been able to reach her.

'Richard, I am sure you know what has happened.'

He marvelled at the steadiness of her voice.

'We need to talk. Can you come at once?'

The secretary showed him in. He had orders that they were not to be disturbed.

As soon as the man had closed the double doors behind him, Richard took Noella in his arms.

'Oh, my love . . . '

She clung to him silently for a moment. Then, gathering her composure, she drew back and said quietly and evenly, 'You see, Richard, how critical the situation has become.'

'It was cold-blooded murder!' Richard's shock and fury were obvious. 'There will be a world outcry!'

The Ambassador had rung to tell him the news. In one of Martiguay's western provinces, where the government had been successful in luring the peasants out of the cocaine industry and back to legitimate agriculture, a village of more than three hundred people had been massacred at the hands of Olivero's private army.

The cartel's message was chillingly clear: the same fate awaited any others foolish enough to accept the government's inducements.

'Christ, Noella,' Richard went on, 'this is all-out war! I wish . . . ' His expression had changed to one of anguish. 'I wish sometimes that I had never encouraged you this far, that — '

'Richard.' There was resolution in her voice. 'There is no turning back. I knew the dangers — and I can accept them for myself. But in such perilous times I can't allow myself to be distracted by personal fears. I have had no opportunity to tell you this before, but Eugene has disappeared. It has been almost four days now with no word and my greatest fear is that he has fallen into Olivero's hands — that he will be used to bargain for the release of Jose Condorro, Olivero's nephew.'

She was standing in front of him now, staring up into his troubled face. 'The dangers have escalated so much in the last few weeks, Richard, it is clear Sandro cannot stay in Martiguay. Despite my selfish need for him, it is his safety, first and foremost, that must concern me now. For sooner or later it will be recognised how close I am to Nina and the child . . . and, as I am afraid has perhaps already occurred with Eugene, *all* those close to me will be at risk.'

Her eyes burned into his. 'For myself, I can face anything — but only if I know our son's future is assured.'

For a moment he was overwhelmed by her courage and utter conviction.

'What are you trying to say?' he finally asked.

Quickly, urgently, Noella explained. 'It is something I have already discussed with Nina over these last few weeks and she is in complete agreement. To the world she is Sandro's legal guardian but it is obvious she is no longer young.

'Richard, Sandro can be legally yours. In the States, when one has connections, I am sure these things can be quietly arranged. Do you understand what I am saying?'

Her voice softened and she put her hands on his shoulders. 'This war will not last forever, my darling. And when I win it, as I am determined to do, the people will be much more accepting of a marriage that they might reject so forcibly now. There will be a time, I am absolutely certain, when all we have hoped for, all we have dreamed of, will come true. You must believe that.'

Richard wanted to, more than anything in the world.

CHAPTER FORTY-THREE

And finally, there was just time to say another goodbye.

Once the decision had been made to move Nina and Sandro to the safety of the United States, the details of the departure were handled swiftly.

Inez was on hand to help with the packing up of the house but Sandro, sensing a disturbance to his usual routine, was untypically disruptive.

'Now look here, my little helper,' Inez scolded, shaking her finger in mock anger, 'this is the third time I have taken the shoes out of this cupboard ready to pack and every time I turn my back they disappear inside again!'

Behind the jovial front, Inez was doing her best to hide her pain and disappointment. She knew it was the right step to take but that didn't make it any easier to face; she was losing not only the company of her old friend, but also the child on whom she had come to dote.

Nina and Sandro were to leave the country the evening before Noella and Richard's departure for Washington. Arrangements had been made for Richard's younger sister, Laura, to meet the flight and take the elderly woman and child into her home.

'I placed a call to Laura from the Embassy, Noella,' Richard reported later. 'As briefly as possible I explained the situation and told her that a detailed letter was on its way. She was surprised, of course, but I know we can count on her.'

Married with two children of her own, Laura, Richard knew, was always serene and unflappable. She and her husband owned a large Cape Cod home set amongst five of the prettiest acres in Vermont. There, he assured Noella, their son and Nina would be safe and well cared for until more permanent arrangements could be made.

They all met that last afternoon in the almost bare house. Boxes and packing cases filled the hallway, and by the front door three sturdy suitcases stood in readiness.

Inez had brought salad, cold cuts, and fruit, and they tried their best to be jolly as they ate together on rugs spread out on the lawn.

Security presented no problems. Noella had confided her plans to Paolo. He knew what was being arranged and would personally escort Nina and the child when they left for the airport.

It had never been alluded to, but Noella knew Paolo was aware that Dr Richard Avery of the US State Department was the father of her child. She was thankful that Paolo, with typical quiet dignity, had never made any reference to the fact.

Lunch over, Noella went to help Nina put Sandro down for his usual nap.

'With the change in routine it is unlikely he will sleep on the flight,' Noella commented as she tucked the squirming toddler into his cot.

Drawing the heavy drapes against the bright heat of the afternoon sun, Nina nodded. 'I am sure you are right, *cherie*. In fact, now that everything is in order, I think I too might take a rest.'

'Of course. You must be exhausted after these last few days.' She patted the older woman comfortingly on the arm. 'Inez and I will hear if Sandro awakes.'

*

'Don't waste this precious time, *querida*,' Inez said to her as she returned to the kitchen to help with clearing away the remains of their meal. 'Spend these last moments with Richard. I will listen for Sandro.'

With a silent hug of thanks for her understanding, Noella went to do as she was told.

They lay on the thin counterpane that had been left to cover the mattress. The shuttered room was cool and dark; curled in each other's arms, they savoured the precious moment of intimacy.

Passion consumed Noella as her lover's tongue explored her mouth, as his breath fanned her cheek, and his hands traced a searing path down her nakedness. Then, slowly, in perfect harmony, they made that breathless, spiralling journey that dizzied the senses, dispelled all fears and finally, in a moment of exquisite, shuddering release, dissolved the rest of the world.

Their lovemaking seemed to fill Richard with a new calm and optimism.

'We will find a way, my darling, I know we will.' He held her tightly against him. 'Something can be arranged. I can make regular visits; you will come to the States... And then, as you suggest, perhaps once the threat of Carlos Olivero is removed there might be the chance of a real future together.' His lips brushed her cheek. 'I love you, Noella. I love you so much. It's all going to work out. We're going to grow old together and watch our son become a man in a country without violence and fear.'

The words, with their promise of the future, filled Noella with an almost unbearable tenderness.

A velvety dusk had just fallen when Paolo and his men brought the car to the house.

Inside, out of sight of the soldiers, it was time for farewells.

Now that the moment had actually arrived, Noella struggled to control her emotions. Her throat seemed to close up as she hugged Nina close and whispered, 'Oh, Nina, you've been so good to us...'

Then she was lifting Sandro, feeling his sturdy arms encircle her neck as she breathed in his sweetness.

Words were beyond her and with eyes squeezed tight, she clung to her son, rubbing her cheek against his soft golden hair, feeling the beat of his heart as he snuggled against her. As if somehow he knew this was a different sort of parting, Sandro began to whimper softly.

'It's all right, Noella.' Richard was there, his arm around her, whispering close to her ear. 'Even if you don't manage to see him this trip, there will be other times. And very soon we will find a way to be together always ... the three of us. I promise you that, my darling.'

Then, suitcases stowed, doors slammed shut, the car with its heavily-armed escort moved off into the shadows.

The same tight security surrounded Noella's return to the palace.

Aware of the presence of the soldiers, Richard merely squeezed her hand as he saw her into her own limousine. 'Try to get a good night's sleep, darling. Tomorrow will be a long day. And you have a demanding task in front of you.'

She nodded, feeling drained of all emotion. 'I will be ready at eight, Richard. *Buenas noches.*'

She had asked Paolo to report to her as soon as he returned, and it was in her office, two hours later, that he found her. Her staff long departed for the day, Noella sat alone, rereading the speech she would give to the US Congress.

'All is well, Noella. The flight took off without incident.'

She nodded in weary relief and pushed the papers aside. Suddenly, she didn't want to be alone.

'Can you stay a moment, Paolo? Can we talk?'

'Of course.' He took the seat she indicated.

She was silent a second longer, looking into the shattered face whose disfigurement she now barely noticed. For her, Paolo would always be that eighteen-year-old boy, the handsome youth who had taught her about the mysteries of love.

'I'm so worried about Eugene, Paolo. Is there no news yet? No indication at all where he might have gone? It's been almost a week now.'

'Unfortunately not, Noella. But my men have orders to continue the search and follow up all leads.'

It aggrieved Paolo to have to admit to failure. But despite a full-scale alert, not a trace had been found of Eugene Ravell since his disappearance from the palace.

Paolo saw the strain on Noella's face and knew that her greatest worry was that her brother-in-law might have been taken hostage by the cartels. Eugene Ravell would provide a first-class bargaining counter against the extradition of Olivero's nephew. But, Paolo asked himself, if that was indeed the case, why had they heard nothing?

Unable to reassure Noella, he did his best to change the subject and for a while they talked about her imminent trip to Washington.

It was her unexpected remark as she rose to bid him good night that caught him by surprise. 'Do you know, Paolo,' a vague smile played around her lips, 'I still remember those wonderful days when we rode the plains for hours. Just ourselves, the horses, and the sunshine. It seemed to me then that there might never be a greater freedom ... ' She seemed to be speaking to herself.

Without warning, she turned to face him and clasped one of his hands. 'You were good to me then, Paolo, as you are good to me still. *Gracias, amigo.*'

For a long time afterwards, his ravaged cheek burned where her lips had brushed against it.

The call woke Paolo in his quarters a short time after dawn.

'Major Avende?'

Paolo frowned, shrugged off the last traces of sleep. The voice was familiar.

'Major Avende, it is I... Eugene Ravell. Please! I have vital news! You must listen carefully.'

Noella was dreaming.

A man and a woman, walking hand in hand along a deserted beach... in front of them, a little boy, chasing the waves, his laughter ringing out over the rush of water...

The sense of happiness was almost tangible.

The dream was abruptly shattered by the ringing of the telephone beside her bed.

Sleepily, she leaned on one elbow and spoke into the receiver.

Paolo's voice, the rapid, urgent words he spoke, made her instantly alert.

'Paolo,' her voice was sharp, 'this is a decision I am prepared to make alone. Give me five minutes then meet me in my office.'

Noella moved restlessly around the room as she made Paolo relate again his short conversation with Eugene.

'And that is where Eugene has been all this time? Following up this lead?'

Paolo's gaze came to rest on her questioning eyes. 'I can only report what he said, Noella. He explained that it has taken time. That his informant, naturally enough, was frightened for his life and would speak only to someone at the top.'

'And Eugene is quite sure that the meeting is *today*?'

'Adamant. The imminent extradition of his nephew has caused Olivero to call an emergency meeting of the cartel. As Senor Ravell reports, it is to be held this morning in a villa on the outskirts of the capital. All members will be present.'

'Paolo,' Noella said decisively, dropping into her chair and leaning towards him across the desk, 'we must take this seriously. Eugene would not endanger innocent lives unless he had absolute proof of what he has told us. It is my opinion that we must act without delay on his information. I hope you will agree with me.'

Paolo studied her a moment. 'I am always cautious, Noella, but as the information has come from such a reliable source, and as we have so little time to consider alternatives, then it seems essential to grasp what appears to be a miraculous opportunity.'

He told her what he had in mind. 'I need to mobilise as many men as possible to this location. We must use all our resources to strike the deathblow once and for all to those who control this evil trade.'

As he spoke, Noella could feel her excitement growing. 'It is like a snake, Paolo — with the head destroyed, the body will soon succumb.' Her fingers drummed distractedly on the desk. 'I only wish that this had not happened today, when I must leave for Washington.'

'Your own security today must also not be overlooked, Noella.' Paolo's voice held a note of warning.

She dismissed his words with a wave of her hand. 'What can happen to me when the ringleaders are locked together, distracted by their own problems?'

She stood up, eager to set their decision in motion.

Noella's mind was in a fever as she made ready for her departure for the airport.

Relief at finally knowing Eugene's whereabouts was mingled with apprehension and excitement at the thought that finally there existed a chance to throw the net over those who controlled the drug trade.

As she clipped a row of pearls around her neck, a strange irony occurred to her. The information had been brought to them by Eugene. Such were the twists of fate, that it was her brother-in-law's ties to the drug world that had led the informant to him.

Carlos Olivero snorted in satisfaction as he replaced t.ie receiver.

The bait had been taken as he had been certain it would.

Now the way was clear to achieve both his aims. His men would wipe that *bastardo* Avende off the face of the earth, and he himself would take the woman. By the time he had finished with her, de Bartez would be a name whispered only in nightmares . . .

CHAPTER *FORTY-FOUR*

The bullet-proof limousine left the palace right on schedule. The accompanying security men travelled in the car ahead while two armed motorcyclists took up the rear.

Distracted and on edge, Noella sat in silence as they travelled the route to the airport. She was impatient to know what was happening with Paolo, impatient to tell Richard of this latest development. Again she wished that the timing of her trip to Washington could have been different.

Drenched in sweat, his body racked by spasms and convulsions, Eugene felt as if he were already dead.

For almost a week they had pumped him full of the drug he had so longed for, shot him with a dose he would never have dared give himself but which in its purity had transported him to that peaceful white land of exquisite joy.

Then, three days ago, he had been thrown into hell.

Deprived so abruptly of the source of his pleasure, it was a hell worse than any he had known before. His veins felt as if they were melting, his heart seemed to be jumping out of his chest. One moment he was running with sweat, the next he was freezing cold, while his muscles jerked as though connected to some unseen, high-voltage force.

He screamed for release, begging for salvation from the torture that twisted his body and burnt his mind.

There was only one means of escape.

In the end he took it gladly.

But they had lied. They had given him just enough to ensure he could make the phone call, then scorned his desperate pleas, his screams for pity.

Later, in a rare, short moment of lucidity, he finally realised they had left him alone. A wasted wreck of a human being who had served his purpose. Not even worth the price of a bullet.

In the distance, Noella could see the jet waiting on the tarmac. Richard would have boarded already. And then there would be the few precious hours together before, once again, time and circumstances kept them apart.

Yet over these last few days Richard had affected her with his own optimism and faith. If today's action was successful, if she could rid Martiguay of the scourge of men like Olivero, then the people might forgive her more than she dared to hope.

Slowly, the car entered the airport grounds.

Panting with effort, Eugene stumbled along the overgrown track. He knew where the trap had been laid — he himself had given the instructions.

The thought brought a wild sob from his parched lips. *Dios, Dios* . . . how could he have done it?

And through the black heat in his brain the faces of Gabrielle, Roberto, and his father-in-law rose up to haunt him.

As the presidential limousine moved towards the waiting aircraft, Noella saw that Richard had just arrived. At the foot of the metal stairs, a chauffeur was standing by the open car door as Richard stepped onto the tarmac.

She saw him turn, look towards her, begin to smile, and in that split second it happened.

*

The explosion of automatic gunfire shattered the calm morning air.

Before Noella's disbelieving eyes, the security vehicle ahead burst into flames as a well-placed bullet found its mark on the petrol tank.

Ducking instinctively, she heard a howl of pain and spun around to see both motorcycle escorts picked off before they could reach for their weapons.

'*Quickly*! Get to the plane!' Noella screamed the order. But the driver appeared not to hear as he swerved and accelerated in the opposite direction.

'No!' Leaning forward, she hammered at the man's shoulder. Then, blood draining from her face, she drew back as she caught sight of the pistol he held in one hand.

For a second Richard stood frozen with shock as the bloody scene was played out before his eyes. Then, barely aware of his actions, he knocked aside the paralysed chauffeur and threw himself into the driver's seat of the official limousine.

Swearing, praying, sweat pouring down his face, he slammed the accelerator to the floor in a desperate bid to head off the other vehicle. He had seen the helicopter appear from its hiding place in the jungle that edged the runway. It was obvious that was where Noella's car was heading.

Paolo had relied on his instincts for too long not to trust them now. Something was wrong. He could smell it in the air.

For one thing, he thought, lowering his binoculars, surely no one concerned about security would have chosen such a location.

The house lay at the bottom of the valley, the craggy surrounding outcrops providing perfect cover for easy attack. He could see the expensive cars parked in the shade of the trees, but still it didn't feel right. Surely a man of Olivero's experience would never trust himself to such a place...

Turning, Paolo murmured in an undertone to his lieutenant. 'Before we send in the men, I want to —'

'Major! Listen!'

Paolo froze. The sound was unmistakable. Someone was breaking through the undergrowth, making no attempt at stealth.

'*Don't shoot*! Please, don't shoot! It is I, Eugene Ravell!'

The figure broke through the trees, stumbling and tripping, his face scratched and bleeding.

'Major...' Eugene staggered, almost fell at Paolo's feet. 'It is a trap!' Heart heaving, Eugene gasped out the words. 'At the airport! Noella — They are —'

The first shot snapped Eugene's spinal column as the trees suddenly came alive with gunfire.

Richard braced himself as he slammed on the brakes.

There was nothing Noella's driver could do to avoid the impact. Metal tore against metal, rubber burnt and squealed, as the two cars slammed together in a jarring collision.

Instantly, Richard had leapt from the wreckage and was dragging a shaken Noella from the back seat.

'Quickly!' His hand grabbed hers.

'Richard!' She was looking over his shoulder, her eyes wide with terror.

The driver had recovered from the impact, and was levelling his pistol at them.

In an automatic reaction, Richard spun around, knocked the gun aside and thudded his fist into the man's fleshy face.

'Hurry, Noella!' He caught her hand again. The hangar was just metres away — if they could...

But it was too late. The men in the helicopter had

opened fire as the machine moved inexorably towards them.

Richard saw they had no choice. He pulled Noella down beside him in the poor protection afforded by the wreckage of the cars.

The gun... His eyes were frantically searching the ground for the weapon he had knocked away just moments before. It wasn't much, but...

Then he saw it. Less than a metre away.

Bullets spat off the ground beside him but he knew he had to take the chance.

Heart pounding, he edged forward.

Never in his life had Paolo driven so recklessly. The jeep bounced high in the air as he forced it along tracks that had never been made for automobiles. But this was the shortest route he knew to the airport.

Leaving the majority of his men to engage the enemy at the site of the trap, he led a dozen others in a frantic dash to save the life of the woman he loved.

Paolo sized up the situation immediately as the jeeps entered the airport precincts. He shouted frantic orders to his men.

Richard's fingers closed around the barrel of the pistol. He had caught the sound of the arriving vehicles, the exchange of gunfire. If he could just keep the men in the helicopter at bay until the rescuers reached them...

'Richard, be careful.' He heard Noella's tremulous warning as he inched backwards with the weapon.

He almost made it.

The bullet caught him in the neck. Bright red blood spurted upwards in an arc, splattering Noella's hands and face.

'RICHARD! Oh, *Dios* ... *Richard*!'

There was the sound of a massive explosion but

Noella barely noticed. Ignoring the danger to herself, she crawled to Richard's side, cradled his bloody head in her lap.

'Richard, *querido*...' She choked back her terror, clutching him to her thundering heart.

'It will be all right, Richard... it will be all right...' She gasped out the words, repeating them over and over like a prayer, a plea for divine help.

But the life was draining out of him. She could see it in his glazed and distant eyes — and she felt the ice form around her heart.

The sound of running footsteps made her head jerk up in fear, and suddenly Paolo was by her side. Somehow he had known. Somehow he had come to help them...

'Paolo!' Her dark eyes were wild with panic. 'Oh, please, Paolo. Get help quickly!'

'It's coming, Noella.' But dropping to his knees beside her, Paolo could see it was already too late.

With a moan, Richard moved his lips, tried to speak.

Gripping his hand in hers, Noella leaned closer, desperate to catch the words he was fighting to say.

'Is ... is it all right?' His voice was a breathless whisper.

It was Paolo who replied. 'Save your strength, senor. It is all over for them. Olivero is dead.' He placed a hand on the other man's shoulder. 'Help will be here any second. You will be all right.'

'No.' Richard knew there was little time left but there were words that still had to be said. 'Noella... come closer... ' His voice was fainter now, his blue eyes dark with pain as he stared up into her stricken face. 'Listen to me, my darling... don't — don't be sad... Don't let this change your dreams. You are so close now and —' he drew a deep shuddering breath 'and there is so much you still have to live for.' His hand clutched weakly at her own. 'Follow your destiny, my darling... Have no regrets.'

Still fighting for breath, his face grey with pain, he shifted his gaze to the man beside her. 'Stay close to her Paolo, look after her as you always have . . . '

And then he was once again looking at Noella, his expression suddenly peaceful and full of unbearable tenderness. 'I love you so, my darling . . . I always will . . .'

'Richard . . . oh, Richard . . . Don't leave me. Oh, please . . . ' Noella bent and kissed that beloved face, her anguished tears mingling with the thick, dark blood which was draining his life away.

Her icy lips were still against his skin when he gave a final faltering breath and was gone.

No one and nothing else existed in that moment frozen in time as she knelt there on the rough, warm tarmac, the blood sticky on her fingers, the tears pouring down her ravaged face.

Beside her, Paolo watched in mute, heartbroken sympathy the agony of the woman he had never ceased to love.

EPILOGUE

The crowds had been gathering since early morning to offer their congratulations. It was the second anniversary of the day Noella de Bartez had led her party to victory — the advent of true democracy in Martiguay.

In those two years much had been achieved through the President's sweeping reforms. Best of all, the shadow of violence that had hung over Martiguay for so long had been swept away by the death of Carlos Olivero. The power of the drug cartels had been broken that day. Olivero's audacious attempt to make a martyr of yet another de Bartez had ended in his own death.

As Noella stepped out onto the balcony, surrounded by her ministers, a deafening roar came from the waiting crowd. Their love and admiration were almost tangible as they cheered the serene, smiling woman who had brought them so far.

Beside her stood another of Martiguay's heroes. It was General Paolo Avende who had saved their beloved President's life; he who had thrown the grenade that had brought the life of Carlos Olivero to an end. In the darkest hours of their history, Paolo Avende, the people knew, had never given up the struggle.

As she raised a hand to acknowledge the acclaim of the people — her people — Noella thought about the price she had paid to achieve this moment. So many lives lost ... her father, Gabrielle, Roberto, poor Eugene ... and her beloved Richard.

The cost had been immense.

But there had been rewards. The reward of starting her country on the road to real reform with national prosperity at last a reality; the reward of international admiration and recognition for the role Martiguayans had played in the deadly war against the drug trade. The war was not yet won, but the tide had finally begun to turn.

The sunshine glinted on the silver star pinned to the breast of Noella's pale blue suit. The US Medal of Freedom had been awarded in acknowledgement of the courageous initiative taken by the de Bartez government in combating the evil which had exacted such a heavy toll on both their countries.

Noella was proud of the honour. But she would be prouder still when she opened the Richard Avery Memorial Library at Martiguay Central University later that day. That would be her tribute to the man she loved. She wanted Martiguayans to remember the price a brave American had paid for the country he had taken to his heart.

Glancing sideways, she saw Paolo watching her and gave him a knowing smile. He was her rock. He had made a promise all those years ago and he had never let her down. Paolo would always be part of her future.

At last, with a final wave, Noella turned away from the cheering crowds. The love of her people would always give her the strength to go on. She had given up so much for them, more than they would ever know.

And inside, waiting just out of sight, were the women who had always been there when she needed them. With Inez and Nina, Noella had forged a bond of friendship that was rare and precious, one strengthened and enhanced by their shared love for her son.

As she stepped into the room, the laughing, blue-eyed boy broke away and ran towards her.

Crouching in the ray of sunshine streaming through

the French doors, Noella smiled and caught the child in her arms. Soon, she knew, the time would be right. By his death Richard had won the gratitude and acceptance of the people; in turn, she felt sure, they would accept the truth about her son.

Richard's son . . .

She bent and kissed the child's soft, golden hair.